A SACRIFICE OF PAWNS

Warrior's Path Book 3

MALCOLM ARCHIBALD

Copyright (C) 2021 Malcolm Archibald

Layout design and Copyright (C) 2021 by Next Chapter

Published 2021 by Next Chapter

Edited by Chelsey Heller

Cover art by Cover Mint

This book is a work of fiction. Names, characters, places, and incidents are the product of the author's imagination or are used fictitiously. Any resemblance to actual events, locales, or persons, living or dead, is purely coincidental.

All rights reserved. No part of this book may be reproduced or transmitted in any form or by any means, electronic or mechanical, including photocopying, recording, or by any information storage and retrieval system, without the author's permission.

For Cathy

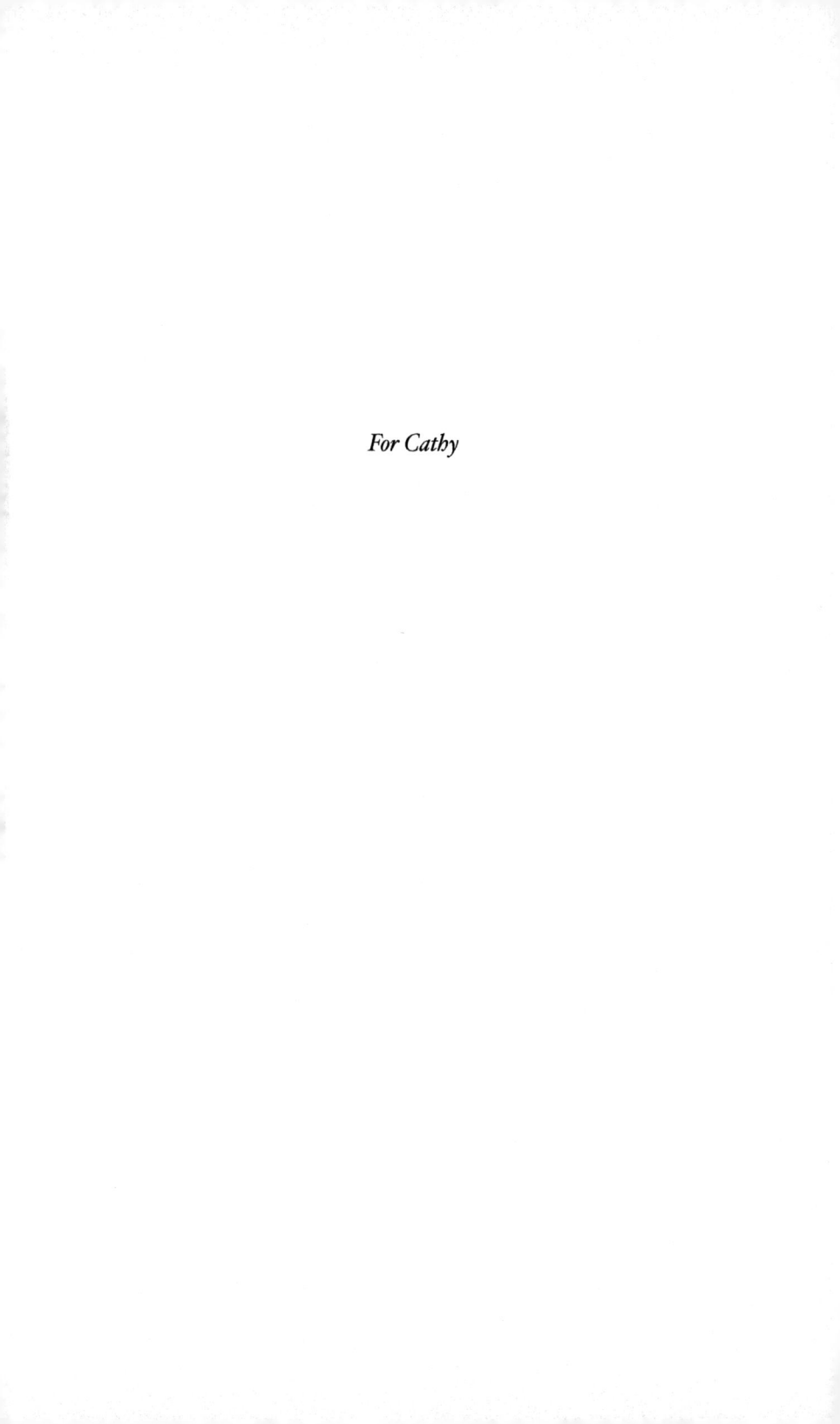

PRELUDE

The Island Of Martinico, Caribbean Sea
June 1761

With her flag of truce limp under the brassy sun, HMS *Temple* sat off Fort St Pierre, Martinico. As the heat bubbled the pitch between the pristine planking, *Temple's* crew stood on deck, studying the fort with its batteries of cannon and white-uniformed garrison. It was seldom that a British ship came so close to a French stronghold without firing, and the officers and men of *Temple* resolved to record every last detail of the enemy fort.

It was June 1761, and the war between His Britannic Majesty, King George III of Great Britain and Ireland, and King Louis XV, Louis le Bien-Aimé, the Beloved of France, had dragged on since 1754. What had started as a minor Colonial dispute in the backwoods of North America had spread across the globe to Europe, the East Indies, and the Caribbean.

"There's the captain going ashore," said Foretopman Harry Squire, tipping back his straw hat as the captain's barge eased from the stern. Captain O'Brien sat erect in the stern beside a smart young midshipman.

"I don't trust these Frenchies!" Daniel Tait was a native Jamaican, a free black man who had joined *Temple* when the warship berthed at Kingston earlier that year. "They are too friendly with the Spanish for me." He shook his head. "I hope the captain is safe."

Squire nodded at the ranked cannon on *Temple*'s main deck, with the gun crews standing ready. "The captain is under a flag of truce to negotiate an exchange of prisoners. Not even the Frenchies will break a truce."

"I don't trust the Frenchies," Tait repeated.

"La Touché, the governor of Martinico, is a gentleman," Squire insisted. "He'll keep his word."

Both men wore the ubiquitous clothes of the British seaman, the white cotton shirt with horizontal coloured stripes—red in Squire's case, blue in Tait's—a dark blue neckerchief, and white canvas trousers. While Tait wore low shoes—"purser's crabs"—Squire was barefoot, and both had seamen's knives attached to their belts.

"Ship ahoy!"

The hail came from aloft, where a lookout was permanently on watch.

"Where away?" the lieutenant of the watch bellowed.

"Just breaking the horizon to the west, sir!" the lookout replied. "Two vessels! One is *Bienfaisant,* and I don't know the other!"

Grabbing the telescope from its bracket on the mizzenmast, the lieutenant scrambled up the ratlines to join the lookout. Perched eighty dizzying feet above the deck, he extended the telescope and focussed on the distant sails.

"That's *Bienfaisant,* right enough," the lieutenant said. "I think she's captured a French prize, the lucky bugger!"

"Is that lucky?" Tait was not yet fully cognisant of the ways of the Royal Navy.

"Yes, Taity," Squire said. "If you capture a ship, it can be sold, and the captain and crew get a share of the profit after the admiral takes his whack."

"Lucky bugger," Tait agreed.

They watched as HMS *Bienfaisant* escorted in her prize, a wave-battered sloop with patched sails and a deck packed with artillery. At her stern, the Union flag hung above the white-cross-on-blue ensign of France, a sure sign she was a prize of war.

"She's a privateer or I'm a Dutchman, although she wears a merchantman's flag," Squire said. "She carries too many guns for an honest merchantman."

Tait studied the captured vessel with calm eyes. "In Jamaica, we call the privateers freebooters," he said. "Or pirates."

"You won't be far wrong, Taity." Squire produced a wad of tobacco, bit off a chunk, and handed the rest to Tait. "Pirates and privateers are much the same in these waters."

Both men knew that privateers were privately owned vessels with an official licence that empowered them to attack the enemy shipping. Fighting for profit more than patriotism, privateers often crossed the border into piracy, attacking even neutral vessels. Some had earned an unenviable reputation for violence and cruelty.

As Tait and Squire watched, an eager lieutenant on the prize ship ushered half a dozen prisoners onto a yawl. Grinning Royal Navy seamen shoved them into the centre of the boat and manned the oars. Within a minute, the yawl was powering towards *Temple,* with the prisoners scowling at the British warship.

"Here come the first of the Frenchies," Squire said.

"All hands!" the first lieutenant of *Temple* roared, and Squire and Tait joined the others in mustering on the main deck. In response to bellowed orders, a file of Marines waited to escort the prisoners below decks until they could be exchanged for British seamen held by the French.

Squire nodded at one of the Frenchmen, a tall, handsome

man in an ornate coat. "A golden guinea to an Irish sixpence that's the captain."

Tait looked and stepped back. "That's a bad man," he said, shaking his head.

"He looks very debonair in his fancy coat," Squire said, still chewing on his tobacco.

"The devil is in that man," Tait said.

As the French boarded *Temple,* the tall Frenchman stopped at the entry port with its elaborate carvings of Neptune. He looked across at his sloop, now a sad sight, and at the flag of truce drooping from *Temple*'s stern.

"Flag of truce!" he shouted the words in high passion, and although he spoke in broken English, Squire understood the meaning.

"The British took me in a flag of truce!" He drew a small knife from his belt and, with a dramatic gesture, he carved a cross in his forehead.

"What the devil?" Squire made to step forward until the second lieutenant ordered him back to his place.

The French captain stood still, ignoring the shouts and pointing bayonets of the scarlet-coated Marines. Blood from his cut seeped down his nose to drip onto the deck.

"You took me under a flag of truce!" the Frenchman shouted. "You broke the rules of war. For that, I will wage raw war on you and your ships. There will be no quarter!" He raised his voice to a near scream. "No quarter!"

When the Marines ushered him forward, the Frenchman replaced his knife, bowed to the first lieutenant, and followed his men.

"Who was that?" Squire asked.

"Captain René Roberval," one of the escorting seamen replied.

The name seemed to strike a chill across *Temple*'s main deck, and not only Tait stepped back in nearly superstitious awe.[1]

I

St Lawrence River, Canada
November 1761

"We're iced in!" Lundey, the mate, swore. "We should have left Quebec a week ago. Now the ice will hold us until the spring thaw."

Captain Stringer looked forward, where the St Lawrence River eased away into the cold distance. "Get the hands forward with poles," he ordered, "and use these damned Rangers as well. It's time they earned their keep."

"Come on, men!" Lieutenant Kennedy hurried forward, with Sergeant Hugh MacKim and the other Rangers only a few steps behind.

The Boston-registered brig, *Martha,* had left Quebec only the previous day, hoping to reach the open sea before the river completely froze over. Now, as the ice closed in, Lundey was not alone in believing they had lingered too long in the British-garrisoned city.

"Can we break through?" Private Dickert asked as he viewed the barrier of ice that stretched from bank to bank of the river.

"We'll give it a bloody good try," Lundey replied.

"Smash the ice with the poles, you men!" Stringer ordered. "It's not too thick yet."

As Dickert lifted his pole, Private Duncan MacRae joined him in the bow of the ship. Both hammered the ends of their staffs onto the ice. A few chips flew upward, and then a tiny crack appeared a foot from *Martha's* bow.

"Break, you bastard!" Dickert said, lifting his pole above his head and smashing the end down on the crack.

"We're winning!" MacRae said as the crack widened and water bubbled through to the surface of the ice.

"Less talk! More sweat!" Lundey shouted. "Get working, you men!"

Martha inched forward, with her weight, the current, and a fortuitous wind combining to ease her slowly downstream.

"We are winning," Private Parnell agreed. "We're moving one tree at a time." He indicated the thick forest on the bank, where rank after rank of trees marched into the limitless interior. "Another six months, and we'll nearly be halfway to the sea."

"We're making poor progress," Captain Stringer said. "Can't you work harder, Rangers? The frost is early this year."

Lieutenant Kennedy nodded. "We'll do what we can." He changed the men in the bow, giving them half-hour shifts at ice-breaking to ensure nobody was overtired.

"At this rate," Private Oxford fretted, "we'll never join with the fleet at New York." He looked around at the snow-covered forests. "We might walk there quicker, sir."

"It's hundreds of miles of bad territory." Kennedy looked over his Rangers, the twenty-five green-clad forest fighters, mostly veterans of the campaigns around Quebec. Only two of them, Privates Oxford and Danskin, were untried replacements.

MacKim read Kennedy's thoughts. "You two," he indicated the new men. "Go forward and help smash the ice."

"Sergeant?" Oxford looked up with a quizzical expression on his face.

"Go and help smash the ice!"

While Danskin hurried forward, Oxford hesitated before moving. MacKim frowned; there was no room for shirkers in Kennedy's Rangers.

"Keep at it, Danskin," MacKim called. "Think how proud your sweetheart will be when you relate your adventures."

Danskin gave a weak smile as he leaned forward with his pole.

"We'll have to watch Oxford, sir," MacKim warned Kennedy as Oxford poked reluctantly at the ice.

"I'll keep my eye on him," Kennedy promised.

MacKim glanced upwards, where the white-tinged sky threatened further snow. "Come on, Oxford, or we'll be stuck on this blasted river until the thaw."

Parnell spat into the wind. "If we are, sergeant, we'll avoid the fighting."

"Aye, and we don't want that, do we?" MacKim said. "We can't let others think we're scared."

"They can think what they like," Parnell retorted. "We'll be alive, and they'll be dead."

"Here!" MacKim tossed over a long pole. "Save your energy for the ice!" He lifted one for himself. "Watch me and learn."

Leaning forward on the sharp prow of *Martha*, thrusting at the ice, MacKim soon found he was sweating, despite the sub-zero temperatures.

"We're slowing down," Kennedy said, half an hour later.

"Rock the ship!" Lundey ordered. "I sailed on the whaling ships. Run from side to side!" Within a few moments, he had all the Rangers and crew not otherwise occupied, racing from port to starboard and back. The motion cracked the ice around *Martha*, so she eased forward another few feet.

"This is the strangest voyage I've ever been on," Dickert said as he ran across the ship. "Join the Army, and play children's games."

"It's working," MacKim pointed out. "We're moving."

"Do we have to rock the boat for the next thousand miles?"

"If we have to," Kennedy replied. "King George needs us."

Parnell grunted. "He should come here then. He can balance his crown on his arse and run around the boat all day long."

"All we need is for the French to fire on us while we're stuck here," Dickert said.

"They've surrendered," MacKim reminded. "Canada is ours now."

"Until the Frenchies change their minds," Parnell said cynically.

Martha continued downstream, sometimes sailing in nearly clear water and occasional spells of ice. On one occasion, when the ice proved particularly stubborn, the captain had the ship's boat brought forward and dropped over the bows. The resulting shock cracked the ice sufficiently for *Martha* to ease through.

"Every delay is costing us time," Kennedy fretted.

"We can't help the climate, sir." MacKim tried to be philosophical, although he thought of Claudette, left behind in Quebec.

"I'm well aware of that, sergeant!" Kennedy's snapped retort proved his tension.

"Yes, sir." MacKim retired to the rail, leaving Kennedy to his worrying. Canada closed on all sides, vast and winter-cloaked in white. MacKim felt inside his coat and pulled out the letter Claudette had placed there when he left Quebec. She had written in French, so MacKim automatically translated the words as he read.

"My dear Hugh,

I have enjoyed our companionship together these last few months, with all your strange Scottish ways and expressions. I sometimes hoped that our friendship might develop into something more. However, it seemed that you were satisfied only with what we have.

Notwithstanding our religious differences, with me a Roman Catholic and you a Presbyterian, and our emotional contradictions, I felt that we formed a bond. My son Hugo also enjoyed your company, and, Hugh, now you have left, I can say this in safety; Hugo often expressed a wish that you would stay, either as a friend or as something more.

I know that I could never follow the drum, as the saying is, and I would never presume to persuade you to leave your military calling, so I allowed our friendship to continue without depth.

I wish it had been otherwise.

Now that you are leaving on another campaign, probably never to return to Canada again, I will say that you take a piece of my heart with you that can never be replaced.

Take care of yourself, dear Hugh, and never forget your friend here in Quebec.

I am always your
Claudette."

MacKim reread the letter, poring over every word before folding it neatly and returning it inside his coat. *Why didn't you say, you distant woman? Why did you hide your feelings from me?*

Martha sailed down the St Lawrence, with every tree they passed taking MacKim further from Claudette and closer to the French and the war.

"THE FLEET'S SAILED."

The news travelled around *Martha* in seconds as men stared at the vast anchorage and the neat little city of New York.

"They've sailed without us."

"That damned ice slowed us down!"

MacKim saw Kennedy's mouth tighten as he heard the news. Captain Stringer swore. "Damn the bloody Army," he said. "I have a cargo to deliver to the fleet." He raised his voice to a bellow. "Rangers! You'll be with us a good bit longer."

"I thought we were joining a transport in New York!" Oxford was not yet tested in battle, so he tried to prove his masculinity by tough talk and an eagerness for action.

"That was the idea, Oxford," MacKim explained patiently. "But the fleet's sailed without us."

"So, what do we do now, sergeant?" Oxford asked.

"Now we follow the fleet and hope to catch them before we reach the Caribbean," Captain Stringer joined in.

"Where about in the Caribbean?" Kennedy asked. "My orders said to join Admiral Rodney's fleet at New York. I know nothing beyond that."

Stringer gave a small smile. "The Army keeps you in ignorance. Well, Lieutenant Kennedy, the fleet has sailed for Barbados, and so must we."

"Barbados? That's far south." Kennedy sounded worried. "The Rangers are forest soldiers. We fight wearing snowshoes."

"Not anymore." Stringer pointed south. "You're headed for warmer climes, Lieutenant. There will be no need for snowshoes in the Caribbean."

"I thought we had beat the French," Dickert said disconsolately. "I thought we were going to New York to get disbanded and go home."

"The French are not beat yet," MacKim said. "We defeated them in Canada, but they're still fighting in Europe, the Caribbean, and India."

"India?" Danskin fastened on the word. "I'm not going to bloody India!"

"No, Danskin. We're not going to India," MacKim said. "The captain told us we're headed to Barbados."

"Why Barbados?" Oxford did not appear the most intelligent of men.

"To join the rest of the fleet," MacKim explained as patiently as he could.

"Are we attacking Barbados then?" Oxford asked.

"No," MacKim said. "We already own Barbados. We are probably using it as a rendezvous and base to attack one of the French-owned islands in the Caribbean."

They spent two days bringing on fresh water and food in New York, with the Rangers sampling the pleasures of the city. MacKim reread the letter from Claudette, scribbled a brief reply, and prepared to send it. But before he ran ashore, he heard Stringer give the order to cast off.

"Ready aft?"

"Ready aft, Captain!"

"Ready forward?"

"Ready forward, Captain!"

"Let fall! Sheet home!"

Martha eased away from New York, and MacKim knew he had delayed too long. Pushing Claudette to the back of his mind, he concentrated on keeping the Rangers fit by regular drills, for sea voyages tended to make men slack.

Rather than sail direct for Barbados, Captain Stringer headed out to the Atlantic before beating south.

"I want a man aloft as a lookout at all times, Lundey," Stringer said, "and change him every two hours."

"Yes, Captain." Lundey did not hide his confusion.

"The French privateers are deadly, even in winter," Stringer explained. "They send out ships from Martinico all across the Caribbean and as far north as Nova Scotia. Bloody pirates!" He spat into the wind.

MacKim and Kennedy exchanged glances.

"Martinico?" Kennedy said. "That would be a logical target for the fleet. I think it's the only sizeable French possession in the Windward Islands."

"We'd better hope it's a quick campaign," MacKim said. The Caribbean islands had a terrible history for previous British military endeavours. As well as the actual fighting against the redoubtable French, the islands had a long-standing reputation for being riddled with disease. Yellow fever and malaria could reduce a regiment of eight-hundred men to a couple of hundred within a few months. To many soldiers, being posted to the West Indies was a death sentence without the possibility of military glory.

The Rangers' morale slumped as they headed south, despite every mile bringing them closer to better weather, so it was a surprise when something disturbed MacKim's sleep.

"Somebody is singing." MacKim struggled out of his tiny cot. *Martha* was a small brig, not designed to carry passengers, and the Rangers crowded into anywhere they could. MacKim and Kennedy shared the tween decks with the carpenter, cook, and sailmaker.

MacKim looked around as the singing increased in volume. "Somebody is drunk."

"It's not one of our men," Kennedy said. "Leave it to the captain."

"I'll look anyway."

It had been a few years since MacKim crossed the Atlantic as a Johnny Raw with the 78th Highlanders. Looking back, it seemed incredible that he had ever been so naïve. Now, with three years of bitter war and three savage campaigns behind him, he was a seasoned veteran, carrying mental and physical scars. MacKim touched the bald patch on the top of his head, where an Abenaki had taken his scalp, grunted, and moved on.

Martha plunged and kicked as she fought her way down the Atlantic towards the Caribbean. MacKim had forgotten how lively a ship could be at sea and how the wind howled fiercely through the rigging. He emerged on deck, staggered as a gust of wind battered *Martha* to starboard, ignored the scornful laugh of the helmsman and listened for the singing.

A seaman emerged from below, grinning vacantly at MacKim and slurring something incomprehensible before he collapsed on the deck.

"Bloody idiot," MacKim muttered and dragged the man to the fo'c'sle. He opened the door and pitched the drunkard into the stinking dark. "Here! Take care of this man before he falls overboard."

Two of the crew looked at their shipmate. "He's been tapping the spirits," one said.

"Does the captain not keep it secure?" MacKim asked testily.

"It's in the cargo hold," the seaman said. "If you want a free drink, lobster, just stick a straw into one of the kegs and suck." He gave a crooked smile.

"What's the cargo?"

"Brandy, rum, and spruce beer for the Army." The seaman laughed. "We're carrying rum to the Caribbean, where they invented the damned stuff."

MacKim shook his head. Even after years in uniform, the ways of the Army were strange to him. "I'll leave this fellow with you," he said.

"Join us, sergeant," the seaman said. "We've always plenty rum in this ship."

"Thank you," MacKim said. "I must decline. I have to show a good example to my men." He heard the crew singing as he returned to his bed, with the night wind keen on deck and *Martha* surging south with the wind now on their quarter—a soldier's wind, as the crew called it.

Claudette. Her image filled MacKim's mind as he lay still. *Will you forget me when I am on the islands of the far south?* He sighed. He was not lucky with women, and despite her letter, he had no reason to believe that Claudette would be any different.

He had met her, a French-Canadian native of Quebec, during the winter of 1759, when the British occupation of the city was raw. Their initial tentative friendship had deepened, yet never extended to romance. They were friends only.

So why am I thinking of you when I am alone?

Because you are something to hold onto, MacKim answered

himself. *You are a reality that there is sanity outside the madness of continual war. That's the only reason. I don't expect anything else, whatever you claim.*

MacKim sighed. Danger, drink, and women were the three constants in a soldier's life.

2

MacKim heard the quick patter of feet on deck, listened to the steady creak of *Martha*, and left the tween decks to check his men. They lay in various corners of the vessel, some silent, others grunting or snoring in their sleep. MacRae was talking in his native Gaelic, Parnell snoring like a bull, Oxford curled in a foetal ball, Danskin holding a letter to his sweetheart, but all present and correct.

MacKim nodded, satisfied that his men were safe. Only a few weeks ago, they had all been quartered in Quebec, secure in the knowledge that they had conquered Canada and hoping their war was over. After years of hard campaigning, MacKim's parent regiment, the 78th Highlanders, had settled into the Canadian city, while Kennedy's Rangers had engaged in routine patrolling and picket work.

MacKim smiled as he remembered these quiet days when he had spent many of his off-duty hours walking with Claudette.

"What are your intentions with that woman?" Kennedy had asked, half-joking, yet wholly serious.

MacKim had considered the implications before he replied. "I'm not sure I have any intentions."

"In the eyes of the rest of the Rangers," Kennedy said, "you two are already married with a brood of children."

"I'm too young for a wedding," MacKim said as the idea of married life slid into his mind. "And a soldier's life is no life for a woman."

"Harriette is happy enough," Kennedy pointed out. Harriette was Private Chisholm's wife, as tough and hardened a campaigner as any soldier in the British Army. MacKim had known her from his early days in the 78th Highlanders when she was married to Corporal Gunn, now dead. Chisholm, a much-scarred veteran, had befriended MacKim when he was a Johnny Raw.

"Harriette was born in the Army," MacKim said. "She knows no other life." He had looked over the ruins of Quebec, which the Army and Quebecers were gradually rebuilding after the British bombardment of two years previously. He liked the spirit of Quebec, although he found city life constraining.

"Claudette favours you," Kennedy urged, smiling.

MacKim temporised. "Maybe after I leave the Army."

"That won't be long now. As soon as peace comes, the king will disband us all. Geordie doesn't need Rangers in time of peace."

Peace. The concept was alien. MacKim could not imagine a world at peace. He knew he could never return to scraping an existence at the whim of a landlord or a clan chief. After fighting with the 78th in the vastness of North America, and particularly after making his own decisions with the Rangers, MacKim would never bow down before imposed authority.

"Maybe then," MacKim said. "It all depends on the Spaniards. If Spain remains neutral, we can force France to the negotiating table, although God knows they've little to negotiate. We've removed most of their colonial possessions from the chessboard."

"They still hold Martinico, Louisiana, and part of Hispaniola," Kennedy said. "Let's hope Spain does not get involved. That would mean another couple of years of war until we can force her to submit." He grunted. "On the other hand, if the Spanish do ally themselves to France, we can grab Florida."

"I don't want to grab anything," MacKim said.

"Except Claudette?" Kennedy said, smiling.

"There are obstacles between us. Claudette is Roman Catholic, and I am Presbyterian."

Kennedy looked away. "That is an obstacle."

"Aye. I'm not giving away my life to the dictates of the Pope."

"Maybe you could convert Claudette to the Reformed Church?" Kennedy asked.

"Claudette is staunch in her Catholicism," MacKim said.

MacKim remembered that conversation as he lay in his uncomfortable cot. The religious obstacle seemed insurmountable, for MacKim's mother had fed him tales of the horrors of the Roman Catholic Church. However, his family had fought for the Catholic Stuarts in the late Jacobite Risings in Scotland, which was always a paradox in MacKim's mind. To him, man had debased the simple teachings of Christ by creating hierarchies of religion, with different factions preaching alternate varieties of the Gospel.

MacKim shook his head. Should people not have allowed the fundamental truth to shine through without confusing the issues for their own ends?

He heard a sudden shout on deck, sighed, and tried not to listen. MacKim had grown used to the crew's nightly raids on the cargo and subsequent drunken return to the fo'c'sle. He ignored the shouts and yells and tried to get back to sleep, but the noise was different this night.

The distinct crack of a pistol brought MacKim to full wakefulness.

"What was that, sergeant?" Kennedy's voice sounded through the gloom.

"It sounded like a gunshot," MacKim said as he controlled

his suddenly increased heartbeat. "Wait here, and I'll investigate."

"Drunken fools!" Kennedy said. "Captain Stringer ought to get them in hand."

With the Rangers' firearms held elsewhere, MacKim only had a bayonet as he slid onto the main deck. He had no sooner emerged when he knew something was badly wrong. A crewman lay dead beside the mainmast, with blood spreading from his chest, and his eyes and mouth wide open.

"Trouble, lads!" MacKim ran below to warn the still-sleeping Rangers.

Before the Rangers could react, a rush of men thundered onto the ship with a pair of pistols pointing at MacKim and others directed at the half-sleeping men.

"What the devil?" MacKim asked.

"Allez!" the man with the pistols gestured for MacKim to return to the main deck. Only then was he aware of the vessel tied up alongside *Martha*.

"Who are you?" A smiling, slender man pushed through the crowd to confront MacKim. "You are not part of this crew." His strong French accent informed MacKim what had happened. Unseen in the cloudy night, a French vessel, either a royal warship or a privateer, had closed with *Martha* and sent a boarding party onto the Boston vessel.

Now that they had control of the brig, the Frenchmen lit lanterns, whose smoky, flickering light illuminated the deck, allowing MacKim to have a partial picture of events.

Looking over the faces of the men who pointed pistols, boarding pikes, and swords at the Rangers, MacKim guessed they were privateers rather than seamen from one of King Louis's ships. They looked more like buccaneers from the seventeenth century than seamen from the more civilised eighteenth —ragged, fierce-eyed, and composed of a multitude of nationalities.

"Who are you?" the smiling man repeated.

"I am Sergeant Hugh MacKim of Kennedy's Rangers. Who are you?" MacKim tried to keep calm.

"I am Captain René Roberval of the privateer *Douce Vengeance*," the slender man gave a sweeping bow as he confirmed MacKim's suspicions. "You may have heard of me?"

"I have not, monsieur," MacKim replied in English.

"You will, sir. You will." Roberval sounded disappointed.

"You appear to have us at a disadvantage," MacKim said as the privateers ushered the Rangers onto the main deck. A glance assured MacKim that the French had complete control of *Martha*, with other privateers holding weapons to the crew. MacKim was aware that the Caribbean and east coast of the Americas swarmed with French privateers, civilian vessels officially licensed to prey on their country's enemies. Some were as disciplined as any French royal vessel, but others were little more than pirates.

"You damned French scoundrel!" Captain Stringer roared from aft. "You'll not take my ship, by God!"

"Oh, it seems that I have taken your ship, by God," Roberval said. "You are the master, I presume?"

"You're damned right I am!" Stringer strode forward, with a grinning black man holding a cutlass to his chest. "Get off my ship, damn your eyes."

"Damn my eyes?" Roberval said. "You'll damn my eyes?" He stepped up to the much shorter Stringer. "You won't damn my eyes, captain, but I'll have yours." The suave voice altered to a deadly hiss.

After years at war, MacKim recognised a dangerous man and sensed the malignant force within Roberval. Behind the polished façade, this privateer was vicious, despite the faint outline of a cross that marred his smooth forehead.

"Hold him," Roberval ordered in French, and two of his men wrapped their arms around Stringer. Drawing a long, slender knife from his belt, Roberval approached Stringer and slowly, deliberately, gouged out the captain's eyes.

"You bastard!" Lundey surged forward, only for two of the privateers to knock him to the deck and kick him into submission.

"Dear God in heaven," MacKim breathed as the Rangers watched in horror. "He's as bad as the Indians."

"Now," Roberval said as Stringer writhed, screaming, with blood flowing down his face, "throw him overboard."

"You monster!" Oxford shouted until MacKim clamped a hand over his mouth.

"Best keep quiet, son," MacKim said. "You can't help, and yelling will only turn Roberval's attention to you."

The privateers pushed the struggling Stringer to the rail, punched him in the stomach until he doubled up, and casually pushed him into the sea.

Even the war-hardened Rangers flinched at the cold-blooded murder.

"Keep quiet," MacKim snarled to his men.

"Why are Kennedy's Rangers on this vessel?" Roberval asked, cleaning Stringer's blood off his knife on the scarf he wore around his neck.

"Captain Stringer was taking us to join the rest of the British Army," MacKim said.

"I have Kennedy," Roberval said. "How many Rangers are there?"

MacKim glanced over his men. If any had managed to hide, he would have given a false figure, but all were present. "Twenty-five," he said. "Including me. Plus Lieutenant Kennedy." He knew that hesitating or lying to Roberval would bring retribution on him or his men.

"Hmmm," Roberval said. "Where are you bound, sergeant?"

MacKim shook his head. "I don't know, captain."

"Hmmm," Roberval said again. "Perhaps the sergeant would not know. It's a small matter."

The tropical night was already easing, with a band of lesser dark along the eastern horizon. MacKim knew that it would be full daylight in fifteen minutes, with the harsh sun ensuring every man would droop in the heat. He was not yet used to the speed of sunrise and sunset this far south, so different from the protracted dawns of more northern climes. He surveyed his surroundings, with the sea rising in a regular swell to north, south, and east, but a dense smudge to the west suggesting an island huddled nearby.

"Bring me Lieutenant Kennedy," Roberval ordered. Within two minutes, three of his men shoved Kennedy along the deck. The lieutenant nursed a heavily bruised eye and left cheek while blood dribbled from a split lip.

"It's nothing serious," Kennedy said with an attempt at a smile. "I've had worse from my mother."

"Join your men," Roberval ordered dispassionately.

Kennedy did so, sinking to the deck in sudden pain.

Dawn came swiftly, with the island now plain. It was a scrap of land with a small hill on the north and a scattering of palm trees catching the horizontal rays of the sun.

"Bring me *Martha's* crew," Roberval ordered in his pleasant voice, and the privateers pushed and dragged forward the twelve-strong crew.

MacKim looked around. The privateer's vessel—a long, fast, black-painted ship—lay alongside, with three steeply raked masts and a row of cannon on her deck, plus a dozen swivels for scything down the crew of any vessel that showed resistance. *Douce Vengeance* must have crept up during the night when most of *Martha's* crew were asleep and half the others lushy with rum. Roberval would have boarded silently, with his more numerous boarders easily overpowering *Martha's* men.

Beyond *Douce Vengeance*, the island was becoming clearer by the minute. However, MacKim's geography of this area was so vague, he could only guess it was an outlier of the Bahamas group.

Roberval smiled as *Martha's* crew huddled before him, with one or two looking at the fresh bloodstains on the deck.

"Who's first?" Roberval asked.

The hands looked at one another without understanding.

"You, I think." Roberval spoke English with a decided accent, as though he was used to mixing with the lowest in society, however resplendent his clothes. He pointed to Lundey, who responded with a defiant glare.

"Me what?" Lundey asked.

In response, Roberval strode forward, drawing his sword. As Lundey lifted his fists in defence, Roberval cut off the mate's left arm. The blood spouted as Lundey stared, too shocked to scream.

"Throw him overboard," Roberval ordered as the remainder of *Martha's* crew stepped back or roared in horror. Two privateersmen grabbed Lundey and threw him over the side.

"And the rest of the crew," Roberval ordered, and a horde of privateers rushed at *Martha's* remaining crew, cutlasses raised as they hacked at the helpless merchant seamen.

"You murdering bastards!" MacRae reared forward, only for two privateersmen to thrust boarding pikes at him, forcing him back.

"Careful, sergeant!" MacRae said.

"Right, men," Kennedy spoke urgently. "This French Roberval's crazed. I'm going to rush him and try and take the boat back. On the count of three!"

"He'll kill you," Oxford said.

"I think he'll kill us all, whatever we do." MacKim balled his fists.

"We've no weapons."

"We have our fists and boots," Kennedy said. "One, two…"

"Allez!" a Frenchman on the upper mast of *Douce Vengeance* shouted through cupped hands. "A British frigate is coming from the lee of the island!"

"Back to *Douce Vengeance!*" Roberval ordered.

In an amazingly short space of time, the privateers fled *Martha*, leaving her crew dead or dying on the deck, or floating overboard in the sea.[1] The newcomer, with the Union flag flying proud, approached at some speed. When she was within three-hundred yards, her gunports opened, and twelve cannons rolled out, their muzzles black and evil.

Douce Vengeance unfastened herself from *Martha*, caught the wind, and danced away, leaving the frigate standing.

"Thank God for the Royal Navy," Kennedy said. "They saved us in the siege of Quebec, and they've saved us again here."

"They didn't save *Martha's* crew," MacKim pointed out.

"Nor did we," Kennedy said.

The frigate came to three cables-lengths from *Martha* with her broadside run out and a row of black-muzzled cannon menacing the brig. Within two minutes, the frigate launched a pinnace, which pulled across the intervening water. A young, gloriously uniformed officer sat in the stern as a dozen men strained at the oars, cutlasses at their hips and pistols prominent in their belts.

"Here they come." Kennedy stepped to the rail. "We're glad to see you!" he shouted.

The pinnace came alongside, with the crew raising their oars at the last possible moment and one man expertly using a boathook to attach the pinnace to *Martha*. The officer scrambled on board, quickly followed by every man save one, who remained in the pinnace.

"Thank God for the Navy," Kennedy said.

"*Qui es-tu?*" Who are you? the officer asked. "British?"

"You're French." Kennedy stepped back.

"Oh, dear God in heaven," MacKim said.

3

"Lieutenant Gramont." The officer gave a slight bow. "Are you English?"

Kennedy shook his head. "No. I am from the colony of New Hampshire. This gentleman—" he indicated MacKim "—is from Scotland, and most of my men are from New Hampshire, with some from Scotland or England."

Lieutenant Gramont gave a slight smile. "Either way, you are now prisoners of King Louis." He indicated his ship just as the Union flag fluttered down to be replaced by the ensign of France. "May I have the honour of knowing your names?"

"I am Lieutenant Kennedy of Kennedy's Rangers, and this gentleman is Sergeant MacKim, late of the 78th Fraser's Highlanders and now of the Rangers. My men are all Rangers and entitled to be treated as prisoners of war."

"The Highland Furies?" Gramont eyed MacKim as if expecting him to pull a broadsword from his stocking and charge forward.

"Will you treat my men honourably, according to the Rules of War?" Kennedy asked.

As he waited for an answer, the French seamen examined

Martha, pointing at the blood-stained planking and talking in low tones.

"The privateers murdered the captain and crew of *Martha,*" Kennedy continued. "I hope you are more civilised, sir."

Gramont frowned. "I am a servant of the king, not a privateer," he spat out the word as if it was a curse. "These men," he continued, jerking his chin in the direction of *Douce Vengeance.* "They were not even privateers; they were nothing more than freebooters —common pirates—not fit to lick the boots of a true Frenchman."

"They were murderers," MacKim said. "Captain René Roberval commanded them, and their ship was *Douce Vengeance.*"

"I will remember the names," Gramont said. "In the meantime, your men shall return to whatever quarters they habitually frequent in this vessel, Lieutenant Kennedy, while you and the brave sergeant shall repair to *Dryade,* his Majesty's ship, so my captain may question you."

With two more boatloads of French seamen arriving on *Martha,* the Rangers, unarmed and outnumbered, could not resist as armed men herded them back into the hold.

"Keep your heads up, lads!" Kennedy shouted. "You'll be exchanged before you know it."

Dryade was a 32-gun frigate, smart, efficient, and dangerous. Captain Marbet waited on the quarterdeck as his men escorted the prisoners aboard.

"Good morning, gentlemen," he commanded as he gently examined Kennedy's bruised face. "My surgeon shall tend to that, Lieutenant Kennedy." Then he snapped an order to a junior officer, who hurried away, returning with a plump and cheerful doctor.

"Ah, two brave British soldiers, lost on the high seas." The doctor examined Kennedy with care, rubbed some foul-smelling ointment on his bruises, and left, whistling a jaunty song.

"Take them below," Marbet ordered. "Ensure they do not escape, and feed them." He smiled. "The fortunes of war have not favoured you, gentlemen, but that does not mean we are not humane."

MacKim found their quarters on *Dryade* more comfortable than their space on *Martha,* with the added refinement of a bottle of fine wine and some bread that their captor sent them as sustenance.

"If this is French captivity," Kennedy said, tasting the wine, "I could get used to it."

"I don't intend to," MacKim said. He pushed at the door, found it was locked, and when he looked through a crack in the wood, saw a marine sentry standing outside. "It may be velvet-lined, but it's still a prison."

Kennedy sat on the deck with his back resting on the bulkhead. "I'll think of something, MacKim. I still want to visit Covent Garden when this war is over."

MacKim touched Claudette's letter in his pocket and said nothing. *This new campaign is not going well.*

Captain Marbet called them up to his cabin later that day, sitting at an ornate desk while he shared a bottle of wine with them.

"I have put a prize crew on your vessel," Marbet told them. "Your men will be gently cared for." He spoke halting English, and MacKim thought it best not to admit he understood French.

"Thank you," Kennedy said.

"Now, gentlemen, I know you are both Rangers and your vessel was bound to the south. Please tell me where you were heading and what you know about the British intentions."

Kennedy glanced at MacKim. "We came from Quebec and meant to join the British fleet at New York," he spoke slowly, enhancing his New Hampshire drawl. "But we were late. Ice on the St Lawrence delayed us."

"And where are you headed now?"

Kennedy screwed up his face. "We were heading south," he said truthfully. "Somewhere south of wherever we are now."

Captain Marbet nodded. "Did you hear the lamented captain of *Martha* mention any destinations? Any islands?"

Kennedy shook his head. "The captain barely spoke to me at all, sir." He looked over at MacKim. "How about you, sergeant? Did the captain mention his destination to you?"

"Not even once," MacKim said.

"You are very reticent gentlemen," Captain Marbet said, smiling. "I will put you with my other guests, and when we arrive at a French port, you will be accorded all the hospitality usual for our prisoners." He called for a guard, and two white-coated marines escorted MacKim and Kennedy down below.

"In there." The marines were rougher than Marbet had been as they thrust Kennedy and MacKim into a reasonably large space lined with furled sails and spars. A dozen men looked up at their arrival with a mixture of resignation and curiosity. The marines closed and barred the door behind them.

"Good morning, gentlemen," Kennedy said. "Can any of you speak English?"

"A damned sight better than you can," a thin-faced man said. "You're a Colonial."

"New Hampshire, born and bred," Kennedy admitted. "God's own country. Are you all British?"

"Some." The thin-faced man sat on the deck, his eyes scrutinising Kennedy. "Some are from the islands—Jamaica, Barbados, or others. We're all masters and mates of vessels that *Dryade* has captured." His bitter eyes scanned Kennedy's green uniform. "How did Marbet net a brace of Colonial Rangers?"

Kennedy explained what had happened as the other prisoners gathered around to listen.

"Roberval," the thin-faced man repeated the name. "I've heard of him. He's a pirate, pure and simple, and a first-rate bastard to boot." He looked up, glaring at Kennedy and MacKim as if at an enemy. "I'm Captain Mansfield, late of *Emma's Pride*, until Marbet captured us off Cape Cod."

MacKim kept quiet as the seamen discussed piracy in the

Caribbean. After a while, he spoke up. "I have no wish to spend months or years as a prisoner. What are the chances of escaping from here?"

"None," Mansfield replied flatly. "We're locked in, with an armed guard outside. Even if we managed to leave the cabin, we're on a French warship packed with hundreds of sailors and marines. What could we do? We're merchant seamen, not fighters."

Kennedy glanced at MacKim. "What do you think, sergeant?"

"I think I don't want to be a prisoner," MacKim said. "We'll get out of here somehow."

"They must feed us." Kennedy squeezed into a corner.

"They treat us well," a stocky man said. "I've no complaints about that."

"How many men come at feeding time?" MacKim caught the drift of Kennedy's words.

"Three," the stocky man said. "One man with food and water, and two marines with musket and bayonet. It's no good, sergeant. Even if we could overpower them, then what? We can't take over the whole ship."

"We don't have to," MacKim said. "We only have to get on a boat. You men are sailors; you can sail to the nearest British island."

Although Mansfield grunted, his eyes lost some of their acidity. "Maybe. Aye, maybe."

Kennedy lifted a finger. "I have a plan." His smile masked the worry in his voice. "I will need all your help, and even then, it may not work."

The stocky man grunted. "That's encouraging. What do you want us to do?" He held out his hand. "Robinson, late of *Bristol Trader*."

"We'll use one of these sails," Kennedy said as he shook Robinson's hand. "And a little bit of guile."

MacKim heard footsteps outside the door. "Somebody's coming," he warned, and slipped behind the old sail Kennedy had draped against the bulkhead.

"Ready," Kennedy whispered.

The prisoners waited, one man chewing tobacco and others holding makeshift weapons or merely clenching their fists.

There was the sound of wood on wood as the Frenchman unbarred the door and pushed it open, shining a lantern inside the room.

"Make way," the Frenchman said in clumsy English. "*Allez!*"

As the prisoners shuffled back, the food-bearer entered with two white-coated marines at his back.

"Monsieur!" Kennedy beckoned them forward, smiling. "Monsieur!" He had picked up a smattering of French from his time in Quebec. "Come here."

As the Frenchmen stepped forward, MacKim emerged from beneath the sail and slipped outside the door. In common with their British counterparts, French marines were brave soldiers, but not trained in deception and original thought like the Rangers. They were disciplined to obey orders immediately and without question. MacKim felt the hammer of his heart and hoped the sound did not echo from the bulkheads of *Dryade*.

Take deep breaths, MacKim. You've faced French regulars in open battle and Abenaki warriors in their native forests. What are a few tarry-backed sailors after that?

MacKim huddled in the thick darkness of the tween decks. On *Martha*, he had belonged, but on this French ship, he was an enemy alien. The surroundings felt more hostile than any Canadian forest—claustrophobic, intense, and with a pervading scent of French cooking. All he needed to do was avoid detection until the hours of darkness, then open the door to release the prisoners. But where to hide? The frigate was crammed with men, far more than *Martha* had held and more than any British warship he had seen. It seemed as if the French filled every available space with men and munitions, leaving no hiding place for fugitives.

Where is the least likely place for a man to hide? If the Frenchies discover I am missing, where won't they look?

In the captain's day cabin. No fugitive would be foolish enough to hide there.

Compared to the crew's quarters, the captain lived in luxury, with two cabins to himself, one for sleeping and another for eating, working, and relaxing. MacKim ensured that Captain Marbet was on the quarterdeck, giving quiet orders that moved *Dryade* efficiently through the sea.

Moving aft, Watters swore when he saw a marine on guard outside the captain's cabin.

Damn! I should have considered that possibility. Distract him, MacKim!

Hiding in the shadows, MacKim called out in French, "Marine! Check the forward hatch!"

As the marine hurried forward, MacKim slid inside the cabin, feeling his heart pounding. If Captain Marbet were as efficient as he appeared, he would remain on deck most of the day. If he returned to his cabin? MacKim shook his head. He would deal with that eventuality if it arose.

The day cabin was beautifully furnished, with an ornate, inlaid desk, a glass bookcase full of books, and half a dozen decanters of wines and spirits. Although *Dryade* was more stable in the water than *Martha*, she still pitched and rolled, causing the decanters on the side table to slide. Possibly to combat the ship's motion, Captain Gramont had placed a heavy paperweight to hold down a neat pile of documents on his desk.

"I'm no spy," MacKim told himself, yet the presence of nautical papers was tempting. The Admiralty would love to have access to a French captain's documents, possibly with sealed orders that revealed the dispositions of the French fleet.

Stepping to the desk, MacKim scanned the papers on top.

One, in particular, took his attention, addressed to the secretary of state in Paris.

It was the work of a second to lift the letter and slide it inside his tunic, and then MacKim searched for somewhere to hide in the cabin.

He heard voices and squeezed against the bulkhead, hoping nobody entered the captain's cabin.

"The British will have to move quickly if they want to take Martinico," somebody said. "The fleet from Brest will shatter their Navy and bring reinforcements to La Touché's garrison."

"I hear the Spanish are with us now," a second voice murmured. "They are sending twenty-five line-of-battle ships to our aid. With our combined fleet, the British will see their acquisitions fall one by one."

The voices drifted away as the speakers passed the door. To judge by their refined accents, both men were officers.

MacKim crouched in the cabin, held the letter he had stolen, and wondered about the snippet of information he'd just heard. Admiral Rodney would be eager to hear of this French fleet from Brest, whether he was headed for Martinico or not.

Am I a spy now? I hope not. Spying is a dirty, dishonourable business, sneaking around and stealing the enemy's secrets.

MacKim shook his head. The intelligence he had in his hand might save thousands of British lives if he could get it to Admiral Rodney. Dishonour or honour mattered little in comparison. A fleet coming from Brest and the Spanish joining the French? Either of these happenings could alter the course of the Caribbean campaign.

Opening the door a fraction, MacKim peered into the gloom. Somewhere ahead, a lantern flickered as it swung to the rhythm of the ship. There was something essentially dismal about a deserted passageway in a ship, an atmosphere MacKim could not fathom, as if the surrounding timber was aware it did not belong so far from land.

Concentrate!

MacKim stepped out of the cabin into the passageway, stooping under the low deck above and nearly choking in the foetid air. A quick search found a marlinespike, which MacKim lifted.

The marine sentry stood at the door where the prisoners were held, half-asleep, with his musket at his side. He stared ahead, his mind numbed by the boredom of his post, occasionally shifting his weight from one foot to the next. When MacKim approached, the marine barely noticed, for his orders were to keep the prisoners inside, not to watch for external threats. MacKim tipped off the man's hat and smashed the marlinespike on his head.

"My apologies, marine," MacKim said, "but our kings are enemies, so we must fight each other."

The door was not locked, but closed with a simple length of wood that MacKim drew from its holders in seconds.

"Right, men," he said. "We're out of here."

A dozen faces stared at him. Kennedy moved at once, with Mansfield a second behind him. "Come on, gentlemen," Kennedy invited.

The seamen merely glanced at the unconscious marine before heading for the main deck. They seemed able to find their way around the ship without effort. Within minutes, Robinson led the Rangers to the longboat that lay between the mizzen and mainmast.

"Qui c'est?" "Who's that?"

The officer on watch leaned forward, peering into the dark from his position on the quarterdeck.

"C'est moi!" Kennedy said, launching himself up the ladder and pulling the officer to the deck. He returned before the seamen had time to think. "He's unconscious, not dead," Kennedy said. "Now, get this boat launched."

"The helmsman will hear the splash," one of the seamen warned.

"Leave him to me," MacKim said. "You get the boat over the side."

The helmsman looked up as MacKim approached, saw a shadowy figure on the dark deck, and presumed it was the officer of the watch.

"My apologies, Monsieur," MacKim said, and hauled the helmsman to the deck. It was the work of an instant to tie him up as Robinson fastened the wheel with a length of rope.

"That will hold the present course until the wind shifts," Robinson said. "We should be alright for ten, maybe fifteen minutes."

"By then, we should be far away," MacKim said.

Dryade was moving slowly before a light breeze, yet lowering the longboat was still a strenuous manoeuvre. Finally, the boat landed in the sea with what seemed a colossal splash, and the seamen followed, scrambling down the ship's side with an agility that MacKim could only envy. He followed as best he could, stepping into the boat and settling on one of the wooden seats as Robinson took the tiller and Mansfield pushed away from *Dryade*.

"Where to?" Robinson sniffed the wind and glanced back at the French frigate.

"The nearest British island," Kennedy said.

"Does anybody know where we are?" MacKim unshipped an oar and dipped it in the water. After years of paddling the light, birch-bark canoes of Canada, the much heavier oars of a European boat felt clumsy in his hands.

"*Dryade* picked us up thirty leagues west of Grand Bahama," Robinson said. "She was headed north and east, so I'd say, given the wind, we're about eighty leagues northeast now."

The other seamen gave their opinions, each of which varied from Robinson's by only by a few leagues.

"If we head south and west," Robinson continued, "we should find the Bahamas by the day after tomorrow. Three days at the worst."

"Three days?" MacKim questioned.

"Three days in an open boat is long enough for anybody," Robinson said. "I was shipwrecked once in the German Ocean. We drifted for thirty-six hours, and I've not recovered yet." He examined the stars, shifted the tiller, and ordered everybody else to row.

"I've brought water." One bearded man held up a keg. "We'll ration it."

"There's a mast here," Mansfield said. "We'll raise it when the wind shifts."

"Row, damn it," Robinson ordered. "Or *Dryade* will see us, and we'll be back on board. Sure as death, Marbet would clap us in irons. Captain Mansfield, keep that damned mast down until we're out of sight. A lookout can spot a sail for miles."

MacKim hauled at the oars, copying the technique of the seamen. The thirst came with the rising sun, and after only a few hours, he felt weak and light-headed. Raising the mast and sail provided some shade while a welcome breeze pushed them southwestward through long swells, with nothing breaking the hard line of the horizon.

"We'll spell each other at the oars," Mansfield said. "And at the tiller. Ration the water."

Nobody argued. The seamen all knew the dangers they faced in an open boat in the Atlantic. The Rangers all realised the seamen were more experienced on the water.

On the second day, MacKim's head pounded with the heat, while his hands were swollen and spongy from the constant friction of the oars.

If Claudette could see me now, she would not be impressed!

"How far now?" Kennedy asked.

"Maybe twenty leagues, if my calculations are right," Robinson said.

"Should we not see land by now? The tip of a mountain, perhaps?"

"The Bahamas are low islands. You won't see them until we're a few miles away."

They rowed on, with a fitful wind filling the sails and instantly falling away, to repeat the procedure throughout the day. Twice, sharks surfaced nearby to circle the boat and submerge again, with the dorsal fin a reminder of the danger that lurked in the water.

"A sail," Mansfield croaked. "I see a sail."

The men peered at the horizon, eyes narrowed against the sun.

"Aye, but is she French or British?"

"At present, I don't care, as long as she has water on board."

Kennedy raised his voice to a croak. "I care. She might be Roberval's *Douce Vengeance*."

MacKim stifled a laugh he recognised as hysteria and pulled at his oar. Rowing had become mechanical now. He could not imagine a time when he had not rowed, when life did not consist of bending forward, dipping the oar into the sea, and leaning back, lifting the oar and repeating the movement, again and again. The sea was a constant, together with the burning sun and the aching abyss of the sky.

"She's a ship...three-masted." The seaman tried to identify the strange sail. "Very sloppy seamanship. She's all over the place. Look at the topsail! It's like mother's washing line on a windy day."

"Spanish then," Mansfield guessed. "Is Spain still neutral?"

"God only knows," Kennedy said.

"She's not Spanish." MacKim stared at the ship as they came closer. "She's from Boston, with a French prize crew. That's either *Martha* or her twin sister."

4

"*Martha's* lookout is either blind or asleep." Robinson appeared to be attached to the tiller. "She's not altered her course towards us."

Mansfield nodded. "Steer for her. We won't survive another day without water."

Martha sailed on, heeling to starboard, and then larboard as the wind caught her, with her sails flapping, filling, and emptying, and a line trailing over her stern into the sea.

"It's not like the French to be such poor seamen," Robinson observed. "Where the devil is the officer on watch?"

"Go alongside," Mansfield ordered. "They haven't noticed us yet."

Robinson eased the longboat alongside *Martha*, with a lanky mate named Kelly attaching them with a boathook. They remained in that situation for two minutes, with *Martha* limping through the dark seas and the longboat attached amidships.

"There's something queer here," Robinson said. "I can't see a damned soul on deck."

"I'll go on board," Kennedy whispered. "MacKim, you're with me."

Martha was much lower in the water than *Dryade*, making it easy for the Rangers to clamber on board. MacKim crouched on the deck, staring forward and aft. The deck was deserted, with nobody on watch and the sails above flapping to the tune of the wind.

Leaving Kelly to watch the longboat, the seamen followed Kennedy and MacKim. "Where is everybody?" Robinson asked. "It's like a ghost ship."

"Ghost ship, my arse," Mansfield gave his sour opinion. "The French have abandoned her."

"MacKim, head aft. I'll go forward," Kennedy ordered, lifting a marlinespike from its rack along the rail.

"Listen!" MacKim hissed as a song drifted from below. "Somebody's singing."

À la claire fontaine m'en allant promener
J'ai trouvé l'eau si belle que je m'y suis baignée.
Il y a longtemps que je t'aime, jamais je ne t'oublierai

As I was walking by the clear fountain,
I found the water so lovely I had to bathe.
I've loved you for so long, I will never forget you.

When MacKim last heard that song, Claudette had been singing as she watched a section of British soldiers march past.

"It is a love song to France," Claudette had explained. "We expect France to reclaim Canada at the peace."

"That might happen." MacKim knew that when the European powers ended their periodic wars, they exchanged acquisitions over the conference table. All the bloodshed and suffering the British and Colonial soldiers had endured could be discarded if Britain handed Canada back to France.

Now the singer was masculine, with the words rougher, yet hauntingly familiar. "He's down below." MacKim pushed aside any thoughts of Claudette. "The singer's below deck."

Lifting a marlinespike, MacKim shoved open the forward

hatch, wincing at the noise, and descended into the stuffy dark. The singing increased in volume, with other voices joining in.

"What the devil's happening?" Robinson asked.

MacKim grinned. "The French have found the cargo," he said as the truth broke over him.

"What bloody cargo?" Robinson asked.

"*Martha*'s carrying brandy and rum for the officer's stores."

"Dear God and all his angels! A cargo of spirits and a prize crew?" Robinson laughed. "That's asking for trouble. Who was in charge? Some young midshipman?"

MacKim nodded. "A youngster. I doubt he was seventeen yet."

They found the first of the prize crew a moment later, lying on the deck in a pool of his own vomit. Kennedy relieved him of his seaman's knife.

"Put this fellow in the cable locker," Mansfield said quietly. "How many men were in the prize crew?"

"About eight or ten," MacKim said. "At a guess."

"Well, you can guess seven or nine now," Mansfield amended. "Were they armed? What about *Martha*'s hands?"

"The privateers killed them," MacKim said. "Captain René Roberval of *Douce Vengeance*."

"Bastards," Mansfield growled. "This lot?"

"No. These are from *Dryade*."

Kennedy found the second of the prize crew a moment later. The Frenchman raised a hand in greeting and invited them to join them. "Come, my friends, we have found a sailor's paradise," he invited in French.

Mansfield crashed a marlinespike on the man's head. "Put him with the other prisoner," he said.

The midshipman was already unconscious, lying full stretch on the deck with a keg of rum rolling at his side. Kennedy relieved him of his dirk and a handy pistol, and ordered one of the mates to take him away.

"We're recapturing the ship without bloodshed," Robinson said.

"Drink is a terrible thing." Mansfield nearly smiled. "Sometimes."[1] The remainder of the prize crew sat in a convivial huddle, some singing, others grinning foolishly as Kennedy burst in on them. It was the work of five minutes to overpower them all and drag them to the fo'c'sle.

"Now," Kennedy said. "Let's get our men, sergeant."

The captive Rangers looked around in disbelief when MacKim opened the door and peered inside.

"What are you lot skulking here for?" MacKim asked. "Get on deck! There's work waiting for you!"

"We thought you were prisoners of the French," Danskin said, following MacKim to the main deck.

"Glad to see you, sergeant," MacRae grinned. "Dickie and I were planning to retake the ship ourselves."

Dickert shook his head. "You'd only be a hindrance, Mac."

The Rangers looked around at the disarray on *Martha* as MacKim gave them a resume of events. He pointed to the blood-stained deck where Roberval had murdered Captain Stringer and the others. "You lads, get this bloody deck swabbed clean!"

"Jesus, it was easier when we were prisoners," Parnell said.

"Welcome back to reality," MacKim said. "Now get scrubbing." He ignored Parnell's expression of disgust as Kennedy joined him.

"What happens now, sir?" MacKim asked.

"Now we resume our old course to Barbados," Kennedy said. "If Admiral Rodney's still there, he'll be interested in your information about the French fleet from Brest."

"I have more than information." MacKim produced the letter he had lifted from Captain Marbet's desk. "I found this as well."

"You kept that quiet," Kennedy said as the seamen bustled about, giving each other orders as they put *Martha* to rights.

"You'd better have it," MacKim said. "You're the officer."

Kennedy handled the document, now sadly stained by seawater and crumpled with its journey within MacKim's coat. He turned it over in his hand. "What does it say?"

"I haven't broken the seal."

"Maybe we should," Kennedy said with a tired smile. The bruises on his face had spread, discolouring one side and twisting his mouth into an ugly sneer. "If anybody complains, we can claim it broke in transit." He slid the blade of his knife through the red seal with the impressive coat of arms.

"It's in French." Kennedy sounded disappointed. "I can't read French."

"I can," MacKim said, recovering the letter. "It's from a Monsieur de la Touché, the Governor of Martinico, to the secretary of state in Paris."

Mansfield had joined them, listening to MacKim's words. "Read it then, man!"

"I will." MacKim read, translating as he did so, halting over some of the words and repeating phrases as others of the seamen crowded around to listen.

"Sir,

Martinico, Jan 18 1762

Doubtless your alarms are great for Martinico, occasioned by the arrogant English nation."

MacKim shook his head. "Why do they insist on calling us English? Don't they know they're fighting all of Great Britain and the Colonies, not only England? Such ignorance deserves to be punished."

"Never mind that!" Mansfield said. "Just read the blasted thing without adding any of your comments!"

"Yes, captain," MacKim said, and continued.

"But on our side, you may rest satisfied, we've a sufficient power to repulse theirs, notwithstanding Admiral Rodney is arrived with a squadron to assist one of the American Heroes who, with thirty thousand men, thinks to make us as easy a prey, as they did the undisciplined Savage Canadians. The arrogance of these invaders is raised to such a pitch of vanity, by a few trivial acquisitions, that I firmly believe they think it sufficient to appear before a place without striking a blow: that their presence alone will make us call for a capitulation. Depend upon it, Sir, we will acquit ourselves to the honour of France, and to the no small disappointment of the enemy. Let the attack be ever so severe, both by land and sea, Fort Royal will render their deepest projects abortive; And should the Brest fleet make a happy junction with that of Spain, and safely appear here, it will be a coup de grace to their naval presumption. We have now 40,000 effective men."

MacKim stopped there. "That seems an excessive force for a small island," he said. "The figure is smudged though, maybe with seawater, so it may only read four thousand."

"That's more plausible," Mansfield agreed. "Carry on, sergeant."

MacKim realised that all the seamen were listening, nodding, and exchanging meaningful glances at the words. Only Captain Robinson was missing.

"Who's working the ship?" MacKim asked.

"Let the damned ship sail herself," Mansfield growled. "Read the bloody letter!"

"Yes, captain," MacKim said.

"Besides the Mariners from the privateers, amounting to 3,000, which I have destined for the defence of the forts. The Gentleman inhabitants are resolved to die or save their isle, having no inclination to trust to the clemency of Ravagers to divide their plantations. All are loyally attached to our Great Monarch and the Isle, and be assured from me, our defence will add lustre to our Flag. In a short time, I hope to return you a large freight of prisoners, with fresh assurances of my friendship and esteem, and a particular detail of our success.

I am Sir, with all respect,
Your very obedient
Le Vassor de la Touché."[2]

"So now we know," Mansfield said. "Admiral Rodney intends to attack Martinico, and the French expect him and are fully prepared to defend their island."

"There is more," MacKim said. "I heard the French say they have a relieving fleet sailing from Brest, and that letter is confirmation. If they get there first, Rodney will have a devil of a job in capturing the island."

"Worse than that," Mansfield chimed in, "if the French line-of-battle ships meet Rodney, whoever wins the battle, the French frigates and privateers will play merry hell with the transports."

There was silence for a moment, as men thought of privateer captains such as Roberval loose with British and Colonial ships.

"The letter says the Spanish may be involved," MacKim added fuel to their fears. "I heard a French officer talk of twenty-five Spanish battleships sailing against us."

"We're at peace with Spain," Mansfield said. "Or we were. They are so volatile and always ready to join the French against us."

"We have to warn the admiral," Kennedy said.

"What are we all standing around here for?" Mansfield had taken on the leadership role with the collected captains and mates. "We've got a ship to sail, damn it. Lieutenant Kennedy! I will borrow your men as Mariners; God knows it's better for them than acting as passengers! Come on!"

5

The memory returned that night, as it did so often. He was ten years old, a helpless child with a brawny redcoated soldier holding him secure as others tortured his brother.

Drawing their seventeen-inch long bayonets, the soldiers circled Ewan, stabbing at him. When one pinioned Ewan's hand to the ground, another kicked away his dirk, laughing. Hughie could only watch as three soldiers surrounded Ewan and began to kick at his shattered leg. Ewan screamed, writhing.

"Leave him," Hughie pleaded. "Please leave him alone! He's hurt."

"Leave who?" A New Hampshire voice sounded through the memory, and MacKim jerked himself back to the present. He was lying on his bed in *Martha* with Kennedy looming over him in the stuffy dark.

"What?" MacKim struggled to sit up.

"Leave who?" Kennedy repeated. "You were shouting to leave somebody alone."

"Ewan," MacKim said. "My brother. He was wounded at the Battle of Culloden, and a group of redcoats tortured him to death."

Kennedy raised his eyebrows. "You must have been young then."

"I was ten years old," MacKim said. "I remember every detail, every pimple on the soldiers' faces, every shift of their shoulders, and intonation of their voices."

Kennedy was silent as MacKim pulled on his boots. "That's a heavy burden to carry."

"Aye. Well, the murderers are all dead now, the blood price is paid, and we're fighting another war."

"Parade in ten minutes," Kennedy said, seeing that MacKim was not inclined to discuss his memories.

"Yes, sir." MacKim rasped a hand over the stubble on his chin. Pushing the past to the back of his mind, he prepared for the day ahead.

Can we ever escape our past? Or does it shadow everything we do and influence all our decisions and actions? Are we the children of our childhood, the result of our history?

※

MACKIM STARED AT THE FLEET AS *MARTHA* JOINED THE assembled ships in Carlisle Bay, on the southwest coast of Barbados. With rank after rank of battleships, a host of busy frigates and hundreds of transports, the British invasion fleet was an impressive sight.

"I've never seen so many ships at one time," MacKim said.

Kennedy puffed at his pipe. "Nor have I," he said. "Admiral Rodney means business. If Martinico is his target, the French had better take care."

"There must be forty warships here," MacKim said, "and hundreds of transports."

Captain Robinson joined them at the rail, busily puffing at a long-stemmed pipe.

"There's *Foudroyant*, Captain Duff—one of your countrymen, MacKim. And beside her is *Temple*, Captain Lucius O'Brien, one of the most active of officers." Robinson used the stem of his pipe as a pointer. "Then there's the 50-gun *Norwich* under Captain McCleverty, and *Vanguard,* Captain Robert Swanton."

"I remember Swanton," MacKim said, looking over to *Vanguard* with interest. "She saved Quebec when the French were besieging us."

"That's right," Kennedy said. "He was the saviour of Canada as much as Wolfe or Admiral Saunders. If Swanton had not arrived, God only knows what might have happened."

MacKim nodded, remembering the dark days when Quebec was under siege. That land of deep snow and endless forest now seemed a world away from the Caribbean.

MacKim stared at the island of Barbados, baking under the sun, bright with colour and life. "It's a beautiful island."

"You won't have long to enjoy it," Kennedy said. "And don't be fooled. The whole area is beautiful, but rife with disease. Yellow jack and black vomit kill more men here than the French and Spaniards combined." He jabbed the stem of his pipe towards the island. "They used to bring in slaves from Ireland and bonded servants from England and Scotland to work the land. When the Europeans died like flies, the plantation owners used African slaves instead."

MacKim nodded. "Where I grew up, we had no idea that such places even existed. We just struggled to survive, trying to raise crops and cattle on poor soil. The idea of settling in such a fertile place..." he trailed off, shaking his head. "We could not even imagine it."

"I doubt one person in a thousand could point to Barbados in a map," Kennedy said.

"Or Martinico," Captain Mansfield said. "Yet, that island has been a major threat to British and Colonial shipping for decades. As well as being the main Caribbean base for the French royal fleet, it's a nest of privateers and freebooters. I'd wager that two-thirds of the ships the French capture in these waters are sold in Martinico."

"Are all the privateers as unpleasant as Captain Roberval?" Kennedy asked. "That's one man I'd like to avoid in future."

"No." Mansfield shook his head. "I've heard of men like him, but most French seamen are like Captain Marbet—brave, skilled, and honourable. I've nothing against the French Royal Navy, except that they're the enemy."

"If La Touché's letter is correct," Kennedy said, "we are at war with Spain as well. So that makes the Caribbean is twice as dangerous."

"All the more reason to capture Martinico," Mansfield said. He eyed the Rangers. "I hope your boys are as good in the sun as they were in the snow, Lieutenant Kennedy."

"So do I," Kennedy said.

MacKim was not listening. He was intoning the words of a song, his mind thousands of miles to the north.

À la claire fontaine m'en allant promener
J'ai trouvé l'eau si belle que je m'y suis baignée.

<hr />

REAR-ADMIRAL RODNEY STOOD ON HIS QUARTERDECK WITH the Union flag flying above him and a gaggle of officers around him, some giving supercilious looks at the two ragged, green-clad Rangers who stood on the white-scrubbed planks. Rodney was a thin-faced man with a prominent nose and a reputation for humanity as well as efficiency.

"A French fleet has left Brest to reinforce Martinico, you say," Rodney said, nodding. "I expected no less, but one does like to hear one's fears confirmed. Did you hear how many vessels there were?"

"No, sir," MacKim said. "I only overheard a snatch of conversation while I was a prisoner on the French frigate *Dryade*."

"The moral of this story, gentlemen," Rodney said to the assembled officers, "is never to listen at keyholes unless you can hear the entire conversation."

The officers convulsed in well-bred laughter. Agreeing with one's admiral was always wise.

"There's more, sir." MacKim produced the letter from the French governor. "I thought it best to hand this to you in person." He waited until Rodney scanned the letter and explained the main points to his officers.

"Thank you, Lieutenant Kennedy, and you, Sergeant MacKim," Rodney said. "You may return to your vessel." The admiral turned to his officers. "Gentlemen, if the French have a fleet coming from Brest, we must make haste to Martinico. I have Admiral Douglas there watching the French already." He rubbed his hands together. "Let's us hope we meet the French and gain prize money, by God."

"The letter mentioned the Spanish as well, sir," one of the assembled captains reminded.

"A letter from a French governor is only hearsay, gentlemen," Rodney said. "I shall deal with the French in Martinico first. The Spanish will have to wait their turn."

The captains laughed again, enjoying the prospect of a war that enhanced their careers and pockets.

※※※

THE MIDSHIPMAN MARCHED UP TO THE RANGERS, GLANCING from MacKim to Kennedy as he touched a hand to his hat. "Do I have the honour of addressing Lieutenant Kennedy of the Rangers?" he asked of the space between MacKim and Kennedy.

"I am Kennedy," Kennedy said, ending the man's indecision.

"Thank you, sir." The midshipman looked relieved. "General Monckton sends his compliments, and asks would you kindly take your men onto the transport *Lucy Swan*."

Kennedy smiled. "Pray thank the general and inform him we will depart immediately."

"Thank you, sir." The midshipman scurried away, with his

dirk rapping uncomfortably on his right hip and his trousers too large for his skinny frame.

Kennedy sighed. "They seem to get younger with every campaign. Soon we'll be fighting this war with babes-in-arms."

Lucy Swan was a Colonial-built vessel of soft pine, light on the water, fast and packed with infantrymen, none of whom welcomed another twenty-five men into their already crowded quarters.

"Bloody Colonials," one bitter-eyed Grenadier said.

"Bloody pork-eaters," MacKim retaliated with the contemporary Scottish term for an Englishman.

"Rebel Sawney bastard." The Grenadier squared up to MacKim, glaring down at him from his four-inch height advantage.

"Don't lean back, or the weight of your tail will unbalance you." MacKim met the Grenadier's eyes, put a hand on his bayonet, and waited. As he expected, the Grenadier backed off, blustering obscene threats.

"Trouble, sergeant?" Parnell had been watching with one hand on his hunting knife.

"Nothing to speak of," MacKim said. If the dispute had escalated, he would rather have had Parnell guarding his back than anybody else. The acidic Ranger was capable of fighting anybody, Grenadier or otherwise.

On January 5th, 1762, the British fleet sailed from Carlisle Bay, with three irregular lines of transports carrying the soldiers while the naval warships acted as escorts and scouted for any French vessels.

"We've fourteen-thousand soldiers," Kennedy said as he and MacKim stood at the rail with the other Rangers, watching the massed sails. A wind had risen from the east, kicking up a choppy sea so that *Lucy Swan* rose and fell in abrupt jerks that had many soldiers spewing over the side. "General Monckton must expect stiff fighting with so many men for one small island."

"How large is Martinico?"

"It's about fifty miles long, I believe," Kennedy said. "But irregularly shaped, and maybe 130 miles in circumference."

"A fair size then," MacKim said. "It's more than just a scrap of land. Will we be fighting in forests, like in Canada? Or is the island as flat as the Bahamas?"

"It's mountainous in the north, hilly in the south, and level in between," Kennedy said. "It depends where the Navy lands us."

"Are there any cities?" MacKim liked to know as much as possible about the terrain in which he would fight.

Kennedy shook his head. "St Pierre is the largest town, or St Peters, as most people will call it. That may be our principal target, for I'll wager the French defend it stoutly. Then there is Fort Royal, maybe seven leagues away from St Pierre, on the east side of the island. Take these two, and all that is left is hamlets, farms, and sugar plantations." Kennedy grinned. "And snakes. The island's forests are notorious for poisonous snakes."

"We had adders in Scotland," MacKim said. "They bit the occasional cow."

"Martinique has the fer-de-lance." Kennedy was not smiling. "Their bite can kill. There are also crocodiles."

MacKim drew in his breath. "I think I prefer Canada."

The fleet sailed leeward of Barbados, passing the Pitons of Saint Lucia and sighting Castries as they headed north. On January 7th, Rodney rendezvoused with Commodore Douglas's smaller fleet in a flurry of flags and greetings.

"More ships!" Danskin marvelled. "I didn't know there were so many ships in all the world."

"That's Jimmy Douglas's squadron," a long-pigtailed petty officer explained between spells of spitting tobacco juice over the side. "Douglas has been blockading Martinico, trapping the French warships and privateers in the harbour, and ensuring no supplies or reinforcements could reach the island."

"Why don't the French give up?" Oxford asked. "They can't possibly defeat us."

MacKim thought of the French fleet coming from Brest, and the determination evident in La Touché's letter. "The French are a tough breed," he said. "They have been in these waters for generations, so they won't want to hand control to us."

Danskin looked thoughtful, checking his bayonet was in place as Oxford turned away to look at the island they were shortly to invade.

Here we go, MacKim thought. *Another piece in the chessboard of war, with fleets and armies only pawns in the game. We, the individual infantrymen, matter less than the Biblical sparrow. If we live, nobody notices, and if we fall, nobody cares.*

MacKim watched as the flagships exchanged signals, and then Commodore Douglas boarded a small boat, with half a dozen smartly uniformed seamen rowing him across to *Marlborough*, Rodney's vessel. After a meeting that lasted an hour, Douglas returned to his ship.

"That's Rodney given him his orders," Kennedy spoke around the empty pipe he held between his teeth. "Now we'll see what's happening."

Within ten minutes, the combined fleet raised anchors and eased away to St Pierre's Bay in the north of the island, a vast convoy that must have raised apprehensions for the islanders. Douglas's squadron took the van and fired the first shots of the campaign.

Oxford and Danskin had never been in action and started when Douglas's ships fired their full broadsides. The sound was like a roll of thunder, louder than the recruits had ever heard, accompanied by clouds of grey-white powder smoke and the orange muzzle flare of the cannon.

The other Rangers watched with professional interest as the warships pounded the island.

"What are they firing at, sergeant?" Danskin asked.

"The French have built fortifications to defend every possible landing place," MacKim explained. "If we come ashore close by, their cannon will hammer us, so the Navy destroys them first."

"I see. Thank you, sergeant." Danskin continued to watch the bombardment with something like awe.

Each warship lined up, rolled out her cannon, and fired, with the force of the broadside sending the ship sideways as smoke rose masthead-high. Although MacKim was too distant to see the result of the bombardment, he saw the orange flare and heard the rumble of the fort's defensive cannon. However, the volume of smoke soon hid everything except the topmasts of the ships.

Within half an hour, the return fire from the island slackened as Douglas's ships overpowered the French.

"Sir Jimmy's hitting them hard," the friendly petty officer said. He gave a cheer that bounced his thick pigtail against his back. Most of the naval seamen had pigtails beneath their straw hats, with the long-service men boasting tails that extended halfway down their backs. When MacKim had asked if the Navy required such hairstyles, as the Army demanded its men had queues, the petty officer had laughed.

"Lord bless your ignorance, green lobster, no! We keep them stiff with tar, as you see, and when we board a French ship, the pigtails protect the back of our necks. The Frenchies' cutlasses can't cut through the tarred hair, you see."

"Somebody's topmast's gone!" another sailor shouted. "I can't see who in the smoke. Damn your hides, Johnny Crapaud! Come on, Sir James! Hammer the Crapauds!"

"Ponchett!" the transport's captain shouted to a red-faced youth. "Get aloft with you and report on the progress of the battle. Sing out if you see anything of importance."

"Aye, aye, sir!" the boy squeaked and scrambled aloft, as agile as a monkey in its forest as he ran up the ratlines to the masthead.

"We're beating them, captain!" Ponchett shouted. "The French are hardly firing back!" His voice rose a painful octave.

"*Raisonable* is leading the line, sir! She is sailing towards a French battery under topsails and t'gallants. Did you hear that roar? That was *Raisonable* firing half her starboard broadside! How did you like that, Frenchies? I said, how did you like that, eh, Johnny Crapaud?"

"Just report what's happening, Ponchett!" the captain ordered. "Or you'll be cleaning the heads for the next month!"

"Aye, aye, sir," Ponchett replied. "You should see *Raisonable*, sir! What a glorious sight! Oh no, no! No, sir! She's struck a rock! Oh, God help them!"

"What's happened, boy?"

Every face in the ship stared aloft, waiting to hear Ponchett's report. The captain, a fifty-year-old man with white hair, struggled onto the ratlines and pulled himself upwards. The officers and crew followed, desperate to see what had happened.

"Stay here," MacKim ordered the Rangers as some moved to the rigging. "We'll get in the way aloft."

A babble of sound came from above as every man shouted his observations until the captain shouted for silence. "Mr Ponchett, continue to report! The rest keep silent!"

"It's *Raisonable*, sir. She was leading the line, firing at one of the enemy batteries when she struck something. It must be a hidden rock or an uncharted reef. Her masts have gone, sir, and she's listing heavily to port. The enemy batteries, what's left of them, are concentrating on her, but Commodore Douglas has sent boats to get her men off."

"That's one ship less," MacKim said.

"We can't help," Kennedy decided. "I wager we'll be landing soon, boys. Get yourselves ready; check your ammunition and ensure the flints in your muskets are sharp." He looked upwards, where powder smoke drifted under a hard blue sky. "Ensure your canteens are full. I reckon we'll need water as much as powder before this day is done."

The Rangers pulled themselves away from the drama at sea to concentrate on themselves. Most were veterans of the war in

Canada and knew what to expect, although conditions on a Caribbean island would be widely different.

"If I get killed," Butler said, "you take my kit, Ranald."

MacDonald nodded soberly. "The same with mine, Will."

Dickert and MacRae exchanged sober glances. They shared the same vow without saying a word.

"May the good Lord help us all," MacRae said as he scrutinised the island.

"We'll show the Frenchies, eh?" Oxford tried to sound tough, then vomited over the rail. The other Rangers understood without criticising. They had learned to control their pre-battle nerves, as would Oxford, if he survived.

The British were at the head of a deep bay. Rising from the sea, steep mountains, in parts seared by deep gulleys and elsewhere by thick forest, frowned over the coast. The smell of powder smoke was acrid in every nostril.

"It won't be fun storming these hills if the French decide to hold them," MacKim observed.

Kennedy frowned. "We'll be fighting uphill against entrenched positions and an enemy who seems determined to fight and with a French relief fleet on its way." He shook his head. "I hope General Monckton knows what he's doing."

A volley of flags lifted on Admiral Rodney's flagship, and half a dozen warships shifted towards the western side of the bay, where puffs of innocent-seeming smoke marked the positions of French batteries.

"That's *Vanguard*," the long-pigtailed petty officer said. "Commodore Swanton."

"Swanton!" MacKim repeated. "We couldn't have a better man!"

"We're going with him," Kennedy said as the captain returned to the deck and shouted a string of commands. Within a few moments, the French artillery doubled their rate of fire, with columns of water rising around the British ships. MacKim watched a cannonball splash onto the surface of the water, then ricochet from wave to wave, appearing as a black blur. It missed *Lucy Swan* by a cable's length and sank into the sea a hundred yards beyond.

"This could be uncomfortable." Dickert smoothed a hand over the barrel of his long Pennsylvania rifle.

Dickert, MacRae, and Parnell were the best shots in Kennedy's Rangers and carried the Pennsylvania rifle. This weapon had more than twice the range of the Brown Bess musket, which was the standard weapon of British infantry, and its rifled barrel gave it increased accuracy. However, there were drawbacks, as the rifle took longer to load, while its longer barrel made it cumbersome to carry in wooded country.

"We're heading south," MacKim said as Swanton shepherded his ships past the green coast of the island. "What the devil's happening?"

"Admiral Rodney's found a secure anchorage and landing spot in the north," the petty officer explained. "Now he's confusing the French by sending ships south, with another squadron of frigates off to Sainte-Marie La Trinité."

"Where's that?" Kennedy asked.

"It's a small port on the windward side of Martinico, sir, opposite Saint Pierre." The seaman grinned. "The Frenchies won't know where to concentrate their forces. They won't know what we're doing."

"I'm sure I don't know either," MacKim said as Swanton's squadron continued to escort *Lucy Swan* and a sizeable number of transports south, keeping out of range of any French artillery posts on the island.

When they reached the southern tip of Martinico, Swanton left three warships to protect the transports while he took the rest of his squadron close inshore.

"This is the time for the French to unleash their privateers," MacKim said, looking at the vulnerable lines of transports. "Three warships can't be everywhere."

Kennedy puffed at his pipe. "You're right, MacKim, but with

the Navy blockading them in the harbour, the French can neither leave nor enter. All we have to worry about is the French relieving fleet from Brest, and hopefully, Rodney has sufficient force to cope with them."

"Unless the twenty-five Spanish vessels also appear," MacKim reminded.

Kennedy removed the pipe from his mouth. "We'll try not to think about war with Spain."

The Rangers watched as Swanton eased into the Bay of Petite Anse in the southwest of Martinico. The convoy followed, with the masters of merchant ships used to independent command and fretting under the Navy's directions.

"What's this place called, sergeant?" Danskin asked.

"Petite Anse," MacKim told him.

"Petite Arse?" Oxford said crudely. "That's what I think of the Crapauds!"

"You'll change your opinion when you smell their powder smoke," Parnell said.

"What's here?" Dickert asked, looking at the surrounding coast and hills.

"Fort Royal is over there." Kennedy nodded to the north. "It's the major French naval base on the island. I suspect that's Rodney's primary objective. If we control the sea and the anchorages, we're assured of eventual victory."

All the Rangers looked up as Commodore Swanton's men-of-war opened fire on the French batteries that defended the bay.

"Maybe this time we'll land." MacRae tested the lock of his rifle, added a touch of oil, sighted along the barrel, and snapped the trigger.

Swanton's ships fired again, the sound of the broadsides echoing from the hills as smoke rose upwards. The French batteries retaliated, with great spouts of water rising around the British ships.

"Thank God for the Navy," Dickert said. "Imagine rowing ashore with the batteries firing at you. One shot from a 24-

pounder would sink the boat, and then the sharks would be waiting."

MacKim ran his gaze over the transports. After three years of war and half a dozen amphibious operations, he was able to calculate numbers. "I'd say there are two brigades here, a sizeable force for a demonstration, but hardly sufficient for a full invasion. General Monckton isn't going to defeat the French today."

"Unless we're the forlorn hope," Kennedy said.

"Sails to the north!" Young Ponchett had returned aloft and shouted the warning.

"Signal the Navy," the captain said, instantly on guard. "Let them know."

Kennedy glanced along the ranks of transports. "If that's the French fleet, we're in trouble," he said as one of the escorting frigates immediately headed north to check the strange sails.

When the frigate signalled that the ships were friendly, relief swept through the fleet.

"Those are Rodney's ships," a seaman said as Swanton finished reducing the enemy fortifications. As the last echo of the cannonade faded, Rodney led the combined fleet south and west to anchor in Sainte-Anne's Bay, then ordered a squadron around the headland to the north and into the bay of Grande Anse.

"I wish that man would make up his blasted mind," Kennedy said. "I'm not sure if it's Monday or Christmas."

"We're creeping closer to Fort Royal all the time," MacKim pointed out. "We'll be landing soon."

The Rangers looked at the bulk of Martinico, thought of the cannon fire, and grew silent. MacRae openly prayed.

Well, Claudette, I hope all goes well with you, MacKim thought. *Remember me fondly if I don't come back.*

6

As the Navy continued to silence the defending fortifications with devastating broadsides, the Rangers waited. Some were outwardly nonchalant, while a few spoke nervously. Danskin reread his last letter from his sweetheart, MacRae prayed, and Dickert oiled his rifle.

"Have you all checked your muskets?" MacKim asked. "Are your flints sharp and spare flints to hand?"

The men nodded.

"Everybody had forty rounds and spare powder? Hatchets and bayonets?"

"We're all set, sergeant," Parnell said, seemingly unaffected by the looming battle.

"You Johnny Raws men, follow orders and follow the veterans' example," MacKim fussed like an older brother.

Then the order came. "Board the boats! Get on board the boats!"

"That's us, lads!" Kennedy said. "You all know what to do!"

The Rangers filed into the long, flat-bottomed boats that would take them onshore, with pigtailed seamen helping them balance inside.

"On you come, lobsters! You, too, green lobsters! Don't fall overboard now, and if you're going to be sick, keep it over the side!"

MacKim winked at Danskin, and then a midshipman pushed them away from *Lucy Swan*. For a moment, MacKim wondered if he would ever see the transport again, and then they were heading for the shore, with the seamen rowing like heroes, waves splashing inboard, and the war seeming suddenly, frighteningly dangerous.

Oxford was vomiting over the side, a seaman was singing some obscene song, Dickert was speaking to MacRae his eyes animated, and MacKim lifted his head.

"God bless Kennedy's Rangers!"

"Rangers, first and always!" Butler shouted, his words lost in the thunder of artillery.

Although they were close inshore, the distance seemed immense when sitting in an open boat in the sun. The Royal Navy ceased firing when they destroyed the defensive batteries, but the French were determined not to allow the British to land unopposed. A dozen musket men disputed the passage.

"They're still out of range," MacKim reassured Danskin, who started when the French musketry began.

A Grenadier in an adjoining boat began to sing, with others joining in as the seamen rowed them ashore.

"*Some talk of Alexander, and some of Hercules*
Of Hector and Lysander, and such great names as these,"

MacKim shook his head, smiling. He had seen the Grenadiers in action and knew them to be formidable fighters, but these men were singing to bolster their courage before the battle. As a so-far-hidden French battery fired and fountains of water rose in front of the open boats, more men began to sing, roaring in defiant chorus to chase away their fear.

"But of all the world's great heroes
There's none that can compare
With a tow, row row row, row row row
To the British Grenadiers!"

"Come on, lads!" MacKim shouted. "Sing! We can sing better than the blasted Grenadiers!"

The Rangers looked at him, with Parnell spitting into the wind. "I'm not one of those murdering dogs!"

"You are today! Sing!"

The next French salvo was closer, splashing water into their boat, although the seamen did not falter at the oars. The Rangers raised their voices to challenge the French cannonade.

"None of these ancient heroes ne'er saw a cannonball
Nor knew the force of powder to slay their foes with all
But our brave boys do know it and banish all their fears
Sing tow, row row row, row row row
For the British Grenadiers!"

The boats eased towards the shore in three divisions, with fluttering flags differentiating the units and officers erect in the stern. The busy seamen were calm at the oars, pulling them lustily as musket balls began to patter in the surrounding water. A man yelled in the boat next to the Rangers, and a sturdy Grenadier sergeant bawled for silence.

"Load up, boys!" the sergeant ordered. "We're the Grenadiers. Once Johnny Crapaud sees us, they'll take to their heels!"

Kennedy looked ahead. "We're landing soon, Rangers."

Sitting in the stern of the Rangers' boat, a kilted major of Montgomery's 77th Highlanders raised his voice. "Montgomerys and Rangers! Listen to me!"

The men in the boat quietened, so only the sound of oars,

the shush of surf on the shore, and the sporadic rattle of musketry disturbed the silence.

"As some of you may have guessed, our objective is the French base of Fort Royal. We would take it by direct assault from the sea, except the mouth of the bay is defended by a heavily fortified island, the Isle des Ramiers—or Pigeon Island, as we call it."

The Rangers looked at each other, pleased to know their part in the landing.

"Pigeon Island is high and rocky, with a battery of heavy artillery that would play merry hell with our ships, so we have to attack Fort Royal overland."

One of the 77th began to cheer until the major cautioned him to stop. "Save the cheering, Gunn, until we're victorious. Then we can celebrate!"

"Aye, sir. I was getting the lads in the mood!"

"We will land here," the major continued, indicating ahead, "the point of Sainte-Luce, only a day's march to Fort Royal Bay. We will remove any insolent Frenchmen from our path, establish artillery posts, and hammer Pigeon Island to submission. Now you can cheer, Gunn!"

"Thank you, sir!"

The 77th Highlanders cheered, with the Rangers following suit. Within minutes, the cheering carried to every boat in the invasion fleet.

The defensive musketry increased as the boats neared the shore, with the Light Infantry and the Rangers first onto land. MacKim clambered from the boat into shallow, warm water and splashed ashore, hearing the Rangers behind him and the crackle of French muskets.

God bless you, Claudette, but I can't think of you for a while.

"Come on, lads!" Kennedy shouted. "Show the Lights what the Rangers can do!"

As the Rangers fanned out into open order, MacKim saw a scatter of French before him, white-coated infantrymen who fired and withdrew without haste. *Trained regulars then, and not a local militia unit.* MacKim knelt behind a rock, fired back, and moved forward, ordering his section to accompany him.

"Push them back, Rangers!" he shouted.

On his left, the Lights of the 77th were doing the same, their dark green kilts rustling as they moved.

The defensive firing stopped, the sound of the surf predominating and the heat hammering on the British like a new enemy.

"They've gone," Dickert said, loading his rifle. "The Frenchies have retreated."

"Keep alert," MacKim ordered. "We don't know how good these Frenchmen are."

With the Rangers and Light Infantry in the van, the landing force moved slowly forward. For the first few hundred yards, they made good progress, but the terrain grew increasingly more difficult. The ground rose, with tangled trees and thick undergrowth impeding their advance and a hitherto hidden gulley forcing them to halt.

"We're to keep to the south of the bay," Kennedy ordered, wiping sweat from his face, "and try to find a route suitable to drag artillery over."

The ground rose before them in a series of steep ridges, punctuated by deep chasms choked with vegetation.

"God only knows what's hiding in there," MacKim said.

"Follow me," Kennedy said. "We'll soon find out." He plunged down the slope, sliding on loose dirt as MacKim followed, the heat striking him as he descended. MacKim saw his first snake as he entered the undergrowth, swore, and banged his feet on the ground to scare it away. The Rangers followed, more nervous about reptiles than they were of the French.

The bottom of the ravine was savage with dense vegetation and alive with whining insects that all seemed intent on biting and stinging every Ranger who invaded their territory.

"We'll never get artillery over this," Kennedy gasped, wiping the sweat from his face. He began the laborious climb up the opposite side of the gulley. "Come on, lads!"

The heat was energy-sapping as the sun bore down on them for hour after hour as one series of ridges and gulleys led to another, each one steep, each one a potential spot for an ambush.

By early afternoon, MacKim knew the landing was abortive, for no army, however good, could drag heavy artillery over these ridges. They might manage with light four or six-pounders, but to damage the strong fortifications on Pigeon Island, the British needed 18-pounders at least—and 24 or 32-pounders if they could.

"We're wasting our time here," Kennedy said.

Dickert crouched down. "I signed up to defend New Hampshire from the French and Indians," he said, "not to die of heat and thirst in some remote island thousands of miles away."

Oxford agreed. "I'd give anything for a day of snow. This heat is killing."

The Rangers halted beneath the crest of a ridge, seeking shade and drinking from their water bottles. MacKim nodded, missing the cool rain and austerity of his native Scottish Highlands. There was nothing in this lush island except humidity, insects, and disease. "Why would anybody wish to come here?"

Kennedy smiled. "It's a stepping stone to the gold and silver mines of Mexico, and a base to attack British and Colonial shipping."

MacKim shifted back from a hand-sized pinktoe tarantula spider that scuttled along the branch of a tree. "Dear Lord! Look at the size of that thing!"

"And look at the fangs on it!" Oxford recoiled in horror. "This place is hellish!"

MacKim heard the crack of a musket. "Tree all!" He shouted the old Ranger warning to take cover. Forgetting about the spider, he slid beside its tree.

"Silence!" Kennedy ordered.

The Rangers kept quiet, listening for the enemy. For most of them, the situation was familiar, and only the terrain and heat were unusual. MacKim peered ahead, holding his Brown Bess like an old friend. In common with most of Kennedy's Rangers, he had shortened the barrel to make the musket easier to handle in close terrain. It meant he had less effective range, but that was no disadvantage when fighting in forests.

The thick undergrowth masked the attackers, and after the single musket shot, there was nothing except the buzz of a million insects and the raucous call of birds.

The shot might have been the branch of a tree catching on a musket trigger, MacKim thought. *Or a man stumbling and firing by mistake.*

"Move on," Kennedy ordered.

The Rangers resumed their advance, warier now, watching every tree, keeping behind cover. They knew how tenacious the French could be, and how brave French infantrymen were when defending territory they considered their own.

"Wait!" Parnell raised a hand. "Over there!" He nodded ahead and to the right.

MacKim saw the movement next, a flicker behind the tree, something shifting when all else was still. He thumbed back the hammer of his musket and checked the flint was still in place.

"There are more," MacRae said.

MacKim nodded. He saw further movement, shadows crossing a sunlit glade, and, more tellingly, a sudden quiet as the birds fell silent.

"Tree all!" Kennedy ordered. He pitched his voice high, so the words carried above the insect-hum while hiding his location from the enemy.

From behind, far back near the beachhead, the sound of digging reached MacKim. He guessed that the gunners were hacking out an artillery emplacement, although, at that moment, he had little concern for such things. The French ahead were the only thing that mattered.

"How many?" Kennedy mouthed.

MacKim shook his head. He was not sure. He waited, ignoring the insects that crawled over his face and hands. If warfare against the Abenakis had taught him anything, it had schooled him in patience and endurance.

Voices sounded from behind as the bulk of the landing force followed in the wake of the Rangers. An officer barked an order, and a drum tapped, rhythmic and martial. Nobody was singing now.

"Parnell!" Kennedy hissed. "Get back there and warn the Grenadiers the enemy is ahead."

Parnell slid away, his slender figure hardly visible in the greenery.

"Over there!" Dickert said.

"Fire if you have a target," Kennedy ordered, his words reaching all the Rangers. Behind them, the drums fell silent. The insects dominated the land.

Dickert fired first, the crack of his rifle distinct from the more resounding boom of a musket. "Got him," he said in satisfaction, and a ragged volley came in return as the half-seen enemy fired their muskets.

The Rangers barely flinched as musket balls ripped through the leaves and tore chips from the trees. They knew how hard it was for an enemy to see a green-clad man among vegetation, as long as the Ranger remained still.

MacKim remained still as somebody reared up twenty yards in front. Broad-shouldered and wearing loose clothing, he carried a musket and ran forward. MacKim waited until the attacker was only ten yards away, then fired, with the force of the musket ball knocking the man off his feet.

More firing came from left and right as the Rangers repelled the enemy, and then silence descended again, except for the insects' constant whine and hum.

"They're retreating," Kennedy said. "Move forward twenty paces, Rangers."

Slowly, cautiously, the Rangers stepped forward, alert for

danger, listening for the furtive moments of enemies in the undergrowth. MacKim stopped to inspect the body of the man he had killed. He was darker-skinned than a Frenchman, but not black.

"A mulatto," Kennedy said. "I don't know much about them. Probably irregular infantry, maybe an island militia."

The Rangers moved on, pushing up the far side of the ridge.

"If we were facing the Abenakis," MacKim said, "they'd have posted men just beneath the summit of the ridge to ambush us."

"Butler," Kennedy ordered, "scout the left flank. MacDonald, scout the right."

The Rangers waited until the scouts signalled the all-clear, and then slithered to the surface of the ridge, hoping for easier terrain ahead.

"Dear God!" More ridges rose ahead, with deep gulleys in between and a jungle of vegetation cloaking the slopes.

"Sir!" Parnell scrambled to Kennedy with sweat spreading in dark patches across his uniform. "Orders from the general, sir. We're to return to the ships. The landing has failed."

7

"We're to return?" Kennedy stared at Parnell, with sweat trickling into his eyes. "Why?"

"We're abandoning the invasion, sir. The general doesn't think the route is practical for artillery."

MacKim nodded. "He's right there. We won't get heavy guns across these gulleys."

"I don't like retreating from the French," Dickert said. "It encourages them."

The enemy agreed, for as soon as the British began to withdraw, they pressed hard on the Rangers with sniping and an occasional minor attack.

"They're not the best of shots," MacRae said as a ragged volley of French musketry passed over their heads.

"They're militia," Kennedy said. "They're not trained soldiers. Only shoot when you have a clear target."

MacKim kept his men under control, preventing Oxford and Danskin from revealing their positions as they fired on the enemy and posting men on the summit of each ridge to slow down the enemy's advance.

"Keep your head down, Danskin! You're a Ranger, not a Grenadier! We don't invite the French to kill us!"

"Yes, sergeant." Danskin fired and slithered into a hollow to reload as MacKim watched him critically.

"Our duty is to kill the enemy and remain alive," MacKim reminded.

Most of the British troops had already evacuated when the Rangers and Light Infantry arrived at the beach. Two officers of the Royal Engineers remained, together with three sappers. A hundred yards inland, a group of Royal Artillerymen working feverishly to dismantle the gun emplacements they had recently built and more recently abandoned.

"Best board the boats, Rangers," a rangy sapper said as he carried away a fascine. "There's going to be an almighty bang here in a minute." Although the Royal Engineers organised any engineering operations, men known as sappers and miners laboured at the manual work.

As always, the Navy was busy, ushering the last of the landing party into the open boats with cheerful jibes while Kennedy led his Rangers to the beach. The Rangers had no sooner filed on board than the sappers and miners joined them.

"Push off, tarry-backs!" an artillery officer shouted.

"And we say farewell to Martinico," Dickert said. "A short and bloodless victory for the Frenchies."

"Farewell?" A grinning seaman shook his head. "Not while our Rodney's in charge. "We're trying again in a few days at Fort Royal Bay."

MacKim looked over his shoulder, thinking of the sweat and toil of the abortive landing and the huge spider scuttling down the tree.

The explosion was like the end of the world. The engineers had blown up the gun emplacements so recently made, with fragments of rock and timber rising high in a dense column of smoke. Even out in the bay, the seamen had to dodge falling pieces as they rowed out to the waiting fleet.

"A fitting farewell." Kennedy ignored the descending debris, lighting his long-stemmed pipe with a flourish.

"Aye," MacKim said as a gust of wind momentarily cleared the smoke from the ruined gun emplacement. He saw two men standing on the shore. One had a musket levelled towards the retreating British, and the other was Captain René Roberval of *Douce Vengeance*.

"Dear God in heaven," MacKim said. "That's the last man I wish to meet."

⁂

"Don't get too comfortable," a Black Watch major warned as the Rangers filed back on board *Lucy Swan*. "You're going back ashore tomorrow."

So soon? MacKim thought. *The boys are exhausted from that landing.*

"It's always the Rangers in front," Oxford complained.

The major threw him an ugly look. "You won't be alone, Ranger. The Forty twa will be there as well. Most of my lads have been ashore for two days now."

As the Rangers settled back down in the transport, MacKim learned that Brigadier Haviland and Commodore Swanton had been busy establishing a foothold further north in Fort Royal Bay. First, Swanton's ships had hammered a French gun battery into submission, and then a force of marines had landed, quelling the remainder of the garrison and occupying the site.

"Now Haviland is leading us ashore," Kennedy said in a quick briefing to his Rangers. "We don't know the conditions or how many French there are to oppose us. We only know we have to secure a position suitable for artillery to bombard Pigeon Island." Kennedy grinned. "Lieutenant Colonel Scott is leading the Lights—with us in front, of course."

"What's the colonel like, sir?" Dickert asked.

"I only met him half an hour ago," Kennedy said. "He seems like a professional soldier, but we can't tell until we see them in action, can we?"

Some of the Rangers laughed, knowing that although Kennedy was an officer, he identified with the Rangers' rank-and-file more than others of his position.

"Rangers, first and always!" Butler shouted, and others joined in.

"Rangers, first and always!"

Again, the British infantry boarded the flat-bottomed boats, and the sailors rowed them ashore, each man wondering what the next few hours would bring. However, with the Royal Marines holding the guardian battery, the landing was unopposed.

"This is more like it!" Butler said. "The Navy's done the work for us."

Parnell grunted. "If they could sail inland and blast the French there, I'd be happier."

"You're never bloody happy, Parnell!" Butler told him.

The Rangers and Light Infantry led the Army into the interior. MacKim smiled when a piper played a rousing air on his highland bagpipes.

"Reminds you of old times, doesn't it, sergeant?" MacRae asked.

"I miss the regiment," MacKim agreed. *I miss Scotland, too, when I'm out here with the heat and the flies.*

"Come on, Rangers!" Kennedy strode ahead, musket in hand.

"Rangers, first and always!" Oxford shouted, but the time for singing had passed as they slogged inland.

Within five minutes, it was evident that the terrain was no easier here. As in the previous landing, the ground ascended in a series of ridges and gulleys, with dense vegetation hampering all movement amid mosquitoes and flies buzzing around the struggling men.

"No wonder the French have held onto Martinico," MacRae said. "This island is a natural defensive site."

"With many defenders," MacKim said, pointing to the militiamen who watched them, always from the next ridge and steadily retreating as the Rangers and Lights toiled closer. The militia opposed the British with sporadic musketry, never coming close and without causing casualties. They were a nuisance more than a danger, although their presence made the Rangers wary.

"Why don't they attack?" Oxford asked. "They should attack before we get established in their bloody island."

"They don't have to," Dickert said. "They're letting us exhaust ourselves toiling up and down these damned ridges while the sun weakens us."

Kennedy nodded, wiping the sweat from his face and glancing behind him, where the remainder of the landing force struggled over the ridges. "I'll wager we lose more men to the climate and disease than we do to French musketry."

MacKim nodded, wordless. He was no lover of heat at the best of times and found heat—combined with an ever-present enemy—exhausting. "The colonel is watching us, sir."

Colonel Scott lowered his telescope and sent a harassed ensign to Kennedy, sweat dripping from his forehead and forming damp patches on his scarlet tunic. "Lieutenant Kennedy!"

"That's me!" Kennedy pushed his hat back on his head.

"Colonel Scott sends his compliments, sir, and asks you to push on ahead to Gros Point and see if the French are defending it."

"Yes, ensign. How will we recognise it?"

"It's the point immediately opposite Pigeon Island, sir." The ensign touched his hat in salute. "And now you know as much as I do."

"Pray tell the colonel we are moving directly."

Kennedy watched as the ensign returned to Colonel Scott and the main body of Lights. "You heard the colonel, men. We continue to do what we've been doing. If anybody finds a signpost that says Gros Point, let me know!"

Some of the Rangers laughed at the attempted humour. They

pushed on, climbing the ridges, sliding down the opposite sides, hacking their way through the tangled undergrowth, and vainly swatting at the insects that tormented them.

"At least there are no snakes," MacKim said.

"Not yet, sergeant," Dickert said. "But there are more militiamen ahead."

MacKim joined Dickert on the top of the ridge, where both lay flat to avoid the enemy seeing them on the skyline.

A company of militia stood on the next crest, some with muskets and others carrying machetes or long knives. They did not attempt to fire at the Rangers, but merely watched in silence.

"As long as they are quiescent," MacKim said, "we'll let them alone."

"Yes, sergeant," Dickert said. "We're out of musket range, although I could reach them with my rifle."

"No." MacKim shook his head. "Let's see this Pigeon Island."

Beneath the Rangers, the ground eased out to a blunt promontory, directly opposite to Pigeon Island. MacKim could see how the island dominated Fort Royal Harbour, with its solid fortifications and the ugly snouts of cannon pointing to the channel between the island and the mainland of Martinico.

"The French can massacre any ship passing Pigeon Island," MacKim said.

"This must be Gros Point," Kennedy joined them on the ridge, glanced at the militia and looked away. "The Frenchies haven't even fortified it."

"Maybe they didn't expect us to get this far," MacKim said.

Kennedy swept the point with his telescope. "Parnell, report back to Colonel Scott that we are above Gros Point and there is only a handful of militia in position, with no artillery cover."

When Parnell hurried back to the Light Infantry, Kennedy inched over the ridge, with his Rangers at his back. More militia appeared, spreading down to Gros Point.

The militia slouched around the rocky ground, holding their

muskets with nonchalant skill. They wore no uniforms, but casual civilian clothes, some with large hats that shaded their faces from the sun.

"They don't expect trouble," Dickert said.

"They didn't expect us to get here." MacRae slid his rifle forward. "Shall I take a shot at them, sir?"

Kennedy shook his head. "That would alert them. We'll move forward a bit." He grinned. "What a coup for the Rangers if we cleared the point ourselves."

"We could capture the island without the redcoats' help," Oxford said.

"I only see twenty men," Kennedy said, passing his telescope to MacKim.

"I agree," MacKim said. "Five on picket duty, ten clumped around that large tree, and the remainder scattered everywhere."

"We can chase them." Kennedy made a sudden decision. "Come on, Rangers."

"Rangers, first and always," Butler chanted.

With Kennedy leading, the Rangers slid down the ridge, moving from tree to tree in a steady advance. They kept within sight of each other, each man covering his neighbour, communicating by signs rather than speech as they neared the militia's positions.

"Dickert, MacRae," Kennedy spoke quietly to the marksmen. "Mark your man, and on my count of three, fire."

Dickert and MacRae lay prone, each selecting a target. The militia remained in position, unaware of the Rangers' approach.

"One, two," Kennedy murmured, "three."

On his final word, Dickert squeezed his trigger, with MacRae a fraction slower. Two of the militia fell, one crumpling to the ground and the other staggering backward under the force of the rifle ball. Even before the echoes began, Kennedy was on his feet. "Come on, Rangers! First and always!"

The Rangers advanced with a cheer, running across the intervening area of rough ground, leaping over rocks and fallen trees, and ignoring the patches of thorn. Taken by surprise, the militia made little resistance. Two of the pickets fled at once, another man fired a single shot, and the other two were already dead, killed by the marksmen.

"Push on!" Kennedy shouted.

MacKim held his musket ready as he saw the militia break and run. Without uniforms, they looked more like farmers than soldiers, with two men dropping their muskets in their haste to escape. One black man opened his mouth in a roar and drew a machete from his belt. He ran to challenge the attackers until Danskin dropped to one knee and shot him. The militiaman fell backwards, tried to rise, and died as he choked on his blood. The man's death only encouraged the other militia to run all the faster.

Some Rangers hastened the militia's retreat with hurried shots, while most were content to capture the position.

"Are you alright, lads?" MacKim questioned the recruits. Both looked slightly shaken, with Danskin looking at the dead militiamen. "You'll learn to accept death and casualties, boys."

"Right, men." Kennedy stopped at a slight rise. "That was easy enough. Now find a position and get ready to repel a counter-attack. The French won't give up as easily as that."

"Come on, Danskin," MacKim said as Danskin continued to stare at the man he had shot. "Leave that fellow for now."

"I killed him." Danskin stood with his eyes wide. "I killed that poor fellow."

"If you hadn't," MacKim said, "he'd have killed you, or me, or the lieutenant. Come on, son, you did your duty."

"I've never killed a man before," Danskin said.

MacKim lowered his voice. "The first is always the worst. You'll never get to like it, Danskin, but it's your duty. You did well, now go and join the others."

"Yes, sergeant." Danskin moved forward as the Rangers settled behind convenient rocks and trees, waiting for Colonel Scott to bring up the Lights.

"Halloa, Rangers!" Private Gunn of the Black Watch was first to swagger up with his kilt swinging and his freckled face damp with perspiration. "I thought I saw you running ahead of us."

"You were so slow, we had to show you the way," MacKim said. "I thought the Forty-Twa were good soldiers."

Gunn laughed. "We're good, right enough, but not stupid enough to race into bad country. That's what we employ the Rangers for."

MacKim put a hand on MacRae's shoulder before he reacted to the Highlander's taunt. Any inter-regimental bickering could wait until later.

Colonel Scott surveyed the position as he brought up the remainder of the Light Infantry. "We'll entrench here until the general decides what best to do. Kennedy, you and your Rangers move two-hundred paces ahead and form a picket line."

"Yes, sir. Come on, Rangers." Kennedy moved forward, with MacKim more settled, knowing that the Light Infantry were supporting them.

"The parole is Wolfe," Kennedy told them, "and the counter-sign is Quebec."

The Rangers memorised the words, knowing their lives could depend on the correct response.

MacKim used his bayonet to hack out a hollow in the ground. "Hell and fury," he said when he found the soil only an inch deep and rock beneath. "There's not much cover in that."

"Do what you can, boys," Kennedy ordered. "Use branches, rocks, or whatever the good Lord has provided for protection."

Night came swiftly, and with the Rangers in position, MacKim crouched in the shallow depression he had scraped out of the ground.

"The French will come now," he said. "I can feel it. Every second man will remain on watch; the others, grab what sleep you can."

Was it experience that made him say that? Or was it a perception inherited from a hundred generations of warriors, men who had fought rival clans, English invaders, and Norse raids? He did not know. He only knew that the feeling was intense.

"Aye," MacRae understood. They shared the same heritage, and there was no need for more words.

The sky was different here, with unfamiliar stars above them, but the hush of the sea was a constant thumping onto the sand, much as it did on the shores of Scotland. MacKim waited with his hands on his musket, aware that the other Rangers were equally alert, each man concentrating on his own arc of vision and peering into the dark.

He heard movement and remained still, working out if it was animal or human. It came again, a soft slither that might be a hunting creature or the scuff of feet on the ground.

MacKim lifted his musket a fraction, controlling the nervous tremble of his left leg. That leg always shook before battle, although it was perfectly alright the second the fighting began.

"Wolfe!" The cry came from MacKim's right, and again, "Wolfe!", followed by the snap crash of a Brown Bess musket. "Would you, you bastard! It's the Frenchies, boys!"

The sudden musket flare momentarily robbed MacKim of his night vision. He swore, blinked, and fired in the direction of the sound. All along the Rangers' line, men were firing and shouting, with orange flashes vivid in the night. The French reply came in a sudden rush of men, mostly in civilian clothes, although a few wore the white uniform of regular soldiers.

"Here they come, boys!" MacKim shouted. "Shoot them flat!" He fired and reloaded hastily, tipping a ball into the shortened barrel of his musket and ramming it home.

The French militia erupted from the dark, yelling and firing their muskets. They seemed surprised to find the Rangers in position, with some halting, barely seen in the sporadic musket flashes. MacKim fired again, bringing a man down, then reloaded with all the speed his training had taught him.

"Are you alright, boys?" MacKim shouted. "Danskin? Oxford?"

"Yes, sergeant!"

MacKim fired at a flicker of white and then clicked his bayonet into place, expecting the militia to press home their attack.

The firing stopped, as men could not see a target. Powder smoke drifted through the trees, acrid and bitter.

"Don't relax, boys," MacKim said as he reloaded for the third time.

"They've run," Parnell said.

"Reload and keep alert," MacKim ordered. "The French are tricky devils."

Silence descended once more as the British waited, men loading their muskets, stamping their feet, and taking deep breaths. MacKim realised his left leg was behaving once more. "Roll call!"

One by one, the Rangers gave their names. Nobody was missing. There were no casualties.

"They'll come again," Kennedy called. "Don't relax, Rangers! That was only a probe to see where we were."

Two hours later, MacKim heard the drums and glanced across at MacRae.

"That's familiar," MacRae said. "The last time we heard French drummers was outside the walls of Quebec, at the Battle of St Foy."

"Aye," MacKim agreed. "And they slaughtered us."

MacRae nodded. "I haven't forgotten."

"They're coming back!" MacKim shouted. "And this time, they're in earnest."

8

The sound of French drumming increased throughout the fading night. MacKim had always thought that drumming was the most sinister of military sounds, a rhythmic tapping that sent shivers through the enemy and stirred men to deeds of valour.

"Lieutenant Kennedy!" A young ensign appeared from the rear. "I'm looking for Lieutenant Kennedy of the Rangers!"

"That's me." Kennedy lifted an arm while still concentrating on the French approaching from the front.

"I'm Ensign Mowat, sir. Colonel Scott sends his compliments, sir." Mowat spoke as if he had been repeating the words on his journey from the colonel to the Rangers. He started from the beginning again. "Colonel Scott sends his compliments, sir, and would you do him the honour of discovering the number of French opposing us?"

Kennedy nodded solemnly. "My compliments to the colonel, ensign, and please inform him that I will attend to his orders." He smiled. "Off with you, Mowat, and give my message."

"Mayn't I come with you, sir? I've never seen a Frenchman."

"They're very much like us, and no, you may not come with us," Kennedy said. "Be off with you."

"I'll go, sir," MacKim volunteered. "And Dickert will come with me."

"Why me?" Dickert asked.

"Because you're about the best woodsman we have," MacKim said. "Swap your rifle for a musket." There was no need to explain to Dickert that muskets were shorter in the barrel and faster to load.

"Look after my rifle." Dickert handed the weapon to Butler. "I'll be back for it."

MacKim led the way, easing through the dark undergrowth. He avoided the crumpled body of a militiaman and moved on, counting the steps.

After five-hundred paces, he stopped where the belt of woodland ended in a scrubby, hard-baked coastal plain of long grass and isolated trees. With their drummers tapping and men disembarking from open boats, the French were forming up, half-seen in the fast-growing light. A group of men clustered around their regimental colours, standing erect and proud.

"I see three companies," MacKim said. "They must have come from Fort Royal across the bay."

"Three companies of French Grenadiers," Dickert agreed. "If I had my rifle, I could peg one or two. This musket hasn't got the range."

"We're here to observe and report, not fight," MacKim reminded.

Grenadiers were the pick of the Army, the tallest, strongest, and often the most experienced soldiers in the regiment. Army commanders used them as shock troops to break down the enemy's resistance or finish off an enemy shaken by artillery or cavalry. The name was historical, from the time that the strongest men hurled grenades at the enemy.

"There are more Frenchies on the flanks," Dickert said.

The formations outside the Grenadiers were only partially uniformed, with some in no uniforms at all. When somebody passed with a lantern, yellow light pooled on one group, and

MacKim swore as he recognised men from *Douce Vengeance* in the ragged ranks.

"Freebooters and militia," he said. "Come on, Dickert." He headed back towards the British lines, circling every few steps to check the rear.

The challenge took him by surprise.

"Wolfe!"

"Jesus!" MacKim's mind blanked. He thought rapidly before the picket fired.

"Wolfe, you bastard!" the challenge came again, with urgency in the voice.

"Quebec!" MacKim said, and moved on. "Bloody Quebec!"

The Black Watch sentry lowered his musket. "I nearly shot you there," he said. "Be quicker next time with the countersign."

Kennedy nodded when MacKim passed on the intelligence. "Dickert, pray convey my compliments to Colonel Scott and inform him the enemy here are French Grenadiers, with freebooters and the local militia."

"Yes, sir," Dickert said, and regained his rifle. "I feel naked without my rifle, and I doubt the colonel would want to speak to a naked Ranger."

"So do I," Kennedy said.

The sinister drumming increased again, a threat of imminent violence. MacKim imagined the Grenadiers advancing in solid ranks, each man determined to conquer or die for King Louis and France. The Rangers and forward pickets of the Black Watch waited in the forest, with the other Lights slightly further back, where the ground was more open. A few Lights stood at the forest fringe, holding their muskets against their cheeks, chewing tobacco, running dry tongues over cracked lips, hiding their nerves as they ran calloused thumbs over the hammers of their muskets.

"Come on, you French bastards. Come on, if you're coming."

The drumming increased with the morning light, with the

occasional deep roar as the Grenadiers encouraged themselves to advance.

"Here they come," MacKim said, and winked to Danskin. "Do your girl proud, Danskin!"

"Her name's Julia, sergeant." Nervousness forced Danskin to gabble. "She's the most beautiful creature in the world."

"Ready, men!" Kennedy shouted. "Fire as soon as you see the enemy!"

MacKim checked the flint of his musket for the third time. He looked up as a Black Watch piper wailed a response to the French drums, the distinctive sound of highland pipes rising high in the Caribbean night.

"You won't have heard that in Martinico, boys!" MacRae shouted.

"Rangers, first and always!" Butler shouted, and then the French were on them.

The militia was in the van, running through the trees, shouting slogans, and waving muskets as the freebooters joined them with cutlass and pistol.

MacRae was first to fire, his rifle carrying further than the Brown Bess musket. "That's one to me, Dickie!"

"And one to me, Mac!" Dickert fired a few seconds later.

As both men reloaded, MacRae gave a low chuckle. "The Frenchies will wonder from where the shots came. They won't have met one of your Pennsylvanian rifles before."

"You talk too much." Dickert completed the laborious loading process first. Throwing himself flat, he squinted into the night, aimed, and fired. "Two to me, Mac."

Three seconds slower, MacRae fired and grinned. "And to me, Dickie."

By that time, the French van was within musket range. The Rangers opened fire, with the Lights on their right also making contact. When somebody yelled a Gaelic slogan, the French responded with a renewed drumroll and a scatter of musketry.

"The Crapaud Grenadiers are advancing against the Lights," Parnell reported. "They're in column, three companies."

"That means we're only facing the militia and freebooters!" Kennedy shouted. "Ten paces into the forest, boys. We're better forest fighters than they are."

MacKim stepped forward, feeling the trees close around him. The militia did not worry him unduly, for although they were dangerous, he did not consider them as skilled as the Indians or Canadians. Instead, he was nervous about standing on a snake or meeting one of the enormous spiders. Until he'd arrived in Martinico, he had not been aware of these fears.

"Sergeant!" Parnell stepped forward and fired, with the ball knocking chips from a tree thirty yards distant. A militiaman darted away, firing his musket. "He nearly got you, sergeant!"

"Thank you, Parnell!" MacKim cursed himself for losing concentration. He stepped forward, trying to push the fear of snakes from his mind.

"Left flank!" Kennedy ordered. "Push forward faster. Right flank, you're the hinge; hold firm. Men in the middle, I want you to support the left and watch your neighbours. We want to repel the militia and hit the Grenadiers in the flank!"

It was a complex manoeuvre in a tangled forest, but MacKim knew the Rangers were capable of such actions. As the NCO in the centre of the line, he was the lynchpin. He had to control his fear of snakes and organise the men.

"Centre on me!" MacKim said. "Men to my right, use me as a marker. Men on my left, keep the line straight and use the lieutenant as your mark."

MacKim heard the ripple of volley fire from his right and knew the Lights were busy. Those were British volleys, firing by sections, aimed and precise. He could only imagine the effect they had on the massed French columns, even in the half-light of the forest.

A musket ball ripped through the air an inch from MacKim's

head and another clipped leaves from a bush on his right. He swore, levelled his musket, and fired at the closest muzzle flare. A second later, the forest seemed alive with flashes as the militia and freebooters fired and advanced, yelling loudly to encourage themselves.

"Right flank!" Kennedy roared. "Stand firm! Left flank, meet them! Sergeant, make sure none of the enemy filters behind us."

The Rangers met the militia head-on, man to man and musket to musket. Using their experience in forest fighting, the Rangers held the assault until the sheer number of attackers began to tell.

"There are hundreds of them!" Oxford fired at a group of militia and slid behind a tree to reload. He looked at MacKim, his eyes wide.

"Fight on, Ranger!" MacKim shot a freebooter in a white shirt, who stood out in the green dim, and swore as two more emerged from the dark. Without time to reload, he snapped his bayonet in place.

"Come on, you French bastards!"

The first freebooter ran with a pistol in his right hand and a cutlass in his left. He levelled the gun, yelling, and MacKim thrust his bayonet into his stomach, twisting the blade to enlarge the wound and withdrew, sidestepping to avoid the inevitable attack from the second man.

MacKim heard the report of a pistol and ducked involuntarily as a ball slammed through the air beside his head. He stepped back to raise his bayonet and looked into the fierce eyes of Roberval.

Accustomed to forest fighting, MacKim attacked at once, feinting for the freebooter's throat, then thrusting at the stomach, but Roberval parried the blade with the barrel of his pistol. For an instant, MacKim and Roberval glared into each other's face, and then the freebooter lunged forward. Taller and heavier than MacKim, he barged into the Ranger, knocking him back.

Roberval kicked at MacKim's musket, then stamped on the barrel, pinning it to the ground. In the dim of the trees,

Roberval appeared monstrous, with his hair in ringlets and his teeth gleaming white. He levelled his pistol and pulled the trigger. The powder flashed in the pan, but the gun did not fire.

Misfire, by God! MacKim thought, and he kicked upward. His boot caught the freebooter on the knee, sufficient to hurt, but not disable. As Roberval winced and lifted his leg slightly, MacKim wrenched his musket free and slashed sideways with the bayonet, slicing through the freebooter's trousers and nicking the skin of his thigh.

Roberval swore, threw his pistol at MacKim, and stepped back to draw his sword.

"Rangers!" Kennedy's voice sounded high and clear. "Push forward!"

The Rangers had held the initial attack and now countered with all the guile they had learned in the North American forests. The militia and freebooters recoiled, and then came a rush of kilted men from the right.

"Forward the Forty-Twa!" Major Ogilvy shouted, and the pipes sounded again, playing a tune of triumph from an earlier war.

Roberval hesitated for a second, looking to the right and left before giving a long, low whistle and stepping back into the shelter of the trees.

"Follow them, Rangers!" Kennedy ordered.

MacKim pulled himself upright and moved forward, fighting the reaction that made his limbs tremble. He knew only a misfire had saved him from death, and he would relive that incident in his nightmares. Without pausing to reload, he stepped into the forest, checking left and right to ensure his men were with him.

"On me, Rangers!"

"Rangers!" Butler echoed. "First and always!"

The British advance was general, with the Light Infantry having repelled the Grenadiers with considerable casualties. MacKim saw a grinning Private Gunn driving four French prisoners before him at the point of a bayonet, with each Frenchman at least a head higher than Gunn's five-foot-nothing.

"I've got a present for Colonel Scott," Gunn said, waving to the Rangers. "Come on, Frenchies, and meet the colonel!" He gestured with his bayonet and ushered his prisoners forward as if he were herding cattle in some Highland glen.

"Well done, Gunn!" MacRae shouted, adding a string of Gaelic epithets that MacKim hoped the French, or even the Rangers, could not translate.

Still shaken from his encounter with Roberval, MacKim mustered his men as Kennedy ordered them to halt.

"We don't know what's out there," Kennedy said. "The French might have mounted swivels in their boats or even landed a battery of six-pounders."

Colonel Scott agreed with Kennedy and halted the surge of his Lights. The British withdrew to their positions, happy with their minor victory.

"Shall we investigate, sir?" Kennedy asked.

"Yes," Scott said. "Report back to me."

"Take over here, MacKim," Kennedy ordered. "Parnell, you're with me."

Kennedy was back within fifteen minutes. "The French are retreating," he said. "They're rowing back to Fort Royal. We'll stand here and wait for orders."

By noon, the position was unchanged, with the British holding Gros Point and no sign of the French, who had all returned to Fort Royal.

Kennedy scanned Pigeon Island with his telescope. "We have them in range now," he said. "If we can get artillery to the point."

Ensign Mowat arrived, face stained with gunpowder and looking slightly older than he had only the previous day. "Colonel Scott sends his respects, sir, and could you prepare to move out."

"Move out?"

"Yes, sir." The ensign looked uncomfortable. "The general

has decided that the country is quite impracticable for artillery. We have all to return to Commodore Swanton's ship's, sir, and Colonel Scott asks that you act as rearguard."

MacKim had rarely heard Kennedy swear, but that morning, the lieutenant made up for his previous restraint with a foul-mouthed tirade that had his Rangers gathering around in admiration.

"We've only just arrived, dug in, reached the correct spot, and repelled a French attack," Kennedy said once he'd composed himself.

"Yes, sir." Ensign Mowat looked ready to burst into tears.

Kennedy took a deep breath. "Thank you for the message, ensign. We will withdraw as soon as is practical."

The Lights were equally unhappy to leave the site of their recent skirmish. They grumbled as they returned to the coast, with an enhanced reputation and Gunn's prisoners all they had to show for their effort. Only when they were in sight of the beach did the Black Watch piper begin to play, and the pipes woke up the French.

"The freebooters are back." MacKim saw the figures flitting through the trees.

"Shoot any you see," Kennedy ordered, still unhappy about a second withdrawal within a few days.

"Yes, sir," MacRae said happily, and winked at Dickert. "I'll help you, Dickie. I know your old eyesight isn't what it was."

Even Parnell smiled at Dickert's response.

As the British advance guard neared the boats, the militia and freebooters pressed on the Rangers, firing the occasional shot and making a rush on any vulnerable man.

"Fire and withdraw," MacKim ordered. "Each man cover his neighbour." He ensured his musket was loaded and looked for Roberval among the enemy. *I'll shoot you the instant I see you,* he promised.

The Rangers withdrew in order, finding cover, firing immediately they saw one of the enemy andmoving to the next tree, confident in their colleagues' skill.

"The freebooters are getting bolder, sir," MacKim reported.

"They are," Kennedy agreed. When they slid over the next ridge, he called for his Rangers to halt.

"When the enemy show themselves on the skyline," Kennedy said. "Give them a volley, and retire. MacKim, you and two men remain for five minutes."

"Yes, sir," MacKim said. "Parnell and Butler, you're with me." He would have chosen Dickert and MacRae, but their rifles were more suited to longer ranges and took seconds more to load. For close action, he preferred the shortened Brown Bess muskets.

The freebooters arrived a few minutes later, advancing up the far side of the ridge to pause at the summit and peer forward.

"Fire when you have a target," Kennedy ordered.

The Rangers fired in an irregular crackling that felled two freebooters and sent the others scuttling to the far side of the ridge. The Rangers reloaded as powder smoke drifted among the trees and foliage.

"Well done, men," Kennedy said. "Give it five minutes, MacKim, and then follow us."

At that moment, five minutes felt like five hours. MacKim held his musket, spaced his men around him and waited. He knew the freebooters would come again; one rebuff would only make them more cautious.

"Over there, sergeant," Butler said, "on the right flank," and fired, with Parnell following a moment later on the left. The freebooters had tried the flanks. They withdrew again, leaving the ridge to the flies and the heat.

"Three minutes." MacKim counted the seconds, with each one seeming to drag. The heat increased, broiling him as he waited for the enemy to appear. "They might try to outflank us."

Something flew over the top of the trees to land in the undergrowth a few feet from MacKim.

"Keep your heads down!" MacKim yelled as the missile blew

up with a loud noise and a flash. "It's a grenade, but only gunpowder."

"Is that five minutes yet, sergeant?" Butler asked. He fired at a movement and swore when he saw a bird rise, squawking.

Although he was tempted to withdraw, MacKim's stubbornness refused to allow him to leave so soon after the grenade had exploded. He did not want Roberval to believe he had forced him away. "Not yet." He watched another bomb come over the ridge to land well short. The moment it exploded, he shouted, "Stay here!" and moved forward, jinking between the trees as he ascended the ridge. He had not reached the summit when he saw the first freebooter lift his head above the skyline.

MacKim fired at once, ducking down to load, and heard his Rangers fire in support. He loaded at speed, tapping down the ball with the ramrod and withdrawing down the ridge as the freebooters threw three grenades at once.

"Time to go, lads," MacKim said.

Butler and Parnell were moving before MacKim finished speaking. They slid down the ridge to the tangled vegetation at the bottom and threw themselves up the next ridge without stopping to look behind them. MacKim halted beside a tree, rested his musket on a convenient branch, and waited. The second the first freebooter exposed himself, MacKim fired and immediately withdrew, not stopping to reload.

"Keep moving, boys; they're at our tail!"

Butler saw Kennedy's Rangers in front and shouted "Wolfe!" quickly as he slid behind the green-uniformed men.

"That was yesterday's word," Dickert reprimanded him. "Today, we're using Saint and Lawrence."

"Nobody told us that," Parnell said, joining Butler in safety as MacKim came last.

"How many, sergeant?" Kennedy had his Rangers formed in a semi-circle, facing outward to protect the withdrawing Army.

"Only the freebooters and militia, sir."

"We heard explosions," Kennedy said. "What happened?"

"Powder grenades, sir. Lots of noise, but no fragmentation." MacKim reloaded. "What's happening here?"

"We're disembarking again."

※

THE LIGHTS WAITED AT THE BEACH, WITH THE REMAINDER OF the Army already on board the transports.

"Well done, Rangers," Colonel Scott said as Kennedy led his men the final few hundred yards. The Navy was waiting with open boats, some with swivels ready to blast any French who appeared.

Two attempts and two withdrawals. The campaign to capture Martinico is not going well, MacKim thought bitterly.

"Where are we going next, sir?" Kennedy asked.

Scott grunted. "I'm sure I don't know, Lieutenant. Either we abandon the attempt on the island, or we try a direct assault on Fort Royal."

"I'd prefer the direct assault, sir," Kennedy said. "I don't like to think of the French holding Martinico."

"Neither do I, Lieutenant," Scott agreed. "Nor do I like to think of the casualties a direct assault would bring."

When the last boat left the beach, the freebooters finally appeared, firing their muskets and jeering as if they had chased the British away.

"We'll be back!" MacKim shouted.

He saw Roberval standing in the surf, with his pistol in his belt, watching him.

9

"Case des Navires." Sergeant Innes of the Black Watch nodded to the coastline. "We landed here back in '58 when we tried to capture Martinico. We failed then, but maybe we'll have better success this time."

The Navy hammered at the shore batteries with broadside after broadside. The bay grew heavy with smoke and the taste of powder lingered in everybody's mouth.

"It's the sixteenth of January," Kennedy said. "It will be crisp and cold in New Hampshire, with a deep layer of snow on the ground." He looked at Martinico and shook his head. "I'll be glad when this campaign is over. It's frustrating, landing and retreating."

"Hopefully, this time, we'll land without retreating."

Sergeant Innes of the 42nd gripped his halberd in a hand that bristled with thick red hairs. "I can't see General Monckton suffering a third reverse," he said. "I think we'll push on this time, whatever the odds."

MacKim watched the ships firing their broadsides, although the volume of smoke meant he could not see the results. When the return fire slowed and ended altogether, he knew the Navy had destroyed the French redoubts. MacKim imagined being on the receiving end of a naval broadside, with the twelve, eighteen, and twenty-four-pound iron shot smashing stonework and sending splinters around the interior of the redoubt. There would be dead men, maimed men, and pieces of men, blood on the ground and the frantic screaming of the wounded.

"Hell on earth," MacKim said.

"Aye," Sergeant Innes said. "War is hell, alright. Only a soldier knows the reality. God help us."

Above them, a flight of birds arrowed away from the island, escaping from the horror to come.

When the Navy had reduced the redoubts to smoking ruins, the Army again boarded a flotilla of flat-bottomed boats. The soldiers stepped aboard, grumbling.

"Here we are again," Parnell said. "Another landing for no reason."

"Back to the island, lobsters," one of the sailors said cheerfully. "Watch how you go now, green lobsters. And you, highland ladies, mind you keep your skirts clear of the oars."

"I'll clear your skirts for you," Sergeant Innes growled.

General Monckton chose Case-Navire Bay for his next attempted landing. Case-Navire was north of Fort Royal, with a road that thrust over the headland of Morne aux Negres towards the town and fortress.

"A road?" Oxford said, hopefully. "We'll be able to march to Fort Royal without climbing up and down those bloody ridges."

Parnell shook his head. "Don't be so sure, younker. Where there's a road, there will be French redoubts, and where there is a redoubt, there will be artillery and soldiers."

"I'd prefer the ridges," Dickert said. "Ridges can't shoot you."

Once again, the Navy escorted the transports as three divisions of invasion barges surged towards the shore. Captain Molyneux Shuldham, Commodore Swanton, and Captain Augustus Hervey commanded the naval part of the invasion, with the ships towering over the open barges.

"Thank the Lord for Commodore Swanton," Parnell said. "He must be the most efficient seaman in the Navy."

MacKim nodded. Ever since Swanton had relieved the French siege of Quebec, the Rangers had great respect for him. Swanton, they felt, was their talisman, and they felt more secure when he was involved.

With the soldiers and sailors now experienced at embarking and disembarking on the boats, the landing was smooth. Within fifteen minutes of boarding the open barge, MacKim was stepping ashore on Martinico, the familiar surge of heat greeting him and the expected cloud of biting insects feeding on his flesh.

"Where are we, exactly?" Dickert asked.

"That's Cape Pilote." Kennedy pointed to a headland. "And that is Negro Point." He looked around. "As far as I can judge, we're only six miles from Fort Royal, so each landing is closer than the last."

"In a few weeks, we'll be sailing up the blasted main street if we carry on like this," Dickert said.

"No." Kennedy shook his head. "This is our third landing, and this time, there's no going back. Whatever the terrain is like, we'll have to meet it head-on. We are at the entrance to Fort Royal Bay at the southwest of Martinico." He drew a rough map on the sand, using his bayonet to indicate the salient features.

"Out there is Pigeon Island, blocking our ships from entering the bay. The Navy has blasted the redoubts to help us ashore; now, we must move inland and create batteries to hammer Pigeon Island to help the Navy. Once we reduce Pigeon Island, we take Fort Royal, and then it's onto St Pierre, about twenty miles to the north, and what's twenty miles to the Rangers? We travelled hundreds of miles in Canada. After we take St Pierre, the remainder of the island must surrender. No more grousing, lads."

"Who's bloody grousing?" Parnell asked.

For once, the Light Infantry trotted in front, with the Rangers behind them. Despite General Monckton's hopes, the terrain was no more accessible at this part of the island, and men swore as they descended the steep gulleys, fought through a tangle of undergrowth, and struggled up the far side.

"What a bloody place," MacRae said. "What the devil are we doing here? The French can have Martinico, and welcome!"

"Keep moving, Ranger," Kennedy ordered, the sweat already soaking through his uniform. "MacRae's right, though," he said to MacKim. "This entire island seems designed for defence. The French have placed batteries and redoubts on every possible point, with these damned irregulars, either militia or freebooters, swarming everywhere. We'll have a tough job even to reach Fort Royal, let alone reduce the damned place."

"If the French have garrisons on these hills, we'll have to take them first." MacKim nodded to three hills that rose inland. "Morne Tortenson, Morne Grenier, and Morne des Capucins." The names sounded very French, as if he were in Europe rather than a tropical island.

Kennedy looked upwards at the mist that drifted across the wooded heights. "I don't think we'll complete this campaign in a few days."

On the 17th of January, with the Lights and Rangers having formed a bridgehead, the remainder of the Army disembarked, with nine-hundred Royal Marines trotting ashore as well.

Ensign Mowat ran to Kennedy. "It's me again, sir!" He straightened to attention. "My apologies, sir. I mean, General Monckton sends his compliments, sir, and could you please establish a forward base of pickets and reconnoitre ahead to see if the French have any ugly surprises waiting for us."

Kennedy could not repress his smile. "Good to see you again, Ensign Mowat. Pray convey my compliments to the general, and inform him that Kennedy's Rangers will comply." He nodded. "Come on, Rangers. Patrolling is what we do better than anybody else."

Once again, the Rangers toiled up steep ridges and

descended into vegetation-choked gullies where flies waited to torment them.

"Over there, sir." Dickert pointed to the side of the next in the interminable series of ridges. "The earth is a different colour, so somebody's been digging."

Kennedy extended his telescope. "You're right. The French have a redoubt there." He gave his usual small smile. "Let's have a closer look. MacKim, you're with me. Corporal Parnell, look after the men—oh, and congratulations on your promotion."

"Which promotion, sir?" Parnell asked suspiciously.

"The one I have just given you, Corporal Parnell. Come along, MacKim."

The French had dug in two six-pounder cannon behind a screen of fascines, with brushwood placed as a cover. The artillerymen stood or crouched in a shallow trench, none smoking, and all looking supremely professional, as French gunners usually were.

"They're confident," MacKim said.

"Look at the vantage point they have," Kennedy said, indicating the redoubt's viewpoint. Their ridge was higher than any in front, giving the artillery an excellent field of fire.

"Aye, they've chosen a good position," MacKim agreed. "But they've neglected their flanks."

Kennedy nodded. "I was thinking the same thing. If we can get around them, so can the Lights. Push on, MacKim, follow the ridge."

There were other redoubts, some with artillery, but most manned only by infantry, either French regulars or militia. Between the redoubts, the freebooters roamed, wild-looking men with ragged clothing and an assortment of weapons, from cutlasses and pikes to muskets.

"Remember what Roberval was like," Kennedy whispered. "We'd better ensure these freebooters don't capture any of our lads."

MacKim nodded. "Aye, I'll warn them."

"We'll look at Morne Tortenson." Kennedy nodded to the closest of the three hills. "If I know the French, they'll have that well-fortified."

They moved on, keeping low, with the sun baking them and insects a constant torment. MacKim checked every movement for snakes, but saw none as they slowly approached Morne Tortenson.

The murmur of voices alerted them to the presence of the French. Kennedy placed a hand on MacKim's arm. They remained still, the tension rising as they peered at the mountain ahead.

The French had prepared well, defending Morne Tortenson with redoubts and gun batteries. The ugly snouts of cannon covered the route the British would have to take.

"The French will slaughter any advance," MacKim said, picturing the effect of 18-pounder cannonballs on a column of infantry and charges of grapeshot on exposed men.

Kenney nodded. "We'll have to report this to General Monckton. This island is better defended than Quebec."

They returned in a sombre mood and pulled the Rangers closer to the British encampment.

General Monckton listened to Kennedy's report with a troubled face. "That's a serious defence. Which regiment is with the guns? I hope it's some local militia force."

"No, sir." Kennedy shook his head. "It's the Cannoniers-Bombardiers de la Marine. We met them in Canada; they're efficient and dedicated."

Monckton drew in his breath. "That's not good news, but better to know about it now rather than meet them at the wrong end of a charge of grapeshot. Thank you, Kennedy; you and your Rangers have done your duty well."

As the general turned to his staff, he spoke again. "We will advance no further today, gentlemen. I do not think it prudent to expose His Majesty's troops until I can erect batteries to cover them, which I wish the artillery to work upon with the utmost expedition."

With their immediate scouting work done, Kennedy's Rangers settled back to watch the rest of the Army at work. As Kennedy's men dug in, Monckton put another company of Rangers to screen the front of the advance, including some Indians.

"It's strange to have these lads on our side," Dickert said. "I can't say I trust them much."

"Do you think they'll change sides?" MacRae asked.

"My experience with the Indians is as relentless enemies."

MacKim took off his bonnet and smoothed a hand over the bare patch. "I've never trusted them since they lifted my scalp. We'll be wary, lads, and watch for the freebooters as well."

Sergeant Innes joined them, sucking on an empty clay pipe. "The 42nd fought with the Iroquois on the advance to Montreal," he said. "We got along famously. They're like the Highlanders, with clan loyalty and a warrior tradition."

"These Indians are from the Carolinas," Kennedy said. "I've no experience of them at all."

As well as the Carolinas' Rangers contingent, around a thousand seamen joined the Army. Laughing, swearing, noisy, and hard-working, they were a unique breed of man and a jovial addition to the force.

"We're a mongrel army," Parnell said gloomily. "An accumulation of bits and pieces."

"An alloy is often stronger than a single metal," said Dickert, the gunsmith.

"Let's hope so," Parnell said. "Let's hope so, indeed."

※

ON JANUARY 19TH, GENERAL MONCKTON ASKED WHO HAD captured the four French Grenadiers on the previous abortive attack.

"One of the Highlanders," an aide-de-camp informed him.

"Ensure the brave fellow is rewarded," Monckton said. "Put that in the General Orders. My men must know that I appreciate their efforts, from the highest-ranked officer to the youngest private soldier."

MacKim was present when Colonel Montgomery assembled his regiment and asked who had taken the four French Grenadiers prisoner.

At first, nobody confessed, until Sergeant Innes nudged Gunn, who stepped reluctantly forward.

"In truth, sir, they are mine."

"What is your name, private?"

"Donald Gunn, sir."

Montgomery looked at the five-foot-tall private and smiled. "You are indeed a brave fellow, Gunn," and passed over a golden guinea.

Gunn made a low bow, raised his bonnet, and returned to the ranks.

"Callum," he whispered to his right-hand man in Gaelic. "If I had known there was a bounty for captured Frenchman, I'd have brought in two more of them."[1] The British Army was static for the next few days, and Kennedy's Rangers were on picket duty, guarding the front and flanks. After their earlier exertions, MacKim found the work little more than routine, standing guard and listening for any French incursion.

"The Lights are attacking soon, lads," Kennedy informed them. "We're not involved this time, but keep alert in case the French try a counter-attack."

Using the information Kennedy and MacKim had collected, the Light Infantry swept forward and captured the French defences with a fine flanking attack. They rolled up the French line, taking redoubt after redoubt at the point of the bayonet, and with only minimal casualties. The Rangers listened to the musketry and cheered on the Lights.

"Good lads, the Lights." MacRae leaned against a tree,

cleaning his already-immaculate rifle and smoking a stubby clay pipe. "We should let them carry on and capture Fort Royal. We'll stay here and guard the camp."

"That would suit you, Mac, you lazy Sawnie bastard," Dickert said. "Some of us want to do our duty and finish the war."

"Don't let me stop you, Dickie." MacRae checked the workings of his lock and added a single drop of oil. "Although I don't think you'd manage without me, a poor shot such as you."

"Poor shot?" Dickert kicked MacRae on the leg. "You couldn't hit a barn door from five paces!"

"Right, lads." MacKim calmed them down before the jesting escalated into violence. "Go and check the left flank picket for me. I have Oxford and Danskin out there alone." He watched his riflemen move out, as alert as a pair of hunting dogs.

As the Rangers relaxed with routine duties, the engineers with their sappers and miners were busy hacking out gun emplacements and fitting fascines and gabions. A fascine was a bundle of twigs or light boughs fastened together to fill in defensive ditches or act as protection for artillery, while a gabion was a large basket filled with earth or stones, often used as a wall. With the soil very thin on the ridges, the engineers required fascines and gabions to shield the guns.

The engineers had chosen a position overlooking Morne Tortenson, with a screen of infantry to protect the emplacement from French counter-attacks and the Rangers patrolling in advance of the infantry.

"This is not going to be a three-day campaign," Kennedy said as he puffed on his pipe. He watched the sailors drag a brace of 24-pounder cannon up the first ridge from the coast. "We'll have to crawl our way over this terrain and batter each French stronghold into submission, one by one. It's a siege, with us as the besiegers."

"Who are these lads?" MacRae pointed to a company of black men making fascines, with a couple of burly civilians overseeing the work.

"Slaves," Kennedy said. "The governor of Barbados sent them to help. They'll do the menial work when the infantry is soldiering."

MacKim stirred uncomfortably. He knew that slavery was an accepted part of life, with the slave trade being important to ports such as Bristol and Liverpool, but he still felt it wrong to enslave fellow human beings. Knowing he was out of step with everybody else, he said nothing.

On the evening of 23rd January, the British gun batteries were complete. The seamen hauled the final gun into position, and the artillerymen took over.

"It's all yours, gunners!" a tattooed seaman shouted. "Hammer the Crapauds!"

"We're attacking tomorrow morning," Kennedy told the Rangers.

The Rangers nodded. Most were sufficiently experienced to read the signs. They knew the British artillery would open fire as soon as they were in position. When the British had destroyed the French batteries on Monte Tortenson, General Monckton would throw forward his pawns—the infantry.

"Do you know the details, sir?" MacKim asked.

"The general has ordered a two-pronged attack," Kennedy said. "As soon as our artillery opens up, a few companies of infantry will advance along the coast, supported by a thousand seamen in boats to ensure the French don't try to outflank them by sea. Simultaneously, Monckton will throw forward a force to turn the French right flank."

"Are we involved, sir?" MacKim asked what everybody else was thinking.

"We're with the coastal party, attacking the French left," Kennedy said.

"Are we with the Lights, sir?" Dickers asked.

"Not this time," Kennedy said. "We're leading the Grenadiers, with Lieutenant Colonel Eyre Massey of the 27th Enniskillens in command."

"We've never fought beside an Irish regiment before," MacKim said. "What are they like, sir?"

"We'll find out tomorrow." Kennedy gave his characteristic smile. "We'll do our duty, sergeant, and we'll depend on others doing theirs."

MacKim found it hard to sleep that night and walked around the British camp, looking for the Enniskillens. Their sentry greeted him with the day's parole: "George!"

"Rex," MacKim replied with the countersign, and entered the Enniskillen's lines. Most men were asleep, with some sharpening their bayonets, or cleaning and oiling their muskets.

"You're with us tomorrow, Ranger," a rangy, red-haired corporal said, eyeing MacKim up and down.

"That's right," MacKim said.

There was silence for a moment as the corporal cut off a quarter of an inch of tobacco and offered it to MacKim.

"Armstrong," he said.

"MacKim."

Corporal Armstrong nodded, spat out a mouthful of tobacco juice, and said. "Aye. Rangers."

"I heard you lads fought in Canada," MacKim said.

"We did," the corporal said. "In the colonies and at the capture of Montreal."

"You'll know how to defeat the French, then."

"We do," the corporal said, deep-voiced and laconic.

They chewed tobacco in companionable silence for a few moments, each taking the measure of the other, and at length, MacKim rose. "I'll maybe see you tomorrow, Enniskillen."

"Maybe so, Ranger."

Shaking hands, MacKim returned to the Rangers.

"How did you find the 27th then?" Kennedy asked.

"Well enough," MacKim said. "I think it will be alright." He settled down for the night, trying not to think of the horrors the next day might bring.

I haven't written to you yet, Claudette, MacKim thought. *If I survive this next attack, I shall. I promise.* He knew he should write tonight, but he lacked the words. He was always tense before action, and his letter would reveal his state of mind. No woman would wish to read that sort of letter, perhaps the last her man ever wrote.

Her man?
Am I her man?
If I am, should I do something about it?
What sort of woman would wish to marry a soldier like me?

10

The artillery barrage began before dawn, just as the drums woke the men.

"I hate these bloody drums," Parnell said. "If this war ever ends, I'm going to buy myself a military drum and hang it on my wall."

"Why?" Butler asked.

"Because every day, I will pass that bloody thing and hit it as hard as I can, to get even for all the times it wakened me at some God-forsaken hour in the morning."

"Get ready, lads!" Kennedy shouted. "Sergeant MacKim, ensure every man has forty rounds of ammunition and his quota of bread. Fill your water bottles, boys, for God only knows when we'll see fresh water again."

MacKim checked every man, inspecting their flints and spare flints, ensuring they had a bayonet and hatchet—and that they had water, not spirits, in their canteens.

"All ready, sir," MacKim reported.

As the Rangers ate breakfast, the British artillery increased its bombardment of the French positions.

"That's our signal, boys," Kennedy said. "Follow me."

The Rangers trotted out, secure in the knowledge that

Colonel Massey led the Enniskillens a hundred yards behind, with colours flying and the red-coated Grenadiers comfortingly solid.

The first redoubt was close by the sea, held by militiamen who fired a single volley before retiring at speed. The Rangers ran past the redoubt without a pause as the Enniskillens gave a great cheer.

"Come on the 27th!" somebody shouted, and the Grenadiers marched onward, unstoppable in their scarlet and pride. The Irish were advancing, and only God could halt them.

"They're nearly catching us with their eagerness," MacRae said.

"Faster boys!" Kennedy ordered and strode in front, with the Rangers in their faded green only a few steps behind, jinking from cover to cover with the slopes of Martinico on their left and the breaking sea to their right. MacKim glanced seaward, where the Navy protected the British flank in open boats armed with small cannon and swivels.

The next redoubt proved a sterner test as French regulars yelled a challenge and then fired a full volley, bringing down Ranger Finchley.

"Flank them, boys! Leave Finchley for the 27th!"

MacKim led his section down to the beach, with the men following him in Indian fashion, a line of green-clad veterans who searched for the best route, returned the French musketry with aimed shots, and refused to be rattled.

"Swing in, Rangers!" Kennedy shouted, and the Rangers moved into the flanks of the French redoubt while the 27th advanced on the front. These French refused to run, firing two volleys at the advancing Enniskillens before Kennedy's pincer movement distracted them, and the Grenadiers marched in with busy bayonets.

There were no French survivors as the Enniskillens finished their work.

"Second round to us," MacKim said.

A SACRIFICE OF PAWNS

Corporal Armstrong of the Enniskillens nodded, his mouth busy with tobacco. "We work well together."

"Push on!" Kennedy ordered, and the advance continued.

Perhaps rattled by the loss of two of their forward positions, the next French outpost gave minimal resistance before the British captured it with another flanking attack.

The advance continued, with the Rangers and Grenadiers pushing through the French, capturing redoubt after redoubt with hardly a pause.

"Are these the same French we fought in Canada?" MacRae asked. "They've got no spirit at all!"

"Don't complain," Kennedy ordered. "Keep moving! Push them back before they reorganise."

Morne Tortenson loomed ahead, with powder smoke rising from the gun batteries and columns of dust and rock the British artillery was hitting.

The British advance halted as the Rangers found cover, with the 27th forming up in a scarlet wall. One man was humming a hymn, another praying, while most were silent, watching the duel between the British and French artillery.

"I hoped our gunners would have silenced the French artillery before we got there," Kennedy said.

"So did I," MacKim said, "but our advance was faster than we expected." He ducked as a salvo of British shells screamed overhead, with one landing just in front of the French battery. The resulting fountain of dust and stones contained fragments of fascines and the pieces of a man. "Poor buggers under that."

"If our gunners were not targeting them, the French would be tearing us and the 27th to bloody shreds," Kennedy reminded.

Another British shell landed, then three twenty-four-pound balls that howled overhead to hammer at the French fascines.

"Are you ready, Rangers?" an Enniskillen major asked.

"Whenever you say, sir," Kennedy replied, glancing at his Rangers. Oxford was shaking, but determined, and Danskin gave a weak smile.

"My lads are ready," the major said. "The French severely wounded Colonel Massey, so the boys want blood."

"Give the word, sir." Kennedy flinched as the French battery returned fire, with the shot ripping the air above their heads.

"I've sent a runner to ask our artillery to cease firing in fifteen minutes," the major said as the echoes of the artillery faded. "We attack the instant our guns fire their final salvo."

Kennedy nodded. "Yes, sir."

"Do you have a watch, Lieutenant?"

"I do, sir." Kennedy checked the time.

"Thirteen minutes now, Lieutenant. We move at fifteen minutes before nine o'clock. I'll lead the Grenadiers in a frontal attack, and you take your Rangers in from the flank. No firing in case we shoot each other." The major's grin showed white teeth. "Bayonets only."

"As you say, sir." Kennedy touched his hat as the major withdrew.

"Eleven minutes, lads," Kennedy said to the Rangers. "We'll move in two waves. I'll take the first, MacKim will lead the second." He told off the men into three groups. "Corporal Parnell, you're in charge of the reserves. Your job is to reinforce whichever of our groups needs the most help."

"Yes, sir," Parnell said.

"Bayonets, lads!" MacKim ordered, ensuring that Oxford and Danskin were ready. "Cover each other and leave the casualties where they fall. We'll care for the wounded once we have the battery."

Kennedy checked his watch. "Five minutes, boys. Check your bayonets are fitted, ensure your muskets are not loaded, and may God be with us all."

The British artillery increased their speed, unleashing a murderous storm onto the French positions. Kennedy crouched under the shelter of a tree, holding his watch. MacKim felt the tension rise, knowing the few moments before action were always the worst, for once the fighting began, his mind would be too occupied to allow him to think.

"Take care, Claudette," he said. "I hope to see you again." He shook his head. "Damn it, if I survive to get back to Quebec, I might as well marry you."

Dear God, did I mean that?

He became aware of the sudden, shocking silence as the British guns ceased fire.

"With me, men," Kennedy said quietly, and strode forward with the Rangers at his heels.

MacKim allowed him fifteen seconds. "Right, my bonny lads," he said. "Let's take these guns." He stepped out of cover to see the thin green line of Rangers in front, bobbing and weaving as they advanced. On his left and to the rear, he heard the rattle of drums as the Grenadiers marched solidly forward, muskets on shoulders and white breeches twinkling in the morning sun.

Kennedy raised a shout, to which the Rangers joined, and rushed forward to the flank of the French gun battery.

"With me, lads!" MacKim yelled, and ran forward. He knew his men were behind him, although he did not look to see. *Today is what soldiering is all about—leading loyal men in an attack on an open and honest enemy, not sneaking around in the dark, fearing a foul death by torture.*

The French in the battery fought. After three hours of pounding by heavy artillery, and assaulted on the flank and in front, the survivors grabbed muskets and tried to defend themselves. Shocked, dazed, scared, but determined, they still fired a dozen shots before the Rangers reached the battery, and then most threw down their arms in surrender or turned to flee.

The Grenadiers arrived simultaneously, chopping down any French who tried to resist, along with one or two who had surrendered, for the loss of their colonel had roused the Enniskillens into a fighting fury.

"Enough, men!" the Enniskillen's major ordered. "They've surrendered!"

The 27th stared at the French and lifted their bayonets as the battle-fury eased. They became men again rather than killing machines.

By the time MacKim arrived, the fighting was over. The battery was a shambles, with two guns off their carriages, and dead men and pieces of men littering the blood-sodden ground.

"Five minutes short of nine o'clock," Kennedy said laconically. The attack had only taken ten minutes.

MacKim nodded. He saw British soldiers moving around Morne Tortenson, ejecting the last French defenders. A sporadic crackle of musketry revealed that skirmishing continued, but seemed unreal on such a beautiful morning.

"Pursue the French," the Enniskillen's major ordered. "Don't give them time to regroup."

The Rangers joined the Grenadiers, chasing the enemy like dogs hunting hares, ensuring the French had no time to recover and reform. The French fled, some running to Fort Royal, which was easily visible less than a thousand yards distant, and others to the prominent mountain of Morne Grenier, which rose higher than Tortenson.

The Grenadiers thundered across the ground in open formation, shouting to intimidate the enemy. "Run, Frenchies, run! We're the dogs of war! We're coming for you!"

One section of the 27th powered ahead of the rest, wrestled a group of French to the ground at the very gates of Fort Royal, and dragged them back as prisoners.

"Halt, Rangers!" Kennedy ordered. "The Grenadiers have their tails up, so let's see what else is happening." He scanned inland with his telescope.

While the Grenadiers had cleared the French from the coast, Brigadiers Walsh and Haviland were also busy. Commanding a pair of Highland battalions plus the Light Infantry, the brigadiers began their advance at two in the morning, crossing a deep ravine to split the French defenders.

After struggling up the steep slopes of Monte Tortenson, the

British captured a series of French redoubts, one after the other. As the Rangers watched, Monckton ordered the Light Infantry and Brigadier Walsh's brigade, along with some companies of Grenadiers, to shift to the British left, where a sugar plantation hugged the lower slopes of the hill. When a company of French regulars contested the British advance, the Grenadiers and Lights swept them away in minutes. Colonel Scott's Light Infantry hurried past the plantation, elbowed aside a French defensive post opposite Morne Grenier, and settled in to await a French counterattack.

Kennedy handed MacKim his telescope. "We're clearing the French positions today," he said.

MacKim focussed the telescope, watching as the separate prongs of the British began to merge. Working in conjunction with the Grenadiers, the Lights pushed the French off Morne Tortenson and onto Morne Grenier. Before any French reinforcement could arrive, Haviland brought his brigade in support, while Grenadiers under Colonel Grant of Ballindalloch, along with Walsh's men, occupied an upper plantation. Finally, the Royal Marines held the road.

MacKim watched the two British forces merge, with the Grenadiers cheering on their comrades. The operation had been a complete success.

"Neat work, General Monckton," MacKim gave his approval.

"We did better than I expected," Kennedy said. "We captured Tortenson and cleared the French in one morning's work."

"Now for Morne Grenier." MacKim pointed to the tall hill that overlooked them. "And then, Fort Royal will be ours."

Neither mentioned the scatter of bodies, in British scarlet and French white, which littered the ground. They knew that every triumph that caused bells to clatter in churches across Britain and North America cost human lives. While the nation cheered at military success, families from Caithness to Cornwall and Newfoundland to Barbados would mourn the deaths of husbands, sons, and brothers. Rule Britannia, wave the flag, paint the map pink, and forget the blood soaking into the baking soil. Nearly four-hundred British soldiers were killed or wounded as they captured that rugged hill on Martinico, and before the smoke cleared, French artillery on Morne Grenier was firing on the victors.

"We'll have to take Morne Grenier next," MacKim said, as the Rangers found cover from the French bombardment and the generals reorganised their men.

Kennedy nodded as a French roundshot screamed overhead. "I think you're right, MacKim. Monckton may try to ignore the French on Morne Grenier while he assaults Fort Royal, but I doubt the French will merely watch."

"Sufficient for the day thereof." MacKim threw himself to the ground and began to clean his rifle.

As if they had been listening to Kennedy's words, the French artillery on Morne Grenier increased their rate of fire, with their intermittent bombardment forcing the British to seek cover.

"Here we go again," Parnell said. "These Frenchies never give us any peace."

Despite the French cannonade, General Monckton planned his attack on Fort Royal, and busy Royal Artillerymen marked areas to site their batteries.

"We're only a few hundred yards from Mount Royal," MacKim said.

"Look at this." Kennedy passed over his telescope. "We can watch the French at work on their defences."

MacKim focussed the telescope, watching the white-coated soldiers busily strengthening the citadel's walls while the Bourbon flag floated overhead.

"The French have held Martinico for a long time. They won't give up easily," Kennedy said.

MacKim nodded. "Nor will we, sir."

Kennedy lit his pipe. "I heard another rumour that the French fleet was due any day now. Some of the French prisoners claimed the fleet from Brest had joined the famous Spanish fleet of battleships. The combined Franco-Spanish fleet would sweep Rodney from the seas, they think."

MacKim shook his head. "We have Swanton, sir. Do you think he'll be afraid of a few French sailors? And we've James Douglas as well. He knows this coast better than any Frenchman."

"I agree with you, sergeant." Kennedy recovered his telescope. "But be prepared for all kinds of wild rumours."

As the Rangers dug themselves in, Royal Navy sailors dragged artillery up the hill to bombard Fort Royal, and the French targeted the redoubts the engineers built.

"This will never do," Lieutenant Knight of the Royal Artillery said as roundshot crashed onto his fascines. "Every time we create an entrenchment, the French destroy it. Their guns are more elevated than ours and take us in flank."

"We have to capture Morne Grenier before we advance on Fort Royal," Kennedy said. "The artillerymen know that, and our veterans realise that. Now the general has to learn."

Monckton was no fool and ordered the artillery to concentrate on the French on Morne Grenier, granting Fort Royal a reprieve. Once again, Royal Naval sailors, with their unrivalled skill at hauling heavy objects with ropes and pulleys, dragged artillery up Martinico's hills to combat the French.

All the 26th of January, as the engineers and artillerymen toiled to position the guns, the French proved their efficiency. The French artillery destroyed all the engineers' work, breaking down the British trenches and shattering the fascines.

"We're getting nowhere here," Lieutenant Knight swore, kicking at the wheel of a gun in frustration. "It's time the general did something about it, damn his eyes!"

"Rangers!" On the morning of the 27th, Kennedy gathered his Rangers around him. "Orders, boys! General Monckton wants us to scout the French positions on Morne Grenier." He grinned at them. "The general must be planning to attack. Come on, boys, we've had a nice rest. Time to save the Army again."

Dickert laughed without humour. "Where would the British Army be if it wasn't for the Rangers?"

With one man killed during the previous battle and four down with Yellow Fever, only twenty Rangers followed Kennedy down Morne Tortenson and into the deep ravine that separated the two hills.

"This undergrowth is worse than ever," Parnell grumbled. He suddenly pointed. "I see water ahead!"

The stream at the bottom of the ravine provided welcome coolness, despite the hordes of insect life that waited in ambush. The Rangers drank, filled their water bottles, and began the climb onto the lower slopes of Grenier.

"We should have done this at night," Dickert complained. "The Frenchies will be watching everything we do."

"Maybe that's the general's idea," MacRae said. "They'll expose their positions when they fire at us, and he'll be able to target them in his assault."

"Our sacrifice won't be in vain," Parnell said. "Well, that's a comfort."

"Not to me, it isn't," Dickert replied.

The musket ball whined past MacKim's head, missing by six inches.

"Who fired that?" The Rangers found cover at once, peering over the rugged hillside. "We're far out of range of the French pickets."

"They must have a patrol out," Kennedy said. "Lie low, boys, and look for movement."

They lay in silence except for the drone of insects and the irregular crash of British and French cannon. MacKim felt something crawling over his face, but remained still. He thought that insects were only mildly irritating compared to the danger from French musketry.

"There," MacRae whispered as he slowly pushed forward his rifle.

"If you see it, shoot it," Kennedy ordered.

MacRae's rifle cracked a second later, followed by a scream from ahead. A man reared up, holding his foot, and Dickert shot him in the head.

"Half each," MacRae claimed at once.

"You only winged him," Dickert said. "I got the kill."

"You didn't even see him until I made him jump!"

Immediately MacRae spoke, a fusillade of shots came from the lower slopes of Morne Grenier.

"There they are, boys!" Kennedy shouted. The Rangers aimed at the powder smoke and fired.

A score of men rose from behind scrubby plants and dead ground. They ran towards the Rangers, yelling their hatred and waving weapons.

"Freebooters!" MacKim exclaimed, searching for Roberval's smooth face. In the confusion and powder smoke, he could not make out any features, only gaping mouths and fierce eyes. When the Rangers fired again, the freebooters slid into cover to load and fire.

"Shoot them flat!" Butler roared. "Rangers!"

The firefight continued with the calm professionalism of the Rangers pitted against the passion of the freebooters. After five minutes, the Rangers' efficiency began to tell. The freebooters withdrew ten paces, still firing.

"Don't follow them," Kennedy ordered. "The French know we're here now; the freebooters have done their duty. Everybody cease fire and withdraw by sections. MacKim, your men are the rearguard."

"Yes, sir," MacKim acknowledged.

"Sir!" MacRae said. "The French are moving."

Kennedy lifted his telescope. "So they are."

Three columns of French soldiers emerged from the French positions, heading downhill. Each formation seemed capable of breaking through the thin British line as they marched forward to the tuck of drums.

"They're mounting another attack," Kennedy said.

11

"Back to base, boys!" Kennedy shouted. "We'll have to warn the general!"

The French batteries opened up, firing shot and shell at the British positions as the three infantry columns debouched from Morne Grenier. Seemingly endless, the columns marched down the slope, white-clad regulars interspersed with militia and a host of freebooters, while the drummers tapped their sinister beat.

"How the devil did they get so many men on one mountain?" Parnell asked. "The Frenchies are cunning beasts."

"They're good soldiers," Dickert said, sliding into the gulley and splashing across the shallow stream.

"Stop talking!" MacKim ordered. "Save your breath!" The French drums were louder now, and he could picture the drummers marching in front of the columns, encouraging the men, throwing the drumsticks into the air and catching them again, leading them against their enemy.

"Parnell, take three men and report to General Monckton," Kennedy ordered. "Give him my compliments and tell him that three columns of French are advancing on our positions."

"Yes, sir." Parnell called up three men and hurried up the slope.

"We'll harass the French," Kennedy said. "Fire and withdraw, boys. No heroics, just try and delay them a little."

Even such professional soldiers as the French had to break formation when they entered the tangled undergrowth at the bottom of the gulley, and that is where Kennedy sprung his ambush. The Rangers fired by sections, aiming, firing, and loading with such speed that the French would not know the numbers that opposed them.

Without waiting to see the results of his attack, Kennedy ordered his men back again. "Come on, lads! Up the hill!"

Twice, the Rangers halted to fire, but despite their casualties, the French powered on, thundering up the slope, seemingly unstoppable.

"They're not even hesitating!" Oxford said.

"We're not causing sufficient damage," Kennedy said.

"Sir!" Parnell returned, with his face damp with sweat. "General Monckton sends his compliments, and could you report to him personally, sir, and have the Rangers help protect the guns."

The French columns marched on, with the tails still approaching the stream at the foot of the mountain while the heads advanced on the British guns.

While Kennedy ran to General Monckton, MacKim organised the Rangers. "Open formation, boys!" he shouted. "Riflemen, target the officers and NCOs. Don't expose yourselves. Musketmen, wait until they're in range."

Dickert and MacRae began their habitual rivalry, exchanging grim jests as they fired, with Parnell, the third marksman, a silent companion.

The French thundered on with drums beating and colours flying, brave men in white, intent on defending their island. Frantic British artillerymen altered the angles of some of their cannon and opened fire, with most of the shots wide. A few ploughed into the French columns, knocking down men and sending heads, arms, and legs high into the air. Closing ranks, the French marched on, with the drummers continuing their rhythmic beat as the columns altered direction, still out of musket range.

"They're heading for our left flank." Kennedy returned to take command of the Rangers. "Haviland's brigade and the Light Infantry."

Twice, the French columns halted for the officers to dress the ranks, then they moved on, with the sinister beat of the drums rapping above the intermittent hammer of musketry and the painful crack of the cannon. Acting as a backdrop, the high wail of the Highland pipes rose in defiance as powder smoke coiled above the hot hills of Martinico.

"How many are there?" MacRae asked, smoothing a hand along the barrel of his rifle.

"A thousand? Two thousand?" MacKim hazarded. "It's hard to see with the cover and the powder smoke."

The French batteries on Morne Grenier fired a salvo, with one roundshot hitting the ground a few yards in front of the Rangers, bouncing over their heads, and crashing into the fascines defending the British artillery.

"That was close," Oxford said.

"If any balls hit the ground and roll," MacKim warned, "you might be tempted to try and stop it with your foot. Resist the temptation, Oxford, for the force of the shot will take your leg off at the knee."

The three French columns marched on, hammered by British artillery and now, the controlled volley fire of the British infantry. At regular intervals, the French halted, fired a volley, and marched on.

"Look!" Kennedy said. "The French left-hand column has exposed its flank to Montgomery's Highlanders. That could be fatal!"

Seeing their opportunity, the Highlanders gave a terrific yell and charged, some with broadswords raised as at the Battle of

Prestonpans, others with musket and bayonet. They covered the intervening ground in great bounds, with the very appearance of the yelling, kilted men so unsettling the French that some broke away in panic.

The remainder of the French left-hand column attempted to turn and face the charging Highlanders, but were too late. Montgomery's 77th crashed into the exposed flank, scattering them in seconds. MacKim saw one Highlander hew the head from a French infantryman and run on, chasing half a dozen more.

"The Grenadiers are following," Kennedy murmured.

Colonel Grant of Ballindalloch led the Grenadiers to support Montgomery's Highlanders, and then Lord Rollo sent some of his men forward. Within minutes of the Highland charge, a sizeable proportion of the British force advanced against the crumbling French flank. As one column collapsed in near panic, the other two refused to hold and also ran. Ten minutes after the Highlanders' charge, the entire French advance had turned into a rout.

"See how they run!" Parnell marvelled as the Highlanders and Grenadiers led the British in what was now little more than a frantic pursuit.

The British artillery continued to fire, harassing the French retreat, bringing down a man here and there.

"Cease fire!" Monckton ordered the gunners. "Leave it to the infantry."

"Rangers! Follow the French!"

MacKim did not hear who gave the order, but the Rangers moved at once. Joining the other regiments, they slid and slithered down the ravine and clambered up the slope of Morne Grenier. Although a few brave French turned to fight, most fled, and the British followed, plunging into redoubts with fixed bayonets and investigating every cranny where a man could hide. Some enterprising officer blew a hunting horn, and the view halloo sounded above the intermittent crackle of musketry and shouts of excited men.

"I've never known anything like this before," Parnell said. He rested in the shade of a trench to load his musket. "The French are normally stubborn fighters."

"We've not taken Fort Royal yet," MacKim reminded.

When darkness swooped on them, the British were still clearing Morne Grenier. Junior officers led small groups of men and starlight glittered from bayonets, while the muzzle flare of muskets showed where occasional French units resisted. An hour after dark, the gunfire ended, although Kennedy ordered the Rangers to remain alert.

"It would be like the French to wait until we relax and then counter-attack," Kennedy said. "Form a defensive perimeter, Rangers, and every third man remain awake. MacKim, you have first watch."

Despite Kennedy's caution, the French did not retaliate. General Monckton sent up reinforcements, and by one in the morning of the 28th, the British had occupied every French stronghold on the mountain and were busy creating new redoubts.

"We've captured the hill," MacKim said. "Morne Grenier is ours."

"Fort Royal is next." Kennedy stuffed tobacco into the bowl of his pipe. "Then St Pierre itself, and we can all go home."

Parnell laughed. "I hope you're right, sir, but I heard a whisper that Monckton wants to attack Louisiana next."

☙❧

WITHOUT FRENCH ARTILLERY TO HARASS THEM, THE BRITISH artillerymen and engineers completed the batteries on Morne Tortenson in two days, and then started fresh redoubts closer to Fort Royal.

"I've never known French soldiers run like that," MacKim said. "They didn't even bother to spike their guns."

Kennedy nodded. "We captured a loaded mortar, with nine

unspiked cannons, plus all their ammunition and provisions. Now look at them." He jerked a thumb towards the nearest redoubt, in which the captured guns grinned towards Fort Royal.

"We're nearly touching the French citadel," MacKim said. "We can't be more than four-hundred yards from the walls."

"Strong walls, though," Kennedy said. "And I wish we had taken more of their militia and these damned freebooters. The French regulars don't concern me as they abide by the rules of war; the freebooters could do anything."

MacKim thought of René Roberval. "You're right, sir." *We haven't finished with that pirate yet. He'll be watching for us, I think.*

"The gunners are nearly ready," Kennedy continued. "It's best if the French in Fort Royal surrender now before the carnage begins."

"Aye," MacKim said. "But they won't. They're a stubborn breed."

As the Rangers on Morne Grenier watched, the British batteries on Morne Tortenson opened fire. With fourteen 24-pounder cannon and two mortars, they should have pounded the citadel, but the cannon were at the limit of their range. By the time the shot reached the walls, the balls were dipping and barely marked the target.

"That's why we had to capture this hill as well," Kennedy said comfortably. "We can do more damage from here."

"And they Frenchies know it," MacKim said as the French guns replied. "They have sufficient firepower in Fort Royal to withstand a siege. All they have to do is hold out until the French fleet arrives from Brest or the Spaniards from Cadiz, and they can sweep our ships from the sea."

"If that happens," Kennedy said, "we'll be the besieged as their fresh troops along with the militia and the garrison in Fort Royal and St Pierre come out to attack us."

"We've got a bit of work to do yet then," MacKim agreed.

Ensign Mowat approached, smiling and confident. Now

burned by the sun, he trotted up to Kennedy and touched his hat.

"Colonel Scott sends his regards, sir, and could you do him the honour of a meeting at your earliest convenience."

"That means immediately," Kennedy said. "Please convey my respects to the colonel and tell him—no, don't tell him anything, ensign. I'll come back with you." He rose. "Look after the men, sergeant."

"Yes, sir," MacKim said.

Kennedy was back within half an hour. "We're going on patrol, MacKim. Colonel Scott wants us to verify the state of Fort Royal's defences."

"Yes, sir." MacKim expected nothing less. "How many men?"

"You and I. Corporal Parnell can take command here." Kennedy gave his encouraging smile. "It will be a routine patrol, I hope."

They left as the light faded, with short muskets, forty rounds of ammunition, the telescope and pen, paper, and ink.

Pen and ink. I still haven't written to Claudette! Damn my mind. I'll write the moment we return.

The sky was clouded that night, with no moon to help guide the Rangers as they eased forward over territory the enemy controlled by the sweep of their guns. When they heard the murmur of French voices, Kennedy signalled a halt, and they eased into an area of dead ground, protected by a screen of thorny scrub.

"The citadel that protects Fort Royal is earth-built," MacKim observed. "That means the walls will absorb our cannon fire better than stone would."

Kennedy nodded. "If anybody knows about building forts, the French do." He studied the fort through his telescope. "It's on a peninsula with the sea on all sides, except a single narrow neck of land."

"That'll be murder to assault." MacKim painstakingly wrote notes. "The entrance is barely over a hundred feet wide. All the

French have to do is concentrate their cannon on that, and they'll sweep any attacking force away. We'll lose hundreds of men."

"We're already losing too many from yellow jack," Kennedy said. "The sooner we take this damned island, the better."

Sentries patrolled the fort's walls, with lanterns hanging outside and the light reflecting from musket barrels and accoutrements. The Rangers timed the sentries' beats and calculated their numbers by the length of the wall, with MacKim writing down the details.

On either side of the neck of land, the guns of a demibastion waited to hammer any approaching enemy, with a half-moon battery in support. Beyond this formidable array of artillery, the citadel boasted a curtain wall held by infantry, plus a wet ditch and a sloping glacis. The garrison's massed musketry would defend everything if the assaulters survived the cannon.

"Even if we hammer the artillery," Kennedy said, "Fort Royal could still hold out. The longer they hold, the more of our men will die of disease, and we'll be so weakened that the relieving French fleet will walk all over us."

"We'll have to take the damned place quickly then," MacKim said.

Kennedy nodded. He crawled further up the hill and lay on a slight knoll. "I can see inside the fort from here, or at least see part of it."

MacKim glanced upwards, where a warm wind was shifting the clouds. "We're a bit exposed here, sir."

"I know," Kennedy said, "but the more information we bring in, the better. I can see a covered way as well, with palisades, and there's a double wall on the harbour side of the fort, complete with flankers." He removed the telescope from his eye. "Even if the Navy silence the batteries facing the sea and breach the outer walls, any assaulting party would face a defended wall, with flankers to give crossfire."

"We'll lose men that way, too." MacKim swore as he blotted

the paper. "This damned heat is thinning the ink. I think the French have Fort Royal better defended than Quebec or Montreal ever was."

"Even if the ships get past Pigeon Island," Kennedy said, "there are guns mounted on a platform overlooking the harbour, and there is more artillery—heavy stuff—behind a parapet facing the sea."

"I can't see how we'll ever take this place before the relieving fleet arrives," MacKim said gloomily.

"If we try a direct attack on the gate, the French have another gun platform above that," Kennedy said.

"We've three choices then." MacKim put down his pen. "We use our artillery to silence their batteries one by one, or starve them into submission, or have an all-out direct assault and accept the casualties."

"We haven't the time to starve them," Kennedy said, "and they'll likely have greater food and water supplies than we have. That also holds for the slow artillery siege." He shifted backwards. "We'd better get this intelligence back to General Monckton. I'm glad I don't have to make the decision!"

"Sir!" MacKim said, lifting his head slightly. "I can smell tobacco."

They lay still, with their eyes probing the darkness for the source of the smell. The drift came to them again, a sure sign that somebody was between the lines.

Kennedy nudged MacKim with his elbow and nodded to their left, where a glimmer of white revealed the presence of a French patrol.

They waited for a long five minutes, and then began to crawl back towards the closest British position. A laugh sounded from the dark, followed by a murmur in French.

"They're all around us," Kennedy whispered. "Lie low."

A French patrol walked past, seemingly casual despite their proximity to the British positions. Kennedy and MacKim withdrew another few yards towards the British lines when they became aware of a commotion behind them. The British challenge "Barbados!" was not met by the countersign "Jamaica!" Instead, a crackle of musketry broke out.

"The French are raiding our pickets!" MacKim said. "They're behind us."

Such practices were standard during a siege. The besieged would send out small parties to harass the besiegers and destroy as much siege work as possible. Although sometimes the raiding party would be only a dozen strong, the defenders could also send a large force to disrupt the siege.

The Rangers lay still as the firing spread behind them, interspersed with yells and the occasional scream. After twenty minutes, Kennedy lifted his head. "I think we should make a run for the lines, sergeant."

"Yes, sir." MacKim was not so sure.

"Remember, the parole is Barbados, and the countersign is Jamaica."

"Yes, sir." MacKim ducked as the French artillery in the fort fired a volley. He saw the muzzle flash first, then heard the roar of the guns. There was a slight pause, then a shrill sound—not quite a whine and nearly a whistle—that increased in volume as the cannonballs passed overhead. The balls landed in front of the British gun emplacements, with the heavy iron shaking the ground on which MacKim lay. When the British guns replied, MacKim was not aware of any individual noise. The sound engulfed him, controlling all his senses, so he felt like a human fly trapped within a military drum, helpless against the noise.

"Ready?" Kennedy had to mouth the words, as the noise was so intense.

MacKim nodded. The firing increased as both sides fired simultaneously, and then fell into painful silence.

"Now," Kennedy said.

MacKim rose and ran towards the British lines, zig-zagging to confuse any French marksman. The ground was hard and churned with the firing, so he tripped more than once and staggered when his foot caught on a disturbed rock. MacKim swore when he dropped his ink and pen, glanced down, failed to see them in the dark, and ran on. He had his notes safe, and the stationery was replaceable.

A line of fascines loomed ahead, with the heads of defenders protruding. Somebody pointed a musket at him. "Barbados!" he yelled. "For God's sake, Barbados!"

"Jamaica," a hoarse voice replied, and MacKim slid over the parapet and lay in the bottom of the trench. "I'm glad to see you, lads," he said.

"And we're happy to see you," said a familiar voice, and Captain René Roberval smiled at him.

12

"You!" MacKim swore and tried to rise, but two freebooters pointed muskets at him as a third shoved him back down. Three British soldiers lay dead in the trench, two with multiple stab wounds and the third with his head cut clean off his shoulders. Half a dozen freebooters stood watching, with Roberval as suave as ever, despite the blood that smeared his face.

"Me," Roberval said. "I thought I had seen you dancing around in the dark. Sergeant MacKim, isn't it?" Roberval spoke passable English, with only a hint of a French accent.

MacKim lifted his musket, only for one of the freebooters to wrestle it from his grip.

"We'll take you back with us, sergeant," Roberval said. "I want to know what you were doing out there."

"Trying to get back to the British positions," MacKim said.

"Barbados," Roberval said, "and Jamaica. What simple paroles you British create. We listened to your pickets shouting at each other all night." He smiled again. "Listen, sergeant." Roberval raised his voice. "Barbados!"

"Jamaica!" a west-country voice replied. "Who's out there?"

"You see?" Roberval said, grinning.

MacKim did not reply. He only hoped Kennedy had escaped with the information he had gathered.

"Gag him," Roberval ordered in French, and strong hands tied a strip of cloth over MacKim's mouth.

The artillery began to fire, with the sound covering all other noises. Roberval nodded, and the freebooters slid over the side of the trench, shoving MacKim in front of them. MacKim glanced behind him, contemplating escape, but with three agile men eager to shoot and stab him, he had no chance.

Pushed, shoved, and occasionally pricked with the point of a sword, MacKim found himself forced towards Fort Royal. Close up, the defences were even more formidable, with the walls higher and the French gunners looking as professional as their British counterparts. Roberval ripped away MacKim's gag.

"Where are you taking me?"

"You'll see," Roberval said.

The night was fading as the freebooters pushed MacKim past a pair of watchful guards and through the heavy gates of Fort Royal. The town was already busy with soldiers and civilians, with a platoon of regulars eyeing MacKim curiously.

"A prisoner," Roberval explained casually, shoving MacKim into a rundown street, where black people were busy making fascines under the watchful eyes of what MacKim assumed to be slave drivers. The atmosphere was oppressive, as if the clean air of the open sea had never penetrated this area, and hopeless faces watched him without interest. MacKim saw a brawny man lift a whip and beat a youth who could not be more than thirteen years old.

"Hey!" MacKim struggled to intervene, but with two guards holding him, he could not get close enough to help. "Leave that child alone!"

"Save your concern for yourself," one of his guards said. "You'll need it."

The second guard laughed as he propelled MacKim into a squat building with small barred windows near the stone roof.

"What is this place? I am a prisoner of war!"

Ignoring MacKim's protests, the guards shoved him into the building and down three stairs to a stone floor. From the little MacKim could see in the gloom, the chamber was bare and bleak, and within a few moments, the guards chained him to the wall.

One kicked him in the ribs. "We'll be back for you later," he said, and left, leaving MacKim to his thoughts.

The place was choking hot, with rats and other vermin rustling in the dark. The smell was atrocious, worse than the 'tween deck of a troop transport, thick with the stench of human waste and the sickly-sweet aroma of death. MacKim hauled at his chains, testing their strength, wondering if he could work them free from the solid stone of the wall.

Even if I did, he told himself, *what good would that be? I'd still be locked in this stinking dungeon in the middle of the enemy's fortification. They would recognise my uniform the second I stepped into the streets.*

Even so, MacKim worked at the chain, pulling it back and forward, trying to loosen it.

"It's no good," the voice was deep, speaking French with an accent that was unfamiliar to MacKim. "The staples are set deep in the rock."

"Who are you?" MacKim asked, peering into the gloom.

"I'm known as Benjamin," the voice sounded again.

"I am Hugh MacKim. Are you a prisoner here, too?"

"I am a slave," Benjamin said.

MacKim was silent for a few moments. "I've never met a slave before."

"I've never seen a white man chained in here before," Benjamin replied. "What have you done?"

"I'm a prisoner of war, a British soldier," MacKim said, wrestling with his chains.

"Save your energy," Benjamin advised. "Why have the French put you in here? The other British prisoners are elsewhere."

Now that MacKim had something on which to focus, he

could make out Benjamin's shape in the far corner of the dungeon. "I don't know," he admitted. "Some freebooters captured me. Captain Roberval and his men."

"The devil's brother!" Benjamin said. "I know of that man."

"Are you chained as well?" MacKim had not heard the rattle of any chains except his own.

"No," Benjamin said. "The French save the chains for special slaves, men who have tried to escape or who have attacked their owners."

"Has anybody escaped?"

"Some have escaped slavery, but the French recapture most. Martinique—Martinico to you—is a small island."

MacKim had heard of slave revolts in other islands, usually crushed with terrible brutality. "If you escaped, where would you go?"

There was silence for quite a while as Benjamin considered the question. "Maybe Jamaica. The British have a treaty with the Maroons there and have promised to leave them in peace."

MacKim was unsure what a Maroon was, but did not ask. "You'd need a boat," he said. "And a compass."

Benjamin was quiet again. "These things are hard to find."

"Could you not go to Africa?" MacKim had only a vague idea of Africa's location. He knew it was somewhere south of Europe, and was large and hot.

"Africa is too far away," Benjamin said. "Anyway, where in Africa would I go? The chief of my tribe sold my grandfather into slavery. Would I be welcome there?"

MacKim did not pursue the question. "My chief sent me into the Army to fight the king's wars."

"Then we are both exiles, you and I," Benjamin said.

The door opened then, allowing in a blast of fresher air, followed by a rush of slaves, both men and women, with Frenchmen and Martinico planters urging them in with loud shouts and blows. Within minutes, the incomers filled the dungeon, squabbling over every inch of space and talking in a mixture of French and a language that MacKim did not understand. He lay in his chains, an alien among strangers, with some slaves staring at this white prisoner in their midst.

"He's a white man," Benjamin explained. "A prisoner like us. His chief made him a slave of the British Army, and Roberval captured him."

"I want to kill all white men," a burly man said, looking at MacKim with loathing in his eyes.

"We all think like that," Benjamin said. "But best to let them kill each other. Maybe one day there will be none left, and we can live as free men."

MacKim sat quiet, picking up snippets of conversation. He had seen occasional black slaves in North America and more in the Caribbean. The Rangers even had freed Black men in the ranks, but he had never thought much about them. Now he saw them as people like him.

"If we kill him, nobody would know," the burly man said.

"The French would take revenge on us," Benjamin told him. "They'd burn some alive and flog the rest."

MacKim listened as the slaves discussed his life or death. He could taste the resentment and fear in the dungeon, along with the misery.

"He's a prisoner, as we are," Benjamin said. "His chief forced him to fight for his king, and now the French have chained him. He's more like us than against us."

The slaves crowded around MacKim, some pressing close to him, one man prodding with a hard finger.

"We can kill him," the burly man said. "He deserves to die."

"Why?" Benjamin asked. "Kill him for the sins of others?"

MacKim kicked at a man who stood on his ankle. "Get away! You wouldn't dare do that if I was free!"

More slaves crowded around MacKim, prodding and taunting, with one man kicking at him as MacKim swung a fist, swearing in frustration as the manacles hampered his movement.

"Let him alone." Benjamin stepped closer, and for the first

time, MacKim saw his saviour. Benjamin was about thirty, with scars on his chest and humorous eyes. "He's no freer than we are."

The burly man growled at Benjamin, showing his teeth.

"He's done us no harm." Benjamin remained calm as a crowd gathered around them, most supporting the burly man.

"He's white," a man with tribal scars on his face growled.

"He's done us no harm," Benjamin repeated, pushing the scarred man away.

The noise rose as the other slaves began to talk. MacKim listened, wondering how he would feel if he were a black slave.

In their situation, I'd probably do the same.

MacKim stood up. Smaller and slighter than most of the slaves, he knew they could kill him in seconds, yet he refused to be cowed. He rattled his chains.

"Come on, if you're coming," he said in French, and added in Gaelic and English, "I'm Hugh MacKim of Kennedy's Rangers, Wee Hughie of the 78th Fraser's Highlanders!"

MacKim waited, with Benjamin standing at his side, undecided what to do, when an interruption altered the dynamics.

"Allez!" The door opened with a crash, and four men shoved in, clearing a passage with whips and boots. One grabbed hold of MacKim, while another pressed the muzzle of a pistol to his head and a third unlocked his chains.

"Where are you taking me?" MacKim asked as the men dragged him to the dungeon door and pushed him into the street outside. He had not realised how much time had elapsed as the glare of sunlight nearly blinded him. MacKim blinked and looked around at the citadel. French soldiers abounded, most wearing infantrymen's white uniforms, some artillerymen and others were casually dressed militia. Of the infantry, most seemed to be tall Grenadiers, with a sprinkling of Marines. A few Grenadiers looked curiously at this green-clad prisoner in their midst, and then MacKim's captors dragged him through a deep gate into the citadel.

"This way, Sergeant MacKim!"

Somebody kicked his leg. MacKim turned in defiance, and two men pushed him into another building.

MacKim heard the hammer of artillery as the British guns opened up on Fort Royal and felt a slight tremor as a cannonball thumped into the defences. The French retaliated with a volley from a full battery, and powder smoke rose in white clouds.

"Here he is," MacKim's guards said, throwing him to the ground.

"Lift him."

Roberval was perched on the corner of a desk, sipping at a glass of red wine. "Ah, Sergeant MacKim. I trust you are enjoying our hospitality?"

"Your trust is misplaced," MacKim said. "You are most inhospitable, captain, and a disgrace to the good name of France."

Roberval laughed at MacKim's words. "We were going to kill you, sergeant, but unfortunately, Governor-General La Touché learned of your capture and wished to see you. I told him you were only a sergeant, but he will not be gainsaid." Roberval shrugged. "Governor Generals like to think of themselves as very important people."

"So do pirate captains," MacKim said.

"Touché, sergeant." Roberval gave a mocking bow. When he straightened up, the scar on his forehead seemed more pronounced. "If you tell your piratical Captain O'Brien your thoughts, I'd appreciate them better." He raised his voice. "Take him to the governor."

Who the devil is Captain O'Brien? And how is he involved?

Louis Charles Le Vassor de La Touché de Tréville, Comte de La Touché, was a man in his early fifties, immaculately dressed, as all French officials appeared to be, and surrounded by underlings. Scattered among the military officers was a group of planters, to judge by their sun-browned faces, loose civilian clothes, and broad-brimmed hats. La Touché looked in disdain when the freebooters handed MacKim to a grenadier sergeant and stepped further away.

"Who is this ragamuffin?"

"This man is the British sergeant the privateers captured, your excellency," a smooth-faced aide-de-camp replied. "You expressed a desire to interrogate him."

"So I did." La Touché approached MacKim. "Does he speak any French?"

"I do not know, your excellency," the aide-de-camp said. "I rather doubt it. The rank and file are largely uneducated."

La Touché glanced at MacKim. "Ask him if he speaks French."

The aide-de-camp took a deep breath before very slowly asking. "Can you speak French, sergeant?"

"I can," MacKim said.

La Touché gave a little nod.

"If you are a British soldier, why are you wearing green and not scarlet?"

"I serve with Kennedy's Rangers," MacKim explained. "The Rangers always wear green rather than scarlet."

La Touché seemed interested. "I have heard of Major Rogers' Rangers," he said. "Are you part of them?"

"There are various Rangers units," MacKim explained. "We operate autonomously of one another within a Ranging Corps as part of the British Army."

"Are you a Colonial?" La Touché asked.

"No, sir." MacKim drew himself to attention as befitted a British soldier. "I am Scottish."

"A Highlander? A soldier in skirts?" La Touché looked at his aides-de-camp and gave a depreciating little laugh, which they reciprocated.

MacKim fought back his desire to punch La Touché in the mouth. Instead, he smiled. "The same soldiers in skirts who destroyed your army on the Plains of Abraham," he reminded.

"And there are thousands more waiting to do the same to Fort Royal."

"I am aware of the number of your army," La Touché said.

MacKim thought quickly. He had seen the formidable defences of Fort Royal and knew that the French, and perhaps the Spanish, had ships approaching Martinico. If the British had to create a formal siege, the relieving fleet might arrive before Fort Royal surrendered. Even if the British assaulted before the French arrived, the citadel's defences would kill hundreds, perhaps thousands, of the besiegers.

"Including the reinforcements?" MacKim laughed. "While you have been watching this little army surround Fort Royal, another ten-thousand men, including loyal Indians from the colonies and three more battalions of Highlanders, two of Grenadiers, and another thirty pieces of heavy artillery have landed." He saw the consternation in the planters' faces.

"I would have learned of them," La Touché said.

"It seems you have not," MacKim said. "General Monckton intends to storm Fort Royal tomorrow night. Unless you surrender immediately, he will sack the town and put all to the sword, according to the rules of war."[1]

MacKim was unsure what the rules of war said about besieging fortresses, but thought he was correct.

La Touché snorted. "My artillery will tear any attack to pieces."

MacKim shrugged. "Your artillery will kill hundreds of men, but it is better for a soldier to die in an assault than of disease. The longer we linger here, the more of us will succumb to fever. That's General Monckton's reasoning." He raised his voice, directing his words to the planters as much as the military. "A bloody assault always raises the temper of the men. Once we have captured the defences, the soldiers will be in no mood to give quarter. There will be murder, looting, rape, and pillage. And once we have Fort Royal, General Monckton has promised the men free reign over the island."

He saw the planters recoil from the idea of thousands of drunken, battle-maddened British soldiers unleashed on their island.

"The choice is yours, Monsieur." MacKim pressed home his advantage. "You have the lives of your garrison and the good people of Fort Royal in your hands."

Two of the planters approached La Touché, speaking rapidly and gesticulating with their hands. MacKim watched, catching a snatch of their conversation as the planters spoke of their fears of rampant British soldiers and urged La Touché to surrender.

"We are French!" La Touché said. "We will fight on!"

As more planters surged around the governor, the aide-de-camp snapped an order. The Grenadiers grabbed MacKim and hustled him away.[2] *Whatever happens now,* MacKim thought, *I have spread some dissent among the French.*

The Grenadiers marched MacKim into the town and into a substantial building, where a group of other prisoners huddled in stifling heat.

"Are any of you British?" MacKim asked as soon as the Grenadiers slammed the door shut.

"We're all British," an anonymous voice called from the gloom. "I'm Wilce, mate of *Charming Nancy* of Bristol."

"Cunningham, master of *Thames* of London."

"Price, mate of *Prince Harry* of Exeter."

MacKim waited until silence returned. "I am Sergeant MacKim of Kennedy's Rangers, late of Fraser's 78th Highlanders."

"What's happening on Martinico?" Cunningham asked.

"We've advanced to a few hundred yards of the citadel, "MacKim said," and General Monckton has established siege batteries. The French have sent a fleet from Brest to relieve the island, but Admiral Rodney has his ships patrolling offshore to catch him." He heard the murmur of voices as the news starved captives assimilated the information.

"How about the Spanish?" Price asked. "The French told us

they had a fleet of battleships sailing to sweep us out of the Caribbean."

"I heard the rumours," MacKim said. "I don't know the facts. Has anybody seen another Ranger prisoner? I lost touch with Lieutenant Kennedy when the French captured me."

Cunningham replied, "I don't know the name, but the guards boasted they had destroyed a British force and killed a famous Ranger officer."

MacKim felt despair replace his elation of only a few moments before.

They've killed Kennedy? First Ewan, then Tayanita, and now Kennedy?

If the French had killed Kennedy, MacKim knew he had lost not only his commander, but also a friend. He slumped on the ground, striving to come to terms with the news. He was well aware that a soldier's life was precarious, but Kennedy always seemed invulnerable, a man apart from the rest.

"Are you alright, sergeant?" Cunningham asked.

MacKim nodded. "That officer was a friend of mine."

"Ah." Cunningham nodded. "War is a complete bastard."

Even in the dungeon, they could hear the batter of gunfire as the British batteries hammered at the citadel's walls. The French replied, meeting each British gun with two of their own.

"Well," Cunningham said, half an hour later. "We know General Monckton is still out there."

The building shook as a shell exploded outside, with fragments of plaster flaking from the ceiling. Some landed on the prisoners below.

"Wouldn't it be ironic if we were all killed by a British shell?" Price asked with a high-pitched laugh that revealed shredded nerves.

Nobody replied as the men sat in near silence, listening to the pounding of artillery. After an hour, the door opened, and a body of Grenadiers pushed in with water and bread.

"What's happening outside?" MacKim asked.

"We're defeating the assault," a Grenadier told him. "We repulsed a British attack and killed hundreds of your countrymen." He slammed the door and left the prisoners in the dark.

"What did he say?" Wilce asked. "I wish these damned foreigners would learn English like civilised people."

MacKim translated the Grenadier's words. "He was lying," he added. After enduring the siege of Quebec, MacKim could recognise the sounds. "If we had attacked, there would have been shouts and yells and musketry. We've only heard heavy artillery."

The prisoners settled down again, starting whenever an explosion sounded close or a cannonball hammered the citadel walls.

"How often do they feed us?" MacKim asked.

"When they feel like it," Cunningham said. "We try to make the bread and water last."

Another shell burst nearby, and then the door opened, intense sunlight blinding the prisoners.

"Out!" A Grenadier sergeant ordered, gesturing with his bayonet. *"Tout le monde sort!"* (Everybody get outside!)

The prisoners stumbled out, blinking in the sun as the French artillerymen worked their guns. A pall of powder smoke lay thick over the citadel, grey-white and acrid on the tongue.

"Where are you taking us?" MacKim asked, and the Grenadier sergeant responded by pricking his bayonet into MacKim's leg.

"Allez!"

"I think they want us to go with them," Cunningham said, as the Grenadiers used their bayonets and musket butts to urge the prisoners before them.

"I think you are right," MacKim said.

The guards herded the prisoners towards the main gate, and for a moment, MacKim thought the governor intended to free them. Instead, the Grenadiers shoved them into the defensive ditch beneath the walls, so they were under the arc of British fire and within easy range of French muskets.

"Maybe La Touché believes Monckton will stop firing if we're here," Cunningham said.

"I doubt that'll happen," MacKim told him. He looked at the ditch, with its steep slope on either side. "We could scale the ditch and crawl over to the British siege lines."

The prisoners ducked as a British volley hammered the wall above their head, sending pieces of masonry into the ditch.

"Move further along," MacKim said. "We're directly under a French battery here. That's a prime target for our guns."

He led them away until a spatter of musketry sounded from above as a squad of Martinico militia fired at them.

"As you were," MacKim said. "That way is even more dangerous. Try the opposite direction." He led them again, with the same result, as the defenders opened fire on the prisoners in the ditch.

The prisoners returned to their original position, hugging the ground as British cannonballs hammered the French battery above; the French artillery replied with interest.

"How long will the bombardment last?" Cunningham asked.

MacKim had to shout above the batter of the guns. "Until our artillery silences the French battery, or until Monckton orders an assault. The general might decide to blow a breach in the walls right here."

If so, this wall will be reduced to rubble that will collapse into the ditch on top of us.

"I hope he attacks soon," Price said as fragments of masonry rose high in the air to descend in a heavy shower within the ditch.

"Try and carve a scrape in the sides," MacKim advised. He checked that every man was digging. "Come on, Captain Cunningham! It's meagre shelter, but it might save your life." He swore as he saw Cunningham lying prone. "Captain Cunningham's gone, men. A piece of rock's broken his neck."[3]

As if on command, all the guns fell silent. An eerie silence descended, broken only by hoarse shouts from the Fort Royal garrison and one of the British prisoners singing an obscene shanty.

"What's happening?" Price asked.

"Blessed if I know," MacKim replied. "Stay here, and I'll look."

Leaving the prisoners in the ditch, MacKim clambered onto the surface, keeping low and prepared to dodge if any French musketeers decided to shoot him. Nobody fired. He saw a row of faces peering over the battlements of Fort Royal, with artillerymen sitting in the embrasures and a Grenadier sergeant smoking his pipe.

Has the war ended, and nobody's told us?

"Halloa down there!" MacKim shouted to the men in the ditch. "Nobody's firing at me. There might be a truce! Up you come."

The prisoners swarmed out to stand cautiously in the open.

"We can't stay here," MacKim said. "We're an easy target for the Frenchies. Our lines are only four-hundred yards away."

Crossing four-hundred yards of open country in full view of the enemy artillery was a strain on MacKim's nerves. He led the prisoners at a trot that soon increased to a gallop. When he was within a hundred yards of the British lines, he started to shout, aware he was ignorant of the password for the day.

"We're British!" he roared. "We're British!" For the first time in a year, he wished he wore the king's scarlet coat rather than the faded green of the Rangers. "Barbados or Jamaica or whatever today's parole is!"

"Don't shoot!" the seamen joined in with voices accustomed to shouting above the scream of a North Atlantic gale. "We're British!"

"What's the parole?" A young sentry of the 90th asked, levelling his musket directly at MacKim.

"I'm damned if I know," MacKim said. "But a few days ago, it was Barbados."

Ignoring the sentry, the seamen ran past MacKim, desperate to reach the sanctuary of the British lines after so long held as French prisoners.

"It's not Barbados." The sentry aimed his musket.

"I know it's not," MacKim said, and broke in a frenzy of foul language, swearing in Gaelic, Anglo-Saxon, Abenaki, and French until a rangy officer appeared and pushed up the sentry's musket.

"He's British," the officer said with a grin. "No Frenchman could swear like that. In you come, my friend, and tell us who you are."

"Yes, sir!" MacKim said. "I'm Sergeant MacKim of Kennedy's Rangers!" He reached inside his tunic and produced the notes he and Kennedy had taken. "Could you arrange for this document to get to General Monckton, sir, please?"

With his duty done, MacKim slid to the ground, exhausted.

Kennedy's dead. I have to write to Claudette.

13

On the evening of 3rd February 1762, Fort Royal surrendered to General Monckton. The next day, the British Grenadiers and a body of Montgomerie's Highlanders took possession of the gates. The Highlanders marched with the high skirl of bagpipes, while the Grenadiers were silent save for the regular tramp of their boots.

At nine in the morning of the 5th of February, the French garrison marched out of the fortress. As they had surrendered on honourable terms, they carried their colours, and each man held his musket and ammunition.

Fresh out of the hospital tent, MacKim stood with the Highlanders as the French garrison evacuated. Eight-hundred strong, the FrenchGrenadiers marched out first, with the marines next, followed by the militia, and finally the ragged ranks of freebooters.

"Where did they get so many pirates?" MacKim wondered.

"From the privateers, mainly," Private Gunn told him. Short and muscular, Gunn wore his habitual smile as he watched the French march past. "Or so I heard. Privateers and pirates, the scum of the Caribbean, men who owe allegiance to neither a king nor a flag. They're only here for money, rapine, and loot."

He began to sharpen his bayonet as the French colours flapped in the breeze. "I hear the Frenchies lost one-hundred-and-fifty men in the siege, and maybe many more."

"So I believe," MacKim said. He searched the garrison for La Touché. "I can't see the governor."

"That's because he's not there," Gunn explained. "He slipped out by sea and is in St Peters with his picked Grenadiers, leaving the rest to surrender." He glanced at MacKim. "The French held you a prisoner inside the citadel, didn't they?"

MacKim nodded.

"Do you know why it surrendered?"

"I didn't hear."

"I did," Gunn said. "The French captured a Grenadier, and he told La Touché that General Monckton was going to storm the place and put everybody to the sword unless he surrendered."

MacKim allowed himself to smile. "The Grenadier's idea worked, then."

"It did. I know the general was not happy about the strength of the French defences. Ever since that Rangers officer brought back intelligence about the number and emplacement of guns, Monckton was uneasy, so La Touché's surrender was a blessed relief."

MacKim nodded. He knew he could never admit the part he had played, for nobody would believe him. Best let the non-existent Grenadier take credit.

"If La Touché hadn't surrendered, Gunn was in a garrulous mood watching the garrison march past, we would have needed to make at least two breaches in the walls, and that would have taken days, if not weeks. The French relieving force would catch us in the open, and bang! We're caught between two fires."

Something Gunn had said came back to MacKim. "You mentioned a Rangers officer who brought back intelligence. Do you know his name?" MacKim did not allow himself to hope.

Gunn screwed up his face. "Damned if I know," he said. "He

was a true Colonial though, a backwoodsman from some outlandish place right on the frontier."

"Was his name Kennedy?" MacKim asked as hope surged within him. "Lieutenant Kennedy?"

"That's the fellow!" Gunn said. "Captain Kennedy!"

"Captain?"

"Indeed so," Gunn nodded vigorously. "Didn't the general thank him for his intelligence by advancing his rank?"

MacKim felt a mixture of pleasure and relief seep through him. "Well now, *Captain* Kennedy. And I thought the French killed the fellow."

"He's as alive as he ever was," Gunn said, "and based up north to watch St Peters. Where are you going, Sergeant MacKim?"

"Up north," MacKim said. "To watch St Peters."

※

KENNEDY LOOKED UP AS MACKIM BOUNDED OVER THE ROUGH terrain. "Who the devil is that? You there! Keep your fool head down! Not all the French have surrendered, don't you know?"

"I know that full well, Captain!" MacKim shouted.

"MacKim!" Kennedy stood up from behind the tree where he had been sheltering and lowered his musket. "Damn you for a rogue and a scoundrel! I thought you were dead!"

"And I thought the same about you, Captain, sir!" MacKim stopped in front of Kennedy, remembered their difference in rank, and touched his hat in salute.

"I should think so, too, sergeant," Kennedy said, unable to control his grin. "I should break you to private and order a hundred at the halberds for making me think you were dead."

"My profuse apologies, sir, and your captainship. I had no choice in the matter, and may I offer my congratulations?"

"You may," Kennedy said. "And I will accept them, too, for your impudence. Here!" Without another word, Kennedy held out his hand, and the two men shook heartily. "Now, tell me what's to do and how you've come back from the dead."

They were north of Fort Royal, in the high terrain near St Pierre, where the remainder of the French in Martinico continued to hold out. Kennedy listened as MacKim told him a little of his experiences, leaving out much of his interview with La Touché.

"La Touché," Kennedy said. "That's a stubborn man! If it weren't for him, we'd have the rest of this island under the Union flag by now."

"Is that so, sir?" MacKim asked.

"It is," Kennedy said. "No sooner had Fort Royal surrendered than most of the other areas of Martinico sent deputations to Rodney and General Monckton, desiring to capitulate. Monckton agreed to their terms, and only St Pierre holds out, with La Touché and the rump of the French army."

MacKim nodded. "Well, we took Fort Royal handily enough. I am sure St Pierre won't be any harder."

"Aye, and the day after we took Fort Royal, Pigeon Island surrendered," Kennedy said with satisfaction. "Now the Royal Navy has the best anchorage in the Windward Islands. Admiral Rodney was as pleased as a cat with three tails when he accepted the surrender, and he took possession of fourteen-sail of privateers as well."

MacKim smiled at that. "All the freebooters?"

"Alas, no," Kennedy said. "One ship, the wiliest and worst of the bunch, slipped out and escaped the blockade."

"Which one?" MacKim already guessed the answer.

"Our old adversary, Captain Roberval in *Douce Vengeance*," Kennedy said. He shook his head. "No matter. Commodore Swanton is out there, and Jimmy Douglas. Two better seamen never sailed the seas. If they can't catch him, nobody can."

MacKim nodded. He had every faith in Commodore Swanton, while all he had heard of James Douglas had been positive.

Kennedy lit his pipe, puffing smoke into the hot air. "Once

we take St Peter, or Pierre, or whatever the Frenchies call the damned place, the entire island will be ours and Roberval won't have many ports left to refit. He'll be like an old-time pirate, with all men's hands against him."

"What's to do now?" MacKim asked.

"Now, we are spying out St Peters for the general," Kennedy said. "And this time, don't get yourself captured, MacKim."

"I'll try not to, captain, sir," MacKim said.

They crawled forward through thick undergrowth, with Dickert, MacRae, and Parnell acting as an escort, until they were sufficiently close to the town and fort for Kennedy to extend his telescope. As before, MacKim took notes, shielding the paper from a persistent breeze and dipping his quill into the inkwell every few words.

"Damned heat," he said. "I'm sure it thins the ink."

"Keep writing," Kennedy said. "The fort is close to the shore, with the sea nearly breaking on one wall and the St Pierre River guarding the western side."

"Got that," MacKim said.

"This western side overlooks the road and has a battery of cannon," Kennedy reported. "I can't make out how many or the calibre. I'd say at least half a dozen 12-pounders, at a guess."

"General Monckton doesn't like guesswork," MacKim said.

"Then he can damned well come here and count the cannon himself!"

"Yes, sir," MacKim said. "Shall I write that down too?"

"Only if you want my boot up your arse, soon-to-be-Private MacKim."

"Very good, sir. Maybe half a dozen 12-pounders it is."

Kennedy nodded. "Exactly so, sergeant." He swept his telescope around the area. "The main gate of the fort faces east and seems to have a permanent presence of a dozen men, although I cannot see any artillery. However, I'd say the fort is vulnerable to our fire, as high ground overlooks it on all sides except towards the sea."

"Yes, sir," MacKim scribbled, cursing as the ink dried and faded almost as quickly as he wrote. "How do people live in this damned heat?"

"Because they make money here, sergeant," Kennedy said blandly. "There is a terrace at the coastal side of the fort, with eight apertures for cannon and sentry boxes at each end."

"Wait!" MacKim said as a French patrol stepped into view. Commanded by a sergeant, the ten-man patrol marched around the fort's walls, peering into the undergrowth without breaking formation.

"They're no threat," Kennedy said, and continued with his observations, telling MacKim that the 200-foot long wall on the landward side was defended by two towers, with eight cannon on each. In case the wall was breached, two more artillery pieces looked over the parade and nearby town.

"Our artillery will dominate this place," MacKim said.

"The walls are between four and five feet thick, with a stone parapet," Kennedy said, "and I think the ditch and covered way are recent."

Waiting for MacKim to complete writing, Kennedy led them to a spot overlooking St Pierre's while Parnell cursed the flies that descended on them.

"The town is well built," Kennedy said, "and divided into distinct quarters." He moved his telescope. "On the west side, there is a battery based on a hill, with ten—no, twelve guns mounted. There is another battery on the west, overlooking the harbour."

"It's a fine-looking town," MacKim commented.

"It is," Kennedy agreed, sliding backwards. "We have completed our work here, and I've seldom had a quieter day in the field."

"Wait, sir, please," MacKim stared forward. "May I borrow the telescope?"

"What do you see, sergeant?"

"A man who saved my life when I was a prisoner," MacKim said.

"Who? I only saw Frenchmen and slaves."

"It was one of the slaves who helped me," MacKim focussed on Benjamin's face, seeing the lines of sweat and the strain. "That fellow has a noble heart. He acted the Good Samaritan when it would have been far easier and safer for him to do nothing."

Kennedy glanced at MacKim. "You are thinking, sergeant."

"I'm wondering if we could stage a raid, sir, as we did in Canada."

"Canada was forest and wilderness, while St Peters is a walled town," Kennedy said.

"Yes, sir," MacKim agreed. "With your permission, sir, I could go alone, slide over the wall, and free that man."

Kennedy shook his head. "And then what? What the devil would you do with a slave?"

"I don't want a slave, sir. I'd set him free." MacKim faced Kennedy with his chin thrust forward in determination. "He saved my life, sir. The least I can do is try and help him."

"No." Kennedy shook his head. "We're soldiers, not philanthropists. Our duty is to fight the king's enemies, not free French slaves. We can't sort the world's problems."

"Yes, sir," MacKim said.

That night, as the Rangers mounted their usual pickets, MacKim stared into the dark, listened to the insects, and planned how to free Benjamin from French slavery. Years of Army discipline had conditioned him to obey orders without question, yet serving with the Rangers had instilled some flexibility of thought. Rather than follow formal drill patterns that saw armies move across the European theatre in chessboard formations, the Rangers valued individuality and initiative when facing an elusive enemy.

"My apologies, Captain Kennedy," MacKim said quietly. "You

are a good man and a good friend, but some things transcend even friendship."

Although MacKim knew the landscape and where he had seen Benjamin, getting through the French defences would be difficult. He decided to leave the following night when he was not on picket duty. He would carry his shortened musket and a knife, with no other equipment—not even a bayonet or a water bottle.

If the Army charges me with desertion, it's in a good cause.

With that decision made, MacKim could concentrate on his duty, checking the pickets, although he knew it would be hard to deceive Kennedy. *With luck, I'll be out and back before anybody realises I have gone. I won't leave that fellow a slave, but I still haven't written Claudette.*

14

"They've surrendered." Kennedy brought the news. "St Peters is ours, and without a shot being fired."

"That's the sort of victory I like," Dickert said. "One with no casualties. What happened?"

"The inhabitants mutinied," Kennedy said. "They told La Touché they'd rather surrender to General Monckton than have British troops ravaging and pillaging the town." He pushed tobacco into the bowl of his pipe. "I hear that St Peter is stuffed full of goods the privateers captured from British merchantmen."

Dickert grunted. "The planters were quite in favour of ravaging and pillage when they benefitted, but opposed when we would be the ravagers." He spat on the ground. "That's for the fine susceptibilities of French civilisation."

How can I rescue Benjamin now?

Remembering the treatment of the slaves, MacKim agreed. "Civilisation is false," he said, in a rare moment of philosophy that eluded most of the Rangers. "When it's based on greed and exploitation, it's not civilisation, sophistication, or enlightenment. It's only a veneer to benefit the most grasping or luckiest in society." He realised that some of the Rangers were looking at him in puzzlement. "I don't agree with slavery," he said, aware he was speaking out against one of the fundamental principles of society. "I don't agree with some people having authority over the rest, whether they are clan chiefs, aristocrats, planters, or kings."

"Are you alright, Sergeant MacKim?" MacRae asked. "You're talking gibberish there."

MacKim closed his mouth. The ideas were only half-formed in his mind.

"Without leaders and followers, we'd have anarchy," Kennedy said. "Everybody would do as they wished, murderers and thieves would run riot, and the world would lack structure."

"Do you agree with slavery then? Or poverty for most people while clan chiefs and aristocrats own everything?" MacKim was about to argue that wars for a king and flag were equally pointless, but realised he would be voicing sedition and kept the ideas locked in the back of his mind.

Kennedy turned a cold shoulder and changed the subject. "I heard that the French don't care much about the loss of Martinico. They say the Spanish have captured Gibraltar and the French have retaken Belleisle. Compared to these successes in Europe, the French say, the loss of overseas colonies is unimportant. They claim we will gladly exchange all our American gains when peace comes."

Glad to discuss something less controversial than his half-formed philosophy, MacKim nodded. "That's probably true, but only if the Spaniards are willing to relinquish Gibraltar to us."

"Which I doubt," Kennedy said. "My informant also said the allies, France and Spain, have a combined fleet of fifty sail of the line due to arrive in May at Cape Francois, at Saint Dominique."

"Is that official, sir?" MacKim asked. "Has Spain declared war on us?"

Kennedy shook his head. "I haven't heard anything officially yet, sergeant. A ship's master in the harbour told me what he picked up on the quayside in Barbados."

"It might be nonsense then, sir," MacKim said.

"Are there any French left in Martinico, sir?" Parnell asked.

"La Touché is still at large with a few hundred Grenadiers," Kennedy said, "although I doubt he'll be out for long. Admiral Hervey seized La Trinity a few days back, and now we have St Peters; where can La Touché stand?" He glanced at his Rangers. "We're better off here than the Frenchies in Fort Royal. Some of the boys went wild with rum in the town."

MacKim imagined the scenes of inebriated British soldiers rioting in the town. He hoped the planters would experience some of the fear they'd installed in the slaves.

"The Jesuits have banned British soldiers from entering the local churches," Kennedy continued, "so General Monckton ordered the troops to use them as barracks." [1]"Cromwell did something similar," Oxford said, and looked up as Ensign Mowat rode up. "Here's trouble, sir."

"Good day to you, ensign," Kennedy said. "Have you brought us orders?"

"Yes, sir. I hope it's not bad news, sir," Mowat said. "General Monckton sends his regards, sir, and wishes to inform you that Commodore Swanton has requested a force of Rangers for his squadron, sir, as so many of his Marines are ashore on Martinico. The Commodore has specifically asked for Kennedy's Rangers, as he knows them of old." The ensign spoke words he had evidently rehearsed.

"We're going to sea?" Kennedy asked.

"Yes, sir," the ensign said. "Sorry, sir."

MacKim saw the dismay on his men's faces.

"We're not bloody Marines!" Parnell spoke for them all.

*   *   *

HMS SLOOP DOLPHIN IS NOT THE LARGEST SHIP IN THE ROYAL NAVY, MacKim thought as the Rangers filed on board, *but she might be the smallest.* With half a dozen four-pounders as her main broadside, a single six-pounder stern-chaser, a long nine forward, and a couple of swivels, she carried less armament than many privateers. Despite her size, her crew seemed hardly adequate to handle her, and MacKim was sure he even saw a woman on board, stitching a canvas jacket.

Maxwell commanded *Dolphin*. Although he held the rank of Master and Commander, everybody on *Dolphin* addressed him as captain. He eyed the eighteen Rangers with resignation. "We don't normally have passengers, and our accommodation is limited, but welcome aboard. Your men can act as marines until we pass you onto whichever vessel Commodore Swanton chooses."

"Where is the commodore now, captain?" Kennedy asked.

"He is blockading Grenada." Maxwell was in his early thirties, with a prominent chin and deep eyes.

"Begging your pardon, sir." A seaman approached Maxwell, knuckling his forehead. "But there's a signal from the admiral, sir."

"What does it say?" Maxwell asked.

"We've new orders, sir, to join Captain Hervey's squadron off Saint Lucie."

Maxwell sighed. "Thank you. Tell Mr Crabb to acknowledge." He faced Kennedy. "It seems that Commodore Swanton will have to wait for his Rangers. Mr Norman, my master's mate, will help you find accommodation on board." Maxwell stalked away on the tiny deck, roaring orders that saw sails hoisted.

Dolphin eased out of Fort Royal's harbour, past the supine Pigeon Island, and out to meet the fresh Caribbean breeze.

"This way, Rangers." Norman was tall, thin, and cheerful. "Only the best accommodation for our guests."

The best accommodation meant sharing space with kegs, barrels, and rats far below decks, where the air was stifling and the darkness so thick, even a lantern struggled to bring any light. "We'll keep the hatch open for you," Norman promised. "Unless the sea cuts up rough, of course."

"Thank you, Norman," Kennedy said cheerfully. "We're Rangers. We're used to us."

"Rangers!" Butler chanted. "First and always!"

Nobody joined in, but MacKim heard the woman give a high-pitched laugh.

The journey was uneventful, with Kennedy keeping the Rangers on their toes with parades and live firing exercises while the seamen overhauled the cables and masts. Maxwell had two men constantly dangling over the side, scraping the lower hull to remove marine growth.

"It's better than flogging defaulters," Maxwell explained. "They hate it, yet it helps the ship, for these weeds grow at an alarming speed out here and slow our passage amazingly."

Captain Augustus John Hervey had a powerful squadron to watch Saint Lucie as the Royal Navy aimed to reduce the French possessions in the Americas one by one. As well as his flagship, the 74-gun *Dragon*, Hervey had the smaller vessels *Norwich, Penzance, Dover*, and the bomb ketch *Basilisk*, with her eight guns.

"Welcome, *Dolphin*." Hervey signalled as soon as the sloop joined his command. "Sail close to Saint Lucie and investigate the defences."

"That's why he wanted *Dolphin*," Maxwell said. "We're lighter draught than any of them except *Basilisk*, and faster than the bomb if there's trouble."

With Hervey's squadron watching, Maxwell eased closer to the island. "Put a man with a lead in the bow. Give regular soundings! Stand by the starboard battery!" After working with the 24 and 32-pounders of the siege train, MacKim nearly smiled at *Dolphin*'s diminutive four-pounders, although he knew that even such small weapons fired a lethal ball.

MacKim felt it unreal to be on board such a small craft on a beautiful day, warm but not hot, with a cooling breeze, approaching a fertile island, while everybody was expecting hot shot and bloodshed. *War is a terrible thing*, he mused, *to spoil such an idyllic scene*.

The first puffs from the island seemed like clouds rather than gunsmoke, and the cannon reports sounded muted. The crew watched the smoke drift skyward, and then the water a hundred yards away erupted as the solid shot landed.

"Steer for the splashes," Maxwell ordered from the minuscule quarterdeck, sounding as calm as if he were boating off some placid British coast.

The French cannon fired again, with the shots landing a few yards from *Dolphin*'s previous position.

"Two points to larboard, helmsman," Kennedy ordered quietly.

The next French salvo straddled *Dolphin*, with water fountains rising on either side of the sloop and descending to soak the crew. Standing amidships to back up *Dolphin*'s paltry six Marines, the Rangers watched Captain Maxwell try to outguess the French gunners as he brought *Dolphin* closer to the island.

"Six fathoms, sir, sandy bottom!" The leadsman continued to heave the lead and chant the depth, despite the cannonballs that landed close enough to soak him.

"Six guns, I'd say," Kennedy counted the splashes. "What do you think, sergeant?"

"Six, sir." MacKim had concentrated on the muzzle flares. "One fort above and to the right of the harbour."

"24-pounders, I'd wager," Kennedy said, and grunted as the French fired again. "With a hidden battery of 12-pounders in reserve."

"I'd agree, sir," MacKim said.

"This is getting rather hot," Maxwell said as a cannonball ripped a hole in *Dolphin*'s mainsail and another snapped a cable aloft. "Get that line replaced!"

Midshipman Crabb led a team of men up the ratlines as *Dolphin* eased ever closer to the island.

"Four fathoms, sir, sand and pebbles!"

The French fired again, with one shot crashing into *Dolphin*'s hull between the waterline and the main deck.

"Signal from the flagship, sir!" Norman shouted. "Our number, sir, and..."

"And what?" Maxwell asked.

"I'm not sure, sir. I can't make it out. The wind's making the flags fly away from us."

"Well, try," Maxwell said. "Mr Norman, check for any damage that French shot made and repair it. Gunners! Fire at that fort as soon as your guns bear."

"We're well out of range, sir!" a gun captain replied.

"I'm aware of that, Jenks, but the smoke might mask us a little and might even unsettle the French!"

"Aye, aye, sir!" Jenks said, and a moment later, the first of *Dolphin*'s broadside fired, with the others following as the sloop eased towards the fort. None of the shots came close, but Maxwell's idea may have worked, as the next French salvo was far over and wasted in open water.

"That'll do," Maxwell said. "Three points to starboard, helmsman. All sail, lads, and let's get out of here before the French find the range again."

"The flagship's signalling, sir. I can read it now. It says to discontinue action and captain to report to the flagship."

"Signal affirmative," Maxwell said. "Get my gig ready!" The commander looked more concerned at being summoned to see the admiral than he had when under fire. Looking at Maxwell's shabby working uniform and knowing how splendid an admiral could be, MacKim could only sympathise.

"He'll want me to report," Maxwell said. "Damn it to hell, what do I know about forts on a blasted island?"

Kennedy knew that the lieutenant was firmly in command of his ship, but decided to give some advice. "I don't mean to intrude, captain, but Sergeant MacKim and I were counting the guns. We reckoned the fort had six 24-pounders and another six 12-pounders. The latter battery is on a higher level."

Maxwell looked more grateful than MacKim expected from a naval officer. "Thank you, Captain Kennedy. I will convey your observations to Captain Hervey. No, dammit! I want both of you in my gig. You can stand by with your military knowledge if he requires more."

"Yes, sir," Kennedy said.

Hervey was a tall, handsome man. He noticed the Rangers in Maxwell's gig and called both onto the quarterdeck of *Dragon*.

"I hear you Rangers are experts in French forts," Hervey said.

"We're no experts, sir," Kennedy said, "but we do have some experience."

"We'll have to silence that fort before we take the island," Hervey said. "Captain Maxwell has given me notice of the depth of water, so you inform me of the defences." He listened as Kennedy gave his opinion.

"Good," Hervey said. "Now, I'll go and see for myself. Maxwell, return to *Dolphin* and await my instructions. You Rangers can accompany Maxwell. I don't suppose either of you speaks French, do you?"

"I have a little, sir, and Sergeant MacKim is fluent," Kennedy reported.

"Is he, indeed?" Hervey raised a neatly manicured eyebrow. "You can come with me, Sergeant MacKim." He gave a boyish grin. "Wait here."

"Come along, Captain Kennedy," Maxwell and Kennedy returned to the gig, leaving MacKim on *Dragon*'s quarterdeck as Hervey disappeared below. Within a few moments, he came back, dressed as a midshipman, with a long dirk at his hip.

"If the French see Captain Hervey, they will conceal their defences," Hervey said, grinning. "But I doubt they will care what a mere middy sees? You and I will be the interpreters, sergeant."

"Yes, sir." MacKim was not sure if the captain's play-acting was a legitimate ruse of war.

"We'll see if Monsieur de Longueville wishes to surrender," Hervey said. "One of my officers will ask the questions, you and

I will interpret, and we'll have a closer look at the defences." He winked at MacKim. "On we go, sergeant!"

Hervey's launch was larger than Maxwell's gig, with all the boat's crew dressed the same, in striped shirts, white canvas trousers, and straw hats. They rowed ashore under a flag of truce while a French delegation waited to meet them at the pretty little settlement of Castries, below the fortress. Although MacKim could see the gun-muzzles waiting behind the battlements and smell the lingering powder smoke, the scene seemed too idyllic to belong to an ugly war.

Dragon's naval officer, whose name MacKim did not catch, bowed politely to de Longueville as the body of French officers and officials stood slightly apart.

"Monsieur," the officer said. "As you see, His Britannic Majesty has sent a force to capture your island."

MacKim stepped forward to translate, wishing he had better clothes than his battered Rangers uniform while surrounded by the gorgeously uniformed French. De Longueville listened.

"I see your force," de Longueville agreed. "We can match you cannon for cannon with our defences."

"My superior, Captain Hervey of HMS *Dragon*—a man who has already tasted victory at Belle Isle and Martinico—asks that you honourably surrender rather than waste lives in pointless resistance."

De Longueville smiled. "I would ask that you sail away to your northern island rather than throw away your men's lives in attacking my fortress and defences. No, sir, I will not surrender."

MacKim translated faithfully, aware that Hervey was carefully noting the harbour and the defences. War was as much about intelligence-gathering as actual fighting, he realised. Courage and daring played their parts, but knowledge of the enemy's dispositions gave an edge to any combatant.[2] "Thank you, sergeant," Hervey said when they returned to *Dragon*. "Now, please remain aboard while we capture this island." He grinned again, an action so unlike MacKim's preconceptions of naval officers that he nearly stared in surprise.

On the 25th of February, Hervey gave his commands, and his squadron prepared to attack Saint Lucie.

"We've seen their fort," Hervey explained to his officers, "and our resident fort expert, Sergeant MacKim of the Rangers, has confirmed my assessment of the artillery. Lieutenant Maxwell in *Dolphin* checked the depth of water, and we have sufficient under the keel even of *Dragon* to go in and knock the fort to pieces."

The officers nodded, although they were aware that a stone-built fort had advantages over a wooden ship. Firstly, the fort was static and provided a more secure gun battery. Secondly, the fort's cannon could fire red-hot shot, a formidable weapon against a highly combustible ship packed with canvas and gunpowder.

"Send a signal to the squadron to follow me in line astern," Hervey ordered, obviously enjoying himself immensely.

MacKim had been part of a few naval expeditions, but this was the first time he stood on the quarterdeck and saw how efficient a line-of-battle ship could be. No sooner did HMS *Dragon* approach the harbour than a small vessel appeared, with the French flag and a flag of truce flying from its single mast.

Hervey laughed outright. "They seek terms," he said. "And that, gentlemen, is how we capture a French island."

Hervey was correct. Saint Lucie surrendered without another shot fired or a single casualty on either side.

"What's that?" A sharp-eyed midshipman pointed to larboard. "A ship, sir, escaping from the harbour."

"The devil, you say?" Hervey lifted his telescope. "She's painted green and brown, even to her canvas. That will be as a disguise against the land, no less."

"Yes, sir," the midshipman said.

Hervey inclined his head slightly. "You did well to spot her, young snotty! I wonder what devious man commands that vessel."

MacKim stepped forward and, without thought, removed a telescope from its bracket on the mizzenmast. He focussed on the escaping vessel. "She's *Douce Vengeance,* sir," he said. "Captain René Roberval, a freebooter and near as damn a pirate as these seas can boast."

"Is she, by damn." Hervey eyed MacKim thoughtfully. "And how the deuce do you know that, sergeant?"

"She captured our ship, *Martha* of Boston, outward bound from New York to Barbados, sir," MacKim said. "Her master, Roberval, murdered Captain Stringer and her crew."

Hervey nodded, with no trace of humour on his face. "I remember hearing of that incident." He focussed his telescope again. "A tricky devil, Roberval. And dangerous." He watched her for a moment. "I can't let her get away."

"No, sir."

Hervey raised his voice. "Signal *Dolphin,*" he said. "Order her to follow that privateer, and capture or sink her."

"Aye, aye, sir," the signal midshipman said.

"Sir," MacKim asked urgently. "May I return to *Dolphin?*"

"What?" Hervey glanced at him. "Oh, yes. Lieutenant Malvern, take Sergeant MacKim back to *Dolphin.*" The grin was back. "Otherwise, I'd recruit you into my crew, sergeant. You're a handy man to have around."

***

DOLPHIN'S DECK WAS TINY COMPARED TO THE SPACE ON *Dragon,* but the faces were familiar and the discipline less strict.

"So, we've to catch and destroy *Douce Vengeance,* have we?" Maxwell said. "What's her armament, captain?"

"I'd say a dozen guns, Captain Maxwell," Kennedy replied. "Six-pounders mainly, with a nine-pounder in her bows and another in her stern."

"She outguns us then," Maxwell said. "And her crew?"

"Large," Kennedy said. "She was crammed with men."

"Boarding will be interesting, in that case," Maxwell said. "Tell me about her master."

"Captain René Roberval," Kennedy said, and told Maxwell about the capture of *Martha* and Roberval's treatment of her crew.

Maxwell grunted. "An old-fashioned Caribbean sea-rover," he said. "Not the sort of fellow one wishes to leave attacking British shipping." He watched *Douce Vengeance*'s sails for a moment. "He'll be moving from island to island, searching for a safe anchorage, now that we've taken Martinico and Saint Lucie. Grenada will be his best bet, I wager."

"What do you intend to do, captain?" MacKim asked.

"I intend to follow my orders, sergeant," Maxwell said. "Hound that privateer across the Caribbean until we can take or destroy her." He shouted orders that had *Dolphin* increase sail and follow in the wake of *Douce Vengeance*. "Mr Norman, up to the masthead with you and watch that pirate's movements! Bosun's mate! Pipe the men to dinner! It might be a long chase."

MacKim watched the disciplined bustle on *Dolphin*. Despite the disparity of force, not a single man complained about their duty. The Royal Navy was used to fighting against odds, and usually won.

"She outguns and outmans us," Maxwell said comfortably, eating the same rations as the men. "That means we'll have to use cunning and deception."

"Roberval is a tricky man," MacKim said.

Maxwell smiled. "Let's see if the Royal Navy can teach him some new tricks."

Dolphin remained on *Douce Vengeance*'s track for the remainder of that day, never closing and never allowing the privateer out of sight. When Roberval moved north, *Dolphin* was on her track. When Roberval furled *Douce Vengeance*'s sails to make herself a less visible target, Maxwell eased closer so his lookouts could keep her under observation.

"She's heading out to sea," Maxwell said. "Once night falls, she'll douse all lights and double back to the islands. I'd wager a queer penny to a golden guinea that she'll steer for Grenada."

"Is that a French island?" MacKim asked.

"Last I heard it was," Maxwell said. "But Robert Swanton was headed there with a blockading squadron. Our man Roberval might get a fright if he meets Swanton."

MacKim nodded. "We know Commodore Swanton," he said. "He's a good man."

"Let's see what we can do with this French pirate," Maxwell said. "All sail, boys! I want to close with *Douce Vengeance*!"

Dolphin's crew responded eagerly, rushing aloft and handling the canvas as if it was nothing. Within minutes, *Dolphin* was surged in the wake of *Douce Vengeance*, with the lookout giving regular reports of their progress.

"We're closing, sir! All her topsails are visible now!"

"I can see her main course, Captain!"

"She's altering course, heading northeast!"

Maxwell matched each alteration of *Douce Vengeance*, and as the day eased to a close, he came within long gunshot.

"Man the bow chaser," Maxwell ordered.

MacKim sensed the excitement on board as the gun crew ran forward. *Dolphin* had a long nine-pounder in the bow, a weapon designed exclusively to fire at a fleeing vessel.

As the gun crew clustered around the ugly black cannon, one man thrust a bag of powder into the muzzle and rammed it to the base before adding a wad to keep the powder in place. As *Dolphin* rose to a wayward wave, a man rolled the nine-pound iron ball down the barrel, with another adding a second wad to hold the ball steady. Accuracy depended on the gunner's skill in estimating the wind and waves that shifted two moving ships on a heaving sea.

With the cannon loaded, a gunner primed the touch hole with gunpowder, and the gun crew shoved the weapon forward until the barrel pointed towards the privateer, now clearly seen rising and falling to the dance of the sea.

"Fire," Maxwell said softly.

The gun captain waited until *Dolphin* rose to near the apex of a wave, then applied his slow match to the touch-hole. The powder flashed, and a second later, the gun roared and emitted a cloud of white smoke. The ball flew from the muzzle towards the privateer.

MacKim fancied he saw the ball like a black streak in the sky, and then came a splash a cables' length to larboard of *Douce Vengeance*.

"Close!" Maxwell said. "Keep firing, boys!"

MacKim knew how hard it was to be accurate on land when the shot did not fit snugly into the cannon's barrel. It would be much harder at sea when both vessels were moving to the swell of the waves.

As daylight faded, Maxwell kept *Dolphin* on the track of *Douce Vengeance,* with the bow chaser firing at regular intervals and the familiar smell of powder smoke drifting across the deck.

"Hit her, sir!" the gun captain yelled as there was a momentary shudder from the privateer. "I swear I saw splinters rise from her counter!"

MacKim smiled at the fancy, yet hoped the gun captain was right. Roberval's cabin lay right aft, and he had a vision of a nine-pound cannonball crashing right into the cabin, destroying Roberval's floating home. "Keep up the good work!" he shouted.

Ten minutes later, *Douce Vengeance* replied, with two bright flashes from her stern, indicating two cannon. The shots fell well short, raising columns of water a hundred yards in front of *Dolphin* and to starboard.

Dolphin's gun crew jeered and whistled, then redoubled their efforts to fire before the swift tropical night ended the contest.

"Fire again," Maxwell ordered. "As if we think she will maintain the same course for a quarter of an hour, and then make sail for Grenada."

"She might not head there." Kennedy had been a silent watcher of the duel.

"She's little choice," Maxwell said. "She didn't have time to refit and bring in water at Saint Lucie before we captured the island, and her men will be weary after Martinico. We also hit her at least twice, and she'll wish to repair the damage."

"There are plenty unoccupied islands in the Caribbean." Kennedy played devil's advocate.

"Privateer seamen need rum, women, and debauchery," Maxwell said, and added, "I sailed in a Bristol privateer before I joined the Navy. I know what type of men they are. Douse all lights and set a course for Grenada."

"Aye, aye, sir!" Crabb said.

MacKim watched the privateer sail into the night and wondered if he were destined to chase and fight forever.

I still have not written Claudette!

15

The frigate approached from the south, with the Union flag claiming British identity. Aware that unscrupulous seamen could raise any flag that suited them, Maxwell kept *Dolphin*'s distance and ordered the hands to the guns.

"Does anybody recognise that vessel?" Maxwell asked.

"Yes, sir," Lieutenant Holmes said, focussing his telescope. "She's *Narcissus,* sir. One of ours, sir."

"Very well," Maxwell said. "Order the men at the guns to stand down."

"She's summoning you on board, sir."

MacKim watched as Maxwell's gig crossed to the frigate, and Maxwell climbed onto her deck. The crew of *Dolphin* waited in the heat, with the green island of Grenada to larboard and the sails of other ships gradually drawing closer.

After fifteen minutes, the gig returned, with Maxwell looking strained. "Captain Swanton is in charge here," Maxwell said. "They saw *Douce Vengeance* last night, but she evaded them and headed north."

Kennedy groaned. "That gives her the entire Caribbean to escape in," he said. "Have the French any other islands here?"

"The Spanish have a few," Maxwell said quietly. "We're now officially at war with Spain."

The crew heard the news with mixed emotions. Although *Dolphin* was a happy ship, most of the hands still wished to return home. They had hoped the war would end soon, but the entry of Spain could prolong hostilities for years.

"Having a new ally might even encourage the French to retake Martinico," Kennedy said.

As a flurry of flags rose on the frigate, Maxwell sent Crabb to read what was said.

"It's a summons for all captains to report to the flagship, sir," the midshipman reported.

"What the devil is it now?" Maxwell asked. "And where's the flagship?"

"Over there, sir." The midshipman pointed to *Vanguard* as she eased towards them.

"Get my gig ready," Maxwell said, and vanished into his cabin. He re-emerged five minutes later, dressed in his best and, MacKim suspected, his only other uniform, with pinchbeck buttons and shoe buckles, and a cheap sword at his waist.

"Damned flag officers." Maxwell tried to adjust the uniform to the best advantage. "I wish they'd leave me alone." He turned to Holmes. "Try to get fresh water when I'm gone, Holmes, and as many vegetables as you can scrounge."

"Aye, aye, sir." Holmes hurried away, calling for the longboat's crew.

The Rangers waited on *Dolphin* as Maxwell's gig rowed away. MacKim looked to the north, aware that every minute gave Roberval more time to escape, and slipped below.

"Where are you going, sergeant?" Kennedy asked.

"I'm going to write a letter, sir."

Kennedy smiled. "Give Claudette my regards, MacKim."

Finding space on a crowded ship was not easy, but MacKim squeezed into the galley stores, placed a sheet of paper on top of a barrel, dipped his quill into the ink, and pondered.

What can I say? What do I want to say?

"Claudette," he wrote, then added a "Dear" in front, swore, nibbled the vane of the quill, cursed again, and wrote on.

"Dear Claudette,

I should have written earlier. We are off Grenada, on a sloop called Dolphin. We took part in the taking of Martinico, and I don't know where we are going next. I hope you and Hugo are both well.

When we come back to the Colonies, or when the war ends, I will come to Quebec.

I think of you a lot.

Hugh."

MacKim knew it was a poor letter. He read it, waved it in the air to dry the ink, folded it over, and sealed it with a blob of wax from the cook.

"Good luck, Ranger," the cook said. "I hope she's worth it."

"She is," MacKim said, and dashed up to the deck. He was fortunate that Lieutenant Holmes was arguing with a boat from the flagship over fresh provisions while some of the crew were purchasing parrots and cocoanuts.

"Can you take this to the flagship?" MacKim asked the boatman, suddenly desperate to contact Claudette. "Give it to the postmaster."

"One shilling!" the boatman demanded.

"A shilling?" MacKim repeated in dismay, for he carried no money.

"A shilling? You rogue!" Lieutenant Holmes shouted. "Sixpence is twice the price! Be off with you, or I'll have you flogged!"

"Sixpence," the boatman amended, and stuffed the letter in the waist of his ragged trousers.

"Here." Kennedy tossed over the silver coin. "And think yourself lucky, you thieving scoundrel!"

MacKim watched as the loading was complete, and the

boatman rowed away. He wondered when the letter would arrive and what Claudette would think of it.

"It's done now, MacKim," Kennedy said. "Don't think about it again. Let events take their course."

"Yes, sir," MacKim said.

I should have been more affectionate.

※

THE SUN CREPT HIGHER, BAKING THE CREW OF *DOLPHIN* AND bubbling the pitch caulking between the deck planks. When Maxwell eventually returned, he looked serious.

"Gather the hands," he said, and stood on the quarterdeck, which gave him a slight height advantage when he spoke.

"You'll have heard by now that we're at war with Spain," he said, and waited for the murmurs to rise and fade away. "Two days ago, Commodore Swanton captured Grenada from the French. As I heard it, the governor refused to surrender, but the inhabitants capitulated rather than undergoing the rigours of a siege and assault."

The crew murmured again, commenting on the news.

"As Grenada is now ours, we also control the Grenadines, the chain of small islands around us." Maxwell indicated the surrounding seas. "That means the French ships, and particularly their privateers, have fewer bases from which to attack our shipping."

The hands listened, grateful to have a commander who explained the ongoing situation to them. "Less cheerfully, and as we have long suspected, a French fleet has escaped from Brest and is loose in the Caribbean. Commodore Swanton will leave two ships of the line and a garrison in Grenada, and we will all return to Martinico and Admiral Rodney. Our search for *Douce Vengeance* will halt for now. A French fleet is a greater menace than a single privateer."

"So the pirate escapes again," Kennedy said as they stood at the rail watching Swanton's fleet bowl northward to Martinico. "Roberval has a charmed life."

"His options are shrinking, though," MacKim pointed out. "I can't think of any French bases left in the Caribbean. He'll have to find a Spanish port."

"The French still hold half of Hispaniola," Kennedy said. "But a penny to a gold sovereign that Roberval will sail to Havana."

Admiral Rodney was on high alert, posting a necklace of frigates to windward of the Caribbean islands, watching for the expected French fleet, and hopeful of snapping up any Spanish prizes that came their way. In the meantime, Courbon-Blenac, in command of the French squadron, was too wary to fall into the British trap. Unsure of the current situation in Martinico, he sailed to the windward coast of the island, anchored offshore near La Trinité, and sent an officer in a small boat to gather intelligence.

"How many French ships?" Kennedy asked when Maxwell gave the information.

"Thirteen vessels, including eight ships of the line," Maxwell said. "One of our frigates saw them heading south from La Trinité and reported to Admiral Rodney, but then the wind dropped and our ships were becalmed. That left Douglas with his three line-of-battle ships isolated at the south of the island. Douglas prepared to fight, of course, hoping to inflict sufficient damage on the French to slow them until Rodney arrived."

"I've heard that Douglas is a fighting seaman," Kennedy said.

Maxwell smiled. "If he weren't, he wouldn't last in the Navy. When a northerly wind returned, Rodney sailed with six battleships. Swanton and Hervey also headed south from different directions. We hoped their pincer movement would trap Courbon-Blenac, but he slipped away. Rodney believes that the French pretended to head south, doubled back, and steered north for Cap Francois in Saint Dominique, French Hispaniola."

"We'll be taking Hispaniola next, then," MacKim said.
"France's last Caribbean stronghold."

"Maybe; the island of Hispaniola is split between France and Spain," Maxwell reminded. "I'll wager Courbon-Blenac has a pre-arranged rendezvous with a Spanish fleet there to descend on some British island."

"Jamaica?" Kennedy asked.

"That's what I'd do if I were him. I'd leave Rodney chasing his tail in the Windward Islands and scoop up Jamaica."

"How many ships do the Spanish have?"

Maxwell pulled a face. "I heard they had fourteen line of battleships in theHavana, and a few others scattered across the Caribbean and the Spanish Main. If they combine with the French, Rodney will have a tough time defeating them."

MacKim pictured a French-Spanish victory in the Caribbean, with sunk British ships and the French landing troops on the recently captured islands. He thought of Private Chisholm's analogy of war as chess, with armies and fleets like the pieces and the entire globe as the board.

"What are we doing now, sir?" MacKim asked.

"*Dolphin* is returning to St Peter's in Martinico," Maxwell answered for Kennedy. "We're taking on food and water, and we'll get further orders there."

"Are my Rangers remaining on board, captain?" Kennedy asked.

"I've had no orders to the contrary, captain," Maxwell replied. "Maybe you'll all be Marine Rangers before this campaign is over."

By that time, MacKim was used to life afloat. He found the variety interesting, with the constantly changing scenery and fresh breezes as *Dolphin* cruised the islands. All the same, he missed the exercise of marching with his Rangers. Most of the time on *Dolphin*, he was merely a passenger, a witness to events.

"Orders, gentlemen!" Maxwell came back on board from St Pierre.

"Where are we headed now, sir?"

"Jamaica, once we have watered." Maxwell grinned. "We'll sail via St Christopher's."

❧

MACKIM WATCHED THE SURF BREAK ON THE PALISADOES, the long sand spit that protected Kingston's harbour.

"I thought all black people in the West Indies were slaves." MacKim sipped at the neck of the rum bottle, wiped his lips, and passed the bottle back.

"Not all. We have free black men here as well, like me." Mike, the Jamaican sailor, lifted his face to the sun. "You haven't been in the Caribbean long, have you?"

"Less than a year," MacKim admitted. "I had never heard of Jamaica until a few months ago."

Mike shook his head. "How greedy your king is to gulp at much of the world." He sipped at his rum. "Yet, he doesn't teach his subjects about their brother countries." He shook his head again.

MacKim could not argue. He accepted the bottle again. "Educate me, Mike. Tell me about your island."

Mike gave a slow smile, happy to accept the role of teacher. "Jamaica was one of the earliest British colonies. The Englishmen, Admiral William Penn and General Robert Venables, captured the island from the Spanish in 1655, fifty-two years before Great Britain even existed."

Mike was justifiably proud of his knowledge as he sat at the water's edge.

MacKim listened. Exposed to education at an early age, he eagerly devoured all knowledge. He thought of Benjamin and the other slaves toiling on Martinico. "Why are so many Jamaican's slaves?".

"Before the Spanish left, they freed their slaves," Mike said. "As the Spanish sailed to Cuba, the freed slaves headed inland. They had no desire to swap one slave master for another."

MacKim nodded, sipped at his rum, and looked around him. Despite the prevalence of disease in all these islands, he could not deny that Jamaica was beautiful.

"These freed slaves formed settlements in the interior of Jamaica," the old man continued, "and people called them Maroons."

"I've heard a lot about Jamaican buccaneers, but only a little about the Maroons."

The old man chuckled. "The buccaneers were down at Port Royal until the earthquake struck. You have to watch the Caribbean. Between earthquakes and hurricanes, nature is important."

"Are you a Maroon?" MacKim asked. "You're black and free."

"I'm a freedman," the man said. "I was born a slave, but I helped save my master's child in a fire, and he freed me by an act of the Jamaican Assembly. The Maroons are born free. Many slaves escape here and join the Maroons in the mountains, while others try to rebel."

"I'd rebel, too," MacKim said.

The old man's eyes sparkled. "You could have joined Tacky, then. He led a rebellion in 1760. Or maybe you could desert from military slavery."

MacKim nodded. "Maybe. Tell me about the Maroons."

Mike passed the rum again. "The Maroons are good fighters. They fought the British to a standstill in the 1730s, and in 1740, gained their land and rights as free men, as long as they help recapture escaped slaves. It was a Maroon, Lieutenant Davy, who killed Tacky and ended the slave rebellion. Even now, there is another rebellion, with Apongo fighting for the slaves and Cudjoe's Maroons fighting alongside the British." He smiled again. "There is never peace beyond the Line!"

"I thought all the black people would stick together," MacKim said.

The man laughed. "Why? Do all the white people stick together? We are as individual as you are, and as disunited. Even now, there are Maroons hunting down runaway slaves and runaways creating other free communities."

"Sergeant!" Parnell shouted. "You're needed on board!"

Mike smiled as MacKim stood up. "I am freer than you, Sergeant MacKim. You're a slave to your uniform and a servant of the king." He gestured to the sea. "That is my only master."

Dolphin did not remain long in Jamaica. With the ever-present threat of a French fleet worrying the authorities, the admiral sent her on various short cruises to search for alleged sightings of the enemy.

All the time, the Rangers remained on board.

"I think everybody's forgotten about us," Danskin said, leaning against the mainmast. "Maybe we'll see out the remainder of the war on this ship."

"I hope so." Oxford lay at his side.

"Are you two comfortable?" MacKim asked kindly.

"Yes, sergeant," Danskin said.

MacKim smiled. "Good! Danskin, take your boots off and help Oxford clean out the heads. It's time you made yourself useful."

"Why us, sergeant?" Oxford asked.

"Because neither of you is any good for anything else." MacKim raised his voice to a bellow. "Move!"

Suzanne Williams, the cooper's wife and the only woman on board, shook her head. "Poor lads! They're only young, sergeant."

"They'll learn," MacKim said. "And the best way to learn is to work."

Suzanne smiled again. "You're a hard man, Sergeant MacKim."

"And you're a brave woman, Mrs Williams, alone amongst so many men."

Suzanne laughed. "It's because there are so many that I am safe, sergeant. They all treat me like a princess."

A week later, a cutter approached *Dolphin* with a very young lieutenant in command. Puffed up with self-importance, he came alongside and ran to the quarterdeck.

"I have sealed orders for Captain Maxwell!" the lieutenant said.

"That's me." Maxwell broke the seal, scanned the contents, and nodded. "No reply," he said. "You may go." He raised his voice. "Captain Kennedy, could you join me in my cabin, if you please."

MacKim raised his eyebrows as Suzanne listened from the shelter of the mainmast. "That looks interesting," he said. "Something's happening."

"We're off to Cuba," Suzanne said. "This is the best spot on the boat. I can hear everything from here."

Kennedy emerged five minutes later.

"Now where are we headed?" Parnell lay on the main deck, chewing tobacco and watching the sailors scamper around.

"The Havana," Kennedy said. "You've all had a restful few weeks cruising around the Caribbean, sunning yourselves. Now it's time to get back to some real soldiering."

MacKim looked up. "Is the Havana not the main port in Spanish Cuba, sir?"

"It is," Kennedy said. "It's on the northwest coast and is one of the most important ports in the Spanish Empire. Every year, the *Flota*, the convoy of gold and silver from the Americas to Spain, assembles at Havana."

"Is it rich then, sir?" Dickert asked.

"Very rich."

MacRae shook his head. "Aye, trust the Spanish. They got the first choice at the Americas and grabbed the silver and gold. We came last, and got snow and trees."

Kennedy smiled. "Well, MacRae, we can try and take Havana from Spain, and maybe get a share of the gold."

"The officers might get a share," Parnell said. "A thousand pounds for the admiral, sixpence for Private Parnell."

Kennedy said nothing to that, but MacKim knew that Parnell was correct. The men in charge could make a fortune from a successful campaign, while the soldiers who faced the French bayonets would barely earn enough for a night's debauchery.

"We've new commanders, straight out from Great Britain," Kennedy said. "Lieutenant General the Earl of Albemarle will be in overall command."

"What's wrong with General Monckton?" Parnell asked. "He took Martinico handily enough."

"Admiral Sir George Pocock is taking command of the fleet," Kennedy continued, "with Commodore Keppel as second in command."

"I rather liked Rodney," Parnell complained.

"Keep quiet, Parnell!" MacKim used his rank to return some discipline in the ranks.

"Thank you, sergeant," Kennedy said. "Lieutenant General Elliot is second in command, with Colonel McKellar as chief engineer. Some of us may remember McKellar from Quebec, and before that, Louisburg."

"McKellar is a good man," MacKim said.

"Finally, Lieutenant Colonel Leith commands the artillery."

The Rangers were silent, almost sullen. MacKim knew many of them had hoped to return home after the capture of Martinico. This war seemed interminable, with campaign following campaign and no end in sight.

Kennedy glanced over the side, where other British ships were in view. It said much about the power of the Royal Navy that since the capture of Martinico, British and Colonial ships could sail with impunity from Newfoundland to Barbados, despite the presence of a combined French and Spanish fleet.

"Havana is larger than Boston or New York," Kennedy continued. "It has Spanish America's largest shipbuilding yard, holds a powerful force of warships, and is well-defended."

The Rangers were beginning to shift uncomfortably now, and

MacKim realised their attention was waning. They were men of action rather than men who wished to listen to theories. He frowned at Kennedy, signalling that he should close the lecture.

"One last thing, Rangers," Kennedy said. "We have been involved in previous amphibious operations, such as Louisburg, Quebec, Montreal, and Martinico."

The men nodded; they did not need Kennedy to remind them of their past.

"Every time, we've only been passengers until we landed on the ground. This time, we may be a little more active. We may help in preparing the way for the rest of the fleet."

Those words caught the Rangers' attention; they began to listen again.

"We will be training for action again, Rangers, so expect early mornings and hard work. Dismiss."

The Rangers broke up, with the experienced men thoughtful and the younger boasting of the great deeds they would do.

"What's happening, sir?" MacKim asked.

"Come with me, and I'll show you."

Kennedy brought MacKim into the tiny cubbyhole he called a cabin. Canvas screens formed the bulkheads, and there was room only for a cot and a chest, but the privacy was welcome. Kennedy pulled a nautical chart from his pack and unfolded it on the cot.

"This is Cuba, with some of the neighbouring islands," Kennedy said. "Our fleets are rendezvousing here," he pointed to Cape St Nicholas, at the extreme west of Hispaniola, the large island immediately to the east of Cuba.

"I see." MacKim studied the map.

"The most normal and safest approach to the Havana is by the south coast of Cuba, north of Jamaica." Kennedy traced the route with his finger. "The channel is broad and deep and well-known. Ships sail around the south of the island and come to Havana from the west, beating against the prevailing winds."

MacKim guessed what was coming next.

"We are not using that route," Kennedy said. "We're using the Old Bahamas Channel, along the north coast. Few ships use that route, and I don't believe that any fleet has approached Havana from the north since the days of Frankie Drake."

MacKim studied the map. "It's a very narrow passage full of shoals."

"That's correct," Kennedy said. "The Spanish won't expect anybody to sail that way, but our Royal Navy is the best in the world. Nobody expected us to force the St Lawrence, and nobody will expect us to chance the Old Bahamas Channel." He looked up with a grin. "There are advantages as well. The prevailing winds are easterly, and as no other ships use that passage, nobody will warn the Spanish of our approach. We'll fall on the Havana before the Spanish even realise what's happening."

"I see." MacKim knew there was worse to come.

"The Admiralty has searched for a pilot, but only two men are known to have used that channel. One is over eighty years old and is nearly blind."

"A perfect pilot."

"The Admiralty decided not to use him," Kennedy said.

"And the other?"

"He is French," Kennedy said.

"We are taking a fleet and thousands of men along a dangerous channel with no pilot?" The audacity took MacKim aback. "Where do the Rangers come in?"

Kennedy's grin widened, so he looked like a schoolboy contemplating a piece of mischief rather than a war-hardened veteran of the North American frontier.

"Admiral Pocock has decided to send some smaller ships in front to mark the shoals. As *Dolphin* has experience of such work, we're leading them." Kennedy's grin could have split his face. "The Rangers are leading the Navy, sergeant, as we've so often led the Army!"

16

The weather was hot and clear as the fleet gathered at Point St Nicholas at the extreme west of Hispaniola. Some vessels sailed from Jamaica, others from the Windward Islands, North America, and Great Britain. As the fleet gathered, Captain Maxwell grew increasingly restless.

"We must be off," he said, looking at the clear sky. "We must start to mark the channel. The longer we linger here, the more time the Spanish have to organise their defences. We'll have to capture Havana and have the fleet safely in the harbour before the hurricane season begins."[1]

MacKim had heard that the hurricanes were savage in the Caribbean, although the weather had been kind so far.

"We're working with Captain Elphinstone in HMS *Richmond*," Kennedy said. "Do you expect any opposition?"

"It's not the Spanish that concerns me," Maxwell said. "It's the shoals and hidden reefs, the sudden currents off the points and the passage of time."

As the British fleet slowly gathered off Point St Nicholas, HMS *Richmond* signalled *Dolphin* to head west.

"About time," Maxwell gave a string of orders to take *Dolphin* to the west. "Put a man in the bows with a lead, and take over, Lieutenant Holmes. I'm going aloft."

Dolphin eased ahead of *Richmond*, with Maxwell changing the man in the bows every two hours. MacKim grew used to the monotonous sound of the leadsman as he called the depth.

"No bottom with this line. No bottom with this line. Ten fathoms, sandy bottom. Ten fathoms, sand and shells. Eight fathoms."

Whenever the leadsmen shouted that the ground beneath *Dolphin* was shoaling, Kennedy called for a slight alteration in their course and shortened sail to prevent the sloop from running onto a sandbank or other navigational hazard.

"*Richmond* is dropping back," Lieutenant Holmes reported.

"Good," Maxwell said. "I don't like anybody watching me work." He raised his voice. "Keep marking these soundings, Snotty!"

Midshipman Crabb looked up. "Aye, aye, sir!"

"Why call the poor lad Snotty?" MacKim asked.

"He's no pockets in his bum-freezer jacket," Suzanne explained. "So no handkerchief."

"I see," MacKim said. "You have strange practices in the Navy."

Surveying was tedious, although necessary, as *Dolphin* crept slowly along the north coast of Cuba. After the first day, *Richmond* was the only ship in sight. The frigate followed a few miles astern, checking the breadth of the channel that *Dolphin* pioneered.

"Signal from *Richmond*, sir!" the midshipman reported. "Go ahead. Report back tomorrow."

"Acknowledge!" Maxwell ordered, and rubbed his hands together. "Captain Elphinstone knows he's slowing us down. He's an Orkney Islander, of course, and understands nautical matters."

Freed from the restrictions of hourly signals to *Richmond*,

Dolphin made better time, finding and charting shoals and offshore rocks as she sailed westward toward Havana.

"Admiral Pocock is a daring man, taking the fleet along this passage," Maxwell said. "I'd be happier if we could physically mark these shoals rather than place them on a chart."[2]

"By the deep, ten!" the leadsman chanted.

The report of a cannon took them by surprise, although nobody saw the fall of the shot.

"Where the devil did that come from?" Maxwell asked.

"The headland there, captain." MacKim had been watching the land. A slow drift of smoke rose in the clear air.

"Nobody told us the Spaniards had a battery on this coast!" Maxwell sounded surprised. "That could impact on the fleet, so let's have a look. Leadsman, continue to take soundings. Take us closer, Mr Holmes!"

Dolphin slid towards the Cuban coast, with the leadsman's monotonous intonation informing them of the depth of water. The cannon fired again, raising a column of water three cables' lengths to starboard.

"Not bad shooting for the range. What calibre would you say, captain?" Maxwell asked.

"12-pounder, Captain Maxwell," Kennedy replied.

The gun fired again, with the smoke sliding westward with the wind.

"Let her drift with the wind, Mr Lieutenant," Maxwell said. "Try a shot with the long nine."

The gun crew hurried forward, squeezed beside the leadsman at his perch in the bows and readied the nine-pounder. The men looked happy to be doing something more interesting than surveying on this hot coast. A ship's master could see the survey results in the map he created, but to the crew, surveying work was only a monotonous crawl in dangerous waters.

The Spanish cannon fired once more, with Maxwell fixing his telescope on the smoke.

"Aim to leeward of the smoke and fire," Maxwell ordered, as

the Spanish shot slammed into the sea three cables' lengths to larboard.

Dolphin's nine-pounder fired a moment later, with the smoke remaining on deck as the gun-crew hurried to load again. The leadsman resumed his chanting as Midshipman Crabb noted the soundings in his log.

"That shut her up," Maxwell said with satisfaction. "Captain Kennedy, I think your Rangers could benefit from a run ashore."

"I was thinking the same thing myself, captain," Kennedy said. "They're getting stale as passengers on your yacht." He raised his voice. "Sergeant MacKim, prepare the men. We're going to look at that Spanish battery."

"Yes, sir," MacKim said. He did not like looking for trouble, but even a single Spanish cannon could cause damage. Although the Spanish gunners may not hit a small sloop, if the entire British fleet of some two-hundred vessels—including slow transports and supply ships—crawled past, even a poor shot could hit something and cause casualties. It was better to check on the threat or remove it rather than have the fleet in danger.

Under the command of very young Ensign Regan, *Dolphin's* six Marines joined the Rangers on the main deck. The Marines looked like solid professionals as they stood at attention, with the ensign fussing over them, checking their equipment, and worrying over their stocks and uniforms.

Kennedy took the ensign aside.

"They're looking fine, Regan," Kennedy said. "But it's not a parade. Better to let them prepare for the assault by ensuring that their ammunition pouches are full and their musket flints are sharp." He winked to remove any sting from his words. "Have you seen much action?"

"No, sir." The ensign looked a little overawed to be addressed by a veteran Rangers' captain. "But I hope to! My father was a major in the Royal Marines."

"I'm sure you'll make him proud," Kennedy said.

The Spanish cannon fired again, the shot passing between

Dolphin's masts without doing any damage. The long nine barked in reply, although nobody could mark the fall of shot.

"The Spanish are getting better," Maxwell said.

MacKim saw that the coast curved into a deep bay, with the Spanish cannon at the easternmost point, where the land jutted out for five-hundred yards. *Dolphin* eased towards a shelving beach, with the leadsman continuing to take soundings.

"By the mark seven! Sand and shells."

He swung the lead again and pulled up the dripping line. "By the mark six, sand and shells."

"Take in the topsails," Maxwell decided. "Drop anchors, bow and stern! We're close enough here. Landing party, off you go and silence that cannon—and hurry, men! We're an easier target for the Spanish gunners here."

Dolphin only possessed two small boats—the light, narrow captain's gig and a larger longboat. Maxwell crammed the Marines into the first and most of the Rangers into the second.

"We won't all fit," Kennedy informed Corporal Parnell and the six men left on deck. "The longboat will return for you."

"Yes, sir," Parnell replied, expressionless as the Rangers checked their muskets and ensured the bayonets were loose in their scabbards.

The Spanish adjusted their cannon to fire at the boats, so their next shot landed perilously close to the gig. Ignoring the water spout, *Dolphin's* seamen rowed on stoically, although Ensign Regan ducked and one of the Marines shifted in his seat.

"Missed!" Oxford shouted. "You couldn't hit a barn door from ten paces!" The Rangers' laughter broke the tension.

The gig came ashore first, with the heavier longboat ten seconds later, and the Marines and Rangers filed ashore. While Regan kept the Marines close together, the Rangers adopted a much looser formation as they extended into a line and marched inland.

"Dickert and MacRae, take the centre," MacKim ordered.

"The others spread out on either flank. The Spanish know we're coming, so watch for ambushes."

The Spanish cannon fired once more, and then the Rangers saw the position. MacKim had expected a redoubt with formal defences and fascines. Instead, the gun stood on a rising piece of ground with only a primitive loose wall as a barrier.

"Flank attack, Rangers!" Kennedy shouted. "MacKim! Right flank. I'll take the left! Ensign Regan, I want your Marines in the centre. Extend your formation and draw the Spanish attention. Don't close with them."

"Why not, sir?" Regan asked.

"One blast of grapeshot will remove all of *Dolphin's* Marines and put your mother in mourning. Let us do the fighting."

"But, sir!" Regan looked downcast.

The Spanish gunners fired a single shot when they saw the Rangers advancing from both flanks, and they fled into the surrounding open forest.

"That was too easy," Kennedy said as he moved forward cautiously to inspect the Spanish cannon. "Take your section around the area, sergeant; the Spanish may have an ambush planned. The parole will be Dolphin and the countersign Derry."

"Yes, sir. Come on, boys," MacKim said. "Watch for stray Spaniards. MacRae and Dicker, wait behind. If you see anybody that's not us, fire."

The Rangers moved out in short rushes, each man covering his neighbour. After five minutes, MacKim heard the distinctive crack of a rifle, followed shortly by another shot.

"The riflemen have seen something," MacKim murmured.

"If they both fired," Butler said, "then they've hit something. These two are too good to miss, although don't tell them I said that."

"I won't say a word." MacKim peered into the tangled undergrowth. This Cuban forest was vastly different from the cool woodland of North America. The heat distorted vision, the ground was hard underfoot, and the insect life was as prolific as on Martinico.

"There, sergeant." Butler levelled his musket as he spoke. "Dolphin!"

The movement was fast as somebody broke cover ahead of them. When there was no countersign, Butler fired immediately, with other Rangers a second later, so the forest echoed to the reports.

"Cease fire!" MacKim ordered. The powder smoke hung heavy, tainting the air. He peered forward, seeing only something white lying on the ground. "I'll look," he said. "Cover me, Butler."

MacKim slid down low and crawled forward, holding his musket in his right hand as he kept his eyes focussed on the shimmer of white. He knew Butler and the Rangers were watching over him, with half a dozen of the best marksmen in the world ready to fire, but still, his nerves were jumping by the time he reached the object.

The man was stone-dead, with a musket ball through his chest and another in his head.

"You don't look like a Spanish soldier or an artilleryman," MacKim said. The man was short and stocky, with brass rings in both ears and nothing on his feet. The palms of his hands were calloused as if he were used to constant hard labour, and there were traces of tar on his fingernails.

"You're a seaman," MacKim said. "A freebooter, perhaps. What the devil are you doing on land, firing a cannon at a British ship? And more importantly, where is your vessel?" He raised his head slightly to see another body a few steps further on. A single shot had ended this sailor's life, entering at the left side of his neck and exiting at the right. The man had died instantly.

"One seaman could be a stray, two argues for a crew somewhere," MacKim said. He looked up as Kennedy's voice sounded through the trees.

"Rangers! Rally to me, Rangers!"

"That's us, lads!" MacKim withdrew to join his men. "Back we go."

They approached cautiously. "Dolphin!" MacKim called.

"Derry!" The reply was reassuring, and green-clad men appeared from their concealment.

"We've spiked the cannon with a rough wooden plug," Kennedy said. "What did you find?"

"They were seamen, sir. Butler shot one, and MacRae and Dickert another."

Kennedy nodded. "Why would seamen fire a land-based ship's cannon at a passing British ship? Something's not right, but there's nothing more to do here, men. We're returning to the ship."

Picking up the Marines on their way, the Rangers returned to the beach just as Parnell's section jogged to meet them.

"About turn, Parnell," Kennedy said. "We've done our job here. You can act as a rearguard while we return to the ship."

"Yes, sir," Parnell said laconically. "Tree all and form a defensive ring, boys."

"That didn't take long," Maxwell said as Kennedy led his Rangers back on board *Dolphin*.

"No, captain," Kennedy reported. "There was just one cannon, manned by sailors."

"Probably from that vessel there," Maxwell said calmly, nodding to the long, lean ship that emerged from behind the headland. "We've seen her before."

"That's *Douce Vengeance*." MacKim felt the sickness in his stomach.

17

"The whole thing was a deception," MacKim said. "The cannon was to lure us into the bay so *Douce Vengeance* could trap us here and pound us with her superior firepower."

"Nearly correct, sergeant," Maxwell said. "She's launching a host of small boats. That means she means to board and take us undamaged as a prize."

Kennedy grunted. "A French privateer taking a Royal Navy sloop! What a coup that would be."

Maxwell gave a string of orders. "Break out the cutlasses and pistols! Mr Holmes! Man the larboard battery! Let's give the Frenchies a hot reception."

As the seamen hurried to obey, Maxwell addressed Kennedy. "I'd be obliged if you'd take your men to the rails, Captain Kennedy, and prepare to repel boarders. Roberval won't know we have Rangers on board, so that will be a nasty surprise for him."

Kennedy nodded. "Come on, Rangers. MacRae and Dickert, use your rifles as soon as they get in range."

Douce Vengeance had sent six boatloads of men to board *Dolphin*, with each boat crammed with freebooters.

"Aim well, gunners," Maxwell spoke without raising his voice, "and sink those damned pirate boats."

Roberval had been clever, blocking *Dolphin*'s exit from the bay while sending in his boarding parties. The boats spread in an arc, making it difficult for Maxwell to decide which part of his ship was most vulnerable.

"Fire any time you like, boys," Kennedy said.

Now it was *Dolphin*'s gunners' turn to find that shooting a mobile target at sea was no easy task, and the sloop's first broadside failed to hit a single French boat. When the splashes receded, the privateers were noticeably closer, and then *Douce Vengeance* fired her broadside, with the balls howling onto *Dolphin*'s rigging.

"She's trying to distract us," Kennedy said. "Ignore her fire. Concentrate on the boarders."

Dickert aimed at the steersman in the leading boat, firing as soon as he judged he was in range. The ball took the man high in the chest, knocking him back, so he released his grip of the tiller. The vessel veered to larboard and slowed until another man took the steersman's place.

MacRae fired then, hitting the new steersman on the shoulder and spinning him around.

"Next time, Mac," Dickert said, "Try to kill your man."

"Shut your mouth and concentrate on shooting." MacRae was annoyed by his lack of accuracy.

"They're too close for the cannon, sir," Holmes reported.

"Four men to man the swivels," Kennedy ordered. "The rest grab the boarding pikes, cutlasses, and pistols."

As Holmes issued weapons, the Rangers and Marines opened fire on the incoming boats, causing casualties. Surprised at the volume of musketry, the oarsmen on the leading vessel hesitated.

Kennedy gave a sardonic laugh. "That's where naval discipline counts," he said. "A French Navy crew would have ignored the musketry or rowed all the harder. Keep firing, men!"

The Marines fired an aimed volley that slammed into the

boat, killing or wounding three men, while the Rangers preferred to fire as individuals, choosing their targets. MacRae and Dickert competed to hit the men in the most distant boat, while the other Rangers fired and loaded as if they were at a firing range, ignoring the long-range cannon fire from *Douce Vengeance*. Only a few of the freebooters fired back, with their shots buzzing past the men on *Dolphin*.

"We're slaughtering them," Oxford said, firing like a veteran.

At that moment, the first of the privateer's boats hooked onto *Dolphin's* hull, and a swarm of men clambered on board.

With savage faces, waving cutlasses and machetes, the freebooters charged straight at the quarterdeck, where Maxwell stood with the helmsman and two seamen at the swivel. When the first seaman tried to fire, the boarders killed him before he succeeded. The second seaman swore and slashed with his cutlass. He cut one of the privateers across the face and screamed as two privateers plunged blades into his belly. Maxwell fired a pistol into the mob, drew his sword, and advanced to face the boarders.

"MacKim!" Kennedy shouted. "Remain on the main deck with your section. My section, fix bayonets and follow me!"

"Stand fast, lads!" MacKim ordered. "Dickert and MacRae target the leaders. The rest, fire away! Send the bastards back to their ship!" He watched as Kennedy led his Rangers forward, their carbine-cut muskets as suitable for the close fighting on board a ship as they were for battling in a forest.

"That's another for Dicky!" Dickert exclaimed as he shot a steersman.

MacRae grunted his acknowledgement. "Even you couldn't miss that one!"

When another boatload of privateers closed with *Dolphin*, MacKim ordered his section to fire a volley together, saw half the privateers crumple, and then the others were clambering over the bulwarks, yelling as they wielded swords and machetes.

"At them, men! Bayonets!" MacKim fired at a huge man, saw

his ball take effect, and then plunged forward, with *Dolphin's* crew screaming defiance as they met the privateers with boarding pike and cutlass.

In a moment, MacKim was involved in an affray as bloody as anything he had ever known, with panting seamen thrusting and slashing at each other, Rangers firing and bayonetting, and Marines in a disciplined line thrusting, parrying, and stepping forward. Ensign Regan laughed as he fought, with blood on his slender sword and his face.

All was confusion and noise, and then suddenly the deck cleared, the privateers withdrew, and the Rangers and *Dolphin's* men stood panting on bloody decks. Regan cleaned his sword and counted his Marines.

"Smith! Your tunic is undone!"

"Sorry, sir!" Marine Smith fastened the offending button.

"Dear Jesus," somebody said. "The pirates have gone."

MacKim looked at the dead and the groaning, writhing wounded that sprawled across the deck.

"Rangers!" Kennedy's voice sounded from the quarterdeck. "Keep firing!"

"That gig there!" MacKim stepped over a corpse and pointed to the closest of the privateer's boats. "Fire!"

Loading with speed, the Rangers fired, with Regan sending the Marines to add their firepower. As the storm of shot hit the gig, some of the privateers crumpled while others jumped overboard, leaving the vessel filled with dead and wounded men.

"Cease fire," Kennedy ordered. "They're out of range. You too, Dickert and MacRae. Save your ammunition."

With one boat drifting and the others returning to *Douce Vengeance* with dead and wounded men, the privateers had been badly hit.

Lieutenant Maxwell cleaned his bloody sword. "They didn't expect such a rough reception. Well done, Dolphins and Rangers. I want a list of casualties and the ship cleaned up. Get these damned pirates off my deck!"

There was no rest as the Rangers helped the seamen throw the dead privateers overboard and carried *Dolphin*'s wounded to the already-crowded cockpit, the only space available for a hospital on the sloop.

"How about the wounded pirates, sir?" the midshipman asked.

"Take care of them," Maxwell ordered. "If they're no danger to us, then they are no longer an enemy."

"We won that one!" Oxford was jubilant. "We showed them, didn't we, sergeant?"

"We did," MacKim said, looking at the carnage on deck and the groaning wounded. He counted the Rangers. Two had died in the brief fight, and two more were seriously injured, with others nursing minor cuts that might fester in the tropical heat.

"We're down to fifteen men, sir," MacKim reported to Kennedy. "Grimes and Butcher are dead."

"They were good men," Kennedy said. "We'll miss them."

"We won!" Oxford said again, surprised that nobody else shared his jubilation.

"Never look back, lad." Maxwell sounded more like an old man than an officer in his thirties. "Always prepare for the next problem."

"Yes, sir, but we won," Oxford said.

"Not yet," Maxwell nodded to *Douce Vengeance*. "That ship is larger than us and carries three times our number of men and more than thrice our weight in her broadside. She is also blocking our exit from this bay. Unless we can move her, we're trapped."

"Well, that's a bugger." Suzanne voiced the opinion that they all shared.

With the blood washed from her decks and the wounded down below, *Dolphin* sat in the bay as the sun set over the rough Cuban hills.

"What do we do now, sir?" Midshipman Crabb asked.

"We hold a conference of officers," Maxwell said. "Captain Kennedy, I'd be obliged if you would attend as well."

"Yes, captain," Kennedy said, glancing at *Deuce Vengeance* as she sat in a splendid silhouette, with the dying sun behind her.

"Sergeant MacKim, you may also come."

With insufficient space in Maxwell's tiny cabin, they stood on the quarterdeck as the velvet night caressed them and the surf boomed in the background.

"Well, gentlemen, I am receptive to ideas," Maxwell said. "We are trapped in this bay, and either we fight our way out, or we remain here and wait for Captain Roberval's next move. I don't like allowing the enemy to take the initiative."

"Permission to speak, sir?" Crabb asked.

"You don't need to ask permission, Snotty," Maxwell said. "I wouldn't have invited you if I didn't want your opinion."

"Yes, sir. Thank you, sir." The midshipman took a deep breath. "Can't we do to them what they did to us? Can't we put a gun ashore and bombard them from land? Make them believe there is another force attacking them?"

Holmes raised his eyebrows and shook his head while Kennedy nodded, narrow-eyed. "It's worth considering, Snotty. Try to work out some details."

"Yes, sir." Crabb looked pleased that Kennedy had not ridiculed his idea.

"How about trying a fireship?" MacKim said. "The French sent them against the Royal Navy when we were besieging Quebec in '59. They brought up rafts full of gunpowder and floated them down the river."

Lieutenant Holmes shook his head. "We don't have a river here," he said. "Or a raft. That won't work." Holmes was a lugubrious man with grey hair and a grey personality. MacKim could not imagine him in command of anything other than a guard ship or a convict hulk.

Maxwell pondered for a moment. "Bays are strange places where the current can play all sorts of tricks depending on the tide." He stepped to the rail and looked out to sea, where the lights of *Douce Vengeance* flickered. "Captain Roberval is letting us know he is still there."

"Maybe he's planning something," Kennedy said.

"I'd imagine he is," Maxwell agreed. "A fireship, eh? Like Frankie Drake used to singe the King of Spain's beard. Well, I'm no Drake, but I do like the idea."

"We don't have a raft," Holmes repeated.

"No, we don't," Maxwell agreed. "But we do have one of Roberval's boats." He jerked a thumb over the side. "The Rangers and Marines emptied it of the enemy, and now it's drifting free. The problem is how to get it to *Douce Vengeance* without her noticing, and then set it alight."

"*Douce Vengeance* will slip her cable and escape," Ensign Regan said. "Unless we set the boat alight when it touches her."

"Her lookout would see it right away," Holmes said.

"Not if we can distract her first." MacKim began to pace the quarterdeck as he cudgelled his mind for ideas. "We might take Midshipman Crabb's ideas here. Put men on land with a cannon and fire on *Douce Vengeance*. While she's occupied with the gun, we set the fire ship on her."

"Burn her to the waterline," Regan said, suddenly bloodthirsty.

"We already have a cannon on the land," Kennedy reminded. "The 12-pounder that lured us here."

"Did you spike it?" Maxwell asked.

"I put a peg in the touch hole," Kennedy replied. "A good carpenter could remove it in an hour."

"Private Dickert is a gunsmith," MacKim said. "I am sure he could drill a peg from a cannon's touch hole."

"And my men can shift a cannon with more efficiency than

any French privateer." Maxwell became suddenly animated. "Gentlemen, we have the makings of a plan. Now we must work on the details. We'll need to take the privateer's boat on board and pack it with explosives, find a landing party—and a volunteer sufficiently foolhardy to sail a fireboat." He looked around the quarterdeck. "We have work to do, my friends, and then Captain Roberval can whistle for his supper!"

"Sir?" Crabb lifted his head. "May I volunteer for the fireboat?"

Holmes grunted something about young fools thirsting for glory as Maxwell studied the boy for a minute.

"How old are you, Crabb?"

"Eighteen, sir," Crabb piped.

"And what was the year of your birth? Quickly now!" Maxwell snapped. "I thought so! You're no more eighteen than I am. Sixteen, I'd wager. Isn't that correct?"

"Yes, sir," Crabb whispered.

"If you lie to me again, Snotty, I'll order you a round dozen over the gunner's daughter," Maxwell said, and suddenly grinned. "That is, if you survive navigating your blasted fireboat!"

Crabb could not restrain his smile. "Thank you, sir!"

MacKim wondered at this strange world when a youth was grateful when a superior officer allowed him to sail a boatload of explosives to an enemy ship.

Maxwell glanced at his silver watch. "Gentlemen, we will move at sunset tomorrow. Get some sleep, and we'll have all day to work out the details. Mr Holmes, you have the ship."

"Aye, aye, sir," Holmes said, and dragged himself away.

They began work before dawn, and for the remainder of the following day, the officers and men on *Dolphin* sweated under the Caribbean sun. Maxwell, Kennedy, Crabb, and MacKim altered and refined their original plan, swearing when things went awry and grunting in quiet satisfaction when parts clicked into place.

"We'll have to fetch the pirate's boat." Kennedy nodded to the empty gig, which bobbed on the water, caught in some hidden current. "All my Rangers can swim, but I am as good as any of them."

"Sir?" Ensign Regan lifted a hand as if he were addressing his master in some peaceful English school. "I was a champion swimmer, sir."

"Off you go then, Regan," Maxwell said.

Regan stripped off and slipped into the water, swimming with powerful strokes to the boat.

"Sometimes one forgets how young these boys are," Maxwell said. "I feel like their father rather than their commander." He gave a sad smile. "Except that in this service, one doesn't have much opportunity for wives and children."

When Regan rowed the gig to *Dolphin*, Maxwell placed it on the lee side of the sloop, away from prying eyes, and packed it full of gunpowder. "This better work," he said, "for we're leaving the ship dangerously short of powder. If it comes to a gun-to-gun battle with *Douce Vengeance,* we'll be at a serious disadvantage."

"Let's hope it works, then," Kennedy said softly.

"Let's hope so," MacKim agreed. Yet, even as he eyed the sinister shape of *Douce Vengeance,* he thought what Maxwell had said about marriage.

I hope you receive my letter, Claudette. And I hope I live to see you again.

18

"Ready, men?" MacKim commanded the shore party, comprising ten Rangers and half a dozen seamen under a petty officer, Charles Williams, who also acted as the ship's cooper. The seamen took the oars and pushed off, with the stars brilliant overhead, but only a sliver of a moon.

"Easy, men," Williams cautioned.

Phosphorescence from the surf highlighted the shoreline as the bulk of Cuba was dark and mysterious in the background.

The seamen rowed with muffled oars, pieces of canvas in the rowlocks to blanket any sound. When one man raised a splash, Williams snarled in a savage whisper, threatening dire consequences if any seaman caught a crab that might alert *Douce Vengeance* a quarter of a mile away.

"Keep it steady, boys." MacKim looked over the familiar, sun-browned faces of his men. They met his gaze, some chewing tobacco, others pensive, all aware of what they had to do.

The longboat eased towards the shore, with the men now quiet and the night sounds of Cuba no longer unfamiliar after months of roaming Caribbean waters. Dickert and MacRae cradled their long rifles while the others held their cut-down muskets, wondering if the enemy was waiting.

For a moment, MacKim thought of his distant Highland glen, and Claudette with her serious eyes and Canadian-French accent. Then the boat's keel kissed soft sand, and he had no leisure to think of anything but the task in hand.

"Pull the boat beyond the high tide mark and cover it with branches," MacKim ordered. "We don't want the Frenchies to find it."

"Frenchies!" Williams grunted. "They're blasted pirates, rot them!"

Unable to disagree, MacKim ensured they hid the boat before leading his men towards the 12-pounder. The island felt different in the dark, even more hostile, and MacKim had to push aside his fear of snakes as he pushed on.

The cannon sat where they had left it, with the fast tropical growth already throwing green creepers around the carriage wheels.

"Dickert," MacKim hissed. "Do something with the touch hole. Williams," he spoke to the petty officer, "We have to move this gun to aim at the French ship."

"Aye." The petty officer spat a stream of tobacco juice onto the ground. "The pirates have made it easy for us. They chose a prime site here, sergeant, well-elevated and with a good field of fire out to sea." He shrugged off the rope he had looped around his shoulder. "Come on, *Dolphins*!"

"Rangers," MacKim ordered. "Form a defensive screen and be ready to help the sailors if they call for us."

The Rangers moved out, finding cover to crouch or lie behind. Then everything depended on Dickert as he inserted a small drill into the cannon's touch hole to remove the plug Kennedy had inserted.

Already an hour had passed since they left *Dolphin*. The stars retained their brilliance, but the wind had altered, a subtle shift that the seamen noticed immediately.

"Wind's backing westerly," Williams said, looking up.

"Is that bad?" MacKim asked.

"Could be." Williams fingered the tremendous pigtail that extended down the length of his spine. "Is your man not finished yet?"

"We can't hurry these things," Dickert said as he prised up a small section of the wooden plug. "Captain Kennedy used pine to block the priming vent, and it's expanded and split in the heat. I can only extract a small piece at a time."

MacKim swore. "Do your best, Dickert." He knew that Maxwell could not launch the fireship until the cannon distracted *Douce Vengeance,* yet he needed the cover of night to hide the launch. Everything depended on Dickert's skill with the drill.

Twice, a Ranger gave a low whistle, which was their signal for possible danger, but one alert was for a giant, night-hunting tree frog, and the second was for an even larger iguana.

"What a bloody country," Danskin said. "Give me New Hampshire any time."

After another half hour, MacKim glanced at the sky, which, in his mind, was noticeably lighter. He felt the seamen's impatience and could only imagine what the men on *Dolphin* were thinking. He heard Dickert softly swearing, fought down his temptation to hurry the gunsmith, and peered into the dark.

"That's it, sergeant," Dickert said, holding up a sliver of wood. "That's it, cleared."

"Right, boys!" Williams hissed. "Five degrees to starboard, and handsomely now!"

Using the handspikes and ropes they had carried from *Dolphin,* the seamen jumped to work, easing the cannon around until the muzzle pointed in the direction where *Douce Vengeance* lay.

"Let's hope she's not moved," the petty officer said. "She's doused her light, rot her hide." He gave rapid orders that saw the seamen bring powder and shot from the French supply.

"French gunpowder isn't the same quality as ours," Williams

said, "so we'll increase the quantities slightly and crank up the barrel a point or two."

"Do what you think best," MacKim said, feeling superfluous as the seamen worked the gun.

"Load her up, boys," Williams ordered, and the seamen prepared the cannon. He glanced at MacKim. "There's no match!"

MacKim swore. *There is always some problem in this bloody war.* "Can't you make something up?"

"Do you think I can magic one out of fresh air?" Williams's tension was evident.

"Here!" MacKim lifted a length of rope. "Will this do? Light the end and press it into the touch hole."

"I can try." Williams swore as he scattered loose powder onto the end of the rope, scraped a spark with his tinderbox, and applied it to the powder. It fizzed and smoked before emitting a dull red glow.

"The tar on the rope causes the smoke," Williams said, and dragged the smouldering end over the touch hole. "Stand clear of the cannon, boys. God knows how she will react."

The powder in the touch hole flashed, then a second later, the cannon roared and lunged backwards, gushing smoke.

"I'm not sure of the fall of shot!" MacRae, the lookout, shouted. "I might have seen a splash. It was a speck of whiteness."

"That's alright, MacRae. We're only a diversion anyway."

"Keep firing lads." Williams adjusted the cannon's angle slightly. "We won't know if we've hit her."

"Let's hope we don't hit the fireship," MacKim said.

"That's a chance Midshipman Crabb has to take," Williams said. "He's only young, but he's got a head on his shoulders. He knows when to duck. Load her up, boys!"

Firing blindly into the night was a new experience for MacKim. He looked away from the gun, lest the muzzle flare ruin his night vision, and hoped they were at least catching the attention of *Douce Vengeance*.

"I saw something, sergeant!" MacRae said. "Out at sea. I'm sure I saw something."

"What?"

"A flash of something, like the shutter of a lantern being opened and then shut."

"Thank you, MacRae. Keep alert." MacKim fingered the lock of his musket, checking that the flint was still in place. Why would anybody open and shut a lantern at night? There could be a hundred reasons, but the one that jumped to MacKim's mind was it was a signal. Somebody on *Deuce Vengeance* had signalled. To whom? To somebody on *Dolphin*? Unlikely. It was much more likely that Captain Roberval was signalling to land.

That meant there were Frenchmen, or their allies, in Cuba and probably near the cannon.

"Keep alert, boys!" MacKim warned. "There may be a French landing party!"

"There is," Dickert said, just as the 12-pounder fired again, its roar temporarily deafening MacKim. "I saw movement down near the beach."

"If you see anything, fire," MacKim ordered. "Don't wait to identify it. If it's not one of us, it's an enemy."

"Or one of those lizards!" Parnell said.

A moment later, there was a crackle of musketry, with the muzzle flares twinkling in the dark and a variety of subdued curses.

MacKim nodded in grim satisfaction. The privateers may be skilled in attacking merchant ships at night, but the Rangers had learned their skills in one of the most dangerous schools on Earth. After fighting Indians in the forests of North America, facing a few dozen privateersmen was not going to daunt them.

The firing flared up for a moment, then died away. MacKim peered into the dark with the muzzle flashes having starred his night vision.

"A score of them." Parnell had already reloaded and lay comfortably behind a tree. "We downed three, I think, and the rest withdrew."

The cannon roared again, and then MacKim saw the glow. At first, he was unsure what it was, and then it spread until he knew it was the fireship. Down there, on the dark sea, a brave young man was sailing a boatload of gunpowder and combustibles towards a French privateer who could kill him with a single gunshot.

"God bless you, Royal Navy," MacKim said, not for the first time in this war. "Williams, fire as fast as you can, but ensure you don't hit that fireship."

Williams had come to the same decision without MacKim's help, and the 12-pounder barked again, and then again, as the sailors worked like demons to sponge, load, and fire.

A sudden surge of firing from the privateer heralded a hurricane of sound and shot. *Douce Vengeance's* broadside smashed into the ground around the cannon. MacKim threw himself down, hugging the earth as iron balls thudded and bounced around him while pieces flew from the trees. Something pinged from the barrel of the cannon and ricocheted high into the air.

"Dear God! Is anybody hurt? Roll call!"

There were no casualties.

MacKim looked back out to sea. The fireship was closing on *Douce Vengeance,* with the flames lighting the scene. MacKim watched, hoping to see the French vessel catch fire, but she seemed inviolate.

"The French bastard's cut her cable," Williams snarled. "We'll never hit her now."

MacKim nodded. "That's our signal to return, boys. Leave the cannon and everything else, and get back to the beach."

"Should we spike the gun, sergeant?" Dickert asked.

MacKim thought for a moment. "Yes. It's unlikely we'll need it again, and the fleet will pass this way. Spike it, Dickert."

"After all my work," Dickert grumbled as he thrust a length

of wood into the priming vent and sheered it off flush with his knife.

"Come on, Dolphins!" Williams said. "Back to the shore!"

The seamen moved first, heading at a steady trot, with the Rangers covering the rear. MacKim was last, counting his men as they slipped and skidded to the beach, where Williams signalled for the longboat.

"Not a single casualty," MacKim said.

"No, sergeant," MacRae agreed. "These French gunners couldn't hit a bull's arse with a musket butt."

"Probably not." MacKim saw the longboat was returning, and with the oars raising phosphoresce on the waves, realised it must be growing lighter. He looked out to sea. The fireboat was still burning fiercely, but alone. Despite all their efforts, *Douce Vengeance* must have escaped the flames.

"Hurry up, lads!" the petty officer in charge of the longboat shouted as he steered her onto the beach. "The captain wants to get out of here while the Frenchie's away!"

"Where is the privateer?" MacKim asked as the Rangers boarded.

"I don't know, Ranger, and I don't care as long as she's out of our way."

Kennedy was on the quarterdeck, waiting for them. "You missed all the excitement, sergeant."

"Did I, sir?"

"When the midshipman took the fireboat against the privateer, Roberval sent his boats. They rowed halfway and sent a dozen swimmers against us. We were lucky because Snotty in the fireship shouted a warning."

"Is that why *Douce Vengeance* got away?"

"That's why. Snotty was a brave lad. He's disappointed he couldn't fire the ship, but he saved us."

All the time Kennedy had been talking, Captain Maxwell had been shouting orders that saw *Dolphin* ease out of the bay and into the Old Bahamas Channel beyond.

"Hands to the guns!" Maxwell ordered. "I can't see *Douce Vengeance*, but we're taking no chances."

Daylight blessed the sea as the lookouts cast anxious eyes for the French privateer. "Sail to the eastward!" Lambert, high on the mainmast, shouted. "I can't make it out yet, sir, but I saw the sun reflect on canvas."

"Keep an eye on her, Lambert," Maxwell ordered. "Pipe the men to breakfast! Leadsman, to the bows. We have a passage to sound."

Within fifteen minutes, Lambert shouted down again. "Deck, there. It's *Richmond*, sir."

MacKim felt the relief surge through *Dolphin*.

"Stand by to go about," Maxwell said. "We'd better report."

"She's signalling, sir!" Lambert called a few moments later and made room beside him for the midshipman.

"Return to Cape St Nicholas, sir," Crabb read the signal.

Maxwell grunted. "Damn it all," he said. "I much prefer an independent command to working as part of a fleet."

MacKim eyed the sea and the landmass of Cuba. He knew that *Douce Vengeance* was out there somewhere, and wondered if their tracks would cross again. Somehow, he thought they would. His life seemed to follow a pattern, with an enemy he repeatedly met. He had little doubt the same would happen with René Roberval, although he could not imagine how.

19

The Royal Navy waited off Cape St Nicholas, with Hispaniola to the east and Cuba to the west. The merchantmen and troop transports lay in massive columns, with red-coated soldiers lining the decks, gesticulating and staring at each new arrival as their flags drooping idly. Bustling around the transports, the frigates and smaller craft of the Navy fussed over details, gave orders that the merchantmen occasionally obeyed, and scoured the surrounding seas for the enemy.

The Rangers crowded *Dolphin's* deck, mingling with the crew as they joined the fleet.

"Admiral Pocock must expect trouble from the Spanish," Maxwell said. "There's *Namur,* 98. I've never seen a 98-gun ship before. *Namur* is Pocock's flagship. And there's *Valiant* and *Culloden,* both 74s, and *Cambridge,* she's an 80."

To MacKim, all the ships looked similar, while the seamen recognised them by their rigging, sails, or some difference of their hulls.

He listened as the seamen spoke of the warships as if they were old friends. "Look at the 74s; *Temeraire, Dublin,* and *Dragon,* and there's *Temple,* with her 70 guns." The seamen were excited, as if discussing living people rather than floating gun batteries. "We lost *Hussar*, though," Williams informed them. "She went down off *Cape Francois*."

"There must be a hundred and fifty transports and supply ships here," MacKim said.

"At least," Kennedy agreed. "And I don't know how many Royal Naval ships. Imagine being able to assemble a fleet this size thousands of miles away to strike a blow at another European enemy."

"War is the most stupid thing," MacKim said. "One bunch of politicians and kings in Europe argue with another bunch of politicians and kings in Europe, so thousands of men who have no quarrel with each other sail halfway across the world to fight."

"How would you settle national squabbles, MacKim?"

"Have the kings and politicians fight each other. Give them a sword and pistol each, and let them duel in a field somewhere, with somebody from a neutral nation acting as referee. That way, the large, powerful nations can no longer bully the smaller."

Kennedy laughed. "King George fighting King Louis face-to-face! I can imagine the crowd cheering them on. That would put tens of thousands of soldiers and seamen out of a job."

"It would save tens of thousands of lives and make our esteemed rulers think twice before they start a war if the danger affects them personally," MacKim said. "The admiral is signalling. Something is about to happen."

"We're moving!" Parnell said. "The entire British fleet must have been waiting for Kennedy's Rangers."

"Naturally," Butler said, puffing at his pipe. "Rangers! First and always!"

The fleet sailed out in three divisions, with smaller ships in front to mark the shoals and reefs that *Richmond* and *Dolphin* had charted and the Navy acting as a protective screen.

"I don't think any fleet has ever sailed the Old Bahama Channel before," Maxwell said. "Pocock is a daring man."

The fleet moved slowly, with the Navy escorting the

ponderous convoy, and every time the scouts arrived at shoal water, they left a manned boat with instructions to warn the ships away.

"I remember that shoal," Butler said whenever the scouts raised a signal to ward off the fleet. "The Rangers were here first."

"Maybe Captain Maxwell was also involved," MacKim suggested.

Butler nodded. "He helped, I suppose."

When the scouts arrived at the headlands or the dangerous rocks that Maxwell had marked on his chart, they built a fire to act as a temporary lighthouse, with Maxwell nodding to see his work put to good use.

Day after day, the fleet crawled through the Old Bahama Channel, following the route that *Dolphin* and *Richmond* had pioneered, watching for any Spanish fleet, cautious of a shore battery opening on them. When they passed the bay where *Douce Vengeance* had trapped them, Admiral Pocock sent *Dolphin* to check for any Spanish. The bay was clear, and the fleet sailed on unmolested.

"The Spanish must be asleep to not notice a fleet this size sailing past their back door," Danskin said.

"It's the heat," Oxford responded. "It rots the brain. That's why people from northern climates are more vigorous."

"The Spanish were vigorous enough to grab most of the Americas before the northerners even knew America existed," Danskin reminded. "Never underestimate Spain."

On the 6th of June, 1762, Pocock's fleet arrived off Havana without encountering a single hostile ship. Pocock immediately organised his warships into a blockade, trapping the Spanish ships in the harbour and ensuring no merchant vessels entered.

"When it comes to economic warfare and starving out an enemyKennedy murmured, the Royal Navy are the masters."

"The Spanish hadn't even heard we were at war," Maxwell

said. "One of our frigates captured the Spanish ship that carried the official declaration to Cuba."

"Is that fair?" Kennedy asked.

"If it saves hundreds of British lives, it's fair," Maxwell said. "We have achieved total surprise, for by using the Old Bahamas Channel, the admiral has ensured that nobody warned Don Juan de Prado, the Spanish governor, of our approach."

"We must be a shock to de Prado," MacKim said.

"The poor fellow was in church," Maxwell said. "He and the city authorities were celebrating the feast of the Trinity when a messenger told him the British had arrived. He refused to believe it, saying it was only passing ships until he saw our fleet."

"That's a lesson on the importance of gathering intelligence," Kennedy murmured.

MacKim noted the governor's name. "Apart from de Prado, who else is in charge here?"

"Commodore El Marquis del Real Transporte is the commander of all the Spanish warships in Havana," Maxwell said. "And commander in chief of all his Catholic Majesty's Ships in America."

"How many men are we facing?" MacKim asked.

"I don't think even Lord Albemarle and his generals are sure," Kennedy said. "I believe something between five and ten thousand, with both regular Spanish soldiers and militia."

Maxwell scanned the coast through his telescope. "However many there are today," he said, "you can guarantee there will be more tomorrow. Prado will arm every available man to repel us, and he'll offer the slaves freedom if they fight against us."

"That's a good incentive," MacKim said. "I wonder if they'll stand against regular, trained British infantry."

Kennedy smiled. "We'll soon see. We have a mixture of veterans from the North American campaigns and the capture of Martinico, and untried units fresh from Great Britain." He focussed his telescope on a boat that was ferrying men ashore. "And I don't know what that lot is."

Ensign Regan joined them, looking less nervous now that he had tasted enemy powder smoke. "I heard that is Freron's Regiment, sir," he said. "They are all French Protestants, men who were prisoners of war, but volunteered to fight for us rather than remain in confinement."

"Good God in heaven," Kennedy said. "Can we trust them not to shoot us in the back when we're going forward?"

"We'll soon find that out, too," MacKim said. "I can't see Albemarle keeping the Rangers in a ship when there's fighting ashore. There's not many of Kennedy's Rangers remaining, but we're the best."

"Rangers, first and always, as Butler keeps telling us," Kennedy said.

"Well, gentlemen." Maxwell wiped the sweat from his forehead, adjusted his queue, and pointed at the land. "Enough speculation. We have reached the Havana, possibly the most heavily defended port in all the Americas."

"Where is it?" MacKim asked. "I can only see a water channel with forts."

"We can't see the city from here," Maxwell explained, "because it's on the other side of that passage, which is a mile long and heavily protected. The harbour is superb, or so I'm told."

Two forts defended Havana harbour. On the west was the Puntal Fort, which was tall and dauntingly impressive, yet overshadowed by the eastern fortification of El Morro. This latter stood on a high headland, dominating the harbour entrance and the surrounding land.

"Cuba is the key to the Caribbean, Havana is the key to Cuba, and El Morro is the key to Havana," Kennedy said. "The castle's artillery can blast any ship entering the harbour. El Morro also defends Puntal and covers the northern walls of the city. We'll have to fight our way in by land before the ships can enter."

MacKim studied the terrain through a telescope while comparing what he saw with their map.

"There is a weakness in Havana's defences," MacKim said. "This ridge, the La Cabanas ridge." He prodded the map with his finger. "It overlooks the city, the harbour, and even El Morro."

"That's how I see it," Kennedy said.

"Have the Spanish fortified La Cabanas?"

"I don't think so," Kennedy said.

"Then that's our way in. I expect General Albemarle will know that."

"Oh, I expect the general has even more knowledge than a Rangers' sergeant," Kennedy said.

"Colonel McKellar, the engineer, has studied all the available maps and plans of Havana and its defences," Maxwell said. "I believe he got his intelligence from Admiral Knowles, who visited the city."

"El Morro Castle is what matters." Kennedy pointed to the grim fortress. "I suspect that place will figure in our nightmares for years to come."

"Sergeant!" Danskin asked anxiously. "Are we going ashore today?"

Even from *Dolphin*, MacKim could hear the regular boom of breakers on the beach. By now an expert in amphibious operations, he shook his head. "There will not be any landing today; the surf is too high. Settle yourselves down, boys, and enjoy a night's rest. Tomorrow, we may invade Cuba."

"And may God have mercy on our souls," MacRae whispered as he checked the lock of his rifle.

※

ON THE 7TH OF JUNE, 1762, THE BRITISH PREPARED TO LAND IN Cuba. As always, the Navy provided a feint, with Admiral Pocock taking a strong squadron to Chorera, a mile or so to the west of Havana, while Commodore Keppel commanded the genuine landing at Coximar, two miles east of the city. The Rangers examined the coast between the Coximar and Bacuranao Rivers, where a white line of surf marked the beach.

"Divide and conquer," Oxford said.

"Yes." Parnell bit off a chunk of tobacco. "But we're also divided." He nodded to an ugly fort that guarded Coximar. "The Spanish are waiting for us."

Commodore Keppel commanded seven line-of-battleships, with four frigates and three bomb-ketches, to protect the landing. With the giant Captain Duncan in command, HMS *Valiant* served as the pivot, taking Keppel's orders and sending them to the other vessels.

"There's the first signal," MacKim said as *Valiant* hoisted a blue-and-yellow flag to her fore-topmasthead.

"Six in the morning." Kennedy consulted his large, very battered silver watch.

When the signal appeared, every ship in the fleet burst into activity. Busy seamen hurried to swing the flat-bottomed open boats over the side and gently lowered them into the sea. A young midshipman scrambled to take command of each, with a petty officer and sixteen hands clambering down boarding netting to take their places at the oars. Seabirds circled, hopeful for scraps of food as the soldiers stood in formation on the transports' decks.

The Rangers looked at the boats rising and heaving on the waves, and wondered what sort of reception would greet them ashore.

"Dear Lord, protect us on this perilous adventure," MacRae muttered a short prayer, glowered at the other Rangers to ensure nobody ridiculed him, and checked the flint of his rifle.

"Danskin," Oxford said in a harsh whisper. "If I fall, you get my possessions."

"And you get mine, Oxford," Danskin hesitated. "Could you tell Julia what happened?"

"I'll do that," Oxford said.

All over the boats, men made similar promises to their colleagues, exchanging final messages for wives or sweethearts, paying old debts of tobacco, or hiding their fear behind dark humour.

Valiant hoisted a red-and-white flag, the signal for each midshipman to steer his boat to a transport. With boarding nets drooping from the side of the transports, soldiers—laden with musket and pack—climbed clumsily down for the sailors to help them to their place. Every open boat flew a small flag, showing which unit was aboard, allowing the regiments to remain together.

To MacKim and the Rangers veterans, the procedure was bitterly familiar. The Royal Navy seamen ushered the soldiers onto the flat-bottomed assault boats with good-natured insults while the warships readied to blast any enemy interference.

After three hours of organising, it was nine in the morning before Duncan hoisted a chequered red-and-white flag and the open boats, formed in divisions, steered for the shore. By that time, many of the soldiers were heavily seasick, while others were white-faced with apprehension.

"Rangers, first and always!" Butler shouted his inevitable challenge, to be met by whistles and jeers from other regiments.

"We're the Grenadiers! Dogs of war!" A group of redcoats responded.

"You can watch us march in front!" Butler yelled.

With the blue sky above and the blue sea breaking in silver-white surf along the shore, MacKim glanced around at the invasion fleet. The boats seemed endless, wave after wave of scarlet-coated men rowed by pig-tailed, nonchalant seamen, crashing into Spain's premium island colony in the Americas.

"Four-thousand men, so I'm told," Kennedy said. "Not many to capture an island half the size of Great Britain."

"Let's hope the Spanish decide not to fight," Dickert said.

"Check your muskets, boys!" MacKim shouted. "Make sure the flints are sharp and keep your cartridges out of the water."

He spoke from habit, for the veteran Rangers did not need his advice.

Cuba was closer now, shimmering under a heat-haze. The sailors grunted with effort as they rowed, and the smell of man-sweat was powerful in the heat. MacKim took a deep breath, thought of the green coolness of Scotland, and pushed the memory away. Behind them, Navy ships began their bombardment of the small fort at the entrance to the River Bacuranao, while others fired broadsides at the dense woodland behind the landing beaches.

"Good lads," MacKim said. "If the Spanish are preparing a counter-attack from the woods, they won't be happy having scores of cannonballs crashing around their heads."

"Make ready, Rangers!" Kennedy shouted as they neared the beach. He checked his watch. Thirty minutes past ten.

The surf was still high, beating on the Cuban coast to make landing dangerous, but the young midshipman on the boat knew what to do. "Drop a grapnel astern," he ordered, to enable his men to drag the boat off the land once the Army had disembarked.

MacKim watched with only a fragment of his attention. He knew that seizing Caribbean islands was important for the British economy, but also knew that they were bloody to capture and expensive to hold. For every hundred pounds the islands made, a soldier or sailor would suffer. He took a deep breath, thought of his native glen, thought of Claudette, and put both images behind him.

"Remember to look after each other, boys!" MacKim shouted, examining the landing beach, looking for any defence. "We're about to land in Cuba!"

20

"Follow me!" Kennedy was first ashore as the boats slid onto the sand, with the Rangers following him, green-clad men leading a scarlet army under the bright sun.

The Rangers fanned out onto the beach and ran into the scrubland behind, ready for a Spanish defence, waiting for the staccato crack of musketry. There was none. The British invaders had the beach to themselves as the Rangers formed a defensive perimeter. Behind the Rangers, more landing craft slid onto the sand and additional units filed onto the land, with officers and sergeants ordering the ranks.

"Keep in formation, men! Light Infantry, to the front! Grenadiers, form in the centre!"

The sun reflected from burnished equipment as young men who had never been away from their rural parishes stared around them in wonder.

"Form up!" Harsh-voiced sergeants ordered the men, using familiar discipline to keep control. "Face your front!"

"This way, Rangers!" Kennedy headed slightly inland from the beach, where the Spanish flag hung limply from the fort. "We'll show the Army where to go."

"Rangers, first and always!" Butler yelled, with the younger men echoing his words.

As the Rangers trotted in front of the Army, MacKim glanced over his shoulder. The redcoats marched in perfect formation, with drums tapping to keep them in step, and the regimental and king's colours carried in the centre of each regiment. It was a beautiful sight to gladden any martial eyes while the reality of war waited behind the ramparts of Coximar Fort.

"There's a breastwork in front of the fort." Kennedy had sent Parnell ahead to investigate the Spanish defences. "Manned by hundreds of Spanish soldiers and militia."

The crash of a cannon interrupted them, with the feather of powder smoke from the fort appearing a moment before the shot landed a hundred yards from the Rangers.

"Well short," Parnell said with satisfaction.

"Here come the Navy," MacKim said as two frigates and a line-of-battleship cruised close to the coast, ahead of the advancing British force. The frigates fired first, unleashing their broadsides at Coximar Fort and the forward breastworks, with the battleship a few moments later. As powder smoke enveloped the ships and the thunder of their cannon rose to the sky, a nightmare descended on the Spanish defenders. Dust, fragments of rock, and pieces of men and equipment scattered above the breastwork as the ships' broadsides hammered at the fort.

"Halt," Kennedy ordered. "We don't want to get caught in that."

The Rangers obeyed, automatically finding shelter.

"Poor buggers." Oxford stared at Coximar Fort.

"Rather them than us." MacKim watched as the ships continued the bombardment.

As the frigates sailed on and the battleship returned, the Spanish withdrew from their battered positions, running out of the gate in a long, straggling line of scared men.

"Will the last man out close the door," Butler repeated the tired old joke.

A SACRIFICE OF PAWNS

Only Oxford laughed, but stopped when he realised he was laughing alone.

"They're off to these hills." Kennedy pointed to the low wooded ridge that overlooked the sea. "The Cabana Heights, according to the map." He raised his voice. "As soon as the bombardment stops, lads, double forward. We'll take Coximar Fort before the Spanish return."

When the Rangers moved in, the interior of the fort and associated breastworks was a shambles of smashed masonry, upended guns, and broken bodies. The Lights were only minutes behind, happy to have secured their bridgehead with no casualties. Major-General William Keppel, in charge of the land operations, sent the Light Infantry across the Coximar River to consolidate the British position.

"Kennedy," Keppel ordered, "join the Lights and report to Carleton."

"Yes, sir." Kennedy jogged after the fast-moving Light Infantry.

"Where are the Spanish?" Danskin wondered. "Why aren't they trying to defend their island?"

"They'll come," MacKim said. "Just be thankful we have time to settle in."

Colonel Guy Carleton was an Ulsterman and a veteran of the European and Canadian campaigns. He commanded the Light Infantry. "Probe inland, Rangers," Carleton ordered. "Keep the Spanish on the hop. Investigate Guanabacoa village and report back to me."

"Yes, sir." Kennedy and his Rangers were glad to be outside the rigid regime of the main British force. Pushing inland in extended formation, they found the small village baking in the heat, with movement all around.

Settling on a slight rise, Kennedy ordered the Rangers to form a defensive circle around him and scanned Guanabacoa through his telescope.

"Regulars, I'd say." Kennedy passed the telescope to MacKim. "What do you think?"

MacKim refocussed, scanned, and nodded. "Smart uniforms and all with muskets. Undoubted regulars, but look at the flanks, sir. I think these men are local militiamen."

Kennedy reclaimed the telescope. "Cuban irregulars," he agreed. "And cavalry in the distance. We've found the Spanish army."

MacKim nodded to the left. "They've found us, too, sir."

A group of Cuban militiamen stood on a rise to the left, observing the Rangers.

"Time to withdraw," Kennedy decided. "Take the rearguard, Corporal Parnell. Return by sections, men."

Colonel Carlton pursed his lips when Kennedy reported. "Cavalry," he said. "We haven't seen much of them in this hemisphere. Thank you, Rangers. Find yourselves some rations now, and encamp until I need you again."

When the Rangers heard the sound of pick and shovel, they knew the infantry were already strengthening the defences to prepare for any possible Spanish counterattack.

"They're also burying the Spanish dead," Kennedy said. "They swell and stink in the heat."

"The Cubans don't need soldiers here." Parnell wiped the sweat from his face and swatted at the flies that swarmed around his head. "The heat and mosquitoes do the fighting for them, and disease kills more men than the enemy in these bloody islands."

"Let's hope we aren't here long enough to catch yellow jack."

The Rangers set up camp near the Coximar River, sufficiently close to fetch fresh water while avoiding the worst of the flies. MacKim took advantage of the rest to borrow paper, pen, and ink from a harassed clerk, and scribed a letter to Claudette.

"My dear Claudette,

I do not know if you received my last letter, or if you will receive this one. I think of you every day when I have time."

MacKim read that small paragraph, scribbled out the final four words, and started again.

"My dear Claudette,
  If you are reading this letter, then I must tell you how much I think of you. When this war is over, or if we are posted back to Canada, I will seek you out. Please do not forget me."

That was short and brutal, MacKim thought. Yet, with the heat pressurising him and the flies a constant torment, he could do no better. *Damn it! Tell the woman what you'd say if she sat beside you.*

He put pen to paper again. *"If you were here, I'd ask you to consider being my wife.*

Your friend,
  Hugh MacKim"

MacKim read his letter, shook his head at its faults, and knew he could do no better. The ink was already dry, so he folded it, borrowed a simple seal, added an address, and asked the clerk to put it with any other letters he had.

"You should pay for postage," the clerk said doubtfully.

"Here." MacKim fished in his pocket for his few remaining coppers. "We haven't been paid for a while."

The clerk sighed. "Alright. Put it in that box and leave it to me." He jerked a slender thumb at a wooden box half-filled with similar letters.

MacKim dropped in his letter, had a momentary panic attack when he doubted the sanity of his actions, and turned away quickly.

It's up to you now, Claudette.

On the 8th of June, with the Navy's boats busy landing the Army's baggage, tents, supplies, and ammunition, Carleton organised his Lights and ordered the Rangers to join him.

"We're heading inland, boys," Kennedy said.

"Where to, sir?" MacKim asked. He looked to the east, where the sun was straining to rise above the horizon.

"That village we reconnoitred, Guanabacoa," Kennedy said. "But this time, we're not alone."

The Rangers moved inland, with the Light Infantry matching them step by step and the rising sun hammering at them from above.

Without the support of naval guns, the Army was more cautious as it approached Guanabacoa. A single cannon fired on them, the shot falling short and bouncing on the hard ground. It raised a large fountain of dust before the ball rolled to a harmless stop.

"They're going to fight," MacRae said.

"I've never fought Spaniards before." Oxford sounded nervous.

"Neither have any of us," MacKim said. "Remember your training, Oxford, and depend on your colleagues. The Spaniards haven't fought us, either."

"Extended order, Rangers!" Kennedy ordered, and the Rangers stepped apart, muskets ready, and moved forward from cover to cover, looking ahead at the village. Beside them, the Lights moved, equally spread out and determined.

"Watch the flank!" Parnell shouted. "Cavalry!"

The Spanish were ready to fight, drawn into formation and holding rising ground in front of the village. About six-thousand strong, they outnumbered the British force by three-to-two and raised a great yell when Carleton drew near.

"They look a formidable bunch," Oxford said.

"So do we," MacKim told him.

Sunlight flashed on Spanish swords, bayonets, and accoutrements as the defenders waited, cheering. For the first time, MacKim had a clear view of the Cuban militia and the freed slaves that supported the Spanish infantry. Agile, tall men, these latter carried long machetes that they held with the expertise of long practice.

"These lads look handy," Dickert said. "We'd be best keeping them at a distance." He aimed his rifle.

"Hold your fire, Dickert," MacKim said. "We're under Carleton's orders here."

"It's the cavalry I dislike most," Kennedy said.

"Here they come." MacRae lifted his rifle as the cavalry left their position to advance on the British.

"Mostly mounted militia," said a slim Light Infantry major who had joined the Rangers, "with some regiments of dragoons."

"They all look dangerous to me," Kennedy said.

MacKim swore. Despite his years of experience in warfare, he had seldom met cavalry. He waited for Kennedy to give orders.

"Lights!" Carleton shouted. "Form squares! Rangers! Join the nearest formation!"

MacKim felt grateful for the presence of trained British soldiers as the Lights opened up to bring in the Rangers. They closed their formation, with the front rank kneeling and the rear rank standing, their bayonets fixed and extended as the Spanish cavalry approached.

"Steady, boys!" The Light Infantry major said. "Glad to have you with us, Rangers. Fix bayonets, if you please."

The Rangers obeyed, with MacKim cursing that he had not given the order; he had almost forgotten this method of soldiering. The square waited, men standing or crouching under the broiling sun, sweaty faces tense or nonchalant, eyes slitted against the glare as the cavalry circled them.

The Spanish wore white uniforms and carried long swords, their faces swarthy, with some sporting moustaches.

"Fire by sections, men," Carleton ordered.

"You heard the colonel," the major said. "First section, fire!"

The Lights fired a section at a time, with the Rangers joining the rest. Now Kennedy's Rangers were part of a whole, a segment of an army rather than an individual unit.

Powder smoke drifted, stinging at eyes, irritating noses and mouths, staining already-dirty uniforms, and darkening faces. The Rangers loaded hastily, thumping musket butts on the hard ground to help the balls slide up the barrels, working the ramrods like Trojans.

The cavalry backed off, leaving a scattering of casualties. A horse screamed, kicking its legs. One man crawled away, trailing his left leg and with his sword dangling from his wrist. Blood soaked into the ground, attracting insects.

"Load!" Carleton shouted. The Lights obeyed, ramming cartridges down the barrels of their muskets. MacKim winked at Oxford, who was pale under his tan. Everything seemed unreal, as if it was happening to somebody else. MacKim could nearly look down on himself from above.

"Here they come!" Carleton warned. "Prepare to receive cavalry!"

The Spanish were brave men, trotting and then galloping through a volley of musketry and approaching right to the bayonet points. Now the Rangers found their shortened muskets gave them a disadvantage over the conventional muskets. It was worse for Dickert and MacRae, whose Pennsylvanian rifles did not have bayonets and who could only thrust their slim barrels at the cavalry.

"Rangers! First and always!" Butler roared, and then the cavalry was on them.

Suddenly, the whole world was composed of screaming horses with flailing hooves, moustached men slashing with glittering sabres, and gasping, blaspheming infantrymen thrusting with bayonets. MacKim parried the down-swing of a sword, felt the shock of impact, flinched as Butler on his left fired his musket, and saw a horseman fall in front of him, blood spurting from his chest and horrified disbelief on his face.

And then, the cavalry was retreating, the Lights fired a final volley and reloaded, and the drums were beating to advance in extended order.

The British stepped over the casualties of horses and men as jets of smoke from Guanabacoa revealed determined defenders in the village. One of the Lights on MacKim's right gave a little grunt and crumpled to the ground, with his colleagues stepping over his body, closing ranks, and marching on.

"Extended order!" The drums tapped out their message, and the Lights and Rangers advanced. The defending militia did not remain to cross bayonets, but retreated quickly, leaving the British to occupy Guanabacoa.

"Stand and fight!" Butler roared as Oxford tried to control his shaking limbs and Danskin gave a weak smile.

MacKim saw that even that short skirmish had taken its toll, with men searching for shade and collapsing in every nook and cranny of the village.

"First round to us," Kennedy said.

"Aye," MacKim agreed, reaching for his water bottle. "But it's a long way to Havana."

Albemarle left Lieutenant General Elliot in command at Guanabacoa with over two-thousand men and orders to scour the surrounding country for water, vegetables, and beef cattle. Men with memories of the terrible winter siege of Quebec feared scurvy more than the Spanish.

As the Lights and Rangers marched back from Guanabacoa, news filtered through that de Prado, the Spanish governor, had bolstered Havana's defences. He'd sent infantry and artillery to the wooded heights of La Cabana and dragged a chain boom across the harbour mouth, with three ships sunk behind it to further impede the British passage.

As the British blockade trapped the Spanish vessels in the harbour and rendered them useless as an offensive force, de

Prado ordered many of the ships' guns removed and added to the city's defences. He also sent other cannon and seamen to El Morro Castle, further strengthening an already-strong fortification. Finally, in a stroke of genius, de Prado sent Don Luis de Valasco, the captain of the battleship *Reina*, to command El Morro.

"A naval officer in charge of a castle?" Parnell sneered. "What's he going to do? Sail El Morro into the Caribbean?"

"From what I've seen of naval captains," MacKim said, "Valasco could be a very dangerous opponent."

Parnell grunted and began to polish his rifle.

Lord Albemarle entrenched his position, thenon the 8th of June, sent out patrolsto test the Spanish troops on the woods of La Cabana. The Rangers listened to the sporadic sputter of musketry as British and Spanish clashed and saw the slow drift of powder smoke above the trees. When more British marched in column towards the heights, the Spanish met them with stubborn musketry.

When the roar of cannon joined the crackling muskets, Carlton sent the Rangers to reinforce the Lights on La Cabana. MacKim suspected that Carlton was less worried about the outcome and more an impatient man who wished to know what was happening.

Although the Rangers arrived too late to join the fighting, they witnessed the end of that first encounter at La Cabana. The British finally pushed most of the Spanish off the hill, with the defenders rolling their cannon into the great harbour and abandoning other items of equipment. Only a rump remained, well-entrenched and too stubborn to retreat.

"We've to remain on La Cabana until reinforcements arrive," Kennedy informed the Rangers. He looked around. "At least there is a modicum of a breeze here, away from that terrible heat further down."

The Rangers dug in five-hundred yards from the Spanish,

watched the enemy, and held their position on La Cabana until the 10th of June when a company of Lights relieved them.

"Have all the Spanish gone?" a cheerful corporal asked.

"No," MacKim said. "Some are holding on up on the ridge."

"We'll soon shift them," the corporal said.

Within hours, engineers and gunners began digging into the thin soil and creating artillery emplacements.

"What's the objective?" MacKim asked a gunner.

"El Morro Castle," the artilleryman said. "Until we take El Morro, we can't get into the harbour, and if we don't get into the harbour, the first hurricane of the season will play the devil with our ships. That castle is the key to Cuba. We'll invest the landward side and leave the coast to the Navy."

The now-familiar sound of naval broadsides soon came from the west as Admiral Pocock led his ships to the attack. "Heavy gunfire, there," MacKim said. With a nod from Kennedy, he climbed a tree for a better view.

"The Navy is busy," MacKim reported. The firing lasted for hours as the Navy bombarded the forts of Chorera and St Lazaro on the opposite side of Havana. The Navy hammered the garrisons and any supporting troops who occupied the forest behind the forts.

"The ships are bombarding Havana as well." MacKim watched a couple of bomb ketches fire their mortars from close inshore, the shells arcing up over Havana's walls to explode in the northern quarter of the city.

He remembered the British bombardment of Quebec back in 1759, and the terrible destruction that had caused.

I haven't forgotten you, Claudette, although I'll wager that you have forgotten me.

When the cannonade beyond Havana ended, there was a short period of silence, then some irregular musketry. MacKim learned later that the Spanish had evacuated the fort of Chorera, and Admiral Pocock had sent the marines in temporary occupation.

MacKim started back as a musket ball smacked against the bole of his tree, followed by another that scored the bark beside his hand.

"MacKim!" Kennedy shouted. "Get down! The Spanish are getting restless!"

MacKim slid and clambered back down, barking some skin from his knuckles and knees on the way. "These boys on the ridge are too stubborn for my liking."

"These Spanish want to stay," Dickert reported. "They know that these heights are vital to Havana's defence."

"Captain Kennedy!" Ensign Regan huffed up. "Colonel Carleton sends his compliments, sir, and could your Rangers scout the Spanish defences."

"Good to see you again, Regan," Kennedy said. "My compliments to the colonel, and we will move directly."

"Here we go again." Parnell checked his flint.

"Let's have a look then, boys," Kennedy said. "We've fought the Canadians, French, Abenaki, and pirates. Let's show the Spanish what the Rangers can do."

"On you go, Rangers," the Lights cheered. "Do our work for us!"

The Rangers advanced along the wooded heights in extended order, moving from cover to cover as they came closer to the Spanish positions. The Spaniards had skirmishers out in front, native Cubans who knew the terrain as well as any Indian knew the North American woods, and who fought just as stubbornly to defend their land.

"This campaign might not be as easy as we had hoped," MacRae said, diving behind a tree as two musket balls burrowed into the ground at his feet.

"These Spanish are a dour breed," MacKim agreed. "They didn't conquer most of the Americas by being soft."

"They're on the flanks!" Kennedy said as he saw movement on the left. "MacKim, wheel your section to meet them!"

The Cuban militia came at speed, communicating with each other by hand signals as they slid through the leaves.

"Tree all!" MacKim roared. "Fire when you see a target!"

There was sudden silence except for the persistent hum of insects. MacKim waited, calling on all his reserves of patience. He knew the Cuban militia were out there, invisible in the foliage, and his Rangers were waiting.

When the fighting began, it was sudden, bloody, and brutal. A rush of men descended on Ranger Grainger, who fired one shot, then died as the militia hacked at him with broad-bladed machetes. MacKim fired a single shot, and before he fixed his bayonet, the militiamen had vanished back into the trees.

As if on a signal, the half-hidden Spanish position opened fire, with artillery blasting grapeshot towards the Rangers and half-seen men firing volleys of musketry.

"Retire, Rangers!" Kennedy ordered. "Back to our positions."

Faced with overwhelming firepower, the Rangers withdrew to lick their wounds as they sat in their original lines, with a growing respect for their Spanish and Cuban adversaries.

"We lost two dead and two wounded," Kennedy said. "We can't afford many more losses out here without any reinforcements."

"Aye, and the heat and disease have weakened us all," MacKim said.

"Parnell," Kennedy said. "Take a message to Colonel Carleton." Extracting his pen and ink from his pack, he wrote a short note. "Hand that to the colonel and tell him that the Spanish hold the summit ridge in some force still, with artillery and Cuban militia."

"Yes, sir," Parnell said, and slipped through the trees.

"Now we wait," Kennedy said. "And hope the Spanish don't counterattack tonight."

MacKim looked up at the ridge, wavering in the heat, and agreed. He could do no more.

21

Nighttime was always the worst, MacKim believed. During the day, he was busy looking after his men, marching, fighting, or creating a redoubt, but at night, most operations finished, and he had time to think.

That night was even worse than usual, for while MacKim tried to keep alert in case of a raid from the Cuban militia, his mind wandered. He remembered the death of his brother on Drummossie Moor, sixteen years ago, a murder that had begun his career in the Army. Then he thought of his passage of revenge as he hunted down the attackers and all the other men he had fought and killed in North America, and here in the hot Caribbean islands. He thought of Tayanita, the Indian woman he had loved and who had died in a sudden ambush, and he touched his head where the enemy had taken his scalp.

MacKim was only twenty-six and had been campaigning for four years. Now he was weary of death and suffering. A man could only accept so much horror in his life, and then he was surfeited. MacKim thought he had reached his limit. He did not want to see any more killing or hear the anguished scream of a man wounded beyond human endurance.

Please, God, he prayed for the first time in many months.

Please God, let this nightmare end soon. I am not a career soldier. I joined the Army for a purpose and have achieved that objective. Give me rest now, and a peaceful life. I want to come home to a smiling wife. I want to tend my own land and raise my own cattle.

For a moment, MacKim was home in the glen, with the friendly hills around him, as they had caressed a hundred generations of his family back to time immemorial.

MacKim jerked himself awake. He was a sergeant, damn it all! He had to set an example to his men, not fall asleep on the job.

What had awakened him? It must have been something out of the ordinary, or he would have continued to sleep.

"MacRae." MacKim tapped the man at his side. "Wake up. Something's out there. I'm checking the pickets."

Oxford lifted his musket as MacKim slid into his trench. "I heard something, too, sergeant." His eyes were huge in the night.

"Keep alert," MacKim said, and moved to the next man, a dim shadow in the night. "Danskin!"

But Danskin did not move. He stood at his post, his head neatly removed from his shoulders and placed at his feet.

"Oh, dear God in heaven!" MacKim raised his voice. "Stand to!"

The Rangers responded at once, men springing from sleep to face forward, each man checking that their neighbour was alive and awake. Only Danskin was dead. Danskin, the young man who spoke incessantly about his girl back in New Hampshire. Danskin the Johnny Raw with the eager expression on his face. Danskin, who would never see Julia again.

The Rangers remained alert the remainder of the night, their nerves jangling and each sound seemingly magnified until it became the footsteps of a hundred Cuban militiamen.

MacKim was not alone in greeting the dawn with relief.

"We're getting lax," Kennedy told them the following morning. "This island-hopping has blunted our edge. As of tonight, we stand picket in pairs, two hours on, with paroles and countersigns unique to the Rangers. We issue a challenge for any unidentified sound and shoot if there's no immediate response."

"What if it's only a lost redcoat?" MacKim asked.

"Then it's his own damned fool fault for blundering near our position," Kennedy said. "We're the Rangers, so let's get back to our best. That's all. Dismissed."

MacKim could not remember when he had seen Kennedy so angry and so upset.

"I liked Danskin," Kennedy said. "He was a decent man and due to be married. Fighting the French and Indians is one thing, but the Spanish or Cubans never threatened New Hampshire, and I don't know why Danskin died in this baking corner of hell."

"Sir!" Parnell slid beside them. "I have a message from Colonel Carleton."

"Spit it out, man!" It was evident that Kennedy had not yet recovered his temper.

"Colonel Carleton sends his compliments, sir, and would like to inform you that he will lead the Light Infantry and Grenadiers onto the La Cabana heights at one of the clock this afternoon."

"Thank the Lord for that," Kennedy said. "Does the colonel require a reply?"

"He didn't say, sir." Parnell looked slightly troubled.

"Alright. Pray carry my compliments to Colonel Carleton, thank him for his kindness, and inform him that Kennedy's Rangers will support him to our utmost extent."

MacKim watched Parnell return downhill. "I'll make sure the men are fed and watered," he said. "And ensure they have full knapsacks, sharp flints, and oiled muskets."

"After the murder of Danskin," Kennedy said grimly, "I don't think there's any chance of them being unprepared."

At one in the afternoon of the 11th, drums began to roll, and the Lights headed for the La Cabana Heights. Kennedy's

Rangers remained where they were, licking their wounds and watching for any incursions by the Cuban militia.

"Here comes Carleton," MacRae murmured, polishing his rifle. "Thank the Lord."

MacKim nodded. "Thank the Lord indeed." He had felt the strain of the previous night hanging over him, so his eyes were heavy and his heart still pounded. "Get ready, boys. The Spanish may try one last attack."

MacRae looked skyward as the weather broke, and a tropical storm threw torrential rain onto the soldiers. He opened his mouth to catch as much rain as he could. "Thank you, God," he said.

The Rangers settled down, with the pickets drawn into the main British line. The men watched their flanks as much as their front, apprehensive, yet ready.

The Grenadiers marched behind the Lights, a solid body of scarlet soldiers who were afraid of nobody. These men would march on whatever the opposition, and God help anybody and anything that stood in their way. The drums encouraged the advance; the flags acted as rallying points as the British thundered up the wooded slope. The enemy might kill them by the score or the hundred, but the Grenadiers would march on forever.

"Give the boys a hand, Rangers," Kennedy ordered quietly, and the Rangers began to inch forward, one tree at a time. They knew where the Spanish positions lay and expected opposition, so they moved warily, recalling the skills that had brought them survival and success against the Abenaki and Canadians.

MacKim saw the flicker of movement ahead and fired, ducking behind a tree to reload, knowing his men would cover him.

As he loaded, the first of the Lights made contact, with an individual musket shot coming from lower down the hill, followed by another, and then a confused spatter as the Spanish and Cuban militia replied.

"Push slowly, Rangers," Kennedy called. "Hold their attention while the Lights probe."

Taking a tree each, the Rangers aimed and fired, then loaded and moved forward to the next cover, never allowing the enemy to mark where they were.

The Spanish fought with volley fire while the Cuban militia flitted between the trees, replying with musketry. Now aware of the threat of the deadly machetes, the Rangers did not allow the Cubans to close, but fired at the first sign of movement.

"There go the Lights!" Dickert shouted as a ragged cheer came from their right.

"And the Grenadiers," MacRae added, as a more resounding roar followed.

The firing rose to a single rolling volley, and then there was a hammer of artillery and another cheer. Powder smoke rose, choking and white from the Rangers' right, for the teeming rain to press it down to the trees.

"The Grenadiers have charged," Kennedy said. "Follow me, Rangers!" He fixed his bayonet, stepped from behind his tree, and strode forward with his Rangers at his back.

MacKim felt the old elation of the charge as his Highland blood rose within him. Moving up a Caribbean hill in the heat was not the same as running across a Scottish moor in the mist and rain, but the result would be similar. He followed Kennedy, then broke into a run as the ancient Gaelic slogans burst unsummoned from his mouth. MacRae was at his side, eyes wide and mouth open as he ran towards the enemy. In a second, all the Rangers were charging, shouting, yelling, and cursing as the battle-lust overcame their fear.

"Rangers! First and always!" Butler gave his habitual cry.

"Danskin!" Oxford shouted. "Remember Danskin!"

A trio of Spanish soldiers fired from a hidden redoubt, but the Rangers leapt among them, firing and bayonetting in a frenzy, then moved on, leaving bloodied corpses in their wake.

While some Spanish tried to fight, the Cuban militia fled.

They were irregulars, not trained to contest regulars toe to toe, but masters of the ambush who killed lone sentries and fell on isolated parties. The Rangers killed any militia they caught, remembering Danskin. The conflict was short and merciless, and when it ended, the British held La Cabana.

MacKim stopped on the apex of the hill, panting as the sweat flowed into his eyes. "We took the hill," he said.

"We did, sergeant," a corporal of the Lights said in a thick West Country accent.

MacKim did not recognise his regimental insignia, but broke off a twist of tobacco and passed it over. "That's one step," he said.

The corporal nodded his thanks. Long-jawed and lean, he bore the marks of smallpox on his face and an old scar on the back of his hand. "That fort is next," he said, nodding to El Morro Castle. "Once we take that, Havana will fall." A sudden laugh lightened his eyes. "That will be a day to celebrate, bringing the treasure of the Spanish Main back to old England."

They stood side-by-side for a moment, men from the far reaches of Great Britain on a Caribbean hillside, sharing a moment of triumph amidst the smoke and agony of battle.

The rattle of drums interrupted their reverie. "That's the recall," the Light said. "God be with you, Ranger."

"And with you, Corporal."

They parted, and the moment was gone.

With La Cabana firmly in British hands, the engineers and artillerymen became the essential components of the Army.

As in the campaign on Martinico, the Navy sent agile seamen ashore to help drag the guns into position, and strange nautical curses and expressions echoed on the wooded slopes.

"The gun's starboard wheel is stuck, lads! Avast hauling!"

"Handsomely now, boys! Stand clear from under!"

Still at the forefront of the Army, Kennedy's Rangers helped the Lights form a defensive screen to keep the Cuban militia and Spanish regulars from delaying the work of the artillery. Once again, MacKim found himself crouching in cover, peering into the dark and hoping the enemy remained behind Havana's stone walls.

"Rangers!" Colonel Carleton appeared in person, a dashing figure with a feather in his tricorne hat and his attention everywhere at once. He stood erect on the very summit of the ridge as the sappers worked like demons at his back. "You have a fine view of El Morro from here."

"Yes, sir," Kennedy agreed.

Carleton borrowed Kennedy's telescope and surveyed the walls of the castle, then the blue waters of the harbour with the anchored ships, and then the spreading city beyond. "Havana will make a fine prize," he said, snapping shut the telescope. "A fine prize indeed." He handed the telescope back.

"I wish you to defend the guns for now," Carleton ordered. "The Lights will be on your immediate left."

"Yes, sir," Kennedy said.

"Very shortly," Carleton continued, "I'll have you and your men survey the defences of El Morro. That castle is crucial to the campaign. As long as it holds out, we cannot progress."

MacKim listened as Carleton explained the strategy that even the youngest Johnny Raw already knew.

"It's all about time, Kennedy," Carleton said, as if revealing a great secret. "We must take Havana before the hurricane season makes our ship's position here untenable, or disease ravages our forces to such an extent that we are too weak to fight."

MacKim nodded. Yellow jack was already decimating the British Army in Cuba and spreading through the fleet. The longer the British remained, the weaker they would become. All the Spanish had to do was hold on, and their victory was assured.

At that period, nobody realised that the mosquitoes carried both malaria and yellow fever. However, some observant men discovered that the lower, damper areas of the tropics were the unhealthiest. Current thought blamed malignant air for spreading the killer diseases that reduced healthy regiments to skeletons within a few months.

"We have until the middle of August at the latest," Carleton said. "After that, the seasonal hurricanes will render this coast untenable for the fleet and unless we have access to that harbour," he nodded downwards towards Havana, "we will have to abandon this enterprise."

The engineers swore as they worked along the ridge, for as well as having to hack down the thick trees, they found another problem.

"We can't dig any depth in this," an officer said. "Look at it! Half an inch of soil, and then we hit solid rock."

"The Spanish had artillery here," MacKim said.

"The Spanish had light field pieces," the gunner corrected. "We need siege artillery, 24 and 32-pounders. We need to protect them. We'll need fascines by the hundred if we can't dig down."

The Spanish soon became aware of the British artillery, and El Morro's guns probed the besiegers' lines. The initial cannon fire was short, with the heavy iron balls landing on the facing slope, but the Spanish soon found the range. The sappers cursed, ducking as Spanish cannonballs fell among them.

Admiral Pocock countered the Spanish threat by a diversionary attack, sending two bomb ketches, *Basilisk* and *Thunder*, to shell El Morro. Simultaneously, a naval squadron demonstrated off the harbour entrance, drawing Spanish fire from the struggling gunners on La Cabana.

The siege stagnated into an artillery duel, with both sides hammering at the other. The Royal Artillery formed a howitzer battery, firing at the Spanish shipping, and forced them deeper into the harbour. The Spanish in the castle, with the warships, retaliated by firing into La Cabana, causing few casualties, but disrupting the work and keeping the men on edge.

"Sweet Lord!" an artilleryman swore as a roundshot ripped

through the trees above him. "Whoever said that the Spanish could not fight was a damned liar! I'd like to bring him here for half an hour, wouldn't I just?"

As the gun emplacements took place, with mortar batteries on the shore and lines of fascines along the flanks to protect both gunners and infantry from the Spanish shot, the Rangers patrolled without incident. Kennedy told them that William Keppel had taken personal charge of the siege of El Morro. "He's Lord Albemarle's brother," Kennedy explained. "The powers that be in Britain want to ensure that the officers in charge don't fall out, as they did in a previous campaign, so they're all related."

"Keep it in the family then," Parnell said. "Like incest."

"Sir." Ensign Mowat appeared once more.

"Ah, Mowat," Kennedy forced a smile. "We haven't seen you since Martinico. What bad news have you brought this time?"

"Sir." Mowat looked pale with fever and sported a bloody bandage around his wrist. "Major General Keppel sends his regards, sir, and could you reconnoitre the walls of El Morro."

Kennedy nodded. "Pray convey my respects to the general and tell him the Rangers will be there." He raised his eyebrows at MacKim. "What's left of us."

22

Kennedy led the Rangers towards El Morro, creeping through the thick wood with its near-impenetrable undergrowth. With the sun filtering through the leaves, everything appeared as a green haze, in which swarms of insects hung, constantly moving, whining black dots that swooped to bite and sting any exposed flesh.

"This woodland is a defence all of its own," Kennedy said. "I thought it might conceal our attack, but it will hamper any advance."

"Like the Highlanders at Ticonderoga," MacKim agreed.[1]

They moved closer, alert for any roving pickets of Cuban militia, careful not to be seen by sentries on the walls above.

"That parapet isn't as strong as it looks," Kennedy said. "It's old; older than Quebec or Montreal, I think."

MacKim nodded. "Maybe from the early days of the Spanish settlement."

"Maybe," Kennedy said. "It's thin and built of masonry, with no earth to absorb our balls. I doubt it would stand a prolonged bombardment from siege artillery."

"We'd have to get the guns fairly close," MacKim said.

"We have the old Spanish positions on at La Cabana, the entrenchments the sappers are having such fun with."

"That's probably a good place to start," Kennedy said. "The gunners will know best. I see this fort as a triangle of stone, with powerful bastions."

MacKim scribbled notes, cursing the necessity of carrying pen, ink, and paper on a scouting expedition. "Got that, sir."

"About forty pieces of artillery," Kennedy continued. "I've heard the Spanish call them the twelve apostles." He grinned. "Maybe the Spanish can't count any higher than twelve."

"Forty is not too bad," MacKim said. "We faced more at Quebec and Martinico."

"It all depends on the quality of the defenders and their commander," Kennedy said. "I reckon the heaviest Spanish heaviest guns are 32-pounders, or maybe even 36-pounders."

They moved on, keeping level with the walls, but on the opposite side of a defensive ditch. The Spanish had erected a covered way, or rampart, on the British side, but fortunately, they only had intermittent patrols. Kennedy and MacKim inched closer and mounted the rampart to inspect the defences.

"Look at that!" MacKim exclaimed. The bank of the ditch on the El Morro side had been hacked from the living rock, making it impossible for British sappers to dig approach trenches underneath. "How the devil can we take this place?"

Kennedy indicated the ditch. "Why has that not filled with seawater? We're on the coast; the sea should run straight in there."

"The Spanish must have left a barrier," MacKim said.

"If there's a barrier to the sea, then that gives us a bridge across the ditch," Kennedy pointed out.

The Spanish on the walls were becoming curious, with one man lifting a telescope to observe the woods beyond the ditch.

"He's seen something moving," MacKim said.

The Spaniard shouted a challenge, and a sergeant bustled up, grabbed the telescope, and scanned the woods.

"Lie down," Kennedy ordered as a section of smartly dressed Spanish soldiers arrived and formed into a line, with every man facing his front. No sooner had MacKim lain down than the Spanish fired a volley, with musket balls cutting through leaves and branches all around the Rangers, but too high to be dangerous.

"Keep still," Kennedy whispered as the sergeant continued to study the woodland. The lone sentry returned, then both marched away, and the Rangers moved on.

They were close enough to the coast to hear the surf breaking on rocks. Thorny branches protruded over the ditch and finally exploded in a riot of shrubbery and bushes that completely concealed the defences and even sent groping fingers onto the base of the wall.

"Our boys will be torn to shreds hacking through this," MacKim said as he disentangled himself from a monster branch complete with an array of hooked thorns.

"Maybe." Kennedy looked thoughtful. "Follow me, sergeant." He inched forward until he reached the edge of the ditch. The ground plunged downward to a tangle of thorns and weeds at the bottom, while the opposite slope was sheer rock stretching to the base of the fort.

"We'll need hundreds of fascines to fill that," MacKim opined. "It must be seventy feet deep." He imagined the scene as British troops descended the ditch and tried to clamber up the other side as the Spanish fired into them.

Without replying, Kennedy inched along the edge of the ditch, heading to the profusion of vegetation at the end. He stopped, grunted, and stopped.

"Got them, MacKim! Look! The ditch ends here. We were correct; the Spanish have left a shelf at the coastal side to keep out the sea."

"That's their weakness," MacKim said.

"It could be," Kennedy agreed with satisfaction. "It could well be."

They stared at the slender ridge for some time, contemplating an assaulting force creeping across, necessarily in single file and under fire from the defenders.

"That's our way in," Kennedy said, "but it will take brave men to cross that."

"It would be a slaughter," MacKim agreed.

"Come on, MacKim." Kennedy inched back from the ditch. "Our duty is to scout and report. The general makes the decisions."

※

As the gunners and sappers continued to hack out batteries opposite El Morro, the Navy was not idle. Their original anchorage at the mouth of the River Coximar was adequate in fair weather, but dangerously exposed if a storm arrived, so Admiral Pocock sent light craft to scout for a safer harbour. Simultaneously, General Albemarle wished for a diversion to draw the Spanish attention from El Morro, using both the Army and Navy to probe west of Havana.

Accordingly, on the 15th of June 1762, Colonel Carleton led two-thousand Light Infantry and Grenadiers, plus eight-hundred Marines to the mouth of the River Chorera, a few miles west of Havana. When Carleton's men found the Chorera water sweet and plentiful in an island that seemed short of that commodity, they immediately set up camp. The Navy also found a safer anchorage than Coximar, which reduced Pocock's anxiety with the hurricane season fast approaching.

Meanwhile, the British gun ketches continued to bombard Havana, with the Royal Artillery erecting a mortar battery on the shore.

※

"THINGS ARE MOVING," MACKIM SAID AS THE SPANISH IN Havana harbour fired another volley and a score of cannonballs hammered the woods. One thirty-two-pound ball smashed into the barrier of fascines around the nearest gun emplacement, sending wood splinters into the sky. El Morro joined in the bombardment, with the heavy balls thundering through the trees.

"Who is under siege here," Parnell asked. "Us or them?"

"Both," MacKim replied. "Somebody told me once that the Spanish in the Americas couldn't fight."

"Send that liar to me," MacRae said. "I'll blacken his eyes for him."

"They've got the range of the Cabana Heights perfectly," MacKim said.

"So they should," Kennedy said. "They've had two-hundred years to perfect it." He ducked as the Spanish guns roared again.

As men filled sandbags and created fascines at the Chorera bridgehead, ships transported the finished articles to the mouth of the River Coximar. From there, working parties of seamen, soldiers, marines, and others carried them to where the sappers toiled to make gun emplacements. While hundreds of sweating sailors sliced at the trees to create roadways, others dragged the heavy siege artillery along these rough tracks. The Army listened to the seamen chanting shanties and exchanging curses and banter in a language only sailors could understand. It was two miles from the ships at Coximar to the gun batteries, and the seamen dragged the guns every inch.

"We're lucky to avoid the labouring," Dickert said.

"We're too valuable," Butler told him seriously. "There's nobody else who can scout like the Rangers."

Parnell grunted and spat onto the dry ground. "Mebbe. The 60th Royal Americans are nearly as good, and some units of the Lights."

"Nearly," Butler said. "But we are the best. Rangers, first and always."

On the Spanish side, boatmen ferried supplies to El Morro from Havana. The Spanish changed the garrison every two days, ensuring the soldiers and gunners did not endure the Royal Naval bombardment for too long. The castle held out, stubborn and enduring, stalling the British advance, and Admiral Pocock cast worried eyes at the skies, wondering when the hurricanes would arrive.

In the meantime, the weather alternated from tremendous heat that felled men with sunstroke, and sudden and heavy tropical rain that hammered down on the workers and filled the emplacements with warm water. One day, a sudden storm caught everybody by surprise, and a lightning bolt set a Spanish ship ablaze.

"Maybe the disease and the climate are fighting on the Spanish side," MacRae said, "but God's sending his thunderbolts to help us."

Patrolling in the ground between the artillery of both sides, the Rangers watched the fire arc above them, dodged the balls that fell short, and perfected their pragmatism.

"The Spanish Battery is coming on well," MacKim said to Kennedy.

"The sappers are working like Trojans," Kennedy agreed. "Let's hope the hurricanes are late this season."

Every man on the British side referred to the main British gun emplacement as the Spanish Battery, mainly because it was situated on the same spot as the battery the Lights had captured from its original Spanish garrison.

Every morning, men checked the sky, dreading the onset of the hurricane season, and then looked over their colleagues, asking who had fallen sick. Every day, men carried off their comrades to the hospital tents and hospital ships. Few returned to duty as fever thinned the ranks of the Army and Navy.

Before dawn on the 29th of June, the Spanish struck back.

"I HEAR SOMETHING," PARNELL SAID.

"Pass the word," MacKim alerted the Rangers. If Parnell said he had heard something, then there was a reason for alarm.

The Rangers woke and struggled to their positions, rubbing their eyes and checking their weapons. They stared into the dark, listening for anything untoward. In the night, ears were as important as eyes, and sometimes one's sense of smell was enough. The whiff of tobacco or the stench of an unwashed body could give a man away as much as the crunch of clumsy feet on crumpled leaves.

Dickert fired first. Kennedy's standing orders were to fire immediately when they saw anything suspicious, rather than waiting for confirmation or orders. Dickert's muzzle flare cracked open the dark, and for an instant, MacKim saw the tangled undergrowth with the cleared spaces the Rangers had hacked to create a firing zone. If the Cubans or Spanish blundered into these areas, the Rangers knew the range to an inch. Now one Cuban militiaman was dead even before he knew the Rangers were awake.

Dickert's shot had hardly faded when the Spanish and Cubans charged forward. MacKim did not know if they intended a quick raid to disrupt the gun emplacements or a fully fledged assault. He only saw the rapidly advancing men, and aimed, fired, and quickly reloaded.

"Here they come, boy!" Dickert shouted.

"Rangers, first and always!"

A force of Lights joined the Rangers, some fully dressed and ready, others in their shirts, but with muskets oiled and loaded. They came from various regiments, each under their own unit commanders, but united in a cohesive whole.

Commands snapped out.

"Extended order!"

"Form a skirmishing line!"

"Fire when ready, Forty-Twa!"

"Extend your right flank, sergeant!"

"Come on, the 90th!"

The Lights and Rangers met the attack with levelled muskets, not firing in volleys by section, but as individuals, targeting any enemy who exposed himself.

The initial Spanish rush faltered in the face of the British musketry, with men falling here and there. A hush descended, broken by the agonised groaning of a wounded man.

"They've fallen back!" Oxford reported.

"Stay where you are, Rangers!" Kennedy ordered. "Don't let them draw you out. Wait for the signal!"

Only when the drums tapped the advance did the British move forward, each man supporting his neighbour and each section supporting the next.

"We've repelled them," a lanky major said. "Halt, boys, and reload."

The British learned from a wounded prisoner that the Spanish had been over 250 strong, a diverse force of seamen and soldiers. While one Spanish body attacked the gun emplacements, a much larger company filed out of El Morro to destroy the British mortars that battered Havana. In both cases, the British infantry repelled the attacks, with over seventy Spanish casualties and less than ten British.

"Hot work," MacKim said as the powder smoke died away, leaving only the memories and the sobbing cries of the wounded.

"Whoever said the Spanish could not fight never met them," Parnell said. "They are as brave as any men I've ever met."

"Who are those lads?" Parnell asked as a new force joined the British Army. "Have we recruited the locals?"

Kennedy shook his head. "Slave labour," he said. "Lord Albemarle bought five-hundred black slaves at Martinico and Antigua to help us carry the ammunition."[2] MacKim watched the slaves toiling up the track, carrying cannonballs and munitions for the besiegers. He wondered how they felt, working in perpetual bondage, and then grunted. He could not afford to think of others' problems.

"Poor buggers," the soft-hearted MacRae said. "Our lives are bad enough."

MacKim gave a start when he saw a familiar face. Benjamin trudged past, bowed under the weight of a keg of gunpowder. One second, MacKim had a clear view of the man's sweating face, and then he was gone, lost in the anonymity of the mass.

※

On the 1ST of July, 1762, the British began their bombardment of El Morro. After weeks of hard labour, the gun emplacements were complete and the siege artillery in place, with a stock of balls and powder. The gunners had worked out their angles and stood ready, staring at the target as the dawn light grew.

"What are they waiting for, sergeant?" Oxford asked. "Why don't they fire?"

"They'll have their reasons," MacKim said. "The generals don't tell me what they plan."

The sudden hammer of gunfire from the coast answered Oxford's question.

"There we are," MacKim said. "The artillerymen were waiting for the Navy to begin."

"Why?" Oxford asked.

"The Navy's the senior service." MacKim was tiring of Oxford's questions. "Or some other reason. Just shut your mouth, watch for a Spanish counter attack, and do your duty."

Three weeks previously, Captain Hervey of HMS *Dragon* had surveyed the seaward base of El Morro and suggested that the Navy could bombard the castle. Despite doubts by both Albemarle and Commodore Keppel, Admiral Pocock decided to press ahead with the idea. A further reconnaissance had found deep water, but failed to ascertain whether the Navy could elevate their cannon sufficiently to batter at the castle walls. Now, the Royal Navy would test Hervey's theory.

While four land-based batteries opened up on El Morro, the Royal Navy attacked by sea. From his position in front of the gun batteries, MacKim could watch the progress of the sea battle.

Four battleships approached the castle, and after working with the Navy so long, MacKim recognised them. The leading vessel was Captain James Campbell's 64-gun HMS *Stirling Castle*, followed by Captain Hervey's 74-gun HMS *Dragon*, with the 74-gun HMS *Cambridge* and the smaller 68-gun HMS *Marlborough*. As they approached, *Dragon* slowed.

"*Dragon*'s lost the wind," MacRae murmured.

"Come on, lads," MacKim urged as the Spanish Battery beside him opened fire, and the iron shot howled towards El Morro. "That's not the Royal Navy I know!"

"That ship there, *Stirling Castle*." Kennedy had joined MacKim. "She is meant to lead the line and draw fire so the others can get closer and bombard the castle."

"Is she?" MacKim had to shout above the roar of the land guns as El Morro returned fire. "She's not doing well at present!"

Stirling Castle seemed reluctant to sail, allowing the other ships to brave the castle's guns while she fell to the rear.

"What the devil is she playing at? Come on, Captain Campbell! Get ahead!" MacKim began to shout. "Bloody Campbells! They fought against us at Culloden as well!"

"Wrong war," Kennedy reminded sharply.

"Aye, but same Campbells," MacKim said as the old memories resurfaced.

With *Stirling Castle* well to the rear and out of the firing line, the remaining three ships braved El Morro's fire to close with the fort. Their broadsides hammered out, covering everything with a blanket of grey-white smoke.

"Go on, tarry-backs!" MacKim encouraged.

Under attack from two sides, the garrison of El Morro fought back, with the fort's guns firing like demons.

"Damn this smoke," Kennedy said. "I can only see the tops of the masts!" He extended his telescope for a better view. "I don't think the ships' broadsides are effective."

"*Stirling Castle* is well out of it," MacKim said. "I think Campbell is afraid."

"Forget her," Kennedy advised. "Oh, Jesus! One ship's lost her topmast. It's tumbling down, taking a whole pile of rigging with it."

"Which ship?"

"Damned if I can see in the smoke," Kennedy said. "I can only see bits of masts and sails protruding. There's another hit on our ships, and another! The Spanish are fighting hard!"

Kennedy was correct. The ships could not elevate their guns sufficiently to damage El Morro, with their broadsides wasted on the cliff on which the castle stood, while the Spanish fire caused havoc on the spars, sails, and rigging of the attackers. The Spanish fire also hit the decks of the British ships, with HMS *Cambridge*, in the lead, having some guns dismounted.

MacKim could only imagine the carnage on deck as the thirty-six-pound shot crashed into the timber, sending deadly splinters flying, throwing cannon around, and knocking spars down to arrow onto the crowds of men below.

"Look, *Dragon*'s hit a rock! Captain Hervey's aground! The Spanish can pound her to pieces; God rot them!" Kennedy was visibly upset. "Get out of there, lads; the fort's murdering you!"

"Brave men," MacKim said, and turned to the land-based battery. "Go on, lads! Pound El Morro! Help the Navy!"

"*Dragon*'s signalling something." Kennedy focussed his telescope on the flags fluttering from the stranded ship. "Look there, a boat sailing from *Trent* to *Cambridge*. There's an officer on board...her captain, I think. He must be taking command!"

"Here comes *Stirling Castle* now," MacKim said. "Limping

along as if next Tuesday will do. You're late, Campbell, you yellow bastard!"

"He's trying to help *Dragon*," Kennedy said.

Stirling Castle fussed around the stranded ship for the next few moments, but Hervey seemed to despise Campbell's assistance and kedged herself away from danger with a stream anchor. *Dragon* was wounded and battered, but safe.

After hours of unequal combat and three of the British ships damaged, Commodore Keppel ordered them to withdraw. Hervey's ships limped away, damaged and frustrated, but still firing; still the Royal Navy.

"Look," Kennedy said, handing MacKim his telescope. "There's blood dripping from *Cambridge*'s scuppers." [3]MacKim nodded, depressed by the reverse. He was not used to witnessing the Navy fail.

"At least they diverted attention from the land batteries." Kennedy sought some consolation for the sacrifice of so many seamen.

"That's true," MacKim said. "But the Spanish won that round. We can't take El Morro by sea, so it all depends on the land batteries now."

"At least the Royal Artillery are successful," MacKim said.

The primary British batteries—the Spanish or William's Battery and the Grand Battery with their 24-pounders and thirteen-inch, ten-inch, and Royal Mortars—fired continually. The supporting artillery on the Left Parallel and Beach Batteries fired less often. Although the Spanish had more numerous guns, they were mostly lighter pieces, six or 12-pounders and a single eight-inch mortar. The British barrage seemed to have put their heavy guns out of action. The British artillery was also better protected by earth-filled sandbags and fascines, while the Spanish sheltered behind thin masonry walls, vulnerable to heavy cannon.

"Carry on, lads!" MacKim encouraged.

Behind him, the most significant British battery—the Grand Battery—continued to hammer at El Morro, with its eight 24-

pounders firing solid shot at the stone walls. Simultaneously, the two thirteen-inch mortars hurled shells inside the fort.

By evening, the fire from both sides was slackening. The Grand and Spanish Batteries had dismounted many of El Morro's guns, while the British were running short of ammunition, despite the constant column of seamen carrying powder and ball from the base at the Coximar River.

"Get some rest now, lads," Kennedy ordered. The constant hammer of artillery, combined with the sun, had given most of the Rangers headaches, which the lack of water did not help. "It should be a quieter night while the gunners replenish their ammunition."

MacKim stared at El Morro. Despite the damage the British had caused, the Spanish flag hung proudly above the smoke, and Spanish soldiers manned the battlements. With every day precious, the rugged Spanish defence seemed to defy everything Albemarle and Pocock threw at them.

23

With his head pounding, MacKim found it hard to sleep. Although the Rangers had built themselves a string of small redoubts, using the felled trees for shelter and adding a few stolen fascines and sandbags to plug any gaps, they knew that a hit from a Spanish cannonball could splinter their defences. They lay uneasily as the artillerymen shouted orders to one another, and El Morro fired the occasional shot to disrupt the besieger's work.

"If I were the Spanish commander," Kennedy said, joining MacKim in his post, "I'd send out a raiding party tonight."

Both men blinked through eyes that were red-rimmed and irritated with powder smoke.

"We'll watch in shifts," MacKim said. "The gunners will be tired after yesterday."

With four hours on and four hours off, the Rangers endured the night, no longer startled by unfamiliar animals. It was early in the morning when Parnell reported hearing a sound.

"Where?" MacKim asked.

"To the right," Parnell said. "In front of the Spanish Battery."

"Sit tight, and I'll look. The parole will be New and the countersign Hampshire." Taking a deep breath, MacKim slid into the dark. He moved forward slowly, listening for any sounds.

MacKim heard an artillery sentry cough nervously and smelled the pipe tobacco of a second sentinel. He moved on and stopped, sniffing the air.

Somebody's close. I can smell human sweat.

MacKim lay quiet with his eyes probing into the dark.

"New!" The word was whispered. "New!"

"Hampshire," MacKim replied softly.

Kennedy joined him. "Anything?"

"I smell somebody," MacKim said.

They moved on, one at a time, covering each other as they probed into the undergrowth.

"Look!" Kennedy hissed. Immediately underneath the Spanish Battery, somebody had placed two kegs of gunpowder, with a trail of coarse black powder reaching towards El Morro. "That's the trick we used during the siege of Quebec. They're going to try and destroy our powder magazine."

"Clever devils." MacKim began to brush away the gunpowder just as he saw a sudden flare from ahead. "They've lit the fuse!"

"Break the trail!" Kennedy said quickly, and both Rangers brushed away the powder, hoping that the dark hid no more trails. The bark of a musket sounded from the left, and the muzzle flare flashed through the trees.

"They're close!" MacKim said as a ball whizzed past his head. He glanced at the kegs of gunpowder and swore. It was unlikely that a lead ball could ignite the powder, but he did not wish to take the chance. He fired at the muzzle flash, lifted a keg of powder, and threw it towards the enemy. He had no intention of hitting the Spanish, only of throwing the gunpowder as far from him as possible.

Kennedy followed his example with the second keg, and then they dropped into cover as British sentries and Spanish raiders opened fire for a hectic few moments.

When the firing died away, MacKim and Kennedy checked for further kegs and made their way back to the Rangers.

"These Spanish are a clever people," MacKim said.

"They've been in Cuba for centuries," Kennedy said. "They won't give it up to us without a fight." He shook his head. "This campaign is far from over, and the hurricane season is getting closer every day. If we don't get the ships into Havana harbour soon, we'll have to abandon the enterprise."

MacKim looked upward. "I never thought I'd miss the Scottish weather, but I'd do anything for a cold downpour just now. When did it last rain?"

"About two weeks ago," Kennedy said. "Get some sleep."

As MacKim lay on the hard ground, his head pounded with the day's bombardment; yet, when he closed his eyes, he could still see Benjamin's sweating face as he toiled up the steep hill with a keg of gunpowder on his back.

※

"Fire! The Grand Battery is alight!"

MacKim struggled from a nightmare and stared as the flames rose from the Grand Battery, with smoke pale in the heated air.

"What's happened, sergeant?" Oxford asked.

"How the devil should I know, Oxford. Try and find some water before the blasted thing spreads!"

"Sparks from the guns ignited the wooden parapet!" a gunnery officer cried. "We've had days of hot sun, and that, combined with the heat the guns generate, made the place vulnerable."

"Rangers!" Kennedy shouted. "Help the gunners! MacKim, take your section to beat out the flames. Parnell, your section can take over the perimeter. My boys, go and fetch water!"

As the gunners and Rangers tried to keep the gunpowder clear of the flames, the fire strengthened, enveloping most of the battery and sending coils of smoke skyward.

MacKim had never been in such an arid environment as Cuba. Kindle-dry, the wood burned with a fierce crackle, spreading to the fascines and the structure of the Grand Redoubt, the largest and most effective of the British gun emplacements.

High on the ridge, the British struggled to get sufficient water for the men's daily needs, let alone find extra to put out a large and spreading fire. Sweating men had to carry every pint for two hot miles from the Coximar River.

"Use half the drinking water," MacKim ordered as the gunners cleared away the last of the gunpowder. "Haul the fasces away to make a firebreak!"

However hard the British struggled, the flames were faster, leaping from fascine to fascine, smouldering and then breaking out again a few feet away as a treacherous wind carried red-hot sparks. As they observed the flames, El Morro's garrison increased their rate of fire to bombard the now-silent Grand Battery and add to the difficulties.

"We can't save it," a sweating, smoke-streaked gunnery officer said as the fire erupted for the fourth time. "We've lost the Grand Battery."

MacKim swore. He wondered if the fire had been an accident or if some Cuban or Spanish raiding party had set light to the timber the previous night.

The artillery officer looked close to tears. "We've done all we can do," he said. "We've used water and earth, but the fire has taken hold where water cannot reach it." He shook his head. "That seventeen days' labour by five-hundred men—gone in one day."

"We can rebuild it," MacKim reminded him. "The five-hundred men are still here."

"Maybe," the officer replied. "One day's bombardment was amazingly successful. Three more days like that, and we'd be in El Morro."

"There are other batteries," MacKim said. "And the Grand

Battery is not totally destroyed. There are two embrasures on the right remaining."

"Yes, and the mortar position on the left." The officer recovered some of his composure. He sighed. "We'll carry on as best we can."

After the failure of the naval bombardment, the loss of the Grand Battery was doubly difficult. Augmenting the constant loss of men to disease, the disasters depressed some of the men.

"We'd be best to leave now," Oxford said. "We've done all we can."

MacKim thrust his face hard against Oxford's nose. "I'll tell you when we'll leave, private. We'll leave when we've captured Havana and not before. Now get out on picket duty, you bloody Johnny Raw!"

Kennedy had been watching. "The lad has a point," he said quietly, pushing tobacco into the bowl of his pipe. "That's two victories in a row the Spanish can celebrate. If they carry on like this, we can kiss goodbye to Cuba. I hear Albemarle has already given up the plan to take Louisiana from the French."

"Do you think the Spanish caused the fire?" MacKim asked.

"Undoubtedly," Kennedy said. "Don't you?"

"I do," MacKim said.

"That's another success to them," Kennedy slumped down. "They only have to delay us until the hurricane season," he reminded.

With the Grand Battery out of action, the garrison of El Morro strengthened their defences, remounted the guns the British had previously knocked out, and increased their rate of fire. They also mounted several offensive patrols to hit the British besiegers and make life dangerous for the British pickets.

Even more worrying was the disease that ravaged the British forces. The Army losses mounted daily, so the Navy had to strip their crews of seamen to man the guns and carry supplies to the besieging lines.

"We're withdrawing from Guanabacoa," Kennedy reported.

"Why? Have the Spanish attacked?"

Kennedy shook his head. "Not a bit of it. What the Frenchies and Spanish cannot do, the fever has done. We're losing so many men to disease, we can't afford to remain there. We have to maintain our force at La Cabana in strength." He lowered his voice. "I heard that Lieutenant-General Elliot has only four-hundred fit men from a force of two and a half thousand."

MacKim grunted. "It's the bad air at Guanabacoa," he said. "It's low-lying and swampy. That's what malaria means, of course —bad air. It affects the men at night."

Kennedy nodded. "The generals should have known that. We'll have to avoid the swamps and keep on the high ground."

"A bit late for the men who are sick or those who have died," MacKim said. "This campaign is not going well."

Despite the losses from fever, the artillerymen slowly regained the initiative. They hacked out more redoubts and replaced the guns they had lost to increase the numbers hammering at El Morro. With the help of the Navy, the engineers and artillerymen rebuilt the Grand Battery, renaming it the Valiant's Battery after HMS *Valiant*. The giant captain of that ship, Adam Duncan, was frequently on shore, encouraging his men and carrying sandbags as if they were nothing.

Sheer perseverance told, and one by one, the British cannon knocked out the Spanish guns. The crash of artillery was a constant, with the cannon firing ten times an hour, sixteen hours a day.

"Why are you adjusting the range?" MacKim asked as the nearest gunner altered his cannon.

The artilleryman snorted. "You're not very clever, are you, green lobster? When the guns fire in the heat of the day and then fires on the same range at night, the alteration in temperature makes the balls fall short. We have to compensate."

MacKim nodded, adding that fact to his store of knowledge.

By the middle of July, the Spanish only had a handful of

working cannon in El Morro, with none on the northeast bastion, the corner closest to the sea.

"We'll be assaulting soon," Kennedy told the Rangers. "One final effort, boys, and this siege will be over."

As the cannons exchanged fire, the engineers enlarged the British lines, using the labour of soldiers, Marines, sailors, and slaves to create a long breastwork of sandbags and fascines opposite El Morro, facing the castle ditch and covered way. The 40th Regiment put aside their muskets to make gabions, while others built mantelets – mobile shields. The Navy brought in bales of cotton to add to the defences, and day by day, the British batteries grew more formidable. Unable to dig into the thin soil, the engineers and artillery built the barriers above ground, daring the Spanish to knock them down.

With the distance between the two forces narrowed to a hundred yards or less, the British and Spanish troops blasted each other at short range. Mortars fired their savage shells over the walls, and the marksmen of each army became the most effective soldiers.

Kennedy ducked as a Spanish ball whistled past him. "These Spaniards are getting too good now," he said. "MacKim!"

"Sir." MacKim arrived, keeping his head below the parapet. Another Spanish ball thudded into the fascine a foot away.

"I want your section to keep those Spanish marksmen at bay; nothing else. No picket duty, no water-carrying duty. You have the finest marksmen with the most accurate rifles in the British Army."

MacKim grinned. "That's the sort of order my men like, sir."

"Order them to find the best cover they can and fire whenever they see the enemy. I want the Spanish to be so scared of the Rangers that they leave us alone."

MacKim's marksmen were already a breed apart, but Kennedy's order gave them free rein to follow their natural hunting instincts.

Ignoring the Standing Orders, roll-calls, and most of the

uniform requirements of the British Army, MacKim's riflemen made their niche in the British lines. They dressed like scarecrows, carved out hides from where they could observe the Spanish on El Morro, and began a personal campaign that took a steady toll on the enemy.

"I got two today," MacRae said in satisfaction. "One sergeant with a flamboyant moustache and a Cuban militiaman who was relieving himself over the parapet."

"Three for me." Dickert gave his quiet smile. "Two sentries with one shot." When MacRae showed professional interest, Dickert explained further. "I watched them on their rounds, and there was one spot where they crossed each other's beat. I waited until they were lined up and bang! I got both through the head."

MacRae gave grudging approval. "And the third?"

"Oh, he was a fool who shouted threats at us and fired his musket. I got him as he reloaded."

Parnell was quieter. He rarely mentioned his kills, except one day when he raised his head. "I got an officer," he said. "He was shouting at his men, really yelling and roaring, so I blew his head off."

"You probably raised the morale of the fort doing that," Dickert said.

Parnell began to clean his rifle, saying no more.

As MacKim's marksmen continued their campaign, the Spanish opposite the Rangers' section of breastwork became wary and rarely showed themselves. Other units asked for the Rangers riflemen, and their reputation grew.

The besiegers stuffed fascines into the gabions and advanced the saps towards the walls of El Morro, step by dangerous step, with the Spanish musket men trying to pick them off.

As the siege continued, the slaves worked beside the British soldiers, ate British Army rations, and slept under the canvas of British Army tents, yet lived in a different world behind a screen of armed sentries. When MacKim patrolled near their quarters, he sometimes heard them singing, the tunes mournful, yet strangely moving, although he did not understand the words.

They're homesick, MacKim told himself. *They're singing songs about the home they left behind.*

That realisation brought memories of the Highland glen and the mist drifting across the rugged hills.

No. I'll weaken myself if I allow such thoughts.

MacKim lingered near the slaves, looking for Benjamin among the toiling men.

"What are you doing here, soldier?" The overseer possessed a weather-tanned face and the accent of Barbados.

"Watching for the enemy." MacKim disliked the man on sight.

"Well, there's none here. Be off with you."

MacKim looked the man up and down. Taller than MacKim by a head, the overseer was beefy, with imperious blue eyes and the attitude of a man used to being obeyed. MacKim decided to remain a little longer. He found a seat on a tree stump and began to stuff tobacco into the bowl of his pipe.

"You won't see many Spanish sitting there," the overseer said.

Ignoring him, MacKim allowed his gaze to pass over the tents, wondering what the slaves were thinking.

"Didn't you hear me?" The overseer stepped closer so he towered over MacKim. "I said you wouldn't see any Spanish sitting there."

"Probably not," MacKim said. "I won't hear them either, with the noise you make."

The overseer touched the whip he wore coiled in his belt. "Who do you think you are?"

"Sergeant Hugh MacKim of the 78th Fraser's Highlanders," MacKim said. "And Kennedy's Rangers. Who are you?" He raised his eyes to meet the overseer's gaze.

"I am Abel Lonelly, the overseer of this section of slaves."

"Well, Lonelly, if you try to intimidate me again, I'll put my bayonet in your gut," MacKim said. "And if I see you maltreating any of these poor fellows, I'll blow your brains out the back of your head."

Lonelly paled beneath his tan and took a step backwards, automatically reaching for his whip. MacKim drew on his pipe and shifted his musket, so the muzzle pointed directly at the overseer's stomach. He was aware that their raised voices had attracted the attention of some of the slaves. He sat tight, smoking.

"I'll report you to your superiors," Lonelly said.

"Hugh MacKim," MacKim reminded. "Of the 78th Highlanders and Kennedy's Rangers. Now run away and *ifrinn mend thu*—that means Hell mend you, as it surely will when you arrive, you hectoring bastard."

MacKim felt revolted by the presence of Lonelly. He knew that more slaves were watching, and rather than have Lonelly vent his frustration on men who could not retaliate, he stood up. When he saw Lonelly had not moved, MacKim spat on the ground at the man's feet. "Run," MacKim said quietly. "Or as God is my witness, I'll shoot you where you stand."

Seeing the menace in MacKim's eyes, Lonelly stepped back. When MacKim followed, Lonelly moved faster until his nerve broke, and he ran.

"Dirty bastard." MacKim found he was trembling with anger.

"Don't you like that man?" Benjamin had emerged from a tent.

"Why the devil don't you run away?" MacKim asked bluntly. "Or smash that bastard's head with a rock, and you can all desert?"

"The sentries have orders to shoot any of us who leaves the perimeter," Benjamin said. "And if we get away, where can we go? I don't even know where we are."

"You're in Cuba," MacKim told him, as others gathered around, casting nervous glances for the return of the overseer. "You're helping us besiege the Spanish in Havana."

"Lonelly's coming back," somebody said, and the slaves

melted away, leaving only Benjamin beside MacKim.

"You can't stay here," MacKim said.

"Where can I go?" Benjamin asked, with a half-smile on his face. Only then did MacKim realise that Benjamin had lost hope. A lifetime of servitude and harsh usage had killed his spirit.

"Surely anywhere is better than being a slave," MacKim urged. He sensed Lonelly walking towards him, with two soldiers at his back. "You'd better disappear," he said, and turned to face the overseer.

"That's the man!" Lonelly said.

"Good evening, sergeant." The first soldier was a sergeant of the 90th Foot, a brawny, freckled Irishman with the skin peeling from his nose.

"Good evening, sergeant," MacKim replied.

"Whatever are you doing here?" the Irishman asked, smiling. "MacKim, wasn't it?"

"Hugh MacKim of the 78th and Kennedy's Rangers."

The Irishman switched to Irish Gaelic, which was so similar to Scots Gaelic that MacKim understood without difficulty. "Walter Byrne of the 90th and County Clare. You're here to fight the Spanish, MacKim, not to annoy the slave driver, bastard though he is."

"And so are you, Byrne, not to herd men like cattle."

Byrne kept his smile. "We do our duty, sergeant, although there's little love in me for this part of the bargain. I didn't take the King's shilling to harass my fellow man."

"What are you saying? What gibberish are you talking?" Lonelly looked from one to the other in incomprehension.

"The sergeant says he is just leaving now," Byre said. "He's had his pipe and thanks you for your hospitality. Isn't that right, sergeant?"

"That's correct, Sergeant Byrne," MacKim said. As he had been speaking, he noted which tent Benjamin occupied. Tucking his pipe inside his tunic, MacKim sauntered away.

24

The nights could be lovely in Cuba, or they could feel like the inside of a furnace, with no air and the heat escaping upwards from the dry ground. The night of the 16th of July was one of the latter, with men struggling to sleep, despite their exhaustion, and sentries emptying their water bottles and thirsting for more. MacKim found it a novel experience when British soldiers hunted for water rather than something with more of an alcoholic bite. However, there was no humour when the sweat dried on every uniform, leaving a white film of human salt.

"Where are you going, sergeant?" Kennedy asked.

"I can't sleep, and I can't settle," MacKim replied.

"Don't wander too close to the Spanish lines," Kennedy warned. "Those Cuban militiamen could be out there."

"I'll be careful," MacKim promised, hefting his musket and lifting the bundle he had prepared at the edge of the Rangers' lines.

He was fortunate that clouds shielded the stars, making recognition difficult as he moved directly to the slaves' encampment, dropping his bundle in a dip in the ground. The 90th was on guard, with most of them in tight scarlet uniforms despite the heat, and a few in shirt sleeves, with muskets and equipment ready to fight.

MacKim watched the sentries for half an hour, listened to their quiet parole and countersign, and passed through a gap in their beat. For an experienced Ranger, it was easy to crawl unseen through the slave encampment to Benjamin's tent.

The flap was laced shut from the inside, so MacKim sliced it open with his knife and peered inside to see the men packed head to foot.

Benjamin opened his eyes when MacKim roughly woke him. "What?"

"Come on!" MacKim hissed.

Benjamin tried to shake away the sleep from his head. "What's happening?"

MacKim put a hand over Benjamin's mouth. "Escape!" he hissed. He saw the fear in Benjamin's eyes. "Yes or no?"

MacKim knew he was putting Benjamin in danger. A slave who obeyed the rules could live to old age, while a slave who tried to escape could be abominably tortured.

Benjamin nodded and followed MacKim out of the tent, shaking with understandable fear.

One of the sentries glanced over his shoulder as MacKim left the encampment.

"Britannia!" the sentry challenged, dropping his musket to the on-guard position.

"Rex!" MacKim gave the countersign in a bored mumble and continued walking, with Benjamin a yard behind him. "Keep moving," MacKim hissed.

"Where are we going?"

"Follow me!" MacKim slid into a hollow in the ground. "Put these on!" He pointed to the bundle he had left there.

Ten minutes later, dressed in the battered green uniform of Kennedy's Rangers, Benjamin followed MacKim into the Rangers' lines.

"Who's this?" Kennedy stared at Benjamin the following morning.

"A recruit, sir," MacKim said boldly. "We're always short-handed, and another man might be an asset. He doesn't need pay, only food and shelter."

"And protection from the slave catchers," Kennedy said. "I know an escaped slave when I see one."

"Other Rangers units have freed slaves in their ranks, sir, and even Indians. This fellow saved my life in Martinico."

Kennedy took a deep breath. "Stealing other people's property is a serious offence, MacKim!"

"Yes, sir. He's a man, sir."

"I know he's a bloody man! But legally, he's the property of somebody."

Benjamin had been listening to the conversation, struggling to understand the words. "Tell your officer I can return if I am trouble," he said in French.

When MacKim translated, Kennedy grunted.

"I have a mind to take him back and have you disrated and sent back to the 78th as unsuitable for the Rangers," Kennedy said. "I warn you, MacKim, if his owner comes looking for this slave, I won't protect you."

"I understand, sir," MacKim said.

On the 19th of July, the siege moved forward. First, the Spanish mounted three cannons on El Morro's wall and fired on the advancing British sap until the Royal Artillery smashed them into silence. At noon that day, British infantry charged forward to capture a section of the covered way in front of the right bastion. Another limited assault snatched more of the covered way, with a barrier of fascines erected to keep the Spanish at bay.

Simultaneously, men noticed that the wind was strengthening, and the sky was ominously dark, with rapid cirrus clouds. At sea, ships were moving more jerkily, and white caps appeared on the waves.

"There's a hurricane coming," Benjamin said. "I can smell it."

"When?" MacKim asked.

Benjamin shrugged. "Tomorrow, next week—I don't know yet, but it's on its way."

As MacKim watched the sky, Kennedy approached.

"Do you recall that ridge we discovered?" Kennedy asked.

"The one near the sea?"

"That's the one. The engineers are going to use our ridge to cross the ditch and begin mining under the bastion of El Morro."

"That will be a terrible task," MacKim said. "They'd better hurry before the weather breaks."

The engineers knew the difficulties more than MacKim realised. Understanding the magnitude of the operation, the engineers trawled the ranks of the Army and the Navy crews for Cornish miners, experts in their field. The engineers and miners gathered on the narrow ridge's British side, then ran across under fire. The Spanish musketeers killed four, but the remainder found comparative safety under the walls of El Morro. They started to mine where Spanish musketry could not reach them. Now it was a race to see if the miners could bring down a section of the wall before the hurricane season arrived, or before so many men died of disease that the British Army was too weak to continue the campaign.

※

"The general wants a reconnaissance." Kennedy gathered the Rangers together. "He thinks the Spanish have a minuscule garrison in El Morro because only a few guns fire at our besieging lines." Kennedy looked tired when he smiled. In common with the others, the lack of sleep and debilitating heat had aged him. "Somebody has to look inside the fort."

The Rangers were quiet for a few moments as they digested the information. "Inside the fort?" MacKim repeated.

"Yes."

"Us?" MacKim said.

"We're the best," Kennedy reminded. "The orders are for a sergeant and twelve men, no officers."

"Why is that, sir?" MacKim asked.

"If the intelligence is incorrect, the general doesn't want the Spanish to capture a British officer."

"When do we go?" MacRae asked.

"The night of the 21st," Kennedy said. "That's tonight." He looked at MacKim. "Pick your best men, sergeant." His smile lacked any humour. "Twelve willing volunteers, if they like it or not."

I'm still here, Claudette, but I might not be here tomorrow. We only have twelve men fit for duty.

"Right, boys." MacKim gathered them in a small group. "We're going over the wall to the right of the mine. Short muskets, no rifles, and bayonets—nothing else. Take nothing that rattles, pad all the equipment, spread soot over your faces, and ensure your bayonets are browned. I want nothing that reflects starlight."

The men nodded. Veterans all, they understood how to move quietly and avoid the light. Parnell spat tobacco juice onto the hard ground while Butler gave his usual refrain.

"Rangers, first and always."

MacKim halted at the edge of the narrow ridge that led to El Morro, remembering his feelings when they had discovered it. He padded onto the bridge, aware he was exposed to any Spanish sentry as he moved quickly across. He took a relieved breath when he reached the shelter of the wall and glanced behind him. His men carried ropes, complete with grapnel hooks that the Navy had supplied. They were lighter and more portable than scaling ladders.

The wall loomed above them, with close-fitting stonework rising to a dark sky. MacKim took the first rope, spun it two or three times, and threw it upward. The grapnel clicked against the parapet, failed to catch, and fell back down with a clatter. He tried again, and on the second attempt, the hook held. MacKim tugged it three times to ensure it would bear his weight.

"Parnell, you put up the second rope."

Parnell's hook caught on the second attempt.

MacKim was first up, with his musket across his back and his bayonet pushed behind his right hip. He rolled over the top of the battlement and lay still for a moment, looking around with his heart hammering inside his chest.

El Morro was quiet, showing signs of the siege, with dismounted artillery along the parapet and craters where shells had exploded. Pieces of equipment lay abandoned on the ground. Only fifty yards away, a section of Spanish infantry lay behind the battlements, sleeping with their muskets at their side. The Spanish flag hung above them, defiant on its pole.

Parnell joined MacKim, with his musket in his hand and his eyes narrow in his blackened face.

"Follow me," MacKim whispered, and moved a few yards along the parapet.

"*Quién está ahí?*" (Who is there?") A Spanish NCO looked up, staring towards the advancing Rangers.

"*Amiga!*" (Friend!) MacKim used one of the few Spanish words he knew.

"*Soldados Británicos!*" ("British soldiers!") Not fooled for an instant, the NCO shouted, kicking his men awake. They were running before MacKim could reach them, scrambling down to the stone-built barracks within the walls.

"Back we go, boys," MacKim said. "We've achieved our purpose. El Morro still has a garrison."

The Rangers scrambled back to the wall and down the ropes, thankful to escape with no casualties.

Colonel Carleton frowned when MacKim made his report.

"How many men did you see?" Carleton asked.

"Nine or ten," MacKim reported, "but they ran to fetch reinforcements."

"Did you see the reinforcements?"

"No, sir."

"They might have been bluffing. Get back up and check!"

Refuse! The colonel is sending us to our deaths!

"Yes, sir," MacKim said automatically, as years of iron discipline demanded. "Come on, boys!"

Aware of the Rangers' suppressed fear, and their hard looks directed at Colonel Carleton, MacKim led them back over the ridge and across to the rope. He looked up to see a dozen heads on the wall as a Spanish sentry asked, *"Quién está ahí?"*

The sentry pointed his musket, shouting, as both ropes came clattering into the ditch.

"They've seen us, sergeant!" Parnell said.

"So they have," MacKim agreed.

"Quién está ahí?" the sentry shouted again, and when the Rangers stopped, cursing, a scatter of musketry followed them, raising vicious chips from the rock.

"Back, lads," MacKim ordered, and they withdrew at haste, with the ditch a yawning black chasm on one side and the castle wall solid on the other.[1] "If I had a hundred men rather than twelve, sir," MacKim said, "I might have made an impression. As it was, we were lucky to escape without casualties."

"You're a sergeant," Carleton reminded savagely. "Leave strategy and tactics to your superiors."

Kennedy shook his head when Carleton stamped away. "Where's Pikestaff Wolfe when we need him?" he asked. "These generals may well capture Havana, but at a terrible cost of lives. If they threw away the textbook and tried something a little different, we might capture this damned place quicker." He touched MacKim on the shoulder. "You did well to bring your men back, MacKim."

"Thank you, sir." *Did I? Or am I becoming shy of danger? Everybody has a limit, and perhaps I have reached mine.*

※

THEY CAME IN THE DEEP DARK BEFORE DAWN ON THE 22ND OF July, a triple attack by one-thousand, three-hundred Spanish soldiers, sailors, and Cuban militiamen from the fort to disrupt the British siege.

"Something is happening in the water!" a Light Infantry sentry reported. "Boats crossing from Havana!"

"Are you sure?" Ensign Mowat, with the advanced picket, called.

"I can see the reflection of moonlight on their oars, sir!" the sentry shouted.

"Sound the stand-to!" Mowat ordered, and within a minute, tousle-haired drummers were rapping urgently on their drums, with the sound carrying the length of the British siege lines. Although the Spanish must have heard the insistent drums, they continued, landing on the shore below the La Cabana heights, forming up in the dark and marching forward. Brave men determined to fight for their island, they advanced towards the British.

The Light Infantry picket, thirty strong, met the unknown number of attackers with a prepared volley, a sudden crash, and a flare of fire in the night. Before the powder smoke had time to rise, the Spanish had retaliated with musketry of their own.

"The Spanish have attacked." MacKim roused the Rangers, further along the siege lines. "Load and check your flints, boys. We may be needed."

As the Rangers ensured they had sufficient ammunition, that their flints were sharp and, their bayonets loose in their scabbards, the fighting to their left raged fiercely. Veterans all, the

Rangers knew by the volume of fire and hoarse orders what was happening.

"That's a picket of the 90th engaged." Parnell crouched behind the breastwork, holding his rifle in his right hand with the barrel pointing to the starry sky. "And the Spanish replying."

The firing grew more intense, with volleys replying to volleys in a crashing chorus, and a sudden roar from scores of voices.

"The general has sent reinforcements," Parnell said, chewing tobacco as if the speed of his jaws could help the 90th.

Parnell was correct. After Lieutenant Colonel Stuart and the 90th Foot held the initial assault, a hundred sappers joined him, and the 3rd Battalion of the 60th Royal Americans marched up in reinforcement. The arrival of fresh men turned the tide. Advancing along the ridge, the Royal Americans faced the Spanish, fired two volleys, and pushed the enemy before them. Many drowned in the water in their haste to escape, while the 60th and 90th fired into the mass.

The firing died down, flared up for a moment, and faded to a spatter of isolated shots. A British officer's voice sounded, passed by the wind, and the drums sounded the recall.

"And that's that," Kennedy said. "They didn't need us this time."

The Rangers had begun to relax when a renewed burst of firing began, this time at the northeast bastion.

"They're after the miners and engineers!" Kennedy said.

The Rangers dragged themselves awake again, some screwing up their eyes as they peered towards the muzzle flares that showed where the fighting took place, and others concentrating on their front in case the Spanish should launch a third attack.

"The Spanish are pushing hard," Parnell said.

The firing increased. Somebody screamed—loud, long, and hopeless—and MacKim shivered, imagining some young man from Madrid or Massachusetts or Manchester dying to defend or attack a fort out here in Cuba without being fully aware of the politics behind the war.

"They are," Dickert agreed.

Again, the firing rose in volume as British reinforcements rushed to the spot, and then the Spanish withdrew, with only a few casualties on either side. MacKim heard the tune of "Dumbarton's Drums" and the crash of regular volleys sounding along the lines, but was too far away to make out details.

"That's the Royal Scots involved," MacRae said. "I know their march."

"Can we get to sleep now, sir?" Oxford asked. "I was on duty half of last night, and my eyes are about closing."

"Yes, MacKim and Parnell will keep watch," Kennedy agreed. "I can't see the Spanish trying three assaults in one night."

Within the hour, the Spanish proved Kennedy wrong as they launched their third attack that morning.

The sound of oars hitting the water was the first indication that the Spanish were returning, and then a challenge from an alert sentry, followed by a single musket shot.

"That was closer!" MacKim said. "Stand to, Rangers!"

"What is it now?" Oxford scrambled to his position, musket in hand.

"They're right beneath us!" Parnell shouted, and fired on his last word.

A Spanish cheer came in reply and a surge of white-uniformed men through the woodland.

"Meet them, Lights!" A stentorian voice sounded, and the Light Infantry responded with a ragged volley.

The Spanish, reinforced with Cuban militia, had crossed the harbour to land at the base of La Cabana and pushed uphill in the growing light of dawn. Perhaps the previous abortive attempts had dispirited the Spanish, for when the Light Infantry met them with controlled volleys, they remained only a few moments. Before the powder smoke had cleared, the Spanish were back in their boats, and the Rangers and Light Infantry sent patrols forward to search for wounded and stragglers.

"They've all gone," MacKim reported to Kennedy. "We only found a few dead and a single wounded man."

Kennedy nodded. "Keep alert, MacKim. Parnell, convey my respects to Colonel Carleton and inform him that there are no Spanish on our front."

"That must have disheartened them," MacKim said. "Three attacks and three failures in one morning."

"Perhaps," Kennedy said. "But do you see how our men responded? We have so many sick, now that our strength is failing. We win the battles, but we could lose the campaign."

"It depends on the speed of the sappers and miners," MacKim said.

"I can fight." Benjamin lifted an arm. "Give me a musket, and I will help."

"You're no soldier," Kennedy told him.

As soon as the Spanish realised the attack had failed, they opened up with their artillery from the west bastion of the castle and the ships, killing some of their own men. Boatloads of Spanish reinforcements, ready to exploit any breakthrough, sat in Havana harbour, only to disembark when the first wave returned in defeat.

By eight in the morning, the smoke had cleared, with the miners and sappers already hard at work. The Spanish and Cubans had lost about four-hundred men to around fifty British killed and wounded.

"I can fight," Benjamin repeated.

"What do you think, sergeant?" Kennedy glanced at his depleted ranks.

"It won't do any harm," MacKim said. "I doubt Benjamin will know much about warfare, but every musket helps."

Even in the short time he had been with the Rangers, Benjamin had picked up a little English. Now he spoke in a mixture of French and English. "I know something of the militia's methods," he said.

When MacKim translated, Kennedy looked interested. "Tell us," he invited.

"They fight with machetes, which is a technique they brought from Africa," Benjamin explained. "Men learn it from childhood, fighting with sticks. In parts of West Africa, the method is called *Abariba*."

Kennedy and MacKim glanced at each other.

"The machete is the symbol of Ogun, the war god, in Kongo, an African nation," Benjamin continued.

"It is religious then." MacKim struggled to understand this insight into a new culture.

"We call our fighting sticks *bangalas*," Benjamin said. "And use them in dances, as well as to defend ourselves from snakes."

MacKim nodded. "I hate snakes," he said with a shudder.

"We learn *tire bwa*," Benjamin said, as MacKim noted he used the first person. "*Tire bwa* is the art of stick-fencing; then we progress to *tire coutou*—knife-fighting—then *tire machet*. The Cubans will be similar to us. The true masters can fight an opponent when he is blindfolded."

MacKim met Kennedy's eye. "Do you have this skill?"

"I have some skill," Benjamin admitted.

"Then you'll join the Rangers," Kennedy said. "You can teach us the basics, in case we meet more of the militia."

Benjamin grinned even before MacKim translated, proving he knew more English than he'd admitted. "Yes, sir!"

"We'll start right away," Kennedy decided. "It will stop the lads from becoming stale."

As Benjamin cut fighting sticks from the forest and began to teach the rudiments of stick-fighting to the Rangers, the siege continued.

Commanded by Patrick McKellar, the sappers sank a shaft outside the covered way that protected the ditch, hoping to plant a mine. When the mine exploded, it should blast rubble from the counterscarp into the deep stone-cut ditch, so a besieging force could charge across, through the breach in the walls, and enter the fort itself.

Besiegers had used the same technique for centuries.

However, the Spanish had not given up.

"Sir!" Parnell reported. "The Spanish ships are on the move!"

25

Kennedy scrambled up the lookout tree and focussed his telescope on the harbour. "Join me, sergeant!" MacKim climbed beside him, watching the Spanish ships raise their anchors. "Maybe they're going to sail out and challenge Admiral Pocock," he suggested hopefully.

"They'd have to move the boom first," Kennedy said.

The Spanish ships crossed the harbour, moored with their broadsides facing the British batteries, and opened fire. Ship after ship rocked under the pressure of a broadside, with jets of flame and smoke issuing from their hulls.

"Tree all!" Kennedy yelled and scrambled back down to cover as cannonballs hammered at the British positions.

Within a few moments, the British batteries returned fire. Once again, the Rangers found themselves between both forces, with Spanish balls crashed around them and the British reply arcing overhead.

"I wonder how the ships are faring," Kennedy said as their redoubt trembled after a Spanish near-miss.

"Hopefully, not well!" MacKim said when the Spanish bombardment slackened and died.

"Come on, MacKim," Kennedy said. "We'll have a look."

The Spanish ships were limping back across the harbour, each with massive damage to masts and rigging, and one frigate, *Perla,* already sinking.

"Another round to our gunners," MacKim said.

As the endless round of patrolling continued, and Benjamin taught the Rangers the rudiments of stick-fighting, both Spanish and British won victories. One Spanish frigate proved a persistent menace to the miners until the 26th of July, when a British howitzer landed a shell directly on her deck. MacKim saw the resulting explosion and the fire that followed.

Spanish seamen scrambled to escape, some burning as they jumped into the sea, with small boats pushing out from Havana to rescue the survivors.

"Aye." MacRae slipped beside MacKim, who sat on a tree, watching.

"Aye, aye, MacRae."

"Poor buggers," MacRae said. "What are we doing here, Hugh, killing men with whom we have no quarrel?"

MacKim opened his mouth to remind MacRae of their respective ranks, but shook his head instead. "I don't know, Duncan." They were no longer soldiers, but fellow Gaels, men with similar backgrounds and cultures stranded in a strange land.

"As I sit on the hill of tears.

Without skin on toe or sole," MacRae began the ancient Gaelic poem of exile in a distant land.

MacKim joined in, murmuring the words.

"O, King! O Peter and Paul!

Far is Rome from Loch Long."[1] "Further still is Cuba from Scotland," MacRae said. "Where do we belong now, Hugh, in our uniforms of green?"

"If I knew that, Duncan, I would be a wiser man than my mother's son." MacKim's mind drifted to the cool mists and grey hillsides of the Gaeltacht, the Highlands of Scotland.

Will I ever see home again? Where is home now? Where do I belong?

A cannon crashed beside them, breaking the mood and returning them to the present.

"Come on, MacRae, there is work to be done."

"Aye, sergeant, the work never ends."

On the 27th of July, Brigadier Burton arrived with the first of over three-thousand reinforcements from North America, and the fresh troops bolstered the morale of the disease-riddled besiegers.

"Look," Parnell said. "Toy soldiers."

The reinforcements marched in, healthy and fit, with some staring at the haggard, yellowed faces of the besiegers and the long lines of the sick queueing for passage onto the hospital ships. The dead were so numerous that the grave-diggers could not keep up, and many waited for burial, with the stench a sickening reminder of man's mortality in this hot hell.

"It surely can't be long now," MacKim said. "This is worse than being besieged in Quebec. Is Cuba worth the price of sick and dead?"

"Is any lump of foreign soil worth a single dead man, let alone the thousands that are dying here?" Parnell asked.

"For King and Country," MacRae replied, and shook his head. "Aye, well, this isn't my country, and if King George wants it so badly, he can come and fight for it."

MacKim tried to control the pounding of his head, hoping he had not caught malaria or yellow jack. He had seen too many good men die to think he was immune and was scared of such a terrible, undignified death.

"Come on, lads," he said. "We've come too far to stop now."

"Rangers, first and always," Butler said, but without his usual energy.

"What's left of us." Parnell spat on the ground.

On the 29th of July, the news spread that the mines were ready to blast a breach in El Morro's defences.

"We've two mines," Kennedy explained to his Rangers. "One is ready under the counterscarp of the ditch—that's the outer slope—and the second is underneath the northwest bastion of the castle."

MacKim looked at the walls of El Morro, which had defied all their attempts for so long. The Spanish flag flew proudly, a symbol of centuries-long authority. "They're brave men in there."

"When El Morro falls," Kennedy said, "we have the keys to Havana."

"It will be a bloody day, particularly as half our men are sick," MacKim said. He remembered the British counterattack at Quebec when men weak with scurvy had staggered out to face the French. That battle had ended in disaster.

General Albemarle must have shared MacKim's foreboding, for later that day, he had the drummers tap the advance and the artillery hammer at the walls.

"The general's trying to bluff the Spanish," Kennedy said, unmoving. "He wants to force a surrender without bloodshed."

"It won't work," MacKim said. "Velasco is too wily a bird for that. I hope the Spanish are proud of his defence."

They listened to the cannonade, with the artillery firing round after round and the drums clattering their sinister message. After a while, the noise reduced to the now-habitual regular thump of gunfire, and the Spanish flag continued to fly over El Morro.

"We're going to need the bayonet," Kennedy said. "God help us."

"Are the Rangers going in with the first assault, the forlorn hope?" MacKim asked.

"No," Kennedy said. "We're in reserve. There are less than three-hundred men for the forlorn hope. About a third are from the First Foot, the Royal Scots, fifty from the 90th Foot, and the rest from various regiments. We are in reserve, with another hundred and fifty from the 35th Foot. Lieutenant Colonel James Stuart of the 90th is in overall command."

"The Royals? A Lowland Scottish regiment?" MacKim looked up with renewed interest. "I've heard about them." He sucked on an empty pipe as his eyes darkened with memory. "They fought at Culloden, on the Hanoverian side."

"That's an old war," Kennedy reminded. "I don't want you renewing old battles."

MacKim stood up, automatically touching the hilt of his bayonet. "I'd like to speak to one of them."

Kennedy looked troubled. "Let the past take care of the past, MacKim."

"We carry it with us always," MacKim replied. "Our past makes us what we are. If I hadn't been at Culloden, I wouldn't be here." He spoke softly, yet with an edge to his voice.

"I'll come, too," Kennedy said, realising he could not alter MacKim's stubborn mind.

"And me," Benjamin chimed in.

"You'd be better remaining unseen, Benjamin," Kennedy said.

"I know, sir," Benjamin agreed, yet the Rangers' newest recruit accompanied them out of friendship.

All three wandered over to the Royals' position. As befitted men who were detailed to take part in a near-suicidal assault, the Royals were quiet, grimly checking their muskets and bayonets.

"Halloa there," MacKim said, approaching a small group of men.

The Royals looked up, nodded, and continued what they were doing.

"My name is MacKim, from the 78th Fraser's Highlanders, now of Kennedy's Rangers," MacKim introduced himself.

"I've heard of Frasers," one man said. He was short in stature, with broad shoulders and eyes that had seen great suffering. "They did well at Quebec." He made space at his side. "And the Rangers are known."

"You're going into the breach tomorrow," MacKim said.

"Aye." The Royal tested the edge of his bayonet with a calloused thumb.

"We're in support," MacKim said.

"Aye." Satisfied with the sharpness of his blade, the Royal

checked his flints before beginning to clean and oil his musket. "We might need you. The Spanish are a tough bunch."

"This is Captain Kennedy," MacKim said.

"Forgive me for not saluting," the Royal said without moving. "I'm a bit preoccupied at present."

"I understand." Kennedy sat at his side. "We know what the night before battle is like."

"And this is Benjamin. He was a slave."

The Royal looked up with renewed interest as he scrutinised Benjamin. "We have that much in common then, Benjamin."

"Were you a bonded servant?" Benjamin asked.

"No," the Royal said. "I was a slave. Born into slavery, lived in slavery, and expected to die in slavery." He held out his hand. "Welcome to freedom, fellow."

Benjamin shook his hand. "What's your name?"

"I call myself Adam Freeman," the Royal said. "A new man, like Adam, and free."

MacKim glanced at Kennedy, both realising that these two men shared a bond they would never understand.

"I didn't know there were white slaves," Benjamin said.

"Thousands of us." Freeman set aside his musket and stared upwards at the sky. He took a deep breath. "Can you do that? Breathe in fresh air and see daylight?"

"I can," Benjamin said.

"It's the best thing in the world," Freeman said. "That's freedom."

"You're tied to the Army," Benjamin said. "A slave to the officers."

"The pit master owned me," Freeman said. "I started work down the mine at the age of four, and from then until I ran away, I never saw daylight, save on Sundays." He gave a brief, bleak smile. "Generation after generation of us, working underground and never seeing the sun. Soldiering is a thousand times better. I changed my name, so my owner could not trace me and drag me back."[2]"I have only Benjamin," Benjamin said. "A name my masters gave me."

"Choose your surname," Freeman said. "You're free now."

Benjamin nodded thoughtfully. "I am free now."

"Come on, MacKim," Kennedy said. "We're not wanted here."

***

The redcoats mustered behind the British lines at noon, grim men who knew the next few hours could be their last. Some smoked their pipes, others made nervous jokes or swigged Dutch courage in fierce Caribbean rum. A few prayed—some openly, others in secret—fearing the ridicule of their companions.

"MacKim," Kennedy said. "Gather the men. Remind them that we're in reserve."

Although the Rangers were not trained for storming operations, which were generally left to the Grenadiers, MacKim was not surprised the general had included them. The disease that had more than decimated the British Army had left Albemarle shorthanded when it came to potentially bloody assaults.

"We're ready, sir," MacKim said. The Rangers waited behind their fascines and earthworks, muskets loaded and knapsacks full of ammunition. They knew what the day might bring.

Here we are again, Claudette. Another potentially bloody day ahead. Look after yourself.

At two in the afternoon, the engineers fired both mines. The explosions were louder than anything MacKim had heard before, massive blasts of sound that rocked the ground and sent masonry and earth flying into the air. As vast clouds of dust obscured visibility, the noise hammered at MacKim's eardrums, so he had to shake his head to regain his hearing.

MacKim expected an immediate assault, but the officers gave no orders.

"Should the forlorn hope not advance?" Oxford asked.

"Not yet," a sapper said. "We'll have to wait until the dust clears to see if the mines have been successful."

"That will give the Spanish time to recover!" Oxford said. "We should attack right away while they're in confusion."

When the dust settled, it was evident that while one mine had damaged the curtain wall of El Morro, the other had not been entirely successful.

"Damned bad luck," the sapper said while his companion vented in a succession of more obscene comments. "We hoped the mine in the counterscarp would have filled the ditch with rubble to allow the storming party better access."

Although the mine had caused significant damage to the solid rock of the counterscarp, the explosion had only partially filled the ditch. Any assaulting column would still have to negotiate the narrow bridge Kennedy and MacKim had discovered weeks before.

The forlorn hope waited, with tension high, as a group of senior officers debated whether to attack or not.

"Get a move on," Freeman urged. "The longer we wait, the more time we give the Spanish to close the breach."

"Advance!" The confirmation came at last. "Take El Morro, boys!"

The forlorn hope rose to the attack, with "Dumbarton's Drums", the old Royal Scots march, encouraging them forward.

As the Rangers watched, the Royals broke into song.

"Captain Hume is bound to sea,
Hey boys, ho boys,
Captain Hume is bound to sea,
Ho!
Captain Hume is bound to sea,
And his brave companie,
Hey the brave Grenadiers,
Ho!"

"I don't know that song," Kennedy said.

"It's old." MacKim caught the lilt of the words as he watched the Royals advance towards the fort. "From a forgotten war of the last century."

The brave scarlet advanced, with Spanish musketry felling men as they moved, smoke from the explosion and the muskets hazing the scene. Above the rattle of weapons, the Royals continued to sing, men from behind the ploughs of the fertile Lothian fields, townsmen from the ancient closes of Edinburgh, and at least one bitter-eyed collier who preferred the queues and tight scarlet of the Army to the dank depths of the coal pits. Lieutenant Charles Forbes of the Royal Scots marched in front, with the sun glittering on the naked sword he balanced on his right shoulder.

"When we come to Tangier shore
Hey boys, ho boys
When we come to Tangier shore
Ho!
When we come to Tangier shore
We'll make our grenadoes roar
Hey the brave Grenadiers
Ho!"

The men were roaring now, their heads high as the drums hammered their encouragement. The Royals increased their speed as they approached the narrow ridge across the ditch, with Lieutenant Forbes in front waving his sword and two smart sergeants with halberds immediately behind. Above them, a knot of Spanish soldiers stood in the breach, shouting in defiance as they displayed equal bravery to the advancing British.

"Hacket led on the van,
Hey boys, ho boys,
Hacket led on the van,
Ho
Hacket led on the van
Where was killed many a man
Hey the brave Scottish boys,
Ho!"

With that last "ho", the Royal Scots plunged forward. The tune of a half-forgotten campaign in a distant war lingered, and then faded in the roar of battle. The future of El Morro Castle, Havana, and Cuba hung on the outcome of the struggle in the breach.

MacKim put a steadying hand on Oxford, who seemed keen to run forward. "They'll call on us if we're needed."

"I'll come as well," Benjamin said. "I am nearly a Ranger!"

"Look!" Kennedy pointed to the sea. "The Spanish are trying a seaborne assault!"

MacKim saw the Spanish counterattack as their boats appeared around the headland. They fired cannon and swivels into the supporting British infantry, with men falling and looking over their shoulders, wondering if their muskets could reach this new attack.

"Riflemen!" MacKim ordered. "See if you can pick off the swivels."

As the marksmen hurried forward, the Royal Navy arrived. The 64-gun HMS *Alcide*, with several armed boats, took the Spanish in the flank. After a few moments of confused fighting, the Spanish counterattack, vastly outgunned, faltered. The Royal Navy pushed home their advantage, pressing the Spanish back to the harbour.

"It's like Chisholm says." MacKim watched the move and counter-move. "War is one gigantic game of chess, with the admirals and generals moving regiments and ships around like pawns and knights."

Kennedy nodded. "That's so. Us, the little men at the sharp end? We don't matter. If we get killed, there are plenty more to take our place."

"We are the sacrifice of pawns," MacKim agreed, and returned his attention to the assault on El Morro.

The Royals formed into single file and hurried across the slender bridge, tall Grenadiers in mitre caps with long Brown Bess muskets. The Spanish mustered at the gap in their defences, and musketry crackled, picking off men before they reached the breach.

"At them, my Royal Scots!" Forbes yelled. "Scotland forever!"

At last, with a loud cheer, the Royals charged into the gap with the other regiments following.

"Rangers! Move on! Support the assault!"

MacKim took a deep breath. "On we go, lads! Kennedy's Rangers!"

"Rangers, first and always!" Butler shouted.

The fighting in the breach was intense, with bayonets stabbing, officers slashing and thrusting with swords, and men firing at close range, or using fists and musket butts to batter at the enemy. The Spanish fought well, refusing to surrender even after two devastating explosions and an attack by determined Grenadiers.

Fighting furiously, Forbes slashed and stabbed in the carnage of the breach.

"Where the devil did they come from?" MacKim pointed to a body of seamen who had appeared with the Army. "I thought Albemarle gave orders that this was purely an Army affair."

"God knows," Kennedy said. "Maybe his little brother, Commodore Keppel, disagreed. Anyway, the Navy's always welcome, particularly that big fellow."

The officer in charge of the sailors was Adam Duncan. A giant of a man at over six foot tall, he advanced with a flourish.

"There's El Morro's commandant," Kennedy said as Captain Don Luis de Velasco tried to rally his men at the breach. MacKim saw Velasco stagger and fall, and then the British were pouring through, the Spanish defenders were retreating, and the breach belonged to the besiegers.

"Come on, lads!" Kennedy shouted as the reserves poured into El Morro. "It's our time!"

As Lieutenant Forbes kept the Royals in hand, the other besiegers spread out inside the fort that had defied them for so long. They ran along the defensive wall, bayoneting any Spanish soldier who resisted and charged across the interior of the fort. Only thirty minutes after Forbes reached the breach, the British had control of El Morro at the cost of fourteen killed and twenty-eight wounded. As well as Velasco and his second-in-command, Colonel Marques Gonzales, another 130 men died defending the castle. The remainder—around 570 soldiers, marines, seamen, slaves, and freed slaves—surrendered or drowned while attempting to escape.

"Look," Kennedy said. Lying in the breach, bleeding from bayonet wounds, Freeman faced upwards towards the bright sky.

"At least he died in the open air," MacKim said.

"He would have wished that," Kennedy said.

Benjamin knelt beside the body of the miner. "I will bury him," he said.

Even after the loss of El Morro, the Spanish refused to surrender. As the British congratulated themselves on capturing the castle, Lieutenant Forbes spoke with Lieutenant Nugent of the 9th Foot and Holroyd of the 90th when a section of Spanish infantry dashed from a lighthouse a short distance away. The officers reached for their swords as the Spanish reached them.

"Royals!" Forbes shouted, and a platoon charged to his help. Nugent and Holroyd died under the Spanish bayonets as Forbes led the Royals in an attack on the lighthouse, breaking in the door and killing every man inside.

"What a bloody waste of lives." MacKim indicated the two dead British officers from his stance on the castle wall.

MacRae looked around at the interior of El Morro, with its dismounted guns and men in every undignified position of death. "Yes," he said, and began to clean his rifle. "We're all mad, sergeant. The whole of humanity is mad unless we stop this insanity of war."

"War is just collective insanity," MacKim agreed.

I have had enough fighting now. I want to go home, wherever that is.

26

Immediately, the British raised the Union flag above El Morro. The Spanish warships began to bombard the castle, with the guns of Havana joining in. Fully aware of the British lack of water, the Spanish aimed at the castle's water cistern.

"If they can't beat us in the field," Butler said, ducking as a cannonball crashed into the wall a few yards from where he stood, "they'll try to kill us by thirst."

The British retaliated, with the artillery on La Cabana altering their aim from El Morro to Havana, while the force on the western side of the city also fired. Forty cannon, plus five howitzers and ten mortars on the west, joined the La Cabana artillery in pounding Havana.

"Who's the black man?" MacKim heard the Royal Scots wonder as they buried their dead amidst the thunder and fury of the renewed bombardment

"Some Spanish slave, probably," a corporal replied, and dismissed the lone observer from his mind.

Benjamin waited until the soldiers had gone before he approached the graves, and then he thrust a simple cross above Freeman's grave.

"Rest easy, brother," Benjamin muttered.

MacKim nodded, understanding the gesture from one man born into slavery to another. In the short time they had known each other, Freeman and Benjamin had created a bond that only they could fully understand.

"What are we going to do with you, Benjamin?" MacKim asked. "Anybody could grab you as a slave over here, and the situation won't be much better in Britain."

"Could we not send him back to Africa?" Dickert suggested. "Or enrol him into the Rangers?"

"When the war ends," Kennedy said, "the government will disband the Rangers and all the other newly formed regiments. The instant they think they don't need us, the government will resent paying our wages, and what happens to Benjamin then? The rest of us can return to New Hampshire or Scotland or wherever."

"The Navy might accept Benjamin as a seaman," MacRae said.

"They'll be reduced as well," Kennedy said.

"Africa it is, then," Dickert said.

"We could ask Benjamin what he wants." MacKim was growing slightly irritated by the tone of the conversation. "He's sitting right next to us."

MacRae nodded. "You could run into the interior, Benjamin," he suggested. "I'm sure there will be a place where other runaway slaves are free."

"I speak French and some English," Benjamin said. "I'd be as foreign here as you are, whatever the colour of my skin." He sighed. "I did not know that freedom would be so hard."

As MacKim fretted over Benjamin, the war rumbled on. With El Morro captured, the British concentrated on Havana. Despite their rising toll of sick and dying, they redoubled their efforts to build gun batteries aimed at the city. Other cannon targeted La Punta, the last defence of the harbour. Encircling Havana in a ring of artillery, Albemarle ordered more batteries built on the Cabana Heights and strengthened the British position at the Chorera River to the west of Havana.

"The Spanish are quiet," MacKim said. "Except for the artillery."

"They only have to sit tight and wait," Kennedy reminded. "El Morro delayed us by weeks, and the first hurricane will arrive shortly."

Benjamin sniffed the air and nodded. "Not long now, sir," he said.

"Our ships won't survive offshore in a hurricane," Kennedy said. "They'll either have to find a secure harbour or put out to sea. Either way, they won't be able to support us. Without the seamen, and the ships to carry water and supplies, our position will be untenable."

"Checkmate," MacKim said.

"Checkmate," Kennedy agreed.

With the British toiling to build more batteries to bombard Havana, the Spanish showed they had not yet given up. In the early morning of the 2nd of August, a Spanish 74-gun battleship sailed across the harbour to bombard El Morro. The ship's initial broadside hammered at the walls, but the battleship withdrew when the Royal Artillery trained a pair of howitzers on her.

A shortage of entrenching tools delayed the artillery until the Navy again saved the day by remedying the deficiency. When General Albemarle sent parties out to reconnoitre the roads to la Punta, the Spanish burned all the local houses to prevent them from falling into British hands. Albemarle countered by marching out a 200-strong working party, only for the Spanish to scatter them with a brisk cannonade.

"As Chisholm said, it's move and countermove. The Spanish haven't given up yet," MacKim said, feeling the heaviness of the air.

"They know the campaigning season is coming to a close," Kennedy said. "They still hold the king and queen in this deadly game of chess."

Albemarle sent a flag of truce to ask de Prado to surrender, but instead, the governor opened a cannonade. In the meantime, sensing the inevitable, the population of Havana began to leave the town with their possessions.

At dawn on the 11th of August, the British artillery began a systematic bombardment of Havana, in scenes that reminded MacKim of the capture of Quebec three years previously.

As the batteries of heavy 32-pounder and 24-pounder cannon threw solid shot at the walls, mortar batteries arced their shells into the city. Some shells exploded in the air, scattering deadly metal shards on soldiers, civilians, and slaves alike. Smoke and fire rose from Havana as MacKim grimly imagined the scenes of horror.

Simultaneously, other heavy batteries hammered the fort of La Punta, whose walls virtually disappeared under clouds of smoke and dust.

"We're slaughtering them," Parnell said.

"We are," MacRae agreed soberly. "I don't mind killing soldiers or militia. They would kill us if they could, and that's all part of the soldier's bargain, but I don't like this making war on civilians."

"De Prado should surrender now," MacKim said. "Before too many of his people are killed."

Butler nodded. "Even if a hurricane comes now, it will be too late to save them. We'll capture Havana."

The Rangers watched as the Spanish garrison abandoned their fort of La Punta, and gun by gun, the British silenced the artillery defending Havana. As the morning wore on, the British guns began to make breaches in the city walls, preparing the way for an assault.

"You know what that means, don't you?" Kennedy asked. "If we take Havana by storm, the rules of war allow us to sack the place. There will be hundreds of drunken soldiers looting and pillaging, raping, and destroying."

Oxford laughed. "That sounds good to me."

"If you saw the results, you wouldn't agree," Kennedy told him coldly. "Now go on picket duty until I send for you, you bloody Johnny Raw!"

"Yes, sir." Oxford disappeared.

Other soldiers shared Oxford's opinion, and excitement mounted in the redcoats' ranks as they discussed the plunder and women that would soon be theirs. Yet, perhaps the idea of being ravaged did not appeal to the people of Havana, for early in the afternoon, flags of truce rose above the walls and there was movement at the city gates.

"Something's happening." Kennedy extended his telescope as a group of splendidly uniformed men appeared outside the city. "Spanish officers under a flag of truce. I think we've won, boys!"

When the Spanish asked for terms to surrender the city, the British artillery fell silent. There were no Spanish guns in action by that time, and parts of Havana were ablaze, with flames licking orange above the ancient buildings and smoke filling the streets.

"We haven't won yet," Kennedy informed the Rangers that evening when he heard the results of the discussions between the British and Spanish. "We've only got a 24-hour truce, and we can't agree on terms."

"We should storm the place and take it at the point of a bayonet!" Oxford said.

"We might yet have to," Kennedy said, "if General Albemarle doesn't come to an agreement with de Prado. Albemarle is demanding the Spanish warships as well as Havana. De Prado is refusing."

MacKim grunted. "If de Prado refuses, we can sink the damned ships, and that will mean more men killed for nothing."

Both sides were no nearer an agreement by nightfall, and the British soldiers were growing impatient, ready to launch themselves into an immediate assault. MacKim knew by their mood that the result would be a mass slaughter of the civilians.

"Let loose the dogs of war!" shouted one tough-looking Grenadier. "Let the Grenadiers among them!"

The British waited, sharpening their bayonets and drooling over the plunder that awaited, while Spanish civilians seeped from the city, carrying their valuables and family treasures.

Dawn of the 12th brought no end to the stalemate until Albemarle contacted de Prado, telling him that the cannonade would continue unless he accepted the British terms.

"What happens now?" Oxford asked.

"Now we wait," MacKim said, "and restrain our impatience."

Tension mounted within the British camp, with the artillerymen adjusting their aim and the infantry checking their muskets.

"If we have to attack," MacKim said to his section, "the same rules apply as if we were in the forest. Guard each other's back and don't stray away. Havana will be full of frustrated Spanish and resentful Cubans waiting to put a knife into the back of any lone British soldier. So don't touch any spirits. It's not worth getting killed for."

"Here comes the Spanish response." Kennedy was watching through his telescope as a small band of Spanish officers emerged from Havana. "We'll know in a few moments, boys."

The cheering started a moment later, spreading with the news that the Spanish had surrendered. The British had captured Havana and, equally as important, the sheltered harbour. Albemarle's muscular diplomacy also gained the guns, ammunition, and ships in Havana harbour, together with a vast amount of treasure.

"Nine warships and scores of merchantmen," MacKim said. "That's a boost for the Navy."

"Prize money, boys," Kennedy breathed. "The generals and admirals will make a fortune, and we'll get tuppence apiece, but it's better than a kick in the breeches."

"Or a bullet in the head," Parnell added.

With the fighting around Havana finished, MacKim renewed his concern about Benjamin.

"You could join the Navy," MacKim suggested. "Or just join the crew of a merchant ship."

"Wherever I go, I'll be in danger of somebody thumping me on the head, and I'd wake up a slave again," Benjamin said.

"How about returning to Africa?" Parnell asked. "If you take a ship that trades there, you can jump ship and get back to your ancestor's village."

Benjamin gave a gentle smile. "The only ships trading to my area are slave ships. I don't think I'd be safe on them, and if I did get to Africa, I can't speak the language or know the geography. I'd be as big a stranger there as I would be in Britain or the Colonies."

"Stay with the Rangers, then," MacRae said. "At least until the war ends."

MacKim drew a rough map on the Caribbean in the dirt, then quickly scrubbed it out. "When we were in Jamaica," he said, "I was talking to one of the locals. He told me about people called Maroons."

Benjamin looked up with a renewed interest in his face. "I have considered joining them."

"They're black, free, live in the island, and have a truce with the British there," MacKim said.

"They're in Jamaica," Benjamin said. "We're in Cuba."

MacRae frowned. "The sea connects both islands," he said. To a man from the west coast of Scotland, the sea was a highway rather than a barrier.

Benjamin stood up. "You mean, go by boat?"

"Unless you can fly," MacKim said. "I'm not sure how far it is, but I'd guess less than two-hundred miles from the south coast of Cuba."

Benjamin raised his eyebrows. "The only time I've been at sea was when your general brought me from Martinico to Cuba. I was sick all the way and prayed to God to let me live."

MacKim looked away. He had not anticipated that freeing a slave would be so much trouble. At that moment, he regretted his action. *I should not have interfered. Be sure that you'll pay for all your good deeds.*

"I'll think of something else," he said. *But only God knows what.*

※

THE RANGERS WATCHED AS BRITISH REGULARS FILED INTO THE abandoned fort at La Punta, a living scarlet snake that occupied the strongpoint and immediately started to put the place to rights.

"Albemarle doesn't seem to want the Rangers on display," Parnell said.

"Maybe we're not sufficiently smart," MacKim said. "Or he has something else planned for us."

"You must have a spy in the general's tent." Kennedy sounded grim. "I hope you lads weren't looking forward to luxuriating in the whorehouses and taverns of Havana."

MacKim guessed there was bad news coming. "Of course not, sir. We were going to dust off our Bibles and sing hymns to celebrate our victory."

"You might need your Bibles," Kennedy said, "but your muskets will be more useful."

"What's happening, sir?" MacKim asked.

"General Albemarle doesn't entirely trust the Spanish," Kennedy said. "And he certainly doesn't trust the Cuban militia. He wants patrols out south of the town to ensure our foragers are undisturbed."

Dickert sighed. "That will mean us then."

"It does," Kennedy said. "The Rangers, and the Light Infantry of the 42nd and the Royal Americans. We're not Grenadiers to crash into a fortified position or line infantry to stand and trade musketry with French and Spanish regulars, but we're the best in the business at irregular warfare."

Wait for me, Claudette! As soon as this war is over, I'll be back.

And then MacKim saw Benjamin and wondered anew why he had tried to help the man, only to land him in worse trouble and cause himself difficulties.

With drums beating, colours aloft, and the sun gleaming from gold braid and brash scarlet, British troops marched through Havana's La Punta Gate and Land Gate. A hundred yards away, Kennedy's Rangers prepared to return to the field. They ensured they had sufficient ammunition, took triple their daily allocation of water and food, and had their boots resoled by the Royal Scots' regimental cobbler.

MacKim looked over the remaining twelve men of Kennedy's Rangers. The unit had proportionally fewer casualties through disease than most regiments, but the men were tired. They had wanted to return home, and this campaign through the islands had damaged their morale. Keeping his head down and his hat pulled low, Benjamin tried to merge with the rest. Fortunately, no senior officer thought to ask about the lone black man amidst the Rangers, for the Ranger units were known to be a law unto themselves.

"We are marching into hostile territory, gentlemen," Kennedy said. "Although Havana has surrendered and the surroundings are officially ours, the remainder of Cuba remains in Spanish hands."

The Rangers gave sour grunts, reconciling themselves to more hot, uncomfortable, and dangerous days while most of the Army regaled themselves in the luxuries of one of the largest cities of the Americas.

They marched southward in the old way, with Kennedy in the lead and MacKim and Parnell in charge of their respective sections. Kennedy had a map and followed their designated patrol route, checking on farms and villages, replenishing their water from streams, and trying to converse with the locals. The interior was hot, dusty, and surprisingly featureless, but quieter than MacKim had expected, and they returned without incident and a better idea of the countryside south of Havana.

"Will we be going home soon?" Parnell asked. They lay on simple cots in the old Spanish barracks in Havana, enjoying the shade.

"I hope so." MacKim thought of Claudette as he counted his men. He looked up as the first gust of wind rattled the shutters. "It looks like we're in for a blow."

Benjamin shook his head. "The hurricane is here."

The Rangers had been aware of the build-up of pressure, and Benjamin had warned them of the coming storm, but when it arrived, the hurricane took their breath away.

The seamen doubled the anchors on their ships while the locals hurried to fasten shutters on the windows. Still unaware of a hurricane's power, the British and Colonials watched and wondered. Some scorned the Spaniards' supposed timidity.

"Scared of a drop of wind," Oxford said, glowing from his first experience of a brothel. "That's why we beat them all the time."

"De Valasco nearly beat us," MacKim said. "He was as good a warrior as any we've met."

Within an hour, Oxford realised that a Caribbean hurricane was unlike any storm he had experienced before. Soon the British and Colonials sheltered under cover, listening in awe to the howl of the wind.

"The Lord is angry with us," MacRae said, staring at the wildly thrashing palm trees and the litter of wreckage the storm blasted around the streets.

"No wonder the Navy wanted a safe anchorage before the hurricane season began." MacKim watched the wind strip the tiles from a roof in seconds.

Benjamin sang a quiet song, winked at MacKim, and asked if he would like to live in the islands.

"Not ever!" MacKim replied, shouting to be heard above the roar of the wind.

When the storm abated, the Rangers watched the people of Havana begin to clear the debris with a fortitude that elicited only admiration.

"Give them a hand, boys," Kennedy said, and the Rangers happily obeyed. Both New Hampshire frontiersmen and Scottish Highlanders were accustomed to struggling with nature, and all came from a culture where people helped their neighbours.

By the end of that day, a semblance of normality had returned, as other British units had sent their men to help tidy up Havana.

"We're back on duty, boys," Kennedy said, and the routine continued as if the hurricane had never occurred.

It was a week and two patrols later before they heard the news.

The elderly villager looked at the silver coin that Kennedy pressed into his hand in exchange for half a dozen chickens and a bag of corn.

"The man's surprised that British soldiers pay for their provisions," Benjamin said.

"The French never did, and I doubt the Spanish paid, either," MacKim explained.

Behind the elderly man, the nameless village cowered under the lash of the sun, with half the roofs stripped by the hurricane. The man continued to talk in a mixture of Spanish, English, and French.

"What is he saying?" MacKim asked.

"He says that the hurricane claimed a British warship." Benjamin had proved a quick learner, picking up not only English, but Spanish faster than most of the Rangers.

"We'll report that," MacKim said. "Does he know anything of Cuban militia? We've heard there are some bands of malcontents roaming around."

Benjamin put the question to the man, who nodded.

"He says there are some further south and east, but not in this area. He is only a poor farmer and knows nothing about the war."

"Sensible fellow," MacKim said.

The Rangers moved on, seeing the results of the hurricane in uprooted trees and damaged property. After two weeks of patrolling without incident, they were becoming relaxed in the interior. Already the war seemed far away, with the sound of cannon and musketry only echoes in their minds. The Rangers were beginning to contemplate peace and a return to their homes.

"Where will you go after the war?" Kennedy asked MacKim as they camped under a cloudy night sky, with only two men on picket duty. The last of the chickens cooked above a smoking fire, and men puffed at their pipes.

"I don't know," MacKim said. "I'll think about that when peace is declared." He pushed aside his vision of his home glen and Claudette. Both were a dream, far removed from the reality of heat, thirst, dust, and disease. "We still have Benjamin to consider."

"Yes," Kennedy said, staring into the fire. "We have Benjamin."

Claudette? The longer he was parted from her, the more he missed her. *People say out of sight, out of mind; I think the opposite. Being apart only strengthens one's feelings. I see things in perspective out here. Please, God, end this war soon so I can get back to her.*

A day after they had returned to Havana, Kennedy called his Rangers together.

"We have another expedition, boys," he said.

The Rangers looked up. "Where to, sir?" Parnell asked.

"Admiral Pocock sent Captain Maxwell to survey the south coast of Cuba to find safe anchorages, places to water, and any Spanish fortifications."

MacKim nodded. "Maxwell is a good man for the job."

"Lieutenant Maxwell did not return. He is long overdue, so

the admiral believes that the hurricane claimed her. You will recall that a villager told us about a ship driven ashore."

"Was that *Dolphin?*" MacKim asked.

"Perhaps. Admiral Pocock is sending out a frigate to search for any wreckage, but this is hurricane season, so the Navy is cautious."

"Where do we come in, sir?" MacKim asked.

"I volunteered us to scour the southern coast for survivors," Kennedy said, and waited for the Rangers to protest.

"When do we leave, sir?" Parnell asked simply.

27

Laden with a week's supplies and medical equipment, the Rangers marched south of Havana. They moved in open order and at speed, knowing that any delay could be fatal to *Dolphin's* crew.

"We're concentrating on the area around the Bahía de Cochinos—that's the Bay of Pigs—and for twenty miles westward," Kennedy said. "The Lights are searching the twenty miles to the east and the Royal Americans after that."

"Lieutenant Maxwell was a good man," Oxford said.

"Is," Parnell corrected. "Lieutenant Maxwell *is* a good man. If anybody can survive, he can."

Twice on their march, the Rangers saw groups of armed men watching them, but the men moved away on both occasions.

"They look like Cuban militia," MacKim said.

"They might also be farmers out hunting," Kennedy said. "In New Hampshire, we often hunt. It's a way of life."

MacKim nodded, not convinced, but not wishing to delay their rescue mission.

As they neared the southern coast, the weather worsened, and a storm swept over them. It was not a hurricane, but reminded them of conditions at sea as they witnessed massive waves crashing on the shore.

"God help sailors on a night like this," Dickert said.

"God help *Dolphin*." MacKim imagined the sloop battling mountainous waves, with her crew straining at the braces, struggling aloft as the wind howled through the rigging. "I've even more respect for the Navy now."

The morning brought a new freshness to the island and a new purpose to the Rangers. "We'll make a base here." Kennedy stopped at an area of high ground beside a stream of clear water. "MacKim, take your section west until you reach the end of the bay. We'll start at the western end of our area and work our way eastward."

"Yes, sir."

"Take Benjamin with you," Kennedy said. "He might be useful."

The Bahia de Cochinos was a beautiful place, with pristine water and a coastline that altered from quiet sandy beaches to savage rocks. MacKim trotted westward, with his men examining the coast, looking for any signs of shipwreck, spars, scraps of canvas, or *Dolphin*'s shattered hull.

"Watch for the crocodiles," Benjamin warned as the Rangers peered around, shouting.

"*Dolphin*! Ahoy! Any Dolphins here?"

"Sergeant!" Benjamin pointed to a length of timber lying on one of the rocks.

MacKim knelt beside it. "That last storm may have driven it here," he said. The timber was neatly sawn, not natural.

"That could have come from *Dolphin*," Dickert said, crouching with his rifle in his right hand.

"Or any other vessel," MacKim said, watching as a group of giant crabs scuttled across the rocks, waving their pincers.

They moved on, with a hot wind blasting them and the fronds of palms rustling above their heads. In mid-afternoon, they reached a curve of the coast where a couple of wooded islets sat offshore, with the sea breaking around the base.

"There's somebody there." Dickert knelt behind a rock, instinctively bringing his rifle to his shoulder. "I saw someone on the larger of these islets."

"He might be friendly," MacKim warned, stepping forward. "Halloa there!" He could see nobody, only the sea and the rocks. "Are you sure you saw somebody?"

"Sure as heaven," Dickert said, without lowering his rifle.

"You're with me, Benjamin," MacKim said. "Take defensive positions, boys." It seemed strange to prepare for war in such a beautiful place, but after years of conflict, the idea of peace was unreal.

A trio of squawking birds rose from the base of the islet as MacKim shouted again, and then he lowered his voice. "Translate for me, Benjamin."

"Yes, sergeant," Benjamin said.

"We're British soldiers!" MacKim shouted. "We mean you no harm." He waited until Benjamin repeated his words in halting Spanish. "Please show yourself so we know you are no threat to us."

"It might be a Cuban militiaman," MacRae warned.

"I'm going over," MacKim said. "I rely on you lads to watch out for crocodiles." The thought of the aggressive reptiles scared him, but he knew he could not leave an unknown person behind him. This man could tell them about *Dolphin* or reassure them that the hurricane had not driven the sloop onto this section of the shore.

"Translate," MacKim repeated to Benjamin. "I'm coming across," he shouted. "I will not hurt you."

Taking a deep breath, MacKim waded into the sea, holding his musket out of the water, and swam the last few yards, depending on his marksmen to watch for crocodiles.

The islet was little more than a tall rock covered in dense vegetation, with a hundred insects waiting in ambush the second that MacKim pulled himself out of the sea. Still wary of snakes, MacKim scrambled up the rock, checked his musket, and shouted again.

"Halloa!" He heard movement from the seaward side of the islet and moved cautiously round, with his musket ready to fire. "I won't hurt you!" He glimpsed somebody's back and the flash of bare skin, and then dense vegetation blocked his path.

"Stand still!" MacKim was losing his patience. "I won't hurt you!" Thrusting into the bushes, he slipped on a rock, nearly stumbled into the sea, and recovered his balance. "I see you," he lied. "You may as well come out. I am Sergeant Hugh MacKim of His Britannic Majesty's Rangers."

"Sergeant MacKim!" The voice was hoarse, but familiar.

"What the devil?" MacKim stared upward, where a cleft in the rocks created a natural cave, and a woman stood in the entrance, staring at him.

"Sergeant MacKim?" The sun had burned much of the skin from Suzanne Williams' face, and her lips were cracked and blistered. Her hair was bleached and tangled, while the canvas breeches and shirt she wore were filthy and torn to the point of indecency.

"Mrs Williams? What the devil? I didn't expect to see you here."

It was instinct that made MacKim lower the musket and hold out his arms, and within a moment, Suzanne was pressing close to him, fighting to restrain her tears. MacKim held her for a long two minutes until she regained control of herself.

"What are the Rangers doing here, sergeant?" Suzanne wiped away her tears.

"We're looking for any survivors of *Dolphin*," MacKim said. "Are you the only one?"

Suzanne looked confused. "The only one? I don't believe so. Have the others been killed?"

"I hoped you would tell me. Were you shipwrecked? Cast ashore?"

"No."

"You'd better tell us the whole story," MacKim said. "We'll get back to the shore first."

"There are crocodiles," Suzanne said.

"We have the best marksmen in the world watching for them," MacKim assured her. "Come with me."

※

The Rangers crowded round as MacKim brought Suzanne amongst them, with MacRae taking off his tunic to cover her and the other men offering fresh water.

"Come away from the beach." MacKim led them to a knoll slightly inland. "Butler and Parnell, keep watch!"

"Now, Suzanne," MacKim said when she had emptied the contents of his water bottle and eaten ravenously of Army bread and salt pork. "Tell us what's happened."

"The captain knew that bad weather was coming," Suzanne explained, "so he put out to sea, rather than having the hurricane smash us against the shore. I don't know all the technical terms, but when the storm hit us, Captain Maxwell turned the bow to face it. We were riding it out when a freak wave came from astern. It washed away the helmsman, and *Dolphin* presented her broadside to the wind and waves. We lost our mizzen mast, and when the storm subsided, Captain Maxwell put into the land to refit."

MacKim could imagine the confusion and outstanding seamanship required to keep a crippled ship afloat in the hurricane and find a safe anchorage on a hostile coast.

"Carry on," he said.

"Captain Maxwell had surveyed this bay already," Suzanne said, "so he headed straight for here, but as soon as he started to refit, that French privateer appeared again."

"*Douce Vengeance*," MacKim said, looking around.

"Yes, that's her," Suzanne agreed. "She sent a longboat to our starboard side, and with most of our crew on land, the men were overwhelmed. I was ashore and ran away. I hid on that island there."

MacKim looked at the tiny islet, with the sea crashing around it.

"One of the freebooters followed me," Suzanne said. "He was laughing and shouting, but I don't know what he was saying."

"I doubt you want to know," MacKim murmured.

"He saw me on the island and came to follow me, and the crocodiles got him."

MacKim nodded. "I'm glad they got him and not us."

Suzanne shivered. "I think there were three crocodiles. Two, at least. I was too frightened to swim ashore."

"So would anybody be. How long were you on the island?" MacKim asked.

Suzanne looked away. "Three days, I think."

"*Dolphin* is around here somewhere, then," MacKim said. "And so is *Douce Vengeance*." He looked around the bay. "Dickert, fetch Captain Kennedy and inform him what's happened."

"Yes, sergeant." Dickert left at a fast trot.

The night was falling when Kennedy brought the rest of the Rangers, and they made camp a hundred yards inland, with the sea crashing against the rocks and the men alert for crocodiles and freebooters.

"It's unusual for these crocodiles to be in the sea," Benjamin said. "They prefer fresh water."

"Maybe they can't find enough food there," Parnell said. "Or they've developed a taste for human flesh."

Benjamin nodded. "That might be so."

"No fire tonight," Kennedy ordered, "and double pickets if Roberval's men are close."

Suzanne slept within a circle of Rangers, mumbling in her sleep. In the morning, she looked refreshed, but wearied by her experiences.

Kennedy sat in front of her. "Can you take us to where *Dolphin* was captured? Are you strong enough?"

"It's not far," Suzanne said, chewing on a piece of MacRae's Army-ration pork.

Suzanne led them eastward, with the Rangers hugging the ragged woodland at the fringe of the beach, moving quietly in case the privateers were close.

"This way, I think." Suzanne stooped at an inlet of the sea, where dense woodland crowded to the water's edge and brightly coloured birds screeched to each other. "Up this beach."

After ten minutes, Parnell lifted a hand, and they stopped, sinking behind the nearest cover with muskets ready.

Without saying anything, Parnell pointed to the ground. The imprint of a man's boot was evident in the soft mud, with half a bare foot at the side.

MacKim nodded. Officers wore boots; ordinary seamen were often barefoot.

The Rangers moved on, more slowly, watching every tree and bush with fingers on triggers, listening for hostile sounds.

"There." Suzanne touched Kennedy's sleeve. "That's where the captain had *Dolphin*."

MacKim saw nothing except trees. The sloop, and the French privateer, had vanished.

28

"The French must have shifted them," Kennedy muttered. "They might be in Hispaniola by now." He lifted his head, sniffing the air.

"I smell it, too," Dickert said. "Something's cooking."

"If we smell their cooking fires," MacKim said, "they're a lot closer than Hispaniola."

Kennedy moved them a hundred yards away from the water's edge, where the forest belt eased into an area of dry scrub.

"We'll make our base here for now," he said quietly. "Corporal Parnell, take your section along the coast to find out how far this inlet extends. If you find *Dolphin,* report back immediately."

"Yes, sir." Parnell signalled to his men.

"Sergeant MacKim," Kennedy said. "I want you to return the way you came. We're not looking for wreckage now, but for two ships. They may be anchored offshore or beached."

Suzanne lifted a hand. "I can help the sergeant."

"No, Mrs Williams," Kennedy said. "You've had enough excitement for the present. You stay here."

The body was floating at the edge of the sea, naked as a newborn infant and partly chewed by fish.

"Sergeant," Dickert said softly, pointing with his chin.

"I see it." MacKim did not venture close. "Where did that come from?"

MacRae joined them, crouching behind a tree. "The tide's carried it across the inlet, sergeant," he said quietly. "Look at all the other rubbish at its side."

MacKim nodded.

"Sergeant," MacRae said. "Can you see that branch with the serrated fronds at the man's feet?"

"The branch that looks like a palm tree?" MacKim studied the trees on the opposite side of the inlet.

"That's the one, sergeant. Can you see any other similar tree around here?"

MacKim scanned the coast on both sides of the inlet, concentrating on one area before moving to the next. "Only that small group on the opposite side of the water."

"That's all I see, too, sergeant," MacRae said. "So the current, or the tide, runs from there to here. Allowing for the different weight, the tide must have carried that body from near these palm trees."

MacKim looked at him with new respect. "Well done, MacRae. How did you know to do that?"

"I grew up by the sea, sergeant. The tide used to throw up all sorts of things on the Ross-shire beaches."

MacKim nodded. "You're a lad of parts, Duncan. We'll have to get across there to solve the mystery."

MacRae studied the trees on the opposite side of the inlet with a curious smile on his face. "I wouldn't do that, sergeant."

"Why not, MacRae?"

"The Frenchies wouldn't like it. *Douce Vengeance* is moored there, and so is *Dolphin*."

"Where?"

"They've hidden them behind leaves and branches," MacRae

said. "But if you look closely, you can make out the masts, standing too straight to be natural, with branches at right angles."

MacKim frowned and peered closer. "My God, MacRae, you've done it! Dickert! Take my compliments to Captain Kennedy, and ask him to pray step along here. Tell him that Private MacRae has discovered *Douce Vengeance* and *Dolphin.*"

***

"There," MacKim said, gesturing to the other side of the inlet. Even knowing what he was looking for, he found it difficult to make out the ships.

"Where?" Kennedy said.

"Look at the line of trees," MacKim spoke in a low tone, in case his voice should carry above the constant screech of birds. "Do you see the tallest ones, about fifty yards apart?"

"I do," Kennedy said.

"And next to them, on their left, there is a tree nearly equal in height," MacKim said. "Those are not trees, but the masts of ships. One is *Dolphin,* and the other is *Douce Vengeance.*"

"Dear Lord in heaven," Kennedy said. "The French have hidden them well. Now that you point it out, I can see the spars and masts. What clever people the French are."

"They're not as clever as they think," MacKim said. "MacRae found them right away."

Kennedy smiled. "Now, what we have to do is free *Dolphin* and capture *Douce Vengeance.*"

"They outnumber us, sir," MacKim reminded. "We're thirteen strong; fourteen including Benjamin."

"Then we'll have to trim them down," Kennedy said.

That night, the weather altered again, blasting a gale into the inlet and causing the trees to shake and bend. The wind carried warm rain in a deluge that lasted until an hour after dawn, when it subsided, leaving only a heavy swell.

"That's why Roberval is sitting tight," Kennedy said the following morning. "He's anchored nice and snug for the hurricane season. He's not going to try sailing with fickle weather, British patrols out, and few secure anchorages in French or even Spanish hands. He has the supplies of two ships to consume, a river nearby for fresh water and good fishing here, with tortoises and even crabs for fresh food."

"Sir," Dickert said. "Something's happening."

They watched as *Douce Vengeance* released a launch with a crew of four men, who dropped lines into the water.

"It all looks idyllic," Kennedy said.

"Apart from the odd corpse," MacKim reminded.

Kennedy grunted. "I aim to add a few more corpses," he said grimly. "I'd estimate *Douce Vengeance's* crew at about 150. We know *Dolphin* had 64 men on board when we sailed with her, and if we add our Rangers, that's 77 men. They outnumber us by nearly two to one."

"Yes, sir," MacKim agreed.

"And I presume that *Dolphin's* crew are locked up below decks," Kennedy said. "Our best advantage will be surprise."

"We're also land-based, sir," MacKim said. "*Douce Vengeance's* crew are seamen, so they're out of their element here. That, surely, can work in our favour."

A burst of coarse laughter from across the inlet silenced the Rangers, and they slid further into the undergrowth as a second boat joined the first on the water.

"What the devil?" Kennedy breathed as he saw the second boat had a man tied in the middle, with the others prodding at him with knives and cutlasses.

"Dear God," MacKim said. "That's Bearsden, one of *Dolphin*'s crew."

"The privateer's crew is watching," Kennedy said, as the foliage screen across *Douce Vengeance* shook, with a dozen gaps appearing as men shoved the branches aside to create better viewpoints.

The prisoner was tied hand and foot, with a gag across his mouth. The privateers poised him in the stern of the boat, cut his bonds, and pushed him in the water. The prisoner floundered for a moment and then began to swim for the shore, only for the original boat to row past and block his passage.

"What are they doing?" MacKim lifted his musket.

Kennedy placed a hand on the lock, preventing MacKim from firing. He shook his head.

After a few moments, it became evident that the privateers were playing with the prisoner, preventing him from escaping and watching him grow increasingly more desperate in his attempts to swim ashore. As the prisoner's strength ebbed, his struggles became weaker.

MacKim lifted his musket again, only for Kennedy to prevent him from firing a second time.

Eventually, the privateers grew tired of their sport, and one man lifted a boarding pike and thrust it into the prisoner's back, with two others leaning out of the boat to watch. After a short pause, both boats rowed back to *Douce Vengeance*, leaving the prisoner's body floating amidst a swirl of blood.

"Free entertainment," Kennedy said. "Judging by the body we already found, murdering a sailor is a regular occurrence. If you had fired, MacKim, the French would have known we were here."

"I could have saved that man's life."

"I know." Kennedy's eyes were haunted. "And probably condemned the others, and maybe my Rangers as well."

MacKim said nothing. He knew Kennedy would not have made his decision lightly.

"Back to the camp," Kennedy ordered.

The Rangers heard the news with grim faces. Suzanne nodded, looked away, and clenched her fist. "Did you see who the man was?"

"It was Bearsden," MacKim told her. "It wasn't your husband."

Suzanne nodded. "Not this time," she said.

"What are we going to do, sir?" Dickert asked. In common with all the Rangers, he knew that Kennedy would act.

"We're going to free *Dolphin*'s crew," Kennedy said. "And we're going to burn *Douce Vengeance* and all inside that hell ship."

The Rangers gave a savage growl of agreement, with MacKim as angry as any of them. Roberval's crew had stepped beyond the pale of civilisation, and the rules of civilised warfare no longer applied to them.

"How?" MacKim asked the pivotal question.

"We're going to cross to the other side of the inlet and hit them at night," Kennedy said. "I'll work out the details later."

"We could cut the ship free and float her out on the tide," MacRae suggested.

"Do you know the local tides?" Kennedy asked. "I certainly don't, and we've no Cuban seamen here to teach us. We'll do things my way, MacRae." He looked up. "Corporal Parnell, take two men and scout our route."

"Yes, sir." Parnell touched two men of his section and moved off.

"Sergeant MacKim, ensure we have double pickets at all times. I don't want any of our men falling into Roberval's hands."

"Yes, sir."

"Spell the men after two hours, so everybody gets sufficient rest," Kennedy said. "I want everybody to eat, sleep and ensure your muskets are clean and dry, and your flints are sharp. We've got work to do tonight."

29

They moved an hour before dark, following the route that Parnell had pioneered.

"You two." Kennedy picked Dickert and MacRae. "Stay in the camp with Mrs Williams."

"Sir," MacKim protested. "They're the best men we have."

"All the better to guard Mrs Williams," Kennedy said. "God only knows how Roberval's men would treat her. Benjamin, you remain here as well."

"I can fight," Benjamin protested. "Give me a musket and I can shoot, or let me have a cutlass and I'll show the Frenchies!"

"You don't know our ways. Stay here, damn it!" The fact that Kennedy swore proved the turmoil in his mind.

"Yes, sir." Benjamin looked at the ground.

The Rangers slid through the woods—so different from the cool forests of North America—following Parnell. Although MacKim had never found Parnell an easy man to like, he trusted him implicitly as an excellent guide. Parnell's two chosen men guarded the flanks, and the others walked in wary silence. They checked the ground before placing their feet, watching for twigs that could snap, or snakes that could bite, ducked under overhanging branches, and bit down the obscenities that rose to their lips.

"Watch yourselves here," Parnell warned as they arrived at a wide stream. "Crocodiles like fresh water."

They forded two at a time, with the others looking out for crocodiles, then moved thankfully along the far side of the river.

Even with Parnell as a guide, it took nearly two hours to walk around the inlet and arrive at the moored ships.

Roberval's men had erected a camouflaged screen on the landward side of the ships, but now, the Rangers were aware of the signs.

When Parnell lifted a hand to signify they had arrived, the Rangers dropped in a crouch, each man keeping behind cover.

MacKim peered ahead. Roberval had moored the ships stern-to-stem, with *Douce Vengeance* closer to the sea and four-dozen stout cables attaching each vessel to trees. For a moment, MacKim pondered MacRae's idea of cutting *Dolphin* free, but decided that Kennedy was correct and studied each ship.

Two sentinels lounged on the stern of *Douce Vengeance*, looking extremely bored, while another paced *Dolphin*'s deck with a musket over his shoulder and a cutlass on his hip.

"Three men on guard," MacKim reported.

Kennedy nodded. "That's what I reckoned. Parnell, I want your men to remain as pickets here."

"Sir." Parnell nodded.

"MacKim, take four of your people, silence the man on *Dolphin*, and free the prisoners."

"Sir." MacKim had expected the order. He knew Kennedy would give himself the most dangerous task.

"I'll take four men and silence the guards on *Douce Vengeance*."

MacKim knew that the Royal Navy specialised in such daring acts, calling them "cutting out expeditions" as they captured enemy ships from the supposed security of a hostile harbour. The Rangers were the best irregular soldiers in the British Army, but lacked the Navy's knowledge of ships. They could not recapture *Dolphin,* and the best they could do was free the prisoners.

MacKim waited, studying *Dolphin* as he worked out how to remove the guard without alerting the sentries on *Douce Vengeance.* Timing and stealth was everything in such cases.

The guard on *Dolphin* stopped to bite at a chunk of tobacco, then recommenced his beat, walking the length of the deck, stopping to stare at the forest, and walking back again. It was a monotonous routine that bored soldiers had cursed for thousands of years.

MacKim timed the sentry's beat. When the man was at the bow, MacKim led his men onto the stern. They waited in tense silence until the sentry returned. MacKim crept behind the man, clapped a hand over his mouth, and held him while Butler slipped a knife between his ribs. It was murder rather than soldiering, but the freebooters had made the rules and could expect nothing less from the Rangers.

Laying the body carefully on the deck, MacKim moved forward to the foc'sle, where he suspected the privateers would have imprisoned the crew. The door was open and the fo'c'sle empty.

"Down below." MacKim stifled his curse. "Butler, act like you're a French sentry, pace the deck."

"Yes, sergeant." Butler glanced at his battered green uniform uncertainly.

"Take the dead man's clothes!" MacKim hissed. "He's about your size."

Without waiting for Butler to comply, MacKim slipped below decks, with Dickert and MacRae at his back. Tropical heat and the proximity of the forest had made the ship's interior even stuffier than usual. MacKim gagged at the stench as he felt his way below decks.

"Pierre?" the voice cut through the dark

"*Oui,*" MacKim answered, and followed the voice to its source, a one-eyed rogue with a brace of pistols. He sat on a three-legged stool, calmly smoking a pipe. Above him, a slender lantern pooled flickering yellow light. The Frenchman had only time for one startled comment before MacKim smashed him over the head with the barrel of his pistol.

"Halloa!" MacKim raised his voice in an echoing shout, hoping to attract any more guards. The word faded away without a response.

MacRae lifted the lantern, with the light revealing a large spider scuttling across the bulkhead. "Where might the prisoners be?"

"I wish I knew," MacKim said, and called again. "Halloa! Are there any British in here?"

"We're all British!" the reply came. "Who the devil are you?"

"Sergeant MacKim of Kennedy's Rangers!" MacKim replied. "One man, shout out so we can find you, but not too loud! We don't wish to alert the enemy."

"Halloa!" the voice sounded. "We're in the cockpit!"

"This way, sergeant," MacRae said, and led them to the cockpit in the bowels of the ship, with the lantern light bouncing across *Dolphin's* dark timbers.

When MacKim pulled back the wooden bar and opened the door, the smell of foul air caught the back of his throat. The lantern flickered and nearly died with lack of oxygen as MacRae lifted it high.

Nearly sixty men were squeezed into the confined space, and all stared at him. Captain Maxwell pushed to the front, one eye swollen and bruised, with his lips puffed up so he spoke with difficulty. "The French took away Bearsden and Peters."

"Both dead." MacKim did not give details.

"My wife." Williams came forward, his voice anxious. "Have you seen anything of Suzanne?"

"She's safe with the Rangers," MacKim reassured him. "If it wasn't for Suzanne, we might never have found you. Come on now, before the French hear us."

They filed out slowly, with some of the seamen so weak they

needed bodily support, and one by one slipped ashore, where Kennedy and his men waited.

"Are your men fit?" Kennedy asked. MacKim noted the blood on the back of his hands. "Could you cut the cables and take *Dolphin* out to sea?"

Maxwell's face brightened at the thought before he shook his head. "Not this night," he said. "Roberval has placed a boom across the inlet. It's only a few logs chained together, but we'd need to deal with the guards and unfasten the chains."

"Let's have a look," Kennedy said. "We can get you out to sea before the French know we are even here."

Before Maxwell replied, a seaman came to the deck of *Douce Vengeance*. He saw his comrade lying down and, quick-witted, rang the ship's bell.

"Damn!" Kennedy said as the brassy clamour reverberated through the night. "That was bad luck!"

Two of *Douce Vengeance's* crew emerged on deck, half-dressed but alert for trouble. They shouted when they saw *Dolphin's* men, lifted a long pistol, and fired.

"Into the trees, lads!" Kennedy ordered. "Parnell, you're in front; MacKim, look after *Dolphin's* men." He took the rear-guard, the most dangerous position, walking backwards as the Rangers escorted the ex-prisoners back along the trail.

"Here they come, boys!"

The crack of the musket followed Kennedy's warning, and then a medley of shouts in French and Spanish. The privateers debouched from *Douce Vengeance* in a mob, carrying various weapons as they leapt ashore and followed the fugitives. Some held lanterns and flaring torches, with the harsh light throwing darker shadows onto the surrounding trees.

"Captain Roberval must have recruited new hands," MacKim said, walking backwards to see behind him. "There are hundreds of them. Keep moving, Dolphins, and leave the fighting to us!"

MacKim heard the sharper report of a rifle, and then another. MacRae and Dickert had joined the skirmish from across the inlet. They would be aiming just below the French lanterns, with their rifles at extreme range.

"That will confuse the Frenchies," Oxford said, tucking himself behind a tree to fire.

"Keep the Dolphins moving!" Kennedy shouted and ran to MacKim. "I'll take half your section, sergeant, and organise an ambush to delay the French. They won't know how many we are."

"Yes, sir," MacKim said. He pushed the seamen on, helping the weakest and encouraging them all. "Come on, lads! Keep up there! Leave the fighting to the Rangers."

After five minutes, MacKim heard an outbreak of musketry behind him as Kennedy's ambush made contact with the French.

"Rangers!" Butler's voice sounded through the dark. "First and always!"

"Can we help?" Maxwell asked. "My lads want to fight!"

"No, sir," MacKim said. "Keep your men moving, please." He turned around, wishing he was with the rearguard so he knew what was happening. Escorting stumbling men through dark woodland was worse than fighting.

The firing eased away, broke out in a few sporadic shots as imaginative men thought they saw shapes in the dark, and ended again. Acrid powder smoke drifted in the night and a bird called its whistle eerie through the trees.

"Nearly there!" Parnell called, and the seamen gave a collective sigh of relief. Used to the vast horizons from the masts and decks of their ship, the sailors found themselves staggering through the stifling confines of an unpleasantly alien Cuban forest

Suzanne greeted the sailors' arrival anxiously. "Is he safe?"

"Suzanne!" Williams enfolded Suzanne in his arms while the rest of the Dolphins collapsed in exhaustion within the Rangers' perimeter.

"Parnell! Take your section on picket and watch for the

captain," MacKim said. "Captain Maxwell, I'm heading back to help Captain Kennedy."

"No need, sergeant, I'm already here." Kennedy trotted into the camp. "We stopped them dead, but now the French know we are here, they won't be idle, and they still outnumber us more than two to one."

Maxwell held out his hand. "Thank you, Captain Kennedy."

"We couldn't leave you there," Kennedy said. "Admiral Pocock is concerned about your safety. He's sent out a frigate to look for you."

"We lost a spar in the hurricane and came in to replace it." Maxwell repeated Suzanne's description of events.

"Get your men rested," Kennedy said. "There's fresh water in the stream thirty yards to the left; that's larboard to you. Watch for crocodiles."

"Thank you, captain," Maxwell said.

Kennedy grinned. "Now we have to devise a plan to get us home."

"Have you anything in mind?" Maxwell asked.

MacKim checked his men as the officers spoke. Apart from a few minor cuts and bruises from stumbling in the dark, there were no casualties. "Where's Benjamin?" He looked around. "MacRae! Dickert! I left Benjamin with you! Where is he?"

MacRae shook his head. "I don't know, sergeant. He must have run when we were firing at the French."

Dickert agreed. "That must be what happened, sergeant."

MacKim cursed. "Where is he going to go?"

"Is he your slave, sergeant?" MacRae asked.

"No, he's as free as you or me," MacKim said.

"If he's free, then he can go where he likes," MacRae said. "He's not a Ranger."

MacKim frowned, although he knew that MacRae was correct.

Benjamin has made his choice, and I wish him the best of luck.

Kennedy and Maxwell were still discussing the situation.

"I had thought of a fire ship," Kennedy said. "It worked before with Roberval. This time, we could moor it alongside *Douce Vengeance* and set him alight."

Maxwell smiled, shaking his head. "We've had a hurricane and a violent storm. The wood is too wet to burn. Oh, it will smoulder and cause smoke, but that's all."

"Damn," Kennedy said softly. "Then all I can suggest is we leave Roberval here and march you and your men over to Havana."

"I'm not leaving my ship in that damned pirate's hands," Maxwell said. "You take your men to Havana, Captain Kennedy, and leave us here. We'll harass Roberval, and you can bring across reinforcements or not, as you please."

"We're not leaving you here," Kennedy said.

"Sir!" Parnell panted up to Kennedy. "Trouble, sir."

"What's that, Parnell?"

"Cuban militia, sir, hundreds of them."

30

"Show me." Kennedy sounded infinitely weary. "Take over the camp, Corporal Parnell. Sergeant MacKim, you're with me!"

A belt of scrubland stretched inland from the forest, with a few isolated trees marking the course of the stream. The Cuban militia had set up camp on both banks of the river. Some had tents, while others merely sat in groups around small fires, talking together, and practising stick fighting, smoking, or roasting newly killed animals over small fires.

"How many, do you think, sergeant?" Kennedy lay on his stomach beneath a brightly flowered bush.

MacKim contemplated the enemy. "As Parnell said, sir, I'd say there were hundreds."

"So would I." Kennedy gave a taut smile. "We appear to be trapped between the devil's militia and the deep sea of Captain Roberval's privateers."

Lieutenant Maxwell joined them. "Can your Rangers pass through them?"

"We're staying together," Kennedy repeated.

"Maybe the militia won't remain," MacKim said.

MacKim's hope lasted until dawn. With the first grey light, a small party of ten militia left the main camp and marched purposefully downstream along the riverbank towards the Bahía de Cochinos.

"They know where they're going," MacKim said.

"We'll follow them," Kennedy decided.

The militiamen followed the river without hesitation, shouting as they reached the Bahía de Cochinos. A group of privateers met them, and after initial greetings, escorted them to the ships.

"They've arranged this meeting," Kennedy said as the militia and the privateer's crew merged. "Back to camp, gentlemen."

The Rangers and Dolphins heard the news with a mixture of dismay and equanimity, with some men cursing and others merely accepting their position. Kennedy spoke earnestly to Maxwell before calling the Rangers together. The crew of *Dolphin* joined them, with Maxwell and Holmes looking grim.

"We don't know the enemy's numbers, men," Kennedy said. "And they don't know ours; we do know they outnumber us. Lieutenant Maxwell and I have discussed the situation, and here's the plan."

The British and New Hampshire men listened, sweltering in the mounting heat.

"I'll take a party of Rangers and seamen to the boom across the entrance of this inlet," Kennedy said. "Captain Maxwell will take the rest of the seamen and Corporal Parnell with three Rangers to recapture *Dolphin*, while Sergeant MacKim, Private Butler, and the marksmen remain here to harass the French with long-distance rifle fire. Mrs Williams will remain in the camp."

MacKim listened without comment, although he did not like the idea of splitting the force into small segments while near an already superior enemy.

Kennedy waited until the expected murmur of comments died away. "After I free the boom, Captain Maxwell will sail *Dolphin* past *Douce Vengeance*, fire a broadside to cripple her, pick up Sergeant MacKim's party, and then mine." Kennedy took a deep breath. "Then we sail for Havana."

The crowd listened, trying to digest the plan.

"We move at dark," Kennedy said with a forced grin.

As the day passed, more militiamen joined the privateers, either singly or in small groups, making it difficult to assess the numbers on *Douce Vengeance*.

"I estimate 180," MacKim said, "but we don't know for sure how many there were before."

"A hundred and eighty or three hundred," Kennedy said. "They still outnumber us. We're embarking on a risky business, sergeant."

MacKim nodded. "We're the Rangers," he said. "We always embark on risky business." Yet, MacKim felt his stomach churning. There were too many factors that could go wrong.

Lights appeared on *Douce Vengeance* half an hour before dusk, and MacKim saw a group of men sitting in the stern, passing around a bottle of something.

"They seem to be having a party," he said, passing the telescope to Kennedy.

"Privateers and Cuban militia together," Kennedy said. "That's all the better for us. The drunker they are, the less likely they'll be to oppose our attack."

The instant the sun fell, Kennedy and Maxwell's parties departed. MacKim sat tight, knowing he had the least active part in the operation.

He allowed both parties half an hour for their respective journeys, then ordered his men to take their positions.

"Butler, you watch for the militia. Dickert and MacRae, we'll get down to the shore, where your rifles can reach *Douce Vengeance*." He waited until Butler moved inland. "On my word." MacKim had taken Parnell's rifle in exchange for his musket, much to Parnell's disgust. "Clear the Frenchman's deck."

What seemed like a hundred men, both privateers and militia, crowded on *Douce Vengeance's* upper deck, laughing, singing, drinking, and dancing. MacKim selected a stout French seaman, keeping both eyes open as he aimed at the broadest target of the man's midriff.

The Pennsylvania rifle felt beautifully balanced in MacKim's hands. "Fire," he said, and squeezed the trigger. He barely felt the kick of the recoil; it was so much less than the Brown Bess. The stout man staggered back even before the rifle's report reached him, and then MacKim was reloading feverishly.

Two more men had fallen as MacRae and Dickert both claimed their victims, but from now on, the targets would not be as easy as the enemy either returned fire or ran below.

Dickert was ready first, aiming from behind a fallen tree, with MacRae a fraction later and MacKim third. The privateers were either stunned or too drunk to care. Only a few looked at the shore, and many continued to drink and sing. Nobody sought to douse the lanterns, which provided sufficient light for the Rangers to see their targets.

"Bloody part-time soldiers," Dickert said.

"All the better for us." MacRae settled his rifle against his shoulder.

"Look for the officers," MacKim ordered. He desperately wanted to shoot Roberval, to knock some of the fight from the French.

"Which ones are the officers?" MacRae asked. "They all look alike."

"The ones that are better dressed and work less," Dickert replied.

MacKim grunted. All the militia looked hideously dangerous with their loose clothing and the vicious machetes hanging from their belts.

Dickert fired first again, and swore. "Only winged him."

MacRae laughed and fired. "Knocked him flat," he said. "Right through the head!"

MacKim was vaguely aware of Maxwell's men hacking at the mooring ropes as he fired. He had aimed at a man right in the bows, nearest to *Dolphin,* and saw his target leap in the air, holding his side.

The privateers responded, at last, with some scurrying below and others running to the ship's guns. MacKim still could not see Roberval and wondered where he was even as he reloaded, swearing when the ball jammed in the long barrel of his rifle, and he had to ram furiously to drive it up.

Dickert's rifle cracked again, with the whiff of powder smoke drifting quickly past. "Wind's rising," Dickert said. "And that's another Frenchie who won't see Paris again."

MacRae grunted. "I thought *Douce Vengeance* came from Martinico."

"I don't care where they're from." Dickert had reloaded his rifle faster than most men could load a smooth-bored musket and was aiming again, even before MacKim cocked his piece.

MacRae fired and swore. "That bugger ducked at the wrong time!"

The privateers had manned the guns and were loading, with a slender man at the swivels, shouting orders.

"Suzanne!" MacKim shouted. "Get down low! The privateer will fire soon!"

MacKim spared a glance at Maxwell's party. They had cut or unfastened half the cables and were swarming on board *Dolphin.* All seemed to be going well on that front.

"Keep firing! Help Captain Maxwell!"

"Listen! Captain Kennedy's reached the boom!" Dickert shouted.

MacKim nodded. He had been aware of the hammer of musketry from the edge of the inlet for the last few seconds, but had blocked it from his mind as he struggled with his rifle.

"Come on, you bastard! Get where you belong!" MacKim tried to force home the bullet.

"This way, sergeant," Dickert leaned across to demonstrate. "Be gentle with Parnell's rifle. Pretend it's a woman." He gave a sly smile. "Pretend it's Claudette."

With Dickert's help, MacKim tapped home the bullet and wad. He lay on the ground just as the crew of *Douce Vengeance* fired their cannons. The noise of the broadside was like the closing of hell's door as a torrent of shot crashed into the woodland. Most of the balls went high, slicing boughs and branches from the trees to thump down among MacKim's small party, although one hit the water ten yards offshore, raising a sandy fountain of water, and another ploughed into the rocks.

Suzanne gave a small scream. "Sorry, boys!" she said. "That broadside startled me a little. Go on! Shoot them to pieces!"

"We're distracting them!" MacRae exclaimed.

MacKim wondered vaguely why the privateers did not concern themselves with the activity on *Dolphin*. He decided that was Captain Maxwell's business and aimed at the men around the swivel gun.

He squeezed the trigger an instant before the privateers fired, saw his man jerk back, involuntarily raising the barrel of the swivel, which fired far too high. He swore as a rush of men emerged from the hold of *Dolphin* to clash with Maxwell's sailors.

"The privateers were expecting an attack!" MacKim shouted.

One moment, Maxwell's men were on the verge of capturing the sloop, and the next, they were engaged in a desperate fight with the privateers who swarmed from every nook and cranny.

"Help the Dolphins!" MacKim yelled. "Target the privateers on her deck!"

It had been easy to fire at the men on *Douce Vengeance*, but much more difficult to single out a target when British, French, and Cuban militia merged in a furiously fighting crowd on *Dolphin's* deck.

Once again, MacKim searched for Roberval or any other French officer amidst the confusion of struggling bodies. Unable to see the French captain, he singled out a Cuban militiaman bawling orders as he waved a machete.

"You'll do, my lad," MacKim said, an instant before Dickert's rifle banged and the Cuban crumpled to the deck.

The firing from the boom intensified, proving that Kennedy's men were also facing opposition.

"Sergeant MacKim!" Suzanne's shriek came simultaneously with the thud of Butler's musket.

"What the devil?" MacKim looked around to see Butler running towards them, with his musket in one hand and Suzanne in the other.

"The militia!" Butler shouted, then stiffened and crumpled to the ground, blood spreading across his chest. Rather than continue to run, Suzanne lifted Butler's musket and swung it at the horde of men who emerged from the trees.

"MacRae!" MacKim made a hasty decision, "Dickert! Ignore the ships! Help Suzanne!"

The plan had come unravelled as Roberval and the militia countered every move. In this game of chess, Roberval had checked Kennedy's triple attacks.

There were too many Cuban militiamen. They advanced from all sides, surrounding MacKim and his men. MacKim saw grinning black faces and triumphant white faces, men with machetes and men with muskets. The leader was a gorgeously dressed individual with a scarlet sash who could have stepped off the deck of a seventeenth-century galleon.

A swarthy man grabbed MacKim's rifle, while another cracked the butt of his musket on Dickert's head, knocking him to the ground. MacRae struggled, drawing his bayonet and lunging at a machete-waving black man, only for another Cuban to trip him and grab his arm.

Within a minute of Suzanne's warning, the Cubans had overcome the Rangers' resistance.

The fighting on *Dolphin* was also over, with the numbers of privateers and Cubans having prevailed. Only the musketry from the boom continued.

"It all depends on Captain Kennedy now," MacRae said, hauling himself upright and glaring his hatred at the Cubans.

MacKim realised that the short tropical night was passing.

As always in battle, time moved quickly, with incidents packed together, so what seemed like minutes were hours. The clock continued to tick, and dawn was not far away.

When the last shooting died down, a cheer rose from the direction of the boom.

"Who's cheering?" MacRae asked. "Who's won?"

The Rangers listened in sick dismay when somebody began to sing in Spanish.

"They've defeated us!" Dickert sounded amazed, holding his injured head.

MacKim placed a protective arm around Suzanne, who stared around her in evident terror. "Keep together," MacKim said. "We're Kennedy's Rangers." He glanced at Butler, who lay still, with a hundred questing flies already feasting on the congealed blood on his chest.

Sleep easy, Butler. Rangers, first and always.

The Cuban militia pushed and shoved the Rangers and Suzanne to the water's edge, where the privateers had sent across their boats.

"Do as they say, boys." MacKim was suddenly infinitely weary. "There's no sense in getting killed."

Maxwell and his men sat in a disconsolate huddle on the deck of *Dolphin,* surrounded by jeering privateers and militia. Three of the victorious privateers threw the dead and wounded Dolphins into the water.

"Murdering bastards!" MacRae watched in horror.

"Heads up, boys!" Maxwell shouted. "We're not beat yet!"

Roberval strutted across from the deck of *Douce Vengeance* and slapped Maxwell backhanded across the face.

"Maybe Captain Kennedy will save us." Dickert hoped as the militia shoved them into the boats.

"There he is now," MacRae said, as a triumphant company of privateers and Cubans herded Kennedy and the remains of his men onto *Douce Vengeance.* "That bastard French pirate knew everything we were going to do."

A SACRIFICE OF PAWNS

"Somebody must have told Roberval our plan," Dickert said. "That black man, Benjamin, must have run to their camp. That's why he deserted."

"Benjamin wouldn't do that," MacKim said. "Maybe Roberval only guessed what we would do."

The privateers rowed them across the inlet, now smeared with blood. A crocodile arrowed from the river, grabbed a body, and disappeared beneath the surface. Not only Suzanne recoiled in horror from the sight.

The militia herded them onto *Dolphin*'s deck to join the Kennedy and Maxwell. The Rangers and seamen glared at their captors in cold hatred.

"Sorry, boys," Kennedy said. "I guess I wasn't as smart as I thought."

"We were betrayed," Dickert insisted. "That bastard Benjamin must have told the Frenchies what we planned."

"No," Kennedy said, shaking his head. His left arm hung loosely at his side, with a trail of blood dripping onto the ground. "Nobody betrayed us; we were outnumbered. I lost two Rangers at the boom."

"I lost eight men, including Lieutenant Holmes," Maxwell said.

"The militia killed Butler," MacKim added to the gloom.

They succumbed into silence as Roberval conversed with the militiaman in the scarlet sash.

"Flamboyant fellow, isn't he?" Maxwell tried to lighten the situation.

MacKim nodded. He saw Suzanne edge towards Williams, who had congealed blood on his face and right arm.

The privateers were jeering, pushing at the prisoners as the militia flourished their machetes. They spoke together in an astonishing mixture of French, Spanish, and a patois that MacKim recognised as native to the Caribbean.

"Dickert!" MacKim hissed. "You're the best swimmer here.

Jump for it!" He nodded to the water. "While the Frenchies aren't looking. Get to Havana, man!"

"The crocodiles." Dickert stared over the rail at the water. It was a hundred and fifty yards to the other side.

"They're feasting on the dead! They won't want you! Move!"

Dickert glanced at the water, swore softly, and slid over the rail without another word. The splash alerted the privateers, who began to shout and point. When two of them aimed their muskets, MacKim and Oxford barged into them, knocking them sideways. A militiaman retaliated, throwing Oxford to the ground and kicking him viciously.

"Swim, Dickie!" MacRae yelled and added. "Crocodile!"

The creature was over eight feet long as it powered from the river mouth directly towards Dickert.

"Dear God!" MacKim staggered to the rail as every eye focussed on the race between Dickert and the reptile. However fast Dickert could swim, the crocodile was faster and much more agile in the water. The privateers and British were watching in silence, the Cubans with excited yells. Only MacRae had the presence of mind to smash his elbow into the face of the Cuban who held his rifle.

"Swim, Dickert! For the love of God, swim!" MacKim roared as MacRae levelled the rifle.

MacRae fired, with the crack of the shot loud in the inlet and the bullet hitting the crocodile full in the eye. The creature jerked in the water and slowed, which gave Dickert time to scramble onto land and run into the trees.

With their entertainment spoiled, the privateers grabbed MacRae's rifle and kicked him to the deck, with others renewing their attack on MacKim.

MacKim curled into a foetal ball, with his arms raised over his face. After a few moments, the attack eased, and somebody grabbed hold of MacKim's hair and hauled him upright.

Captain Roberval shook his head. "We've met before, sergeant," he said.

"You're a murdering hound." Aware that his life was likely to be short, MacKim decided there was no point in politeness. "A lying, deceiving, murdering bastard. Hell mend you, as it will."

Roberval stepped back, with his smile fading.

"You first, sergeant," he said. "For at noon, we will swim you to death. Unless the crocodiles get you first." Roberval lifted a hand. "Tie the sergeant to the mast, and let the flies feast."

31

MacKim sagged in his bonds. He did not know what time it was or how much longer he had to live. Since the rising of the sun, the morning had been an eternity of torment. MacKim was bound in the heat with no shade as the flies and mosquitoes whined around him, feasting on his blood. His head ached as if it would split, and the cords bit into his body. He remembered the death of Bearsden, swimming until his strength gave up, then drowning as the privateers stabbed at him. It was not a pleasant method of death.

Every so often, one of *Douce Vengeance's* crew, or a Cuban militiaman, would pass MacKim with a taunt, a curse, or a blow, and he could do nothing but endure and hope that Dickert, at least, reached safety. MacKim had no illusions of surviving the day or that Captain Roberval would show mercy to the Rangers. After all that they had achieved in North America, Kennedy's Rangers would end here, murdered by a maniacal pirate in an obscure inlet in Cuba.

"Do you want water, Ranger?" Roberval stood a yard away, drinking from a silver goblet. He smiled. "Soon, you will have all the water you can drink."

Get to Havana, Dickert. If anybody can escape, you can. Tell the world about Kennedy's Rangers' successes. Don't let our story die untold.

As the sun beat on him, MacKim remembered the tales of his childhood, the ancient heroes such as Ossian and more modern stories such as Coll Ciotach Mac Domhnaill of Colonsay, Coll the left-handed, and Rob Roy MacGregor.

I'll be joining the old heroes in Tir-nan-Og soon. Wait for me, lads, and make way for another Highland warrior.

"Here, Roberval!" MacKim forced himself to stand upright. "Where are you going next? The Royal Navy will hunt you down for the murdering pirate you are!"

Roberval smiled and poured the contents of his goblet onto the deck. "Maybe so, Ranger, but you'll be dead long before then."

No. No, I won't die easy or give sport to Roberval and his men. MacKim raised his head. *I am wee Hughie MacKim of Fraser's Highlanders, Sergeant MacKim of Kennedy's Rangers; I won't die easily in some unknown cove in Cuba. Remember me, Claudette!*

"78th! Come to me, 78th! The French are before us!" As the heat pounded on him, MacKim became delirious, imagining himself back on the Plains of Abraham, with Pikestaff Wolfe in command and Montcalm's French army marching towards him. The dawn sun glittered on the splendid white uniforms as the silk colours rustled overhead and the French regiments advanced in columns. MacKim could hear the skirl of the great Highland bagpipes and the rattle of drums encouraging the men forward.

That's the past, MacKim told himself. *I must concentrate on today. When they throw me in the water, I will grab at the first man to thrust a boarding pike at me. I'll hold the pike and pull him in with me. I'll die, but I'll die like a Highland warrior. I'll take the warrior's path home.*

MacKim shook his head, trying to clear his mind from the memory of the pipes and drums. He thought of his brother, wounded and left on Culloden Moor, and of Private Chisholm of Fraser's Highlanders, a veteran of Fontenoy who was so severely scarred, he could not return to civilian life. The pipes were still wailing, calling MacKim back home.

I can still hear them. Maybe I'm already dead. Perhaps I have entered the place of heroes. He opened his mouth, feeling his parched lips crack and tear.

"78th! Come on, Fraser's Highlanders!"

MacKim looked around him. He was not in the place of heroes. He was still tied to the mainmast of *Dolphin* with the Caribbean sun roasting his head and the sea lapping around the hull. Yet, he could hear the pipes, high above all the other sounds. Unmistakable, soul-stirring, bringing memories of cool rain on the heather moors.

There are no pipes in Cuba.

The drumming increased in volume. MacKim straightened up, feeling the ropes scraping the flesh from his wrists, ankles, and waist.

"I hear you!" MacKim shouted, with the words coming as a croak from his tortured throat. "I'm coming, lads!"

The sound increased, a lone piper and the rhythm of three drums beating the assembly, and then the advance. MacKim heard an officer's voice, shouting in Gaelic, and then an undoubted New England accent calling for the Rangers.

"Come on, Kennedy's Rangers! First and always!"

Was that Butler? But he's dead! Where am I? Heaven? Hell? Or somewhere in between?

After the rattle of drums and droning pipes, MacKim nearly expected to hear the rolling volleys of British infantry firing by sections. He struggled against his bonds, knowing it was futile, but determined to fight until he died.

"78th!" he croaked. "At them with the bayonet, Fraser's! Draw your claymores, you dogs of war. Sons of the hounds, come here to get flesh!"

MacKim looked down and saw his green uniform. "Kennedy's Rangers! Rally to me, Rangers!"

Nobody rallied. He was tied to the mast with the sounds of

battle only in his head. The glory was all in the past, while the future promised only humiliation and lingering death. So why was there a kilted warrior emerging from the forest at the side of the inlet? And who were those scarlet-coated soldiers thrusting triangular bayonets into cringing Cuban militia?

The pipes were real. Nobody could imitate the sound of the Highland bagpipes or the high Gaelic slogans as kilted men burst onto *Dolphin*'s deck, bayonetting all who stood in their path. MacKim grinned through cracked lips as Colonials and moustached Germans of the 60th Royal Americans swarmed onto *Douce Vengeance,* brushing the privateers aside. He saw Roberval draw his sword and try to rally his men, only for the green-clad man to drop to one knee and shoot him clean through the cross in his forehead.

"That's done for you," the man said in Dickert's voice.

"I'm dreaming," MacKim said as Benjamin ran to his side, sawing at the ropes with a sharp knife.

"It's no dream." Dickert caught MacKim as he collapsed. "This fellow has a tale to tell."

༺༻

THEY SAT UNDER THE TREES WITH BOTH SHIPS SHELTERING from the gusting remnants of the third storm to hammer Cuba. Officers from the 60th Royal Americans and the Black Watch, the 42nd Highlanders, sat on makeshift chairs on *Dolphin*'s quarterdeck, with MacKim joining Kennedy and Maxwell. Midshipman Crabb, temporarily promoted to acting lieutenant, stood against the taffrail, eagerly listening to the conversation of his elders and betters.

"You've had quite the adventure," Captain Jacobs of the Royal Americans said.

"I'm still not sure what happened," MacKim admitted. "How did you know where we were?" His head continued to pound from the effects of the sun.

"That black fellow, Benjamin, alerted us," Ogilvy of the 42nd said, sipping at a glass of brandy they had liberated from *Douce Vengeance's* stores. "We were heading in quite the wrong direction when he came running out of nowhere, yelling like a fiend. Our picket would have shot him until he said he was one of Kennedy's Rangers."

"One up to Benjamin," Kennedy said. "We thought he had deserted."

"Quite the reverse," Ogilvy said. "He told us where you were and insisted we help you."

MacKim nodded. "That's twice Benjamin's saved my life."

Ogilvy frowned at the interruption. "When he saw we were only thirty strong, he ran off to find the 60th." He finished his brandy with a final swallow. "Good man, that. He'd be an asset in any regiment. I can't persuade you to transfer him to the Forty-Twa, could I?"

"You'll have to ask him," Kennedy said. "Benjamin is a free man."

Maxwell nodded. "He might not remain free for long, with the demand for labour in the islands. I have picked up a couple of volunteers from Cuba and Barbados, prime seamen, but they know that every time they go ashore, they're in danger of being taken as slaves."

MacKim listened without commenting.

"Well, your man Benjamin ran along the coast until he found the Royal Americans and told them his story," Ogilvy said.

Captain Jacobs took up the story. "When he came to us, we thought he was a Spanish spy, and my men were going to shoot him out of hand. Luckily, he mentioned Kennedy's Rangers, and we knew the name."

"He's a brave man," Kennedy said. "I'm glad you came to rescue us."

"So am I," Maxwell said, nodding. "So am I."

That night MacKim approached Benjamin, who sat talking to one of Maxwell's volunteer black seamen.

"You saved our lives." MacKim shook Benjamin by the hand. "And now, you lads are worried about being taken back into slavery?"

"Yes," Benjamin answered for all three.

"We're on the south shore of Cuba," MacKim said. "Two of you are seamen, and Jamaica is about a hundred miles away to the south."

MacKim saw no interest in the seamen's faces.

"Jamaica is a British colony, and the British treat their slaves worse than the French or Spanish," Benjamin explained.

MacKim understood the men's reluctance. "Don't forget the Maroons on Jamaica, free black men and women who owe allegiance to nobody." He felt, rather than saw, their interest quicken.

Benjamin glanced at his companions before replying. "It's a long way to swim, sergeant."

"*Douce Vengeance* has two seaworthy boats quite capable of making the passage," MacKim said. "And the Rangers are on picket duty tonight. I'm the duty sergeant."

Benjamin gave a long, slow smile.

"I am sure a trio of likely lads such as you could manage to ensure one of the boats has sufficient food and water to last the journey. Captain Roberval has armed each boat with a swivel, plus muskets with powder and shot on board." MacKim stood up. "I believe that one of the boats is fastened to the taffrail of *Douce Vengeance.*"

I am helping two Royal Navy seamen desert in time of war and sending reinforcements to the Maroons, who could soon be fighting against King George. MacKim smiled. *What would Claudette say?* He thought for a moment. *She would say that basic Christian decency is more important than kings, countries, or colonies, and she'd be right.*

Benjamin looked sideways at MacKim without saying anything.

"I'll leave you to think about it," MacKim said, and ambled across the deck.

MacKim saw the three men creep across *Douce Vengeance's* deck shortly after midnight and stood erect on the quarterdeck, daring anybody to challenge him. He heard the whisper of voices, and watched the seamen help Benjamin onto the boat and unfasten the painter.

Within minutes, the seamen rowed the boat away, with the oars making little noise in the calm waters. Once they were in the bay, away from the confines of the inlet, the seamen hoisted the sail.

"Safe passage, lads," MacKim whispered. He had given them as much chance as he could, and now their fate was in their hands. Tomorrow, the Rangers, together with the 42nd and 60th Royal Americans, would march back to Havana. The future was in the hands of the generals, admirals, and politicians who acted in the king's name.[1]

"Is anything happening, sergeant?" Kennedy stepped beside him.

"Everything is as quiet as a November Sunday, sir," MacKim said.

Kennedy nodded. "That's the way I like it, sergeant." He glanced out to sea. "Do you think they'll make it?"

"Yes, sir." MacKim guessed that Kennedy had been aware of his plan. "Benjamin's proved himself a resourceful fellow, and the other two are seamen, born and bred."

"That's what I thought." Kennedy lit his pipe and puffed aromatic smoke into the air. "The 60th relieve us at three. We'll let them discover the loss of *Douce Vengeance's* boat."

"As you wish, sir." MacKim resumed his duties as the white gleam of Benjamin's sail faded into the night.

32

Quebec, Canada, December 1763

MacKim stood at the door, fighting the nervousness that threatened to overwhelm him. Taking a deep breath, he raised his hand and knocked, hearing the sound echo in the quiet street.

When there was no reply, he knocked again, harder, and the door opened. Claudette stared at him, with her sleeves rolled to the elbows and flour on both hands.

"Hugh?" Claudette's voice shook. "Hugh?"

"That's right." MacKim took a step back, unsure if he were welcome.

Claudette opened the door wider. "Come in, Hugh," she placed a hand on his arm. "Come in."

The house smelled of soap and fresh-baked bread, with flour spread over the table. Claudette patted her hair into place, leaving white smudges on her forehead. "I don't know what to say. I got your letters." She opened a drawer and produced them, tied in a bundle with red ribbon. "Did you get mine?"

"Only one," MacKim said. He looked around the cosy

domesticity of Claudette's home. "I wasn't sure if you wanted to see me again."

"I did," Claudette said, and corrected her words. "I do. I was never sure how to address them." She held out her arms. "Come here, Hugh."

They embraced clumsily. "You've lost weight, and you're as brown as anything." Claudette smiled, wiped away a rogue tear, and hugged him again. "The place is in a mess." She began to tidy up, making space at the table. "You must be hungry."

MacKim watched her for a minute, then began to help, getting in the way and sharing her laughter.

"Where's Hugo?"

"At school," Claudette said. "He'll be pleased to see you. He talks about you all the time."

MacKim nodded.

"What happens now, Hugh?" Practical Claudette asked.

"That's what I want to talk about," MacKim said. "Shall we sit down?"

"I have some spruce beer." Claudette bustled around, bringing a bottle and two pewter mugs with newly baked bread.

They sat at the newly cleared and cleaned table with the fire crackling in the background. MacKim noted that the walls still bore the scars of the British bombardment. After so long on campaign, he felt like a stranger here, and spoke like a sergeant, telling Claudette of his adventures.

"With the fall of Havana, General Albemarle and Admiral Pocock each pocketed over £122,000 in prize money, with each naval captain gaining £1,600."

Claudette tried to ease the awkwardness with a smile. "How much did you get, Hugh?"

MacKim sipped at his spruce beer. He had developed a taste for the beverage during the siege of Quebec. "Ordinary soldiers gained four pounds," MacKim teased her a little. "Sergeants, six pounds."

"That's not a lot for all the work you've done." Claudette did not hide her disappointment. Already, the barriers of long separation were beginning to ease.

"No," Hugh said. He pulled the small bag from inside his coat and emptied it on the table. Gold coins spun and bounced on the wood as Claudette slapped her hand on a guinea that threatened to roll off the table.

"That's more than six pounds," Claudette pointed out quietly. "Were you looting in Havana?"

"No, I wasn't looting. General Albemarle sent the Rangers on patrol immediately we captured the city." MacKim smiled. "We didn't get the chance."

Claudette raised her eyebrows, gently mocking. "So where did this come from? Was it treasure from the Spanish Main? Captain Kidd's loot, perhaps?"

"Not quite," MacKim said. "We shared in the prize money for capturing *Douce Vengeance*." MacKim watched as Claudette counted the coins, placing them into small piles.

"You're quite rich," Claudette remarked.

"Perhaps." MacKim pulled out a second bag and emptied that, with more gold cascading onto the table. "*Douce Vengeance* was a privateer, with a valuable cargo captured from a score of British and Colonial ships. We shared in that, too."

"How much money is there?" Claudette asked.

"Count it and see," MacKim said.

Claudette did so, marvelling at the feel of so much gold. "What are you going to do with your treasure, rich man?"

MacKim suddenly felt as nervous as he had when fighting the French. "When the government disbanded Kennedy's Rangers, many of us returned to our original formations; in my case, the 78th Highlanders."

"I see." Claudette waited with infinite patience, pressing her fingertips together.

"The government also disbanded the 78th at the peace," MacKim said. "They offered the men the choice to return to Scotland or remain in Canada, with a grant of land."

Claudette listened, saying nothing.

"Chisholm finally left the Army, with fifty acres and Harriette," MacKim said. "Out here, few people will stare at his scarred face, particularly as his nearest neighbour is also a veteran of Fraser's Highlanders."

"Who is that?" Claudette asked, gently smiling.

"Me," MacKim said. "I accepted a hundred acres beside the St Lawrence."

"Why?" Claudette looked up, with hope fighting expectation.

"There's a woman I want to marry," MacKim said. "I want to take her to meet my old officer, Captain Kennedy, then introduce her to my mother in Scotland. After that, we can settle in Canada on our own land, which I doubt I could ever do in Scotland. This money will set us up well in stock and seed."

"That's a good plan," Claudette agreed. "As long as the woman agrees. Have you asked her yet?"

"Not yet," MacKim said.

"Maybe you had better do that first," Claudette said. "She may not be as keen to marry a scarred Scotsman as you believe."

"Maybe not." MacKim rose from the table. "I'll ask her. There is one last thing, Claudette."

"What is that?"

"Will you marry me?"

"Only if you also marry me," Claudette said. "Now, let's plan our farm and our future."

THEMATIC NOTE

All three MacKim books are set in the Seven Years' War (the French and Indian War was part of the larger conflict) and share a theme of revenge. In the first two, *Blood Oath* and *Edge of Reason,* MacKim is the man seeking revenge, while in the third, *A Sacrifice of Pawns,* he is on the opposite side. MacKim would understand the concept, for personal and family revenge runs through Scottish history like a red thread.

The old Highland clan feuds were often based on vengeance for some historical wrong, factual or alleged, while the Border clans were possibly even more bloodthirsty. For example, if a Borderer were killed in a raid or foray, the people of his family would seek revenge against his killer or anybody else who shared his killer's surname. There is a legend that when Borderers were christened, a male child's hand was excluded so it could deal "unhallowed" blows against the enemies with whom he would be at feud. Some of these revenge-based feuds lasted decades, as in the case of the Johnstones and Maxwells. These families were already enemies in 1528, but their feud only climaxed in 1593. Maxwell led two-thousand men against the Johnstones and lost in the bloody Battle of Dryfe Sands.

However, closer to MacKim's era was the case of Sir Thomas

THEMATIC NOTE

Graham, Baron Lynedoch (1748-1843.) Oxford-educated, he was a typical Scottish landowner with no interest in anything military until he was in his mid-forties. In 1792, Lynedoch was visiting France with his wife when she died of natural causes. When he sent his wife's body home in a coffin, the French revolutionaries desecrated her body. Until that point, Graham had sympathy with the Revolutionaries, but after their actions, he swore revenge.

Graham joined the army, raised a regiment of volunteers in Scotland, and took part in many of the opening campaigns of the French Revolutionary War, from Toulon to Italy, Minorca, and Malta. He fought beside his fellow Scot Sir John Moore in the Corunna campaign and led a brigade at Walcheren before being promoted to lieutenant general in 1810. That year, Lynedoch defeated the French at Barossa, despite the feeble efforts of his Spanish allies. He commanded a division under the Duke of Wellington, serving at Ciudad Rodrigo and the slaughterhouse of Badajoz. He also fought at Vittoria, Tolosa, and San Sebastian.

Altogether, Graham was one of the finest soldiers of his generation and a man who only joined the army to take revenge for an insult to his dead wife.

MacKim would have understood and approved.

Dear reader,

We hope you enjoyed reading *Sacrifice of Pawns*. Please take a moment to leave a review in Amazon, even if it's a short one. Your opinion is important to us.

Discover more books by Malcolm Archibald at https://www.nextchapter.pub/authors/malcolm-archibald

Want to know when one of our books is free or discounted for Kindle? Join the newsletter at http://eepurl.com/bqqB3H

Best regards,
Malcolm Archibald and the Next Chapter Team

NOTES

PRELUDE

1. In June 1761, HMS *Temple* was at Martinico (now Martinique), exchanging prisoners under a flag of truce. During the procedure, another British warship, possibly *Bienfaisant*, captured a French prize and took the prisoners on board *Temple*. The French prisoners claimed that one of *Temple*'s boats was involved, which created a diplomatic incident between the French governor La Touché and the British.

CHAPTER 2

1. Some privateers had a reputation for near piracy. This fictional incident is based on a report in the *Leeds Intelligencer* of the 2nd of February, 1762, when two Martinique-based privateers captured the British merchantman, maltreated and murdered the captain and at least one of the crew, and took the others to Martinique.

CHAPTER 4

1. Although this incident is fiction, the idea came from the experience of the Leith whaling ship *Raith* in 1794. A French privateer captured *Raith* and placed a prize crew of 16 men on board. All the whaling ship's crew, except three men, were taken away as prisoners. When the prize crew found *Raith*'s spirits and drank themselves stupid, the three British crewmen, led by the mate—a Shetlander named Burish Lyon or Lyons—recaptured the ship. The ship's owners promoted Lyon to captain on his next voyage.
2. La Touché, the French governor of Martinico, sent this letter. A British warship intercepted the carrier, and carried the letter to Admiral Rodney.

CHAPTER 9

1. This incident happened.
    Extract from General Orders, Island of Martinique, January 19th, 1762,
    "Donald Gunn, of the 1st Highland battalion, or Col. Montgomery's Regiment, took on the 11th of January, four French Grenadiers, with their

NOTES

Arms, Accoutrements, etc. The General has been pleased to order him a reward for his gallant behaviour."

A guinea (£1 and one shilling) may not sound much, but a private soldier was paid around 8d a day, minus stoppages, so a guinea was more than five weeks' wages.

CHAPTER 12

1. According to the 18th century rules of war, when a besieging force had made a practical breach in a city or fortress wall, the defenders could honourably surrender. If they decided to fight on, the attackers had the right to kill all the defenders and sack the city or fortress.
2. There were rumours that La Touché's sudden surrender was due to a British prisoner. When brought before La Touché, the prisoner claimed that General Monckton planned to assault the next day, putting "all to the sword." See the *Newcastle Courier* of 3rd April, 1762.
3. The details of the treatment of British prisoners are from the fragment of a letter published in the *Ipswich Journal,* 3rd April, 1762.

CHAPTER 14

1. Extract of a private letter from Martinico, published in the British newspapers:

   "The Churches belonging to the Jesuits, and the Friars, (which on the 14th instant were shut against our troops and admittance refused even to the officers) are in return for this civility, converted into barracks, as are their convents, their estates too have been seized, and a party of foot quartered on the Jesuits with orders to sit at their tables let who will be there, upon pain of imprisonment."
2. This incident took place. Hervey went ashore disguised as a midshipman and translator to assess the island's defences.

CHAPTER 16

1. The British fleet did take the Old Bahama Channel to the north of Cuba, rather than the better-known and safer route to the south.
2. HMS *Richmond* did survey the passage in advance of the fleet. *Dolphin* is fictional.

NOTES

CHAPTER 22

1. The Battle of Ticonderoga, 8th July, 1758, saw the 42nd Highlanders—the Black Watch—advance against a heavily fortified French fort. The French repulsed the regiment, which lost heavily.
2. "30th this day was chiefly taken up in carrying ammunition and necessaries to the several batteries to provide for their opening next morning, which was done by the soldiers, and 500 blacks purchased by lord Albemarle at Martinico and Antigua for the purpose." – Journal of Patrick MacKellar, Chief Engineer.
3. The attack cost the three ships over 190 men killed and wounded, with much damage to the ships. Campbell was subsequently court-martialled and dismissed from the Navy

CHAPTER 24

1. Journal of Patrick McKellar, Chief Engineer:
    "21st July our sappers and miners continued to carry on their work: in this they were much retarded by meeting often with very large stones, which cost them much labour to remove. In the night, there being a suspicion that there were very few men in the fort, a serjeant and 12 men that scaled the sea line a little to the right of the mine and found only about nine or ten men asleep in that part of the work: they wakened before our men got to them and ran off immediately to alarm the rest: the serjeant and his party then came down, and, being ordered up a second time, found they had taken the alarm and a considerable number assembled and ready to make an opposition; had it been practical to succour them briskly, the fort might have been carried at that time, but the attempt was not to be repeated."

CHAPTER 25

1. This poem is ascribed to Muireadhach Albanach O Dalaigh, a pilgrim veteran of the Fifth Crusade of 1218. The words carry the piety of some crusaders, mixed with the desolation of distance from familiar shores,
2. Colliers and salt workers, the last Scottish slaves, were not wholly freed from bondage until 1799, although their working conditions continued to be appalling.

CHAPTER 31

1. When the Treaty of Paris ended the Seven Years' War, Britain gained Canada and several smaller territories, but returned Cuba to Spain and Martinique to France. Manila, in the Philippines, was also restored to Spain. As Chisholm of the 78th would have agreed, both acquisitions were only pawns in the chessboard of war, and the respective governments hardly considered the men who fought and died to capture these places.